A TIDING OF

A NOVEL BY

RAPHAEL MERRIMAN

*To
Adam + Hannah
 Live Long and Prosper (Together!)
    Reiph*

"A Tiding of Magpies" © Raphael Merriman 2015

Set in Garamond, with a bit of Final Frontier thrown in for good measure. I'm a Star Trek fan... you want an apology?

Dedication

This book is dedicated to my wonderful daughter, Georgia Grace Merriman, without whom life would be much easier, but exceedingly dull.

I love you, Georgia! XXX

Prologue

Hermitage Mining Colony, 2286

Est'Elek-Vultari spread his wings and flapped them gently in the breeze, his way of expressing his annoyance.
"This was not part of the mission brief," he insisted.
Moonchild rolled her eyes.
"Did I miss something, or are you suddenly in command of this team?"
The Arajak liaison officer's face seemed to shift to a deeper blue.
"My concern is that the mission stays on brief," his voice rose in pitch, ever so slightly, as he began to lose control of the situation. "You have a well-documented inability to simply carry out your duties and return to Control. Is it too much to ask that this one time you break with tradition and do as you were told?"
Moonchild sighed and pulled out her communicator.
"Magpie? Are you there?"
"Here, Colonel." Magpie's voice sounded distorted, due to the amount of belgiumite between them.
"How soon do you think we can get finished up here?"
"Not sure, Colonel. Goldfish says he thinks he can defuse the bomb, but historically the mine did collapse. We're trying to decide if we can jury rig it to explode later."
Moonchild considered for a moment.
"Ok, hon, you see if that's possible. I'm coming down there."
"I wouldn't advise that," Magpie warned.

"Don't you start, Will, I've already had as much insubordination as I can take. See you soon."

She closed the communicator and looked back at Est'Elek-Vultari.

"If you want to file a complaint with the Arajak high command, you go ahead, but if we can retrieve any information, it'll give us a better idea of how the Balsari managed to pull this off."

"I am already compiling my report," the Arajak told her.

"Good," Moonchild nodded curtly. "It'll keep you quiet while I'm gone."

Moonchild left before he could respond to the insult. She reviewed the situation, going over the relevant information again. In 2286 the belgiumite mining operation on Hermitage was brought to a standstill for a few days by a cave-in. Had the explosion destroyed the mine, the military expansion of the Terran Empire would have been arrested, leaving the colonies vulnerable and, ultimately, Earth itself. Records from the time suggested it had been a seismic event.

But, when it became clear that the cave-in was caused by a bomb from the future, planted by a Balsari agent, it became the jurisdiction of Moonchild and her team. Using Arajak temporal technology, they had arrived from the late twenty-fifth century to investigate. The problem was the bomb was designed to do more damage than had historically been done, so the team had the task of figuring out a way of defusing the bomb without disrupting the established timeline. But that, she mused, was why they put the team together in the first place, rather than just sending a bunch of grunts to run roughshod through history.

The trouble with belgiumite was it made it difficult to communicate, and virtually impossible to teleport, through it. So she had no choice but to make her own way down to where Magpie and Goldfish were trying to solve the problem.

She paused to let the mine entrance identify her.

"Please state identity," the computer requested in its soulless voice.

"Colonel Elise Washington, Space-Time Axial Response Team," Moonchild responded, placing her palm on the scanner.

"Confirmed," the computer agreed.

The lift door opened and she stepped in. The journey took several minutes, so deep was it beneath the surface. As she stepped out onto the level of the bomb, the floor shifted, almost imperceptibly. She took out her communicator.

"Magpie? Did you feel that?"

The sound of static answered her.

"Magpie? Goldfish? Come on, guys, are you there?"

"...*again......unication......king prop...*"

Moonchild put her communicator away in frustration. Damn this belgiumite, but the Empire had depended on it so heavily in this time.

It took several minutes to get to where she wanted to be. She called in on the two officers as she made her way to the control room on this level.

"How's it going?"

Magpie looked up and grinned one of his lopsided grins at her.

"Well, I got a good story from it," he told her. "I can give you a complete history of who planted it, and where they went afterwards. We can pick him up when we get home. That's the good news."

Moonchild appraised her acquisitions officer. He looked tired, but he always did when he'd been using his psionic skills to read the history of an object.

"Good work, Will," she smiled. "What's the bad news?"

Goldfish hauled himself out from under the device.

"The bad news, boss, is we can't alter the intensity of the blast on this thing. It'll either blow the northern hemisphere off the planet, or it'll be a dud. No middle ground."

He patted the side of the bomb, and the floor shook.

"I didn't do anything," Goldfish's eyes opened with alarm.

"Ok, hon, I believe you," Moonchild said. "You know what I think? I think the place is going to collapse anyway. I felt the same thing a few minutes ago. I think we should get out of here, fast."

"No argument there," Magpie said, clambering to his feet.

"We have to move the bomb, though," Goldfish reminded them. "Especially if the cave-in was natural. Even though I've defused it, seismic activity might well set it off."

Between the three of them, they manhandled the bomb to the lift. It wasn't lost on any of them that Balsari technology had allowed them to place it directly by chronoporter at such a depth, with no problems from the belgiumite. Neither was it lost on them that the device was probably the biggest, bulkiest and heaviest piece of ordnance they'd ever had to shift. Which became relevant when they reached the lift.

"We won't all fit in," Moonchild observed.

"Ok," Magpie said, innocently. "You two go. I'll catch the next bus."

"Stow it, soldier," Moonchild grinned back at him. "You don't get out of it that easily. You two go, and you can move this before sending the lift back for me. Ok?"
"Rank has its privileges," Goldfish smiled at the rumbled Magpie, and the two of them got in with the bomb.
Magpie waved cheerily to Moonchild as they disappeared upwards to the surface. Moonchild waved back, looking smug. A few hundred metres from the surface, something made the lift shake. Magpie and Goldfish exchanged glances.
"Not sure I like the sound of that," Magpie muttered.
Goldfish said nothing, but looked at the bomb doubtfully. Finally, the lift arrived and the two men hauled the bomb out.
"I'm going back down," Magpie said.
Goldfish looked doubtful.
"It's your call, sir, but be careful."
Magpie smiled and got back into the lift. The ground shook again, harder this time. Then the lift was in free fall. It jerked to a halt after about twenty metres or so, and Magpie sprawled across the floor. He gathered his wits about him and sat up shakily, taking his communicator from his pocket.
"What the hell was that?" he demanded of no-one in particular.
Est'Elek-Vultari answered him.
"That was a seismic shockwave, Commander, centred on an area some sixty kilometres south-west of your current position. Are you harmed?"
"No, I'm ok. Sixty kilometres? It felt closer. Any discernible effect over here?"

For an answer, the lift rocked violently, drowning out Est'Elek-Vultari's reply, although he heard enough to make out the fact that the mine was caving in.

Why would I be surprised? It's history.

He switched frequency.

"Control, request emergency extraction for Moonchild. Get her out of there now!"

"*Commander, this is Control. Negative on the extraction, sir. There's too much interference from the belgiumite. And the whole layout of the system has changed.*"

"Dammit, Control, she's trapped down there! Find her and get her out!"

"*Sorry, sir. There's no way to locate her. And if you stay where you are, you might be caught by any secondary tremors. I have a lock on you, sir. Extracting now.*"

"No! Belay that! Wait! Give me a moment, please."

Magpie closed the signal and sat there for a moment. There was a hatch in the ceiling, and one in the floor. He had to decide now. Should he climb up, to safety? Or down to her? Would he make it? Would he find her? Would she even be alive?

For an eternity, he sat on the lift floor and weighed up his chances. The floor shook again.

Then he made his decision.

1

<u>Oxford, England, 2029</u>

There was something wrong with what he was looking at, but he couldn't say exactly what. Nonetheless, something nagged at the back of Magpie's mind. Whatever it was, it wasn't immediately obvious.

The others arrived, shimmering into existence on the pavement outside the shop. Moonchild looked round in surprise.

"Very public," she stated, although Magpie wasn't certain whether this was a criticism or a commendation. He ignored the comment. He hadn't seen anyone since he arrived. Maybe that was the problem.

"Who are you?" Goldfish demanded, his voice rising in panic. "Where am I?"

"Here, read this," Moonchild told him, handing him his mnemonics.

As Goldfish took the card, Moonchild turned her attention to Magpie.

"OK, Hon, you've had time to look round. What do you think?"

"Not sure, Colonel," he answered, slightly distracted. "I'd like to get inside and have a look. Something's wrong, but I'm not confident I could tell you what."

"It's all yours," she told him.

Magpie took his lockpicks from a jacket pocket that Moonchild knew was not regulation issue. But so much about her acquisitions officer was not regulation.

"Wait!" the voice of caution demanded. Exchanging a glance, Moonchild and Magpie turned to face their new Arajak liaison officer.

"How can I be of assistance, your highness?" Moonchild addressed the latest thorn in her side.

If R'sulek-Entah was at all offended by the deliberate jibe, she refused to show it.

"Has it been established that the bomb was placed in this building? And I wish to know why it is considered necessary to enter this property without the owner's permission. Is this not considered illegal within the Empire?"

"She has a point," Magpie said.

"Don't start, hon, you wanted in, you got your chance," the colonel was having none of Magpie's usual banter. "Listen, if the Arajak are so concerned with how we observe the law, they should send a liaison officer to study our justice system, not out here on the front line, ok? You want to play legal pedant with us, fine, just do it quietly, from a distance. Your highness."

Before R'sulek-Entah had an opportunity to counter, Moonchild turned to Magpie and nodded. Magpie nodded back, grinned, and went in, spending no more than a few seconds on the primitive security system protecting the shop.

"Oh, God, Sarah!" Goldfish's anguished exclamation made Gunboy jump. R'sulek-Entah glanced uncertainly at him. The others looked away, leaving the stricken man to his torment.

Moonchild was studying the shop front when Iceman finally spoke up.

"Colonel, the chronographer refuses to calibrate. It does give the date as our target time, but it won't settle."

"Is it a computer glitch, or could there be an outside element?" Moonchild asked.

"I'm still working on it," Iceman said. "I'll let you know when I've recalibrated."

"Ok, keep on it. Goldfish, you back with us?"

The haunted look of the demolitions expert told her the answer before he spoke. He handed her back the mnemonic card. "I'm here, boss."

"Good man," she said, a smile of encouragement for his benefit. "You and Bouncer have a look at this contraption." She indicated a metal construction propped up outside the shop.

The two men set about their examination with some enthusiasm. Moonchild was a bit put out that she'd had to waste Goldfish's talents like that, but every time he came on a mission he needed something to distract him. It wasn't fair that one of her best men had to relive that every time he jumped. She really didn't want to make him suffer, but she needed him and the suffering was necessary.

So she turned her thoughts to the last member of the team, the new guy. Gunboy was a puzzle. A recent transfer from the marines, he'd been a gunner before that. Apparently, he'd had a civilian life prior to joining up. She must check his personnel record after they got back. She hated not knowing everything about her people, but Gunboy was transferred in just in time for this mission. Now, he was getting on quite well with R'sulek-Entah, and Moonchild thought she could detect the first stirrings of a romantic interest there. Oh, well, that should prove entertaining. Time to get back on top of this mission.

"Iceman, how's the recalibration coming?"

"It isn't," Iceman told her. "It's not internal, there's something affecting the signal."

Frowning, Moonchild reached for her temporal communicator. "Control, this is Colonel Washington, can you hear me? Control, can you hear me? Control, answer me, this is Colonel Washington. Are you there?"

R'sulek-Entah approached. "Is there a problem?"

Moonchild looked at her for a moment before answering.

"Yes, there's a problem. We can't get a fix on our coordinates and we've lost touch with control. This mission is compromised."

"Evidently," R'sulek-Entah agreed. "Although the only people we have seen have been members of the team. We have been fortunate."

"I'm not sure," Moonchild mused. "It's April 7, 2029, a Saturday. People should be swarming all around here on a Saturday morning. So we're either at the wrong coordinates or something's seriously wrong here. How are you two getting on with that thing?"

Goldfish glanced up. "Well, it's a vehicle and remarkably efficient in a strange way. You put your feet on these and push. See, it's connected to the wheels, I think the harder you push, the faster the wheels turn, making it easier to balance. The container at the front makes it look a bit cumbersome, but you have to remember the 21st century wasn't a time of particularly important technological advances anyway. They wasted it all on gaming platforms."

Moonchild nodded thoughtfully. "And the fact it's obviously used to transport goods to and from the shop suggests that someone who works here is inside. Dammit! So's Magpie!"

She grabbed her communicator and flicked to Magpie's channel. "Magpie? Are you ok?"

Magpie answered immediately. "I'm fine, what's the problem?"

"There's a potential hostile element in there with you, be careful, ok, hon?"

"Understood, I'm upstairs, there are more stairs leading up, but I'm going to check around here first. Don't worry, if I get attacked I'll scream. You can come and rescue me."

"Yeah, yeah, you're not worth rescuing and, besides, we haven't got the funding for it. Listen, don't take unnecessary risks, ok? Will? I'm serious."

"I know you are, Elise. I'll be careful."

Magpie replaced his communicator, checked his rifle and continued to the front of the building where he looked out of the window. He saw the others on the street below, Moonchild was talking animatedly to Bouncer who was obviously about to come in to give him tactical support. Goldfish was fiddling with the wheeled contraption outside the shop, as if he could discern its secrets by touch alone. Perhaps he's after my job, Magpie wondered. Iceman seemed engrossed in fixing something on his chronographer, while Gunboy and R'sulek-Entah were involved in some kind of conversation. Hardly surprising, he thought, for all she was an Arajak, more akin to an insect than a human, she was very pretty. Her cobalt skin and midnight blue hair marked her as Arajak aristocracy, and Gunboy, he knew, came from a wealthy family. Maybe these were kindred spirits. As long as he could cope with butterfly wings and the antennae. And the sex, of course. But he doubted Gunboy had as much experience with the Arajak as he did, so it was unlikely he was even aware of that aspect of Arajak biology.

Grunting with amusement, Magpie looked beyond them all, trying to concentrate on his job. More shops lined the other side. Something that proclaimed that it sold "Fish and Chips", although Magpie didn't think cybernetically enhanced livestock had been popular at this point in history. A chemist's shop. Well, he knew about those. They were authorised to administer prescribed medications. A jeweller's shop, one of many entrepreneurs who took advantage of human vanity. Of course, gold had gone out fashion after they discovered the motherlode on Taruman VIII and suddenly everyone had it. Paradisium was the choice of the wealthy now, and the Empire held its location a closely guarded secret. You really had to be someone to have an item of Paradisium about your person. Or an expert at acquiring it, like Magpie. And then there was a newsagent's shop. Magpie smiled to himself. In this age, they disseminated current affairs through the cumbersome medium of paper, and it was often old news by then. If the Balsari had attacked Earth in the 21st century, the humans probably wouldn't have known until the next day! But at least this was the pre-Empire period, so it was fairly certain that events were reported without political agendas distorting the truth.

A sound behind him brought him out of his musings. Magpie turned to see Bouncer arrive on the landing.

"Looks very quiet, sir," Bouncer said, looking round. "Hard to believe it'll be a crime scene later today."

"It's already a crime scene, Ibrahim, my friend," Magpie told him. "Did you see those prices? And there's supposed to be a sale on. John Gray should be arrested for daylight robbery, if nothing else."

The two comrades shared a laugh before Magpie turned back to the window. "Watch my back," he said, as he reached out and touched the glass.

The window was made in 1875, in a local factory. And it wasn't. The glass of the lower right hand pane was replaced in 1922, when a local boy threw a brick through it. But it wasn't, and the boy didn't. Magpie saw the brick, but there was no brick.

Magpie took his hand away. He used it to wipe at the sheen of sweat that covered his face. He stared at the window for a few seconds as if it would give up the secret of what he just experienced.

"You ok, sir?" Bouncer asked, clearly worried by Magpie's reaction.

"I don't know," the older man answered. "That was very strange. It was like I was getting two different histories from the glass. I'm not sure I understand it. Let's get out of here."

Magpie led the way down the stairs and out of the shop. Bouncer stayed long enough to do a quick security sweep of the premises before following.

Magpie went straight to Moonchild. "We've got a problem. I'm not sure what exactly, but it's a problem."

Moonchild frowned. "Tell me," she said.

Magpie glanced round, something making his nerves jangle. "There's something not right about all of this, Elise. There's something... I don't know... I just had the weirdest feeling from the window when I touched it. It was like it was two different windows at the same time. I can't understand it. It's never happened like that before."

Moonchild glanced at the vehicle, still standing where Goldfish was studying it. "Would you take a look at that for me?"

Magpie followed her gaze and grunted, moving to stand beside Goldfish. Squatting, he reached out and grasped the rear wheel.

It was an old model, but it wasn't. A young girl rode it for her uncle, but she didn't. There was no uncle. There was no girl. There was a dent here, with the paint scratched where the girl had been knocked over by another vehicle. But she hadn't been. There was no dent. There was no paint missing.

Taking his hand away, Magpie looked up. "Same thing, two histories. I don't understand it. This has never happened before, now it's happened twice in a few minutes."

He stood up and moved in front of the shop window, looking up to the first floor window he'd recently examined. Not finding answers there, he looked back at the vehicle. Still nothing. As if searching for clues he looked in the big window before him. Various articles sat in the display, all of which he assumed were relevant to the 21st century paper and twine industry, all proclaiming they were being offered at sale prices. Despite his joke with Bouncer, he had no idea if these were reasonable prices or not. He looked behind him, then back in the window. Then his mouth began to hang open and his eyes grew wide with realisation.

"Will?" Moonchild came to stand beside him. "What's wrong?"

He turned to her. "It's a trap," he said quietly. "Look."

She looked. At first she couldn't see anything amiss. "I'm not following you," she admitted.

"Not the shop," Magpie prompted.

She looked again. Then really looked. And saw what he'd seen. "I can't see our reflection," she said slowly, then turned 360 degrees before settling again in front of the window. "In fact, that's not the reflection we should be seeing, is it?"

Magpie shook his head. "Those are different shops," he said. "Just Classic, En Vogue... not just the names, the buildings are different. It's not even the same street. We're caught in a temporal refraction. We've been set up."

2

"Ok, so we've been shifted into a temporal refraction," Moonchild whispered. "But the question is, was it the Balsari, or has this been done from the inside?"

"What, someone from S.T.A.R.T.?" Magpie seemed to be struggling with the concept.

"You're the mind reader, you tell me," Moonchild countered. "In fact, you're the mind reader, you tell me. Start with me."

Magpie looked her in the eye. "Elise, you're my oldest friend. I don't need to read your mind. Ok, people gather round."

Moonchild let the age comment go. As the others drew into the circle and listened to Moonchild as she outlined the situation, they were unaware of Magpie stepping back and concentrating on them individually. Moonchild told Iceman to give up recalibrating the chronographer as it clearly wasn't broken, and turn his attention to solving the real problem. Bouncer and Gunboy were given sentry duty, while Goldfish was given the job of defusing the so far hypothetical bomb. Magpie was to concentrate on finding out how and why the situation arose, which he was already working on, while R'sulek-Entah was to try and think of any similar situation in Arajak experience.

"Excuse me, Colonel," Gunboy said. "I'm still new to time travel. So forgive my ignorance, but what exactly is a temporal refraction?"

Instead of answering, Moonchild looked round the group. Ordinarily, she'd have let Iceman explain the science, but there wasn't time for his in-depth analysis, so she gestured to Goldfish instead.

"Oh, it's quite simple really," Goldfish told him. "You know how light travels in a straight line? But if you pass it through a prism, it refracts, you know, bends and splits into its component parts. Well, you can do the same thing with time, splitting it into its component parts. Where each split occurs, there's an area of dead time. That's where we are now. It's impossible for it to happen naturally, it has to be engineered by someone who knows what they're doing."

"Thanks, Goldfish," Moonchild nodded. "Ok, people, any questions?"

"Just one," Gunboy said. "Can anyone else explain what exactly a temporal refraction is?"

When everyone was settled into their roles, Moonchild went back to Magpie.

"Anything to report?"

Magpie shook his head. "Nothing, but that's good," he admitted. "Iceman obviously doesn't give anything away, and her high and mightiness has a brain that no-one can understand, but the others are all either great at masking or they're clean. And given that none of them have tested highly for psi-potential, I'm going with the latter."

Moonchild nodded. "Even Gunboy?"

"Even him," Magpie agreed. "I know we don't know too much about him, but I got so much more out of him than I thought possible. Look at the way he watches R'sulek-Entah. That's no act, he's like a teenager with a crush. And she's a pheromone factory. Whether it's animal magnetism or money magnetism, I can't tell you, but it's rolling off him in waves."

"That's too bad," Moonchild mused. "Does he know about the Arajak mating thing?"

Magpie gave a short laugh. "Well, part of the interest is definitely sexual, so I guess not. Poor boy, he's in for a shock if she lets him get close enough."

Satisfied that at least her team was clean, Moonchild allowed herself to relax. At least if they had an enemy, it was one they could all fight together. But for now, they needed to know what had happened, how it had happened and wait until it was practical to find out who was responsible.

"In the meantime," Magpie changed the subject. "What do we do about the mission? Do we assume the whole thing is a trap, or do we carry on as ordered? Will the bomb still be planted on schedule?"

Moonchild considered it for a moment. "We have to proceed as though our orders stand. But we need to get out of here and back into the right time track first. Bouncer, are you certain there's no bomb in there at this time?"

"As certain as I can be, ma'am," Bouncer replied, as he approached. "It would have to be a pretty good system to get past my sensors." He indicated his ocular implants.

"That's good enough for me," Moonchild concluded. "Take a post in that doorway and keep me informed. Anything suspicious, you let me know."

"Um… everything about this mission is suspicious," Bouncer said, the uncertainty evident. "Is this a new kind of suspicious you want reporting?"

"Whatever," the Colonel replied. "If it moves, report it. If it doesn't move, kick it till it does, then report it."

"Got that," Bouncer saluted and moved to take up his position. Gunboy took up a similar position in a doorway opposite, so he could watch the other direction. But, as dedicated as he might be, his gaze kept slipping from his duty and onto R'sulek-Entah.

Goldfish came and sat in the same doorway. "Don't mind me, I just need to think. You can talk to me if you want, it actually helps."

"Ok," Gunboy said, not sure how it would help, but not questioning the chance to talk. "You know, I didn't understand any of that temporal refraction stuff."

"I wouldn't worry about that, sir, not many people do. I was just giving the explanation that's in the book. 'Temporal Mechanics for Dummies'. Iceman's the only other one here who could explain it properly. I doubt anyone else could."

"Oh, right," Gunboy didn't seem convinced. "You know, you don't have to call me 'sir'. I noticed there's a certain lack of formality in the team, I don't want to be the stickler for rules. Besides, 'Gunboy' doesn't suggest I outrank too many people round here, and I am only here as tactical support."

"Don't underestimate your role here," Goldfish chided. "If you and Bouncer weren't here we'd be left vulnerable. That would never do. Bouncer's pulled us out of some tight spots over the last few years. So did Blade. You've got a tough act to follow, but they wouldn't have drafted you into S.T.A.R.T. if they didn't believe you had what it takes. My name's James, by the way."

"John. Pleased to make your acquaintance. What happened to Blade?" Gunboy had been told he was a replacement, but no details had been forthcoming.

"Ah, that's a sore point," Goldfish was quiet for a moment. "He, um... he's been retired on medical grounds."

"Was he hurt badly?"

"Very badly, I'm afraid. But the damage is in his mind. He's in a top hospital. They take good care of him there. He deserves the best for what he did."

Gunboy changed tack. "What is it with those two?" He indicated Moonchild and Magpie, still deep in conversation. "Are they an item?"

Goldfish laughed. "Hard to tell, really. They've known each other a long time. They have a great deal of affection for each other, but how far it goes is anyone's guess. You'd think they were married most of the time. He's been her SIC since the team was first created. She insisted on it."

Gunboy nodded. "I understand how an acquisitions officer gets called Magpie, but where does she get Moonchild from?"

Goldfish laughed again. "Oh, you don't want to go there, really you don't. Trust me."

"Ok, what about R'sulek-Entah? She's a real touch of class, isn't she?"

"Do you speak Arajak?" Goldfish asked.

"No," Gunboy admitted. "But for her, I'd learn."

"Good for you," Goldfish said, trying to keep the smirk from his voice.

"Hold on," Gunboy said. "I saw something. Movement. From the corner of my eye. It's gone. Maybe it wasn't anything."

Goldfish stood and glanced in the direction Gunboy was looking, but couldn't see anything. He looked across at Bouncer. Nothing. He turned back to where Gunboy was concentrating his search.

"There," Gunboy hissed. "Again, just a glimpse, but I know I saw it this time."

He brought up his rifle and used the scope to search, flicking it to thermal. Definitely something there.

"Oh, crap," Goldfish whispered. "Goblins. Stay perfectly still, but be ready to run like hell when I say, ok?"

Gunboy wasn't sure what Goldfish was talking about, but he was obviously scared, so he didn't question him. Remaining as still as possible, still sighting down the scope, he was aware of Goldfish backing into the safety of the doorway and testing the lock on the door. The door swung open with a slow creak. Goldfish swore quietly and held the door steady.

"Did they hear that?" He whispered urgently.

At first, Gunboy didn't know how to answer that. He wasn't even sure what he was looking for. Then a face appeared in a doorway further along the road. It was like nothing he'd seen before. It was certainly alien, but it looked as though it belonged in a children's animated holovid rather than in the Imperial Species Recognition Database. The face loomed out of the doorway and leered maliciously along the road until it locked eyes with Gunboy. "It's seen us," he said, redundantly.

Goldfish didn't hesitate. "Goblins!" He shouted, throwing the door open and pulling Gunboy in with him, slamming the door after him. Outside, muffled slightly by the door blocking them off from the outside world, they could hear an unearthly undulating scream. The scream was picked up by first several other similar voices, and then it sounded like a whole horde had taken it up. Gunboy was reminded of the old vids he'd seen of the Zulus as they poured into Rorke's Drift, and had visions of thousands upon thousands of cartoonish freaks bubbling and boiling down the street on the other side of the door.

"Upstairs, now!" Goldfish pulled his arm, and Gunboy snapped into alertness. Taking the lead, he pushed his way to the back of the shop, where a further door led into what he presumed was the owner's living quarters. Barging his way through this door, he quickly found the stairs and went up. On the landing, he began moving to one of the front rooms, but Goldfish stopped him.

"No, keep going up, those little devils can climb."

They continued up. There was another floor, then an attic. At the top, they slammed the door and began moving whatever they could to barricade themselves in. Gunboy went to the tiny attic window and looked out. It was set into the roof, so all he could see was a few tiles and the rooftops opposite.

"What are those things?" He demanded.

"Goblins," Goldfish answered. "We don't really know for sure, but they live in the dead time in temporal refractions. We've come across them before. We've just got to hold out here long enough for them to lose interest and go away."

"How long will that take?"

"Hard to say," Goldfish admitted. "Last time, it took a few days."

***

Over the road, events had proceeded much the same way. As soon as Goldfish had given the warning, the others had immediately abandoned what they were doing and hurried into the shop they were camped outside. R'sulek-Entah had been caught by surprise, but recovered quickly with Moonchild's prompting. Magpie was last in and he locked the door behind them, just as the screaming reached the outside. He took an alarmed step back as something heavy slammed into the other side of the door with a sound uncomfortably like splintering wood. Racing after the others, he closed every door he could find. Then he was with them in the attic. He arrived just in time to hear the end of Moonchild telling R'sulek-Entah about the goblins, although her explanation was less than edifying for the Arajak. Her antennae danced with ill-concealed fear and her wings flapped as she listened to the screaming masses outside. The window in this attic sat perpendicular to the floor, and she was able to see into the street below. The street seethed with an abomination of biological implausibility, as she watched beings of all configurations battling for the privilege of being first to get into a building.

"What do they want with us?" She asked, trying to keep control of her rising panic.

Iceman joined her at the window. "To them, we are food," he told her in conversational tones, as if he was merely discussing the weather, or inviting her to a concert. "All they want from us is a good meal."

"Can we escape?"

"If they decide they can't get in, they will give up. But it may take time."

With a show of determination, the team members unholstered their weapons and checked them, reloading them where necessary. They knew they were really only going through the motions. If they needed to use them, then they were already as good as dead. They would probably be overrun by the goblins long before their power packs ran out of charge anyway. But they had to make the effort.

"Here we go again," Bouncer tried to sound calm. "Lock and load!"

Moonchild frowned and glanced at him. "What?"

Bouncer grinned, embarrassed. "Sorry, just something I saw once in a 'vid."

Then the first face appeared at the window, peering in with evil eyes that seemed to rake everyone in the attic. Then others joined it, until the combined mass of bodies outside began to block out the sunlight. The window burst outwards as four Imperial-grade rifles and an Arajak pistol blasted at random into the horde. Limbs were torn off, bodies vanished in a bloody haze and shrieks of agony mingled with the screams of bloodlust as the goblins pounced for the scraps of their erstwhile kin. But for every body that they obliterated, more appeared at the window. They poured in like a rushing tidal wave, an unstoppable force, and rushed forwards to claim their prize.

3

Magpie found himself struggling to keep hold of his rifle as a pair of goblins grabbed it and began a morbid tug of war with it. Realising he was defenceless if he didn't have full control of a weapon, he flicked it onto overload and let it go with a shove that sent the goblins sprawling. They continued fighting for it as they tumbled towards the window, unaware of the fate planned for them. Magpie grabbed his pistol and blasted the new goblins that were approaching him.

"Everyone get down!" He shouted above the noise. No-one questioned him. They all took what cover they could, ignoring the attentions of the goblins as best they could. The detonation of the rifle blew most of the front of the attic into the street. The roof disappeared and the floor blew downwards. Most of the goblins were vaporised immediately. Recovering quickly, the S.T.A.R.T. members were able to pick off the remaining goblins and take stock of their new surroundings.

With the front of the shop gone and indefensible, it was obvious they would have to move out. Magpie hesitated, waiting for Moonchild to give the order, but the order never came. Magpie looked round for her, but she wasn't there.

"Elise!" He called, realising too late that there was too much panic in his voice to make him sound professional.

"Sir!" Bouncer caught his attention and pointed through the hole to the floor below. She was slowly and groggily sitting up from where she had landed. Magpie took in first of all that she was alive, secondly that the goblins were

beginning to gather around the top edge of damaged brickwork, ready to pounce on her. He didn't hesitate; he simply launched himself forwards and downwards. His progress was halted with no warning as he found himself changing direction. He looked up at Iceman who held him in a firm one-handed grip.
"No, Magpie. Let me," he said quietly and calmly.
Magpie nodded once, which Iceman returned before letting go and leaping down to stand by Moonchild. He landed on both feet, straightened and bent to help the colonel to her feet, even as the goblins began swarming in. Magpie watched for a few seconds, then bolted for what remained of the attic door. He hurled himself down the stairs and through the door which led to where Moonchild and Iceman were in the first throes of combat. With a totally unthinking rage, he charged across the room and slammed into the goblins that had knocked Moonchild down again. Then he was in a race against them to regain his balance and get to her first. Aware that they were trying to find purchase on his legs and back, Magpie scrambled to his feet and grabbed Moonchild's outstretched hand, half dragging, half carrying her to the door, to the waiting arms of Bouncer and R'sulek-Entah. He then turned to see if Iceman was behind him, but he was being overrun by goblins. And the goblins chasing him out of the room were deterrent enough against going back in to help. Iceman was doing the best he could to keep the bulk of them away from the others, and Magpie could only watch as his comrade began to succumb to the torrent of bodies, his skin shredding and tearing under their claws and teeth as the goblins screeched their delight. Still he fought on, the goblin corpses piling up around him as he backed slowly towards the door. But

still they came in their droves, clambering over him, cutting off his retreat. Magpie eventually had no choice but to close the door, immediately hearing the scrabbling and scratching as the goblins on the other side struggled vainly to come to terms with the concept of a handle.

"We have to go, now," he said as he turned to the others. "Are you ok?"

Moonchild nodded, still slightly dazed, but recovering quickly.

"Bouncer, get us though that wall," Magpie pointed at the wall opposite, and Bouncer levelled his rifle, flicking up the settings. The thump of directed energy on solid brick sent a shockwave through their bodies, but before the dust settled, they were moving, trusting that the wall was gone.

"Up," Magpie ordered, locating the stairs, concealed behind a door. Still bringing up the rear, he removed his bayonet and jammed it into the wooden doorframe, behind the handle. Even if the goblins managed to fluke the handle mechanism, they'd have difficulty pulling it open. He could do without the bayonet anyway, now he had no rifle to fix it to. Almost as an afterthought, he set the detonator. An extra insurance, not that it would even the odds in any appreciable way, but at least it would be the signal that the door had been breached. As if the screaming wouldn't be clue enough.

When he joined the others, Moonchild was sufficiently recovered to be issuing orders and coordinating their escape attempt. She saw him arrive and broke off her discussion with the others.

"Commander, a word, please," she motioned to the back of the room, and the pair walked over to the far side to take as much privacy as they could. "That was stupid. You should have left me."

"Not an option," Magpie responded. "There was always a chance we could've rescued you, we took it."

"What were you thinking, Will? You tried to come down after me."

"I wasn't thinking, was I? You were there and you needed help."

"I needed help. But at what cost? We lost Iceman. You should have left me, we're all expendable."

"No," Magpie looked straight in her eye. "No, you are *not* expendable. Not to me, you're not."

Moonchild held the look for a moment. Then her glare softened. "I know, hon. What's done is done, we have to live with our choices. We'll see what we can do for Iceman later."

They continued to look at each other for a while, each waiting for the other to speak, then the moment passed and the spell ended. They returned to Bouncer and R'sulek-Entah, who were watching the goblins on the street below.

"Status report, Bouncer," Moonchild said as she came to stand beside him.

"They're all over this side of the street, by the looks of it," he answered. "But they seem to be pretty much leaving the other side well alone. Maybe Goldfish and Gunboy are safe."

"Let's hope so. We're not even considering going home without them, if we can get home at all. We need to move out. What's below us?"

Magpie thought for a moment. "It's still John Gray's shop. It extends through two houses. We're in the second one."

"What's the layout?"

"Obviously the ground floor is a single room, the first floors are connected by a door on the landing. The upper floors aren't connected at all."

R'sulek-Entah joined in the proceedings. "Until Mr Afzal made his own doorway," she looked at Bouncer as pointedly as it was possible for someone who hadn't quite mastered human facial expressions.

Moonchild came to Bouncer's defence. "He was following orders, Princess!"

"Duchess."

"Whatever. Without that makeshift doorway, we'd most likely all be dead, and if it's a choice between losing my people and damaging property, property comes second every time. Have I made myself clear?"

"Your mission…"

"*Have I made myself clear?*"

"Perfectly. I apologise. On Ara'Sayal, we operate differently. It will take me some time to adjust to your methodology. I will endeavour to do so."

"Good. Well, you go ahead and endeavour. In the meantime, I'm going to ask Mr Afzal to make another hole in this wall. Bouncer? It's all yours."

"I wouldn't," Magpie said. He removed his hand from the wall and turned to the others. "The other side is full of goblins. We need to find an alternative exit."

"Suggestions?" Moonchild asked.

R'sulek-Entah sighed heavily. "If I can get onto the roof, I can try and draw them away. If they follow me in sufficient numbers, it should allow you to retrieve Lieutenants Warner and McCallum."

"And how do you intend to do that?" Moonchild demanded.

In answer, R'sulek-Entah flapped her wings. "Despite appearances, they are quite functional. I am able to travel this way for some distance. My intention would be to draw them far enough from you, then double back on myself and meet you at a prearranged location."

Moonchild mulled it over for what seemed like forever, then came to a decision. "If no-one has any better plans, we go with that. No? So, we'll meet in the attic directly opposite, as soon as you can. Ok, Bouncer, new doorway, in the ceiling."

Bouncer took aim as the others retreated into cover. The blast would no doubt attract the goblins, but if the plan worked, it wouldn't be a significant risk to themselves. The hole was large enough for an elephant to squeeze through, so R'sulek-Entah had no problems once Bouncer hoisted her up. Out on the roof, she could see the ragged hole of the attic next door. The screaming of the goblins was slightly subdued, suggesting they had finished their business with Iceman and were either searching for more food or were losing interest. Moonchild attracted her attention from below.

"No heroics, ok? Straight there, straight back. If the plan doesn't work, don't go for a second pass, just hightail it out. Find the others and stay with them. You'd better take this," she held out the signal beacon. "If we don't make it, you find the others and use this to get yourselves home, you don't wait for us. That's an order."

"Noted," R'sulek-Entah acknowledged, and took the beacon from her, secreting it on her utility belt. Standing, she looked all around her. The breeze was cool and it made her hair dance around her face. Pushing it from her eyes, she studied the locations of the highest concentrations of goblins, using her antennae to gain an accurate picture of their densities and movements. Then, with a last brief glance downwards, she took two steps and flung herself from the roof.

The sudden increase in shrieking and screaming was the signal to the others that the goblins had spotted her. Magpie watched as the dark blue butterfly swooped into the street and up again, out of reach of the goblins, before disappearing from view. The shrieks seemed to diminish as a clearly significant number of them followed her. Magpie eased the sash window open and leaned out. There were still some goblins on the street, and some still lurked in the gap where next door's front wall had been, but the majority seemed to have gone to chase down the flying food.

"Time to leave, folks," he said, and began pulling components from various locations on his uniform. As Moonchild and Bouncer watched, he began constructing some kind of launcher for a grappling hook that he just produced from a side pocket they never knew existed.

Moonchild left him to it and took out her communicator. "Goldfish? Can you hear me? Respond please."

"Hello, boss," Goldfish's voice sounded relieved. "We were wondering if you were still there. Are you ok?"

"Mostly," Moonchild answered. "We lost Iceman."

There was a moment's silence as they digested this. "That's bad news," Goldfish eventually managed.

"Where are you?" Moonchild asked.

There was a sound of two people conferring. "We're in an attic two shops west of our original position. Red paintwork. We came the back way, so we missed most of the action. Gunboy says he can see Magpie."

Magpie overheard and broke off his work to offer a cheery wave towards the red window. Then he continued

with the launcher. "Tell them we're about to enter the attic two doors west of their current position," he told Moonchild, who passed the message on. Their reply was lost as the explosion sent wood, plaster and brick up the stairs. All three instinctively dived for cover as the dust and debris washed over them. Moonchild recovered first and ripped her pistol from its holster, shooting on full charge into the dark stairwell. Bouncer also brought his rifle to bear, adding to the firepower. Magpie made the most of the covering fire to finish the launcher. Taking aim, he pressed the firing mechanism and the grappling hook, attached to several metres of flexi-steel cord, fizzed across the street, through the window opposite and punched through the wall at the back of the room before opening out and fixing itself in place. He fixed the other end to the wall. "Let's go," he called, as he pulled his anti-mag gloves on. The others drew back to the window and reached for their gloves, while Magpie laid down covering fire.
Once they were all ready, Moonchild tapped him on the shoulder. "You first, hon."
Magpie nodded. He wasn't happy leaving her, but she was a better marksman than he was, and Bouncer was there purely for his weapon prowess. So Magpie leaned out of the window, caught hold of the cord and felt the anti-mag drives pull him smoothly along the line. He was less than a third of the way when the goblin landed on the other end and began a rapid charge towards him. Another time, he would have marvelled at the acrobatic skill involved, but not when he was sharing the line. He let go with his left hand and carefully drew his pistol, catching the goblin with a raking shot across its chest. The goblin's remains fell from the line, but then there was another one, and

another. They were on the opposite roof, and were converging on the window through which the line had gone. He knew they wouldn't go in because of the repellent attached to the hook, but they were ironically being herded by that repellent onto the line. He hadn't considered that earlier. In a moment of panic, Magpie turned to shout a warning to the others and froze as he saw more goblins swarming over the roof and onto the other end of the line. Trapped, he looked down and saw them massing below, waiting for something to happen. Then, inevitably, the goblins on the line caused it to sway and wobble. Despite his best efforts, he knew there was no way he'd make it to the other side. His hand hit the first goblin, knocking it from the line. But when he collided with the second one, it managed to hold on and dislodge his grip. His stomach flipped as he let go of the line and plummeted to the street, three floors below. The sound of his legs shattering as he hit the street seemed to echo despite the frenzied screeching of the goblins. Then his own scream of unfettered agony, as the nerves in his legs told his brain what had happened, rose above the infernal chorus, before everything went black and the mass of blood-crazed goblins washed over him.

4

R'sulek-Entah turned back. She hadn't been entirely successful, but she knew the majority of goblins had followed her. The problem was, with the thousands that were in evidence, even taking the majority left too many for the others to handle. She made a last low pass, just to get those that she had brought interested, then flew round a corner, blocking herself from their view, and cutting back her pheromone release. By the time they turned that corner, R'sulek-Entah was on her way back. She reckoned that she'd taken the goblins far enough that their return would be too late to affect the others.
She knew she had made herself unpopular with Colonel Washington, but that didn't matter. It was her job to make sure the Arajak commitment to S.T.A.R.T. was not misplaced. She didn't like Washington, or her methods, but trusting her with the signal beacon had been a huge step in the right direction. She was not going to abuse that trust. Nor was she about to abandon her new comrades just because they were low born humans. She concluded the colonel was doing her duty as she saw it. Besides, it was becoming apparent Lieutenant McCallum was from a well-placed family, and was clearly interested in her. Maybe there was a gain to be made in fostering a relationship with him. It was not unknown for different species to become lifemates, but in her experience, it was usually for romantic reasons, at least at first. That was not the Arajak way; a certain order had to be maintained, but her brief was to be liaison officer between her people and S.T.A.R.T., so what better way than to mate with one of

its officers? She tried to picture the resultant offspring: the physiological similarities between human and Arajak were limited to number and positioning of head and limbs, as far as her studies had taught her. Humans were limited to five senses and needed mechanical aid in order to achieve flight. Also, their skin colouring was not based on a complex social stratification, but apparently on geographical heritage. McCallum was from the same racial stock as Washington, but they were from opposite extremes of the social order, while the brown-skinned Afzal seemed to be from somewhere in between. She would probably never understand how the apparently random social order was kept in check, but she decided to make it her next area of study. All thoughts of study evaporated when she arrived back at the landing zone and saw the carnage unfolding below her.

***

The hand had been stripped of most of the flesh, but still it would not release its grip. The face, little more than a grinning skull, moved in close as it searched for the best way to see its target. The goblins naturally did nothing to help in any way. Then a second skeletal hand plunged in and found purchase. With an easy heave, Iceman hoisted Magpie free of the goblins and swung him over one shoulder. The acquisitions officer was a tattered and bloody mess, and his legs swung unnaturally as his body moved, but Iceman could tell he was alive. Using his free hand to bat away the goblins that objected most to the meal being taken away half eaten, Iceman searched for signs of the others. Looking up, he saw the line leading into the attic opposite, and surmised that was the intended destination. He shifted Magpie's position to balance him better, then made his way towards the corresponding door. His progress was slowed by the goblins, as he had to constantly pick them off Magpie's body, although he killed as many as he was able, which at least distracted a few as they went into feeding frenzy on the easier targets. Finally reaching the door, Iceman was able to get in and close it with minimal incursion from the goblins. The few that got in were easily picked off, and as soon as he'd secured the door, Iceman set about getting Magpie up the stairs. The explosion from the upper stories alerted him to the arrival of Goldfish and Gunboy in the building. That was good. Gunboy, he knew, was rated as a field medic, one of the reasons he was drafted to S.T.A.R.T. in the first place.

Laying Magpie down on the bed that occupied the middle of the attic, Iceman stepped back as Gunboy moved in immediately with his med-pac. Goldfish looked on in horrified concern, grateful only that Magpie wasn't conscious. He tore his gaze from the ruins of his comrade and looked at the ruins of his other comrade. Iceman never moved, just stared at the bed. Without a face, it was impossible to tell what he was thinking. With a face, it had been difficult enough. The scraps of flesh that still clung to the adamantium frame were quite nauseating.

"You look terrible," Goldfish said, quietly.

Iceman said nothing, didn't even turn. Goldfish continued. "It's good to see you."

Finally Iceman turned to face him. Goldfish noticed for the first time one of the lights in his optical receptors was dim. "I'm damaged," Iceman said. "Not badly, but I'm unable to operate at optimum efficiency."

"You've been through a lot recently. Want me to take a look at the eye?"

"Unnecessary, but thank you. How's Magpie?"

Gunboy glanced up briefly, only to acknowledge he'd heard, and then turned back to his examination. "I can stabilise him, but I can't save him. He's lost too much blood, among other things. If he doesn't get proper medical attention soon, he's not going to make it."

"Is there anything we can do?" Goldfish asked.

"No, his condition is beyond field medicine, I'm afraid. All I can do is keep him unconscious and hope we can get him home in time."

Goldfish went to sit in the only available seat, in front of an old dressing table. He studied his reflection for a moment, then became aware of Iceman standing behind him. He hadn't even noticed him approach.

"You're right," Iceman said. "I do look terrible." Then he proceeded to peel off the remaining flesh. Goldfish turned away at the sucking sound made by the action and instead went to look out of the window. He could hear the gunfire from the other side, but realised there was nothing any of them could do. The goblins were using the line to approach the window opposite and he realised that if Moonchild and Bouncer were busy fighting off an attack from one front, they might not be aware they were about to be ambushed. He watched as the occasional goblin lost its grip and fell to its death below, but noted with dismay that most held on and were making good progress. Looking for inspiration, he realised what he needed. Now, if 21st century technology included electricity, which he was sure was the case, he only needed a length of wire and a power point.

"Gunboy, is Magpie's top button still there?" He asked as he searched for the socket.

"Er… yes. Is it relevant?"

"Pull it, hard."

Gunboy did so, realising that Goldfish probably had a plan, and wasn't going crazy. The button came away trailing what appeared to be a couple of metres of superthin copper cable. Handing it to Goldfish, he dismissed the entire episode and continued his ministrations with Magpie.

Goldfish, by now, had depolarised his gauntlets and was coiling one end the cable around the line. Then he pushed the other end into the nearest socket. The only sign that this had achieved anything was the slight crackling and elevated, but staccato screeches of the goblins on the line as they were fried. Most fell off, but two remained in place, their death grips preventing them from falling. Iceman had come to see what was going on, and he shot the two cooked goblins off the line.

Goldfish grabbed his communicator. "Colonel, if you can hear this, the line is clear. On my signal, you and Bouncer need to get out of there. Ready… go!"

He pulled the cable from the socket and turned to the window in time to see Moonchild leap from the window and grab the line. Her anti-mag gloves carried her without incident all the way across to safety. Iceman was leaning out to catch her and take care of any goblins who encroached, but that wasn't necessary in the end. Moonchild caught her first glimpse of the figure lying on the bed and went to him. Gunboy stood quickly and placed himself between the two.

"No, Colonel, don't. It's best not to."

She seemed torn between going anyway, and seeing sense. In the end, she turned to watch what was happening outside.

Bouncer was on the line now, but the goblins were following. They were gaining on him too quickly. It was obvious that he wasn't going to make it, and they couldn't shoot the goblins because the angle was too narrow. And, worse, he seemed to understand his predicament. If ever they needed a *deus ex machina*, it was now, and it came in the form of a blue humanoid butterfly. R'sulek-Entah slammed into the lead goblins and smashed them from the line. They tumbled uncontrolled into the street below, where they were soon torn to pieces by the ravenous horde that waited for them. The goblins that remained on the line hung back uncertainly, analysing this new threat. By the time they had decided the prospect of food outweighed the risk, Bouncer was safely through the window. The goblins continued their advance. For good measure, or perhaps just out of spite, Goldfish plugged the cable back in and cooked the lot of them, unplugging it in time to allow R'sulek-Entah to sail in.

Bouncer was clearly relieved to see her. "Thanks, ma'am," he nodded.

R'sulek-Entah nodded her acknowledgement, then turned to Moonchild, offering her the signal beacon. Moonchild took it and handed it to Iceman. "Get this working, let's go home. Good to see you, by the way."

Iceman took it without a word and began making adjustments to compensate for the temporal refraction. Moonchild turned back to R'sulek-Entah. "Good work, Commander. But remind me to have a talk with you about how I define the term 'no heroics' when we get back."

"I look forward to that discussion," R'sulek-Entah noted. "I'm sure it will be an education."

Unsure if she'd just been insulted, Moonchild succumbed to the inevitable and went to Magpie. Gunboy was too busy trying to help him to prevent her approach, and by the time he noticed her, it was too late.

"I'm sorry," he said as sympathetically as he could. "I can't do much more for him. If we don't leave soon, he'll die. I can keep him alive maybe an hour, but not much more than that, maybe not even that long."

"I understand. Thanks for trying," Moonchild patted him absently on the shoulder, but didn't move away. She just stared down at her best friend. Until Iceman fixed the beacon, there was nothing she could do. Then she wrinkled her nose. "What's that smell?"

Everyone else sniffed.

"Something's burning," Bouncer said, at the same time as everyone else realised it. A crackling sound beyond where the hook had punched through the wall accompanied the puff of white smoke that came through the hole.

"What the hell was that?" Moonchild demanded.

"The repellent just failed, and the line is no longer electrified," Iceman explained.

Goldfish went pale. "I overloaded it with the electricity supply. I've burned it out."

Moonchild unholstered her pistol. "Stow the self-recrimination, Goldfish, let's get this line out and secure our position. Iceman, now would be a good time to tell me you've fixed the beacon."

Iceman didn't look up from his work. "It would also be overly optimistic, as well as inaccurate," he said.

The howling from outside intensified as the goblins became aware that a new location had appeared. They weren't interested in why they hadn't noticed it before, only that it was there and there was a large concentration of food inside. Those who elected to use the line were briefly disappointed before they were killed, as the end close to the food source became detached and left them all spinning downwards. Others, though, were converging on the window with renewed enthusiasm, not even slightly dampened by the fact that those who reached it were summarily obliterated by gunfire.

Inside, Moonchild, Bouncer, Goldfish and R'sulek-Entah were maintaining a coordinated barrage of shots that so far was keeping the goblins out. But they all knew there were just too many goblins and not enough of them to defend the attic.

Then the power pack on Bouncer's rifle drained completely. Sensing a necessary change, Goldfish called to him and tossed him his own rifle, converting to his pistol for the duration. Bouncer adjusted rapidly, but even that short delay had been enough. The goblins were getting in, and they were in danger of being overrun. Then Moonchild's pistol lost its charge. Reduced to snatching Gunboy's rifle, she threw the dead pistol at the goblins, who made a scramble for it in case it was edible.

"Iceman, we need that beacon!" She called in rising desperation.

"It's ready," Iceman said with the same level of excitement he would express if he were talking about lunch. The world shimmered and faded for a second, then resolved into S.T.A.R.T. HQ.

"Medical emergency!" Moonchild shouted immediately. "Get Magpie into sickbay now!"

"Where am I?" Goldfish demanded. "What is this place?"

Moonchild handed him his mnemonics and told him to read it, before hurrying out after the medics who'd come for Magpie.

***

R'sulek-Entah opened the door to her quarters. Gunboy stood there, looking slightly awkward with his fist curled around some form of red flowering plants.
"Good evening, Lieutenant, it was good of you to come," she stepped aside to admit him.
"Please, call me John," he told her, momentarily shocked at the differences between human and Arajak living spaces. Somehow, he'd been expecting just an alien-looking version of the standard chairs and tables. The huge twisted tree that took up most of the main room had very clearly designated sitting areas. "Oh, these are for you. It's a human tradition, or at least in my part of Earth, that on a date, a gentleman brings red roses for the lady."
"Thank you, Lieutenant… John… that was considerate." She examined them briefly, then started munching.
Gunboy started to tell her she'd misunderstood, but decided not to. It was up to her. "So, would you like to go and eat, or will that be enough?" He asked. "There's a wonderful restaurant in Italy, overlooking Vesuvius and the bay of Naples, it's quite stunning. And they cater to Arajak diets."
"No, thank you, John, these will be sufficient. Besides, I would rather not delay. You do wish to mate with me, don't you?"
Gunboy coughed and spluttered something about not wanting to rush things, but R'sulek-Entah waved away the protest. "I've consulted with my family on the matter, and

they are quite agreeable to the arrangement." She unhooked her dress, which fell away, leaving her completely naked before him. "I will be in the bathroom for a moment. Please excuse me."

She turned and went to the door at the back of the room, her wings fluttering as she went. Gunboy took several deep breaths, unable to believe his luck. He hadn't been at all sure they would ever reach this stage, however long the relationship lasted. Hastily abandoning all his plans, he undressed. A few minutes later, while he was still trying to work out which part of the tree was the bed, R'sulek-Entah came back.

"Everything is ready for you," she said. "Please take your time." And she smiled, her blue face lighting up. Gunboy nodded, breathless with her beauty, and walked slowly to the bathroom, not taking his eyes off her all the time. In the bathroom he looked around. And saw the bath. And saw the eggs R'sulek-Entah had just deposited for him. *Everything is ready*, she'd said.

And that was when he realised his mistake.

***

Magpie sat up in bed when he saw Moonchild come in.
"Hey you," the colonel said. "How are you?"
"Well, my legs are still tingling, and my skin itches where it's growing back, but apart from that I feel awful. You?"
Moonchild sat on the bed and grinned. "I'm ok, but everyone misses you."
"What, even you?"
"Especially me, Will, you should know that. How long before they let you out?"

Magpie flexed his legs. "Well, with some fairly rigorous exercise, I can be pronounced fit in a fortnight. But if you close the blinds and lock the door, you can get in with me, and I'll see if I can do it in seven days." He moved aside and patted the bed.

Moonchild laughed. "Save your energy, hon, I'm going to work you so hard anyway, you won't even be able to *think* about that, let alone *do* it." Her expression grew serious. "Besides, there's still the matter of the temporal refraction. Someone betrayed us; we need to find out who. I need you for that. Concentrate on getting well, ok?"

And she left him to his own dark thoughts.

5

Tombaugh Station, Pluto, 2507

The military courtroom was not open to public scrutiny, but the galleries were still full. Instead of friends and family, and those with a morbid taste for scandal, those occupying the galleries wore the uniforms of the various branches of the Imperial armed forces.
The accused was enclosed by forcefield, as much for his own protection as the safety of the onlookers. He was flanked by two heavily armed security officers, and was handcuffed, making escape seem unlikely anyway. His lawyer sat to one side, going through his case notes for the millionth time. The prosecutor sat opposite, also studying some notes, but with a slight smile that suggested he was only committing the case to memory, unlike the defence lawyer, who still appeared to be struggling to find some way of getting his client off the hook.
A door opened and three humans entered, flanked by two more armed guards. Admirals Saastemoinen and Chalk, and General N'Komo, the current Chiefs-of-Staff connected with S.T.A.R.T. This was clearly being taken seriously at the highest levels. As soon as the door opened, the court had stood, including the accused, although his handcuffs were attached to the floor by means of a short chain, and he wasn't able to stand straight. Instead, he bent at the knees, to give the appearance of a much shorter person standing to attention.

The tribunal sat, and the court followed suit. The accused sat gratefully, the discomfort in his knees having become quite pronounced.

Admiral Saastemoinen seemed to be the chief judge in the trial and he spoke first.

"Would the accused please stand?"

"Could the accused please have a longer chain?" he countered, but was savagely punched below the ribs by the rifle butt of the guard on his left. Coughing, he stood as well as he was able.

The judge continued. "Will you please state your name and rank for the purpose of verification?"

The accused took a deep breath. "I am Lieutenant Commander William Angel, formerly of the Imperial Navy, for the last five years assigned as second in command and acquisitions officer of the Space-Time Axial Response Team. My team designation is Magpie."

"Verified," said a disembodied voice, clearly a computer comparing Magpie's voice to the sample on file.

"Commander, do you understand the charges that have been brought against you, and the penalty these charges carry, should the evidence result in a guilty verdict?"

Magpie nodded. "I understand."

"Very well. Lieutenant Commander William Angel, you are accused of the unlawful killing of your commanding officer, Colonel Elise Washington. How do you plead?"

Magpie was silent for a moment. He raised his eyes up to the ceiling as if seeking inspiration. In a quiet, haunted voice, he simply said. "Guilty."

***

We had been sent to prevent the Balsari planting a bomb. The Prime Minister of the United Kingdom was scheduled to pass through the area and the bomb was designed to give the appearance of an Islamic terrorist attack. Weeks later, the Prime Minister was involved in negotiations which eventually brought peace and stability to a long-troubled region of Earth's middle east. Only, we never arrived where we should have. We were caught in a temporal refraction, engineered by someone within the higher echelons of the military hierarchy. Whoever it was, they had high-level clearance and an intimate knowledge of S.T.A.R.T. operational procedure. Colonel Washington asked me to work on it when we got back. Well, I had plenty of time; I spent ten days in hospital with broken legs, among other things. In the meantime, the rest of the team had gone on another mission and that hadn't gone especially well. Only the colonel, Iceman and R'sulek-Entah had come back unscathed. It seems Goldfish, Bouncer and Gunboy had contracted some kind of alien disease and were confined to quarantine until further notice. They'd been there for a fortnight already when R'sulek-Entah came to see me in my quarters.

***

The door chimed.

"Door, open," Magpie said. The door peeled away to reveal R'sulek-Entah. "Come in, Commander, how can I help you?" Magpie was aware that social calls were not normally part of Arajak life. R'sulek-Entah would never visit him unless she required something from him.

The Arajak liaison officer entered the room and tried to avoid glancing at the untidiness. She failed. "Please forgive my intrusion, Commander Angel. A matter of some delicacy has arisen and we require your insight."

"We?"

"Lieutenant Vee and myself. Colonel Washington has gone."

Magpie was instantly alert. "What do you mean, gone? Gone where?"

"That is the nature of the insight we require, Commander. She claimed she was on a mission, and instructed us to make no attempt to follow her."

"So why do you need to tell me this?"

"The records show no such mission was authorised. However, she used the temporal projector to go into the past."

"Can you determine where she went?"

"Lieutenant Vee is working on the computer at this moment. It appears she erased all traces of her intended destination. Wherever she went, she clearly did not want anyone to follow her."

"So how do we know she's gone at all?"

"There is a visual record of her entering the control room at headquarters, then there is a record of power usage. No record exists of her leaving the room. Unless you believe she falsified the records, we should take them at face value."

"Well, I'll come and take a look, if you think it'll help," Magpie said, as he rose unsteadily to his feet. R'sulek-Entah took him by surprise by reaching out and supporting him. "Thank you," he said, trying to keep the uncertainty from his voice. She didn't acknowledge her uncharacteristic move, simply made sure he wasn't about to fall and stepped back to let him walk on his own.

***

The prosecutor strode purposefully across the courtroom, nailing Magpie with his glare from the moment he left his seat all the way to a point less than a metre from the prisoner's face. "Commander, I'm a little confused about all this. You have admitted murdering Colonel Washington, but it's common knowledge she was your best friend. What changed in the relationship to cause you to kill her?"

Magpie looked at the floor, unsure if he could answer without his voice catching. "I thought she was a traitor," he said quietly.

"I didn't quite catch that, Commander, could you repeat it for the benefit of those sitting in seats other than your own?"

"I said, I thought she was a traitor. I believed she'd betrayed the team."

"I see. And can you furnish the court with the evidence that led you to this conclusion?"

"There is no evidence. I made a mistake."

"A mistake?"

"Yes. A mistake."

"How long had you known Elise Washington?"

"Most of my life, on and off. We were both from Mars, originally. I knew her by sight when I was a child, before she joined the army. When she left the army, she came back to Mars and spent two years running a bar. I spent a lot of time in that bar, I got to know her quite well."

"Did she ever give you the impression she did not serve the Empire with the utmost loyalty?"

"No, never."

"You're quite an accomplished psi-operative, aren't you, Commander?"

"I'm rated higher on several psionic tables than most humans, yes."

"You have the highest rating for ESP within the Empire."

"For humans, yes," Magpie qualified. "But that only includes those on active duty within the Imperial armed forces."

"Hmm… even so, it's impressively high. So you would be able to read Colonel Washington's mind at any point, am I right?"

"Theoretically, but there are ethical questions regarding the practice. I can't allow myself to be receptive to everyone all the time. I don't habitually violate people's privacy. Besides, the effort can be very tiring."

"So, theoretically, you could have read Colonel Washington's mind prior to killing her, yes?"

"Yes."

"But you didn't?"

"No, I didn't."

"Why?"

"Because I didn't have time. I had to make a decision, I didn't have the luxury of asking too many questions."

"I see. So you killed her on what was, essentially, a hunch."

"Yes."

"But the hunch was wrong?"

"Yes. Elise Washington was not a traitor."

"But you killed her anyway?"

"Yes."

"Thank you. I have no further questions."

***

I couldn't understand what was happening. It seemed she was treating me like a delicate package, one that had to be delivered on time, but which might shatter if handled wrong. I almost fell over and she stopped me. She actually touched me, held me up. I've never known any Arajak do that. It was like she was setting me up for some bad news. Very bad news.

***

The journey to S.T.A.R.T. Control was largely taken in silence. Magpie was trying to make sense of what little information he had, and R'sulek-Entah wasn't offering more than she'd already given.
Iceman didn't look up as they entered the control room. "Thank you for coming, Magpie. Sorry to have to disturb you during your recuperation."
"That's ok, Mark. What have you got so far?"
"Very little," Iceman admitted. "The colonel covered her tracks very well. I have been able to determine only that the projector was used at the time she was in this room, but that is only consistent with the information we already possessed."
Magpie sighed. "Do you want me to see what I can find?"
"That would appear to be our best option," Iceman confessed.
R'sulek-Entah moved to stand beside Magpie. "We do not know where she has gone, or why. But we are concerned for her safety. We would not be asking you to do this if we did not believe it to be essential."
Magpie looked from one to the other, but their faces gave nothing away. And it was pointless probing their minds for explanations, so he simply shrugged and turned to the projector. He placed one hand on the panels that he

imagined Moonchild had touched only recently. Closing his eyes, he concentrated on the machine.

***

At first, it was confusing. There were so many destinations programmed into the projector by Elise. Then I realised what she'd done. She'd covered her tracks to a point, by entering several sets of coordinates, but I could easily determine them all. All I'd have to do was figure out which was the correct one. As each set of coordinates was revealed to me, I repeated them to the others. Eventually, I'd got them all and broke the contact. That was when Iceman began filtering them. Of the twenty some sets of coordinates she'd programmed into the projector, only one was genuine.

***

"The unveiling of the temporal projector?" Magpie was getting an awful sensation in the pit of his stomach.
"Those are the correct coordinates," Iceman confirmed.
"But why would she go there? Unless it was to prevent an attack on it. Could the Balsari be so crude as to attempt that? Preventing S.T.A.R.T. from existing?"
"We have to be prepared for another possibility," R'sulek-Entah seemed hesitant. "If the colonel has made an unauthorised jump…"
"No!" Magpie was emphatic in his dismissal of the idea. "No, whatever else she's doing, she's not working against us. Don't ever say that again. Don't even think it."
"I apologise. I do not know the colonel as intimately as you do. I meant no disrespect. It is simply my job to consider all eventualities."
"Apology accepted," Magpie grimaced.

***

But her words had an ugly ring about them. I couldn't believe Moonchild would even consider betrayal, but the more I thought about it, the less likely any other explanation seemed. There was only one way to be sure. I had to follow her. Five years into the past, the day S.T.A.R.T. was commissioned.

***

The prosecutor placed before the panel of judges the post mortem results. "Unfortunately, Doctor Hanson was unable to attend this hearing, because his duties as the Imperial Navy Chief Medical Officer take precedence, but his report is highly detailed, so his absence will not be a problem. It should be noted that until two years ago, Doctor Hanson was a member of the Space-Time Axial Response Team and was, therefore, familiar with both the victim and the perpetrator. His examination of the colonel's body was thorough and, I believe, answers all questions pertinent to the case. In essence, Doctor Hanson confirms that Colonel Washington died as a result of sustaining a shot at Heavy Disrupt from close range. Facts which will be borne out by the testimonies heard in this court."

***

The corridor was mostly dark, lit only by the service lights that were, in Magpie's opinion, no use to anyone. Barely able to see, he glanced both ways as if his intuition alone was able to determine the direction Moonchild had taken.

Checking the chronographer, the illuminated readout told him he was right on cue. But it refused to point him in the right direction.

"Eeny, meeny, miny, mo...," he scientifically deduced which way to go and then went the opposite way just to be on the safe side. The corridor ended in a T-junction. Biting back a curse, Magpie wished he'd reviewed the information on file about the layout of Control, but for all he'd been a part of the team since its beginning five years ago, he'd never actually been in the computer core, and had seen no need to study it. Naturally no maps would exist down here, the only people who had reason to come here would know the place back to front, and the last thing anyone wanted was to give saboteurs any help. *Saboteurs like Elise?* he wondered, before pushing the thought away. He couldn't afford to think like that. Even so, he unconsciously groped for the holster and pistol Iceman had given him. He hadn't been expecting action, and had arrived at Control unarmed. Fortunately, both his colleagues were armed as they were actually on duty and Iceman had not hesitated to offer his sidearm to his superior officer.

With no real way of knowing where Moonchild was, or how much time he had to find her, Magpie was forced to take drastic action. Closing his eyes, he began to turn a slow circle, seeking her with his mind. Not finding her on the first pass, he was forced to extend his search. This was going to tire him, but he didn't see how he could avoid it. On the fourth turn, he found her. She was in the bowels of the computer core. He could see her attaching some kind of device to the inner wall of the central processor. Cursing, he realised he should have taken the other direction. Even as he broke into a run, his legs screamed their protests. Staggering to a halt, he leaned against a wall for a moment to mollify his limbs, before setting off again at a slow walk. As he went, he reviewed what he'd witnessed. Moonchild was clearly attaching some kind of device to the computer. He could only think of one thing that it could have been. His mind reeling from the implications of his best friend destroying everything he'd believed she stood for, coupled with the exertions of his clairvoyance, Magpie drew his borrowed pistol, checking the setting was heavy stun. As he closed on his quarry, he began to question himself. Did he have what it took to take her down? He would have to have what it took; there was no other option. If she was a traitor, she wouldn't hesitate to kill him, friendship or no friendship.

Then he was at his destination. He entered the computer core, following the only path available to him. But when he got to her position, he was alone. Stepping cautiously out of the shadows, into the central chamber, he located the bomb. Holstering the pistol, he went straight to the device, examining it for any possibility he might be able to defuse it. Where was Goldfish when you needed him? Sat in some hospital quarantine with a dose of Andromedan measles or something equally unpleasant. Magpie's chances of defusing this were somewhere south of zero. Then he looked closer and his heart leapt with relief. The bomb wasn't even primed yet. So, he had arrived in time, after all. He reached up to disconnect it.

"Step away from there, Magpie," Moonchild said quietly from behind him.

Magpie turned slowly to face her. Her pistol was centred on his chest and didn't waver.

"I won't ask you again, Will, please move away from there," she cocked her head in the direction she wanted him to go.

"Elise, what are you doing?"

"You wouldn't understand, Will, you shouldn't be here. I'm only doing what I have to do."

Aware that even now, above them the original members of the team were gathered to be presented to the Joint Chiefs of Staff and their entourages. Enough brass to send the Earth out of orbit if they all shuffled sideways at the same time, he remembered thinking when he first saw them. Now Moonchild was about to blow the whole lot of them into the stratosphere. Along with her own earlier self. And his. He had no intention of being an observer as she tested the Grandfather Paradox Theory. He stepped away, then began a spin and twist that should have brought him back round with his pistol aimed squarely at her. That was the moment his tortured legs gave in and he plummeted clumsily to the floor with a muffled cry of pain, and committed one of the cardinal sins of armed service: he let go of his pistol, which clattered away from him. As he made a desperate scramble for the fallen weapon, he felt the sear of Moonchild's shot hitting him directly in the centre of his back. Then everything went dark.

It could only have been a few seconds. When he opened his eyes, she was still there, concentrating on the bomb, clearly priming it. Her pistol was holstered. Without moving his head, he looked round for his pistol and calculated his next move. As he tensed his muscles to move, she glanced at him, saw his eyes were open, made a grab for her pistol. He was too quick for her this time. He launched himself sideways, hand closing round the pistol.

He had it trained on her, as hers was still only halfway out of her holster.

"That's enough, Elise. Put your hands up."

"Will, you have to shoot me, you know that, don't you?"

"Elise, don't do anything foolish."

"Will…" Moonchild hesitated for the briefest moment, then tried to draw the gun.

Magpie shot her once in the chest. She cried out once and dropped like gravity had only just realised she was there. Magpie stood with difficulty, then his legs gave way and he collapsed again.

He heard footsteps coming towards him. Iceman and R'sulek-Entah appeared in the doorway. Iceman came to help him, while R'sulek-Entah went to check on Moonchild. She knelt briefly beside the stricken colonel, then felt for a pulse. She looked up, across at Magpie and Iceman.

"Colonel Washington is dead," she stated.

"What?" Magpie was incredulous. "But I only stunned her…" He rechecked the setting on his pistol. Heavy disrupt. Moonchild was dead. And he'd killed her.

6

R'sulek-Entah took the stand. "I am R'sulek-Entah, royal duchess of Ara'Sayal. My mother is the archduchess, sister to the queen. I was assigned to S.T.A.R.T. as Arajak liaison officer on 1st February of this year. I hold the rank of sel'ved-ar in the Arajak Defence Force, which equates to Lieutenant Commander in the Imperial Space Navy."

"Thank you for agreeing to testify, your grace," the prosecutor began.

"Please, I was assigned to the Empire in a military capacity, address me by my rank."

"Of course, Commander," the prosecutor seemed a little cowed, but recovered smoothly. "For the record, would you please outline your experience with the Space-Time Axial Response Team."

"I accompanied the team into the temporal refraction, and later to the Molkaraz sector in 2296 to investigate a potential disruption to the timeline. The matter was resolved with few difficulties, although three members of the team were confined to hospital following their return. Latterly, I was concerned with the disposition of Colonel Washington."

"You arrived at the scene after the shots were fired, is that correct?"

"That is correct."

"And you determined Colonel Washington to be dead at the time?"

"Colonel Washington had died sometime prior to my arrival, yes."

"And you believe Lieutenant Commander Angel fired the shot that killed her?"

"Commander Angel admitted as much at the time. He made no attempt to deny it."

"Thank you, Commander, I have no further questions."

***

That was when R'sulek-Entah shot me. I woke up in my cell to find I'd been arrested for the murder. I don't know how the pistol reset itself to heavy disrupt, maybe when I dropped it, it somehow damaged the setting control. Then I learned that Elise had actually been trying to locate several similar devices that all had to be deactivated before any of them could be removed. But, because the real traitor was highly placed within S.T.A.R.T., she couldn't risk telling anyone what was going on. So when she saw me, she must have figured I was the one. She died believing I'd betrayed her.

***

Iceman took the stand.

"I am Lieutenant Mark Vee, assigned as technical coordinator to the Space-Time Axial Response Team. My team designation is Iceman."

"Lieutenant Vee, you are an SMU, is that correct?"

"I am a Mark V Sentient Mobile Unit, constructed by Kayanaga CyberSystems on Xeran IX in 2498."

"Mark V? Hence your name?"

"Yes," Iceman answered, without the slightest hint of irony.

The prosecutor chuckled as though it was the first time he'd been exposed to the joke, but Iceman gave no indication that he shared the amusement. "So, would I be right in saying that you have been programmed without a capacity to lie?"

"The question is irrelevant."

The prosecutor stammered slightly. "I... I'm sorry? What did you say?"

"The question is irrelevant," Iceman repeated, but did not expand, despite the fact the prosecutor and, indeed, the rest of the assembly were waiting.

Eventually, Admiral Chalk broke the silence. "Why is the question irrelevant, Lieutenant?"

Iceman turned to the admiral. "If I were I capable of lying, and wished to conceal the fact, I would still reply that I was programmed without that capacity. Therefore the question is irrelevant."

The prosecutor took a moment to digest this statement. "I see. So, I think we can assume that you can't lie."

Iceman didn't appear to see the need to comment, and waited for the next question.

"Tell me, Lieutenant, you supplied Commander Angel with the weapon that was used to kill Colonel Washington, is that correct?"

"That is correct."

"And when you supplied it, were you aware of its setting?"

"Yes, I checked its power reserve before handing it over. I was able to confirm at the same time that it was set to its default of Heavy Stun."

"Heavy Stun, I see. And the next time you saw the weapon, where was it and what was its setting?"

"It was in Commander Angel's left hand, and it was set to Heavy Disrupt."

"How do you imagine it changed its setting in the intervening period?"

"I am not programmed to imagine, only to observe facts and extrapolate from those at hand."

"Ok, what conclusion do you draw from the facts at hand regarding the change in setting from Heavy Stun to Heavy Disrupt?"

"My conclusion is that the facts support the theory that Commander Angel altered the setting on the pistol between the time I handed it to him and the time he shot Colonel Washington."

"Would it be possible, as Commander Angel has suggested, for the setting to change as a result of him dropping the pistol?"

"It is possible but unlikely that dropping the pistol on its setting adjuster may shift it up to Light Disrupt or down to Medium Stun, but to drop it so it bounces three times on the adjuster would take a level of skill and accuracy I do not believe is available to the commander."

"Thank you, Lieutenant, I have no more questions."

***

Admiral Saastemoinen looked across at Magpie.

"Commander, your plea is on record, and your report of the incident has been made known to the court. Witnesses have corroborated the evidence presented therein. There will be a short recess before a verdict will be reached."

The court stood respectfully as the three judges rose and left by the door they had come in by. Magpie tried to shift his position, but his knees were by now crying out in pain as the ability to endure this much standing was proving beyond them. Once the judges were gone and the door closed, he sat heavily and gratefully back on his seat. He closed his eyes and once again saw only the face of his best friend. Would she never leave him in peace?

***

Admiral Saastemoinen looked sadly at his fellow judges. "Well, gentlemen, it seems our choice is already made. Angel has already admitted his guilt, and there was no-one to disagree. Are we of one mind, here?"
"I think so," General N'Komo nodded. "He's guilty."
"Yes," Admiral Chalk sighed. "Guilty."
"Very well, gentlemen," Saastemoinen said, putting his sherry glass back on the table and rising from his seat. "Let us attend to our duty."

***

The court rose again as they reappeared. This time Magpie remained standing. Admiral Saastemoinen looked up and spoke in a loud but formal tone. "Lieutenant Commander William Angel, you have, by your own admission and the testimony of those called to bear witness, been found guilty of the murder of Colonel Elise Washington. There is but one penalty: total annihilation of your physical being. You will remain in custody for the duration of this night. At dawn you will be taken to a place of execution, there to accept the punishment for your crime."
Magpie didn't move, didn't acknowledge that he'd even heard the death sentence. He simply stood as well as he was able. When the guards unhooked the chain and lowered the forcefield, he followed their directions as if he was sleepwalking. When the forcefield went up in his cell,

he didn't react. He merely sat staring at the wall, as a single tear tracked its way down his cheek.

***

Magpie looked out of his cell window at the approaching daylight as it bled slowly into the night. He knew he looked completely defeated, even without the use of a reflective surface of any kind. The tear tracks still itched on his cheeks and a tic had developed in his right eye, which was distracting him. His underarms itched even more, and he could smell the sweat. He knew other parts of his body were even worse, the result of wearing the same clothes for several days without access to more than the most essential hygiene facilities. He'd been forced to use the toilet water for some of his ablutions but there were limits to how practical this was: he couldn't bring himself to clean his teeth in it. His hair, already longer than was strictly allowed, was matted and he wondered how much of the local wildlife had taken up residence there during his incarceration.

He realised the irony of being concerned over his personal hygiene less than an hour before his scheduled execution. As a boy running wild in the slums and alleys of Olympus City on Mars, he'd had little time for it, preferring to use his time just staying alive, aware that death could come at any time. Now his death was assured, he had nothing better to do than consider the image he was projecting to the world.

He fingered the scar on his abdomen. For eight years he'd carried that badge of honour, one of the many sacrifices he'd made in the name of the Empire. That mission had started with twelve of them, and ended with just two of them left alive. Himself, having received a field promotion to Lieutenant, dying in the knowledge that his first command, inherited as it was, had ended in disaster. Then the only other survivor, the team's medic, had found him among the trees, worked like hell to save him. Six weeks they'd been missing in that jungle, presumed dead. And now all he had left of those six weeks was this scar. He could have had it removed at any point, but he'd become quite attached to it. For some reason, he felt it kept him centred and focused on where his loyalties lay. Now it didn't matter. The annihilation chamber would make scars irrelevant. In little over half an hour, there would be nothing left of him except maybe a few stray atoms. Certainly not enough to call human remains. And everything the Balsari had failed to do, the Empire would manage with no resistance.

***

They came for him minutes later and found him still staring out at the dawn, absently rubbing his stomach. He didn't turn, but continued staring for a few moments. They kept their distance, somehow understanding he wasn't trying to avoid coming with them, but simply preparing himself. After a long pause, he finally drew a ragged breath and looked at them. He nodded once, then stepped between them, through the cell doorway and out into the corridor beyond. One of the guards, caught by surprise, swiftly moved to cover any escape attempt, but Magpie had waited for them. The guards seemed cautiously relieved that the former acquisitions officer hadn't attempted to flee. Magpie was well aware he could have been out of the cell and losing himself on the planet's surface at any time. And on the walk through the facility he was aware of the many opportunities for someone with his abilities to turn a corner and disappear, never to be seen again. But he dismissed all these chances before they'd formed into real plans. Where would he go? And, more importantly, why? What reason did he have to go on living with the knowledge his best friend had died at his hand? No, he would rather die than live with that knowledge eating away at his soul. He knew it would only be a matter of time before he ended it in suicide, unable to live with himself.

So it was that he found himself in the annihilation chamber, in the presence of the three judges, and an assortment of other officials. Looking round, he was aware of several faces he recognised. Many of them were people Elise knew, some were those they both knew. He saw Iceman and R'sulek-Entah among those gathered to watch. Iceman's face was, naturally, impossible to read, R'sulek-Entah's expression seemed to be one of... compassion? He wasn't sure if that was possible from her, especially given the situation. He also recognised Maek Newark, Elise's former husband. Didn't they realise what Maek was? This was supposed to a classified operation, one that would never be brought to the attention of the public. He found Maek's expression equally difficult to interpret and, as he was never going to be able to abuse the information, decided to investigate. He quietly insinuated himself into Maek's mind and explored the man's emotions. There was some excitement that he had a personal link with the victim that had given him access to the story, but nothing close to sadness that his former wife was gone.

Magpie and Maek made eye contact and Magpie stared at the journalist with a contempt so palpable that Maek seemed to turn several shades paler. The room seemed to go quiet for a moment as several of the people around Maek shivered and hunched down as if struck by a sudden draught. Then Magpie was ushered into the chamber and the spell was broken. Admiral Saastemoinen stepped up to a podium and faced the prisoner.

"Lieutenant Commander William Angel, you have been found guilty of the murder of a superior officer, a crime for which the only punishment is total physical annihilation. Within 60 seconds all you are and all you ever were will be erased from existence. You are entitled to a final statement if you wish."

Magpie glanced at Saastemoinen. "The only words I have left are for Elise."

Saastemoinen nodded and proceeded with the execution. He entered a code into the podium then stepped aside to let General N'Komo enter another code. In turn, Admiral Chalk entered his code. Then Saastemoinen stepped up again and entered the final code, enabling the chamber. Finally, with a press of a button, the machine was in motion. Saastemoinen looked at Magpie one last time and saw new tears. Magpie didn't care if people saw him cry. Let them think he cried in the face of death, let them call him a coward if they wished. The tears were for Elise, and her alone.

Then the machine took him.

7

Doctor Hanson operated the door controls. "Well, gentlemen, I'm pleased to announce you've all been given a clean bill of health and you may return to your duties immediately."

Goldfish wasn't buying it. "So what was wrong with us? No-one did any tests on us. And how come no-one else was quarantined as a precaution?"

"Ah, yes, that's the interesting part," Hanson beamed. "It seems it was all an administrative error. None of you actually contracted anything. Never mind, at least you get out of confinement now, that's the main thing."

The three colleagues warily left the hospital and made their way back to Control, aware that something was going on, but no-one wanting to voice their suspicions until they were back with the others. As they entered the transport terminal lobby, Gunboy glanced up at the huge screen that took up the entire East wall. A hologram of a young news anchor woman was talking about something, but what caused Gunboy to tune in to her words was the image beside her of the S.T.A.R.T. emblem. "What the hell is this?" he caught Bouncer's arm and pointed. All three stopped and watched.

"...and now here's our reporter on the spot, Maek Newark. Maek, what can you tell us?"

Newark's smug features thrust to the foreground as the hologram looked out at his unseen audience. "Well, Sophie, I can reveal exclusively that the Space-Time Axial Response Team and, indeed, the Empire's entire temporal programme has completely unravelled before my very eyes within the last half hour. I have just witnessed the execution of the team's second in command, one Lieutenant Commander William Angel, for the murder of the team's field commander, Colonel Elise Washington. The sordid catalogue of ineptitude that has afflicted the temporal programme since its creation five years ago has finally culminated in this most repulsive betrayal. Angel admitted his crime and wept openly throughout the execution, which took the form of total physical annihilation. Surely this is the last straw and now is the time to take stock and realise that temporal tinkering was never meant to be and close down the programme."

There was more to the statement, but they never heard it. Coming out of confinement to discover that, in their absence, their commanders had been victim and killer was too much to take in. Goldfish took out his communicator. "Control, this is Lieutenant Warner, request urgent pick up from these coordinates."

There was no acknowledgement, just the slight tingling that accompanied the shift in view as the busy lobby was replaced by the Control entry port.

The soldier on duty saw the thunder in their expressions and paled visibly. He faced Gunboy, the ranking officer. "Sir, Commander R'sulek-Entah is in the briefing room," he managed to say. "She requests your presence as soon as you report in."

The trio made no sign that they'd heard, and left the port without comment. They headed straight for the briefing room and charged in without ceremony. R'sulek-Entah and Iceman were waiting for them.

"What the hell has happened here?" Goldfish demanded before anyone could speak.

R'sulek-Entah was clearly expecting the outburst and didn't budge, although her antennae danced with alarm as she absorbed the intensity of the venom in his voice. She glanced nervously at Gunboy whose expression softened slightly, but he seemed unsure whether to go to her or to stand and be indignant with his comrades. In the end he elected to stay his ground. He would speak with her later in private.

R'sulek-Entah recovered her composure. "Gentlemen, please sit down. We have much to discuss."

"Damn right we've got much to discuss," Goldfish hadn't finished. "Why have we spent a month in limbo with no visitors, no news, no word from outside and the first thing we find out when we get out is some reporter announcing to the universe that Moonchild and Magpie have been killed?"

R'sulek-Entah drew a breath and weighed her next words carefully before speaking. "The fact that the news has been made public was an unfortunate development. It was always intended that you would be fully informed in this meeting."

"However," Iceman said. "It is possible to use this new development to our advantage. Please be seated and we will explain everything to you."

Clearly unhappy, the three sat and waited for the explanation.

Iceman provided it. "We have all been aware that someone inside S.T.A.R.T. has been trying to destroy us. The faked information that led us into the temporal refraction was the clearest indication that someone wanted the team killed. Moonchild and Magpie had concluded that whoever was responsible was probably working for the Balsari and, as such, was probably versed in mental defence techniques specifically to counter Magpie's probing. So with Magpie out of commission for a few days, Moonchild, Commander R'sulek-Entah and I decided on a course of action to deal with the problem. A human employing mind blocking skills will be tired, especially one who constantly keeps his guard up, even while sleeping, for fear of Magpie checking for vulnerability. If Magpie is no longer here, there will be no need to maintain the mind block, and the traitor has the opportunity to relax."

"So we had to permanently remove Commander Angel," R'sulek-Entah continued. "But the only way to do that without arousing suspicion was to trick him into committing a crime for which he would be executed."

"So you had Magpie killed?" Goldfish was still livid, and becoming more upset as he listened. Bouncer sat in silence knowing that as a lowly trooper it wasn't his place to confront officers, but glad Goldfish was saying the same things he felt. Gunboy was watching the whole thing trying to figure out what was happening.

"There was no alternative," a voice said from behind them. The three of them turned as one to face Moonchild. "Magpie had to be set up. He had to believe he'd killed me for his reaction to be convincing, which is why I had Iceman programme his pistol to change settings after Magpie had fired it. Also, none of you could have been involved because, if at any time Magpie had read your minds, he would have known the truth. That's why we arranged for you to be detained while we made all the arrangements. To be safe, we had Hacksaw keep you until the execution was over."

"I have a question," Bouncer said quietly. "If all this was to get the traitor to lower his mental shield, how will you identify him anyway, now Magpie's dead?"

"Hmm," Moonchild answered. "I wondered when you'd think of that. Follow me."

***

Hacksaw stepped away from the body, shaking his head. "This was extremely risky, far too dangerous for my liking."

"But is he hurt?" Moonchild asked.

"No, but only because Iceman got the timing exactly right. Too early and it would have been obvious. Too late and it would have been… well, too late. I hope this was worth it, Colonel."

For the first time, Moonchild let her mask slip. "I hope so too," she said looking at Magpie.

R'sulek-Entah and Iceman stood to one side, both fully aware of the events leading to this situation, and of their part in it all. The others were ranged around the room, still coming to terms with the enormity of what they'd walked into.

Hacksaw told her. "He'll be coming to in a moment. I think you need to be here when he does. I think the rest of us need to clear the area and deploy the blast doors. Come on, folks, out." He made shooing motions and ushered them all from the room, fixing his former commander with a look that spoke more eloquently than any words, before he followed them out and the door insinuated its way into the gap.

Almost as soon as she turned back to him, Moonchild saw his eyes flicker. Then he frowned slightly and his nose twitched. Magpie blinked and his gaze was directed towards her, but locked somewhere beyond her, as if she were invisible. For a second or two, he held the look, then his eyes flickered closed again. Moonchild thought he'd drifted out of consciousness again, but without warning he sat up and stared into her face with frightening clarity.

"Then he woke up and it was all a dream," he mumbled.
"That's how it's supposed to end, isn't it?"
"Hello, Will," she whispered.
"You're not really dead, are you?" he seemed to be struggling to interpret what he was seeing.
"No, I'm not. Neither are you."
"The court marital…"
"Will," she interrupted him. "Please. I want you to know everything. I want you to understand. It's all in my mind. Take it."

Magpie frowned at her, still not fully comprehending, but realising the only way to change that was to read her mind. He closed his eyes and gently reached out. Fingers of thought caressed her awareness as he searched only for what he wanted. She was leaving herself wide open, but he stepped around the things he didn't need, teased them back into the shadows, brushing against the information he needed long enough to absorb it.

When she opened her eyes, she saw him wracked with anguish. The weeks of hell he'd endured, just to further her plot had finally overtaken him. He wasn't the dependable acquisitions officer with the ready smile and the insubordinate comment anymore. Nor was he the no-nonsense second in command who would fly into the sun and out the other side to be with her. He was just a broken man, capable only of the wrenching sobs that tore themselves from his heart and threatened to shake his body apart. She wanted nothing more than to hold him and tell him everything was better, everything was as it should be, but she didn't know how he'd react. In his position she didn't know how she'd react. So she stood close enough to give support if he wanted it, distant enough to not offer any. She felt the tears on her own face and made no move to wipe them away.

Eventually, the sobbing died down. Magpie's shoulders stopped heaving as he became calmer. Finally he looked up at her, his eyes red and sore, filled with the tears that were just too tired to be cried.

"You put me through all that, just to catch the traitor off his guard," his tortured voice was like ice thrown on a fire, cracking and fizzing in its torment. He looked down again, a clear sign he wasn't looking for her response. After a while, he looked up at her again. "That was… ingenious."

Moonchild blinked as she realised what he'd said. She didn't trust herself to speak. But as he wiped his eyes and made a feasible attempt at a cheerful grin, she took a step forward and hugged him.

***

General Claude N'Komo stepped up to the podium. He surveyed the faces of the Empire's free press, along with those of the Emperor's propaganda merchants and drew a breath. "Citizens, we have called this press conference to make an announcement regarding certain allegations about the Space-Time Axial Response Team. Now, the procedure will be as follows: I will read a short statement prepared by Admiral Saastemoinen then I will open the floor to your questions, but the first question will be Mr

Newark's." Envious glances were aimed at Maek Newark, who arrogantly soaked them up, nodding and smiling at his less well-connected colleagues. N'Komo continued. "But before that, I would like to present to you S.T.A.R.T.'s command team, Colonel Elise Washington and Lieutenant Commander William Angel." As the general turned to beckon Moonchild and Magpie to the stage, more and more faces turned back to Maek, this time with puzzled, then amused, expressions. Magpie waited for Moonchild to take her seat before sitting himself, using the moment to glance at Maek. It didn't take any psionic ability to determine the expression on his face was one of a man whose career had suddenly been destroyed.

***

Alone in his cell, Admiral Chalk pondered the events leading up to his imprisonment. In ancient times, this kind of operation was called a sting. And he'd been well and truly stung. He hadn't yet figured out how Angel had survived the annihilation chamber, but he was guessing someone had tampered with it, connecting a teleporter circuit to kick in as the machine started up. Unwittingly repeating Angel's words, he conceded it had been an ingenious ploy. Once the psi-operative was removed, Chalk had relaxed his mind, as it was straining him to the limit maintaining it, especially within Angel's optimum range. He had just been congratulating himself on dealing the temporal programme a potentially fatal blow, when both Angel and Washington had teleported into his quarters with Admiral Saastemoinen in tow. Caught with his mind open to Angel's scrutiny, he'd lost most of his secrets by the time he recovered and replaced the psychic wall. He knew arrests were going to be made. And all that faced him and his cohorts was another trip to the annihilation chamber.

Chalk lay back on his bunk and closed his eyes. He had known what would happen if he was ever revealed, but the promises the Balsari had made, and kept, had blinded him to the risks. Now, he wondered if they would rescue him or leave him to his fate.

Something was pulling at his awareness. Opening his eyes, he caught the flare of a Balsari teleporter. His eyes opened even wider as he recognised his rescuer.

"Remain silent," the hissed command brooked no defiance.

Chalk complied and allowed the newcomer to tag him with a tracking device. Seconds later he found himself in another room. It could have been anywhere on the planet; there were no windows, no distinguishing features, nothing to hint at a location or time of day. A handful of humans he didn't recognise were waiting for him, but their attitude, appearance and lack of obvious respect for his rank told him they weren't military. They merely bundled him out of the building and into a waiting groundcar. All he saw suggested he was in a rundown area, probably somewhere in Europe, a suburb of a small city, most likely. A blanket was used to cover him, and he assumed it had shielding circuitry wired into it. The journey was taken in silence and he eventually found himself on a small commercial freighter bound for the Tau Ceti system. Once out of his uniform and into civilian clothing he allowed himself to relax and consider his position.

Finally, he was handed over to a Molzhan merchant who conveyed him to a waiting Balsari vessel on the edge of

Imperial space. There, the Balsari captain received him, and that evening dined in fine style, although most of the food was too spicy for him and wriggled too much for his taste. Now, he was truly home.

***

Admiral Saastemoinen looked across his desk at Magpie. "Can we now assume the threat is over, Commander?"

"No, sir," Magpie admitted. "Although, with the arrests, its back has certainly been broken. Unfortunately, Admiral Chalk recovered in time to conceal some of the names, but now we've identified him as the traitor, I can have another go on him in the morning and try and dig up what he's still holding on to."

"Would the others know anything?"

"Unlikely. I would think Chalk was the hub of a wheel and the rest were all spokes radiating outwards. It's more likely only he knew the other names, the rest would only know him, possibly not even that much if he conducted his meetings covertly."

Saastemoinen seemed about to speak when a beeping interrupted him.

"Yes, what is it?" he demanded of the communicator on his desk.

"Sorry to disturb you sir, but you need to be informed, Admiral Chalk has escaped, sir."

In a tone that would have melted pure Paradisium, he said to Magpie. "Find him."

Magpie nodded once and left the office. The team had another mission.

8

Austin, Texas, 2485

As Drill Sergeant Galloway stormed across the square like he was on a mission, his eyes took in the new recruits. Every September, a batch of children was presented to him in the hope he could make soldiers of them. And the way he always began the process was to approach them in this way, let them see he was coming straight at them, watch them flinch as he seemed to single them all out for special attention. Every year, the hundred or so wet behind the ears little runts would be whittled down to those who could best serve the Empire this way. That process would start immediately.

By and large, they were standing in a variety of attitudes they presumed were approximating attention. Such things no longer amused Galloway. Once, he would have laughed at their naïve attempts to be soldiers without training, but as year drifted into endless year, he stopped showing any outward sign of humour. Eventually, even the inward signs went, leaving him dry.

Most of them did flinch as he approached, as he knew they would. They'd all been watching him and calculating the point of intercept, working out who was going to bear the brunt of his arrival. The sighs of relief were reined in, but he knew they were all breathing easier, all but the one he stood in front of. He eyed the boy with a contemptuous sneer. "Who told you you'd be a soldier, lad?" he demanded. The voice, amplified by the vocal enhancers in his larynx, echoed round the entire square. The group flinched again.

The youth cocked his head and met his eyes with a slight smile, clearly not afraid. "My father is the senior partner of…"

"I didn't ask for your family tree reciting, lad, I asked you who told you you'd be a soldier. When I ask a question, I expect the answer to the question I just asked, not some crap about someone who isn't you. Pack your bags and get out, lad, the Heavy Artillery doesn't need smug bastards in its ranks."

The boy stared for a moment waiting for the drill sergeant to move on to the next victim, but he didn't. He stayed in place, glaring at the boy. "Why are you still here?" he shouted. "Is English not your second language, or something? Go on, get out, and take your attitude with you."

Realising this wasn't a joke, or a test, the boy glanced round at the others, as if there would be someone who could countermand the order. No-one even looked at him, for fear of dismissal by association. Left with no alternative, he turned to Galloway. "You're making a big mistake," he told him. "My father is…"

"I don't care if your father is the Queen of Ara'Sayal, you're still a civilian," Galloway bellowed. "Now, for the last time, get out of my sight, or I'll have a medical team take you away in pieces."

The boy seemed to be caught between lashing out in outrage, and crying in frustration. In the end, it was the tears that won out, as he turned and stalked from the drill square, humiliated. Galloway dismissed him from his mind with the same ease as he'd dismissed him from the army, and turned his attention to the others. "Anyone else who feels they'll have trouble answering questions can leave now."

No-one moved. Nodding to himself, Galloway began moving along the line. "When I address you, you will answer first by calling me 'sir'. You will answer the question as accurately and concisely as possible and you will indicate that you have finished speaking by saying 'sir'. Is that clear?"

"Sir, yes sir!" the massed reply resounded, equalling his enhanced voice for volume.

Galloway pushed his way through the crowd and halted before a surly youth with dark hair and hooded eyes. "Did you think I wasn't speaking to you, lad?" he roared. "Did you think maybe you were exempt from answering?"

The boy opened his mouth, but Galloway cut him off. "Too late! On the field of battle, your insubordination could have cost lives and these fine people could be dead now. If you'd been wearing a uniform, your refusal to answer would have got you a court martial. Pack your bags and get out, you're following the other one. Maybe his father could give you a job."

Galloway watched as the youth slowly made his way from the line, then he ignored him and continued on his way. He contented himself with a few disparaging comments made at unfeasible volume to scare the recruits into submission. Until he came to the pretty girl. She probably could have been beautiful, but there was something in her eyes, something that spoke of hardship, of things seen that should never be seen. And she was too small.

"How tall are you, lass?" he thundered.

"Sir, five feet, four inches, sir!" she shouted back.

"You're too short to be a soldier, pack your bags and get out."

"Sir, no, sir!"

The collective gasp was audible. Galloway widened his eyes and his nostrils flared. It was obvious no new recruit had ever spoken to him this way before. "I don't think I heard you right, lass, I thought you just refused a direct order," the voice had dropped to a dangerous whisper as he leaned in close and put his face inches away from hers. "Tell me what you just said."

The girl swallowed, her terror palpable. Her eyes flicked briefly in his direction then centred again. "Sir, with respect, I would ask you to reconsider. I'm only short at the top, my legs reach all the way to the ground, sir!" The girl tried to shout, but much of her reasoning came out in a squeak.

For a long moment, Galloway glared at her. Then, for the first time in years, he laughed. "Are you some kind of moon child? What the hell kind of reasoning is that? What's your name, trooper?"

"Sir, Elise Washington, sir!"

"Well, Washington, you just earned yourself a stay of execution. But understand this: I am going to push you so hard, and I am going to make it my mission to make you fail. I will make you wish you'd followed those two today, and I will break you. If I fail, and you stay the course, you will be the most complete soldier that ever wore the Imperial uniform. But don't be under any illusion that I'll ever cut you any slack. Last chance to walk."

"Sir, thank you, sir!" she answered, but stayed where she was.

***

The canteen was buzzing with the enthusiasm of teenagers who hadn't yet experienced army food. As Elise surveyed her tray, she reasoned it was better than hunting for scraps in the Martian refuse dumps. The tables were being filled from one end, so she sat next to Hannan, the young man on the end of the line. Hannan glanced appraisingly at her.
"You got a problem, hon?"
Hannan held up his hands in a non-threatening gesture. "Hey, I'm only being friendly."
"Really? Try being friendly to my face, and not my chest."
Suddenly, he wasn't so much a man as a blushing boy, caught in the act. Another youth, across the table, rescued the situation. "Hey, don't wind her up, she's the one that took out Sergeant Go-Away. You did a good job, Moonchild, well done. I'm Giovanni di Ravello, by the way. Second year."
Elise rolled her eyes. "Am I going to have live with that? Listen, I was scared and I said the first thing that came to mind to save my career. Now I'd like to forget it and get on with being a soldier. Is that too much to ask?"
Di Ravello grinned. "Sorry, I didn't create the name, I just overheard it."
Elise placed her fork carefully on the side of the tray. "Ok. So who called me Moonchild first?"
Di Ravello looked her in the eye and said. "Sergeant Go-Away. He was talking to Sergeant Fisher. I heard him say how impressed he was with you."
Elise considered this. "You're teasing me," she concluded, and picked up her fork. "I'm not buying it."
"Suit yourself," the senior recruit shrugged and cheerfully tucked into his food. "But I'm not making it up. I didn't even know you existed until he said it. And as you're the

shortest person here by some way, I figured you'd be the one."

Elise narrowed her eyes and gave him a long stare. "Moonchild, huh?"

He nodded, but said nothing, his mouth full.

"Ok, hon, have it your way," she said, and that was the end of the conversation.

***

She hadn't realised there would be so much theory behind modern soldiering. So much of her time was spent in the classroom, learning the philosophy of warfare, learning the Empire's friends and enemies, learning how to think like a soldier. Very little of it actually seemed to involve *being* a soldier. She considered her life before joining up. She'd been a waitress in a seedy restaurant, where too many of the patrons had wanted more from her than was on the menu. But suppose they kept making her *train* to wait at tables, and never let her *actually* wait at tables; that was what she imagined would be the equivalent.

But, in the words of everyone's favourite tutor, Major Pope, regular and diligent application to schoolwork, whether to be done in the field or in the classroom, is an essential prerequisite to scholastic success. Elise recognised his meaning immediately. A good soldier is an intelligent soldier.

She managed to tune in to what Lieutenant Mendelssohn was saying. "There is one element that is, in equal measure, your greatest ally and your worst enemy on the battlefield. Anyone care to tell me what it is?"

A few people mumbled unsteady guesses, suggesting all manner of things from a person's comrades, to darkness, to technology. Mendelssohn ignored all of these, until Elise spoke.

"Fear," she said.

"Explain," Mendelssohn snapped.

Uncertain of the wisdom of committing to an opinion, Elise nevertheless did so. "Fear can cause you to freeze in battle, but it can also spur you on to achieve things you never thought possible."

Mendelssohn smiled. "Absolutely right, Washington. Never let any soldier tell you that fear is a bad thing. Fear is neither good nor bad. It is your reaction to your fear that determines what is good and bad. Whether you run screaming from the battlefield or single-handedly storm an Arajak nest armed only with a toothbrush, it is your fear that drives you. The fearless soldier is a dead soldier. The good soldier is one who controls his fear and directs its energy towards acts of courage. Fear and cowardice are entirely different things. Fear will cause you to weep and shake in the trenches on the Arajak Front. Cowardice will cause you to weep and shake at the *thought* of going to the Arajak Front. That is the subject of the 10000-word dissertation I want you to produce in time for the next lecture. Dismissed."

***

Sergeant Galloway walked briskly back to his quarters. He walked everywhere briskly, he had no knowledge of how to saunter, or not have purpose. He did everything briskly, as his attitude to life was the same. Very little in his life took up more time than he deemed essential, which was why one factor was causing him problems, disrupting the ordered scheme of his life. Galloway couldn't make up his

mind how he felt about Private Washington. He'd purposefully singled her out as a victim, someone to push to her limits and further. But every limit he found, she surpassed. Not always immediately, but soon afterwards. He could reduce her to tears one day, but the next she'd come back with even greater determination to beat his challenges. On one level, it was frustrating. He saw in her success his own failure to break her. On the other hand, every time she rose above his demands, she proved what a fine asset she was to the Empire. He could see two outcomes to their relationship: he destroyed her utterly, or she became one of the greatest soldiers that ever existed in Imperial history. The only way to make her the greatest was to keep trying to prevent it. Aware of the irony in that concept, Galloway knew it was his duty to continue in the manner he had been, and let Washington decide for herself which path she would take.
"Sergeant Galloway!" The voice was unfamiliar to him, but carried enough authority with it to cause Galloway's head to snap round and identify its source. Seeing the officer standing in the shadows, he quickly came to attention.
"Sir!" he bellowed.
The officer stepped forward and Galloway saw he was wearing a Lieutenant Colonel's insignia. "We must have a talk, Sergeant Galloway, you and I. Walk with me."
Galloway didn't question the order. He was well aware that high ranking officers often met with non-coms and grunts for many reasons, most often for the advancement of their own careers. He'd always managed to stay clear of such machinations, but he figured it was inevitable that eventually someone would get to him. He fell into step with the officer and didn't look at him. He'd already

committed every relevant detail to memory and would now wait and hear what he had to say. He would weigh up what he considered to be in the best interests of the Empire and decide on a course of action based on his conclusions. If he decided this officer would best serve the Empire by succeeding in his scheming, he would gladly do what he could to facilitate that. If he felt the Empire would suffer from such action, he would do everything in his power to bring the officer down. Galloway had been a soldier too long now to be fooled by mere words. He got a feel for a person very quickly. Let the officer talk, he would say nothing.

"Sergeant, it's my understanding you have a young lady in your troop who goes by the name of Moonchild."

This wasn't what Galloway had been expecting as an opening gambit.

"Private Washington, sir!" he barked.

"Do you have a volume control, Sergeant? This is intended to be a clandestine meeting," the officer seemed half cautious, half amused.

"Sorry, sir," Galloway growled, as low as he could manage without whispering. When his vocal enhancer had been fitted, it hadn't been anticipated he would need to whisper.

"Thank you, Sergeant," the officer seemed to be laughing. "Let me explain why I've come to see you. You've been going fairly rough on that poor girl, haven't you, Sergeant?"

"She shouldn't have been admitted in the first place, sir, she doesn't meet the minimum height requirements for humans. But I liked her attitude, sir. I think I can turn her into a good soldier, but she needs pushing."

The officer stopped walking and rounded on Galloway. "No, Sergeant, she doesn't need pushing. She needs you to ease up on her. Make no mistake, Sergeant, this girl must not be allowed to progress in the military. She's a dangerous element who will cause no end of trouble to the Empire. She's one of the Martian street urchins, Sergeant. A gang member. She has a criminal record. We don't want that sort in the army, we can't allow the Emperor to be represented by scum like her. She only stays because she won't admit you can beat her. The harder you push her, the more stubborn she becomes. And she's building up her hatred of you, and the rest of us, as a result. One day that hatred will boil over and a lot of people will be hurt, possibly worse. Why? Because you gave her a reason to hate. Cut back on her, Sergeant, don't give her anything to strive for. She'll think she's won, but she'll get bored, and she'll leave quietly. Do you understand what I'm saying, Sergeant?"

"Perfectly, sir," Galloway nodded. "Am I to assume these are my new orders, sir?"

"You can assume that, yes, Sergeant. Dismissed."

Galloway snapped to attention, saluted, then turned smartly on his heel and stalked off into the night.

9

The assembled youths looked around, taking stock of their surroundings. Moonchild immediately picked up on the fact that the first years and second years had formed separate groups. She sniffed the air. Definitely not like Mars or Earth, the only two planets she'd ever set foot on. Sergeant Galloway appeared from the open hatch on the transport ship. "Welcome to New Philadelphia," his voice carried across the starport and everyone heard him, even the techs who were busy servicing other vessels. "For you first year troopers, this is your chance to sample hell for the first time. For you second years, it's the planet's chance to get revenge for what you did to it last year. This time, you will be the experts, and it's your job to get your first years back to base. First years, it's your mission to get to base alive. Make no mistake, this is not a game. Not all of you will survive this exercise. It's up to your second year guides to help you survive, but they won't all make it back either. You must cooperate with each other. Or you will die. Pair off."

Moonchild had realised that this was what Galloway had been building up to, and she'd used the time to locate di Ravello. Somehow, he'd gravitated towards her, and the two of them met in the skirmish and nodded acceptance to each other. Decision made. "What happens now?" she whispered.

"Now they drop us somewhere on the planet and tell us to head for base," di Ravello told her. "We get no help, no map, no supplies, just a canteen of water each. We get six days to get back before the ship breaks orbit. If we're not on it, we stay here for as long as it takes for us to convince someone to take us off-planet. But we go back as civilians. If we don't make it back in six days, the army doesn't take us back at all."

By now, the pairing had been completed. Galloway surveyed the little islands of life before him and knew some of them would never stand before him again. As usual, the small number of women in both years had paired off as much as they were able with other women, but he noticed one of the few exceptions was Moonchild. He wondered what had influenced both their choices. Certainly, the few other such pairings were based on the mistaken belief they were going to find time to have sex in the six days ahead of them. Lovers made terrible battlefield companions in his experience, but it was their choice. For some reason, he didn't think Moonchild and di Ravello had based their decision on anything other than belief that they were each other's best choice for survival. He expected their chances were better than most others could dream of.

"Listen up, people," he bellowed, interrupting their introductions. "You will be taken to an unspecified location and given an objective. You will have six days to reach your objective. Those who are at their objective within that time will be transported back to Earth to resume training. Those who are still here and alive had better make alternative arrangements. Second years will explain what they remember from last time they were here, so you first years had better hope you picked one with a good memory. Good luck." He turned away from them and stalked back into the transport ship. The hatch slithered shut behind him. Moonchild wondered if he really had been looking directly at her when he'd wished them luck. She shook the idea from her mind. The man had been trying to kill her since she'd first arrived on the drill square, why would he change that attitude now?

Within minutes, the ship had taken off and the troops were herded by starport personnel towards what appeared to the main building. There, they were met by a couple of soldiers who handed each pair a small card. As Moonchild and di Ravello approached, and took their card, they were ushered through a door into a teleportation chamber. The card seemed to have a series of numbers on it and di Ravello gave them a cursory glance before handing it to Moonchild as they were directed to stand on the platform. The chamber faded out of existence, to be replaced by darkness. Cold, wet darkness. At first, it seemed they'd landed in the middle of the night, but it soon became obvious the canopy of leaves above them was so dense it simply cut out most of the sunshine. Taking stock, they appeared to be in a swampy jungle, up to their knees in water. Even in winter, it was stiflingly muggy, with the canopy retaining all the moisture from the swamp.

"Let's get out of here," di Ravello said, with a sense of urgency. "There could be things in here that would see us as a threat."

Moonchild laughed. "What, are we on the menu?"

His look froze her. "Yes," he said. "It happened last year. Three entire groups disappeared in the swamp. We need to find solid ground and get our bearings."

They waded towards what looked like a suitable patch of land. "Don't sit down," di Ravello warned her. "We don't have time."

"We've got six days," Moonchild protested.

"And?" di Ravello countered. "You think we're only a couple of days from our objective? No, they've planned this with surgical precision. If we make good time, and don't run into trouble, we'll probably make it in five days, maybe five and a half. If we have problems, we'll maybe make it in time, but if we can't solve any problems quickly, we're here till some merchant takes pity on us and gives us jobs cleaning his cargo holds for the rest of our lives."

Moonchild swallowed. "I won't sit down then," she said.

"Good choice."

She looked round, then up. "If we're going to find our bearings, we probably need to be up there."

"That's good thinking, off you go, then."

Biting back a comment, she selected a tree and began shinning up it. After about ten metres, she encountered branches and foliage. Working her way up, she eventually clawed her way to a level where the light became stronger. Getting herself to a point where she could take in the panorama, she allowed herself a moment to appreciate the beauty of her surroundings, and then began the task of returning to the floor of the jungle.

"That way's east," she pointed. "The jungle goes on as far as I can see in all directions, there are mountains to the north. The sun's directly overhead, so we're on or near the equator. Nothing else of interest."

"Good work, the coordinates are to the north, so we head for the mountains."

"I have a question," Moonchild said. "How do we head north through the swamp if there are things in here that'll eat us?"

"We need some means of crossing the swamp without getting our feet wet. Know how to build a raft?"

"A what?"

"Sorry, I forgot, you're from Mars. Funny, a planet once famous for its canals has no free standing water."
"Why's that funny?"
"Don't worry, the strangest things amuse me, it's nothing personal. A raft is a kind of makeshift boat. I'll show you. We need to find some big branches."
"What do we do with them?"
"You see those creepers? There, on the trees. We gather some of them, we tie the branches together and we're away. Trust me, it works better than it sounds."

***

They spent the rest of the day punting through the swamp, occasionally carrying the raft over land, though fortunately there wasn't much of it to impede their progress. Although it was difficult to tell when it happened, they stopped at nightfall. Di Ravello located a certain type of tree and began peeling bark from it. Handing some to Moonchild, he retained a piece, from which he took a hearty bite. Moonchild stared in horror, so he said. "Can you find anything better to eat?"
She said nothing and took a cautious nibble. It was bitter, it was woody, it was disgusting. She knew she must have pulled a face, because he sat down beside her and said quietly. "If you don't make the most of your environment, you'll die here. You have six days to keep your energy up. If you don't eat, you can't keep going. I admit it's an acquired taste, but you can't afford to wait for something tastier. Listen, I was in the same position a year ago, and I thought the same thing about my second year's choice of food. But you know in the end you have to eat it, so you

just do. At least this stuff doesn't try and escape when you put it in your mouth."

"Oh, please, don't be disgusting."

He grinned and stood up again. "Don't dismiss the idea, we've got a long way to go, and it won't all be jungle."

"So six days last year makes you an expert on this planet, does it?"

"No, but it teaches you to make a point of studying it for your next visit. My second year studied it, and I did the same. If you know what's good for you, you'll study it for next year, and keep your first year from going hungry. And you'll pick strange things up off the floor and eat them like it was gourmet food. Believe me."

"So, did you get the jungle last year?"

He shook his head. "Desert. Very hot, very dry. But there's this animal, kind of like a snake but with legs. Very tasty. And they have something very similar to dung beetles. You can't eat the beetle, but the dung makes a good…"

"Stop it!"

He shrugged, smiled to himself and continued munching on the bark.

Moonchild changed the subject. "So, where are you from, originally?"

"Trisander, a little planet near Arajak space. Heard of it?"

"Nope."

"Can't say I'm surprised, no-one else has. It was settled in the twenty second century and became known for its university. My parents wanted me to go to the university, but I had my eye on a military career. Best way to see the length and breadth of the Empire, I thought. Then, Trisander was hit by a surprise attack from the Arajak, and the university was flattened. So much for my education."

"That's awful, I'm sorry, I didn't mean to…"

"It's ok, my family weren't hurt, they live on the other continent, but the planet took heavy damage. And with the Empire now involved in the war against the Arajak, I don't imagine state assistance is going to come anytime soon. But we'll survive. I know it."

"I know what you mean, when we went to war with the Galkasians, Mars went into recession. My earliest memories are of rioting on the streets. Even though it's one of the core planets, and despite it being so close to Earth, the whole planet seems to be going to pieces."

"Were your family badly affected?"

Moonchild was silent for a moment. "I never knew my family. All I knew was the street. I always assumed I was an orphan, but I honestly don't know. The gangs raised me until I was old enough to branch out. They expected me to start my own gang. Instead, I became a waitress. I raised enough cash to get me to Earth, just so I can join up."

"You must've been desperate, that's why you stood up to Sergeant Go-Away."

"Exactly. I was terrified of him, but I was more scared of not making it. I don't know what I'd've done if I'd left that first day."

Di Ravello stood. "Get some sleep. I'll take first watch, I'll wake you in four hours."

Moonchild nodded. She turned over onto her side and closed her eyes. She didn't believe she'd ever sleep in this place, but she was long gone before she could analyse that thought.

***

She awoke with a start to find di Ravello prodding her. "Hey, sleeping beauty, it's your shift."

For the first moment, almost too quick for di Ravello to register it, her eyes assumed the hostile alertness of one used to waking in Martian doorways with the sound of a jaded spacer looking for an easy score ringing in her ears. The moment passed, but di Ravello had noticed. Although he said nothing, he watched his new partner with an increased level of caution and concern. She, in turn, noticed his reaction. They regarded each other for a moment, before she rose to her feet and went to where he'd just come from. Di Ravello watched her for a moment longer, then decided there was nothing he could say or do to broach a subject that was none of his business if she chose not to share it. Removing his jacket, he fanned it out over himself like a blanket and was asleep in minutes.

***

The jungle eventually gave way to marshy lowlands, then foothills. The sunshine of the first day gave way to heavy rain on the second. The discomfort of their first day together gave way to even greater discomfort as they trudged through the permanent puddle that seemed to be the only feature on their section of the planet. The low cloud had hidden the mountains they were aiming for, which added to the feeling of pessimism that hung between them as they tried to keep a steady pace. Di Ravello had made it clear they wouldn't allow themselves to ease up for the first four days, at least. If they were delayed, they needed as much time in hand as possible. So, aside from a twenty minute rest for lunch, they never stopped except to get their bearings until they made camp in the evening.

"Whoopee!" Moonchild mused with all the enthusiasm of someone who had lived one long anti-climax, as di Ravello broke out their rations. "More bark. My favourite."

Her partner favoured her with a grin, rather than a reprimand. It was becoming obvious to him that her initial complaint was merely to make her point of view known, before settling down to the reality of their situation. She even thanked him when he handed her a piece of bark, and took a healthy bite from it. Even her grimace was only a token effort this time.

"Tell me," he said, as he watched her eat. "Where do you see yourself in five years time?"

"What kind of question is that?" she returned.

"Don't you ever answer questions when you're asked one?"

"Is this one of those games?"

"What games?"

"You've never played this game, then?"

"No."

"Hah! You lose, di Ravello! You're supposed to always ask a question."

Di Ravello laughed, a deep throaty chuckle of genuine amusement. She joined in.

"You're a weird one, Moonchild, you know that?"

"We used to play it in our gang, all the younger kids. I guess I just never grew out of it. Did you play games as a kid?"

"Trisander wasn't the kind of place you played games for amusement," di Ravello said. "You were expected to learn. With its university, it was supposed to be the

highest aspiration for all of us natives to be admitted. They taught me mnemonic games and mathematical tricks. My parents wanted me to be a great scientist, or possibly even go on to teach at the university."
"So how come you never got in? You're not dumb, you could've gotten in."
"I suppose I could've, but I deliberately failed the entrance exam."
They both laughed.
"Well, you got two things out of that choice, hon, you avoided getting flattened, and you met me."
"Yeah," he admitted. "Although this time yesterday, I was thinking maybe getting flattened was better than being stuck in the jungle with you for a week."
They both laughed again. Their eyes met across the space between them. He looked away.
"What?" she asked.
"Sorry," he told her. "I don't want to give you the wrong impression of me."
"Wrong impression? As in, wrong impression? Like, the impression that you like me?"
"Listen, Moonchild... Elise... I do like you, you're a good soldier, and a great person, but you should know... it's nothing personal, it's just... not too many women do that kind of thing for me."
"Oh, you mean you don't think... oh... oh!" she nodded as the penny dropped. "As in, women in general don't do it for you?"
"Like I said, it's nothing personal," di Ravello apologised. "But I didn't want to make you think I was making a move on you."
"Hmm... that's ok, you just stopped me making a move on you, that's all. No apology necessary."

Then they smiled at each other, with proper understanding, and found themselves laughing again.

"How's your bark?" he asked.

"Worse than my bite, hon," she answered. "Oh, you mean this? Not bad, could do with a touch more salt, though."

As she prepared for first watch, and he settled himself under his jacket, she considered the irony of it. Here she was, in the middle of nowhere, with a man who made her body ache with his nearness. And he was untouchable.

"Hey, di Ravello," she called out to him. "You know, there are some things we could do where it doesn't make a difference. You just close your eyes and pretend…"

"Goodnight, Moonchild," he said, rolling over, but she could tell he was grinning in the darkness.

10

They'd found a pass through the mountains, and were making good time. As they gained altitude, it became clear that the weather was changing. The rain of the previous day was turning to sleet, then snow. Moonchild thought she was going to freeze to death. Dusk began to draw in. She squinted into the blizzard.

"How much further before we can stop?" she called to di Ravello.

"You had enough already?" he shouted back.

"No, I was just wondering."

"Hah! You lose, Moonchild. I thought you were good at this game."

She laughed. "You damned cheating son of a…"

Her retort was lost as di Ravello gave a short cry and disappeared from view. Hurling herself forwards, she landed near the spot where he'd been standing. He had uncovered a crevasse and had fallen in. Moonchild searched for him in the gloom, hampered not just by poor light levels, but also by the flurrying snow, already difficult due to the blizzard conditions, made worse by the passage of di Ravello's body.

"Di Ravello? Where are you? Can you hear me?"

"I'm ok," came the somewhat groggy answer. "All this snow, it was a soft landing. Can you… oh!"

"What? Di Ravello, what's wrong?"

"Moonchild, you'd better get down here. I've found something."

"If I do, how will we get out again?"

"There's a way out over here. Come on, this is serious."

Moonchild lowered herself as carefully as she could and let go of her hold, landing with a muffled thump beside di Ravello, who made an attempt to catch her.

"What's up?" she asked.

He nodded to somewhere beyond her, and she turned. "It's Ballantyne," di Ravello told her. "I don't know the first year's name."

"Vasquez," she recognised the younger of the two corpses. "They must have fallen down here like you, but maybe there wasn't enough snow to cushion them."

"I wish that was the case, but I doubt it," di Ravello frowned, moving forward. "Look at this wound. Ballantyne was hit by something sharp."

"You think Vasquez stabbed him? What with? An icicle?"

"Possibly, but it doesn't explain… ah!" he rolled Vasquez over, to find a similar wound in his back. "That might explain how, but it doesn't say why."

Moonchild glanced round. "I don't see anything here that could be used as a weapon. An ice knife wouldn't melt at these temperatures. There has to be another explanation. An animal?"

Di Ravello stood. "I think you're right. And it probably killed them either to defend its territory, or for food. Either way, it'll come back here, so we'd better be gone before that happens."

Seeing no reason to disagree, Moonchild hurried out the way di Ravello had indicated. From there it was an easy task to get back on their path, and when they took stock, they decided they hadn't lost any significant time from the diversion, and at least they would be able to report the loss of Ballantyne and Vasquez.

As they walked, Moonchild had an idea. "Instead of making the canteens filter the crap out of all that swamp water, why don't we pack them with snow? That way, at least we know it's clean."

"Good thinking," di Ravello encouraged, and immediately emptied his canteen onto the snow and replaced it with more snow. The canteen's thermal circuitry began melting it. Between them, they realised that the snow they packed in melted down to about a third of the capacity in water, so they packed one with snow and poured it into the other one once it had melted, eventually filling both without draining both power cells.

"How did you find water last year?" Moonchild asked as they walked.

"Oh, there were plants dotted around the desert. Like cacti, many of them stored water, so it was a case of locating them and sucking them dry. Trouble is, not all of them were healthy to drink from. One plant that's native to New Philadelphia actually converts it while it stores it, kind of like plant pee. It gave my second year cramps. He marched for a whole day nearly bent double. I walked behind him all the way and I have to admit I enjoyed the view."

"Must've been tough to resist the temptation, huh?"

"Nah, it was easy. Considering what else it did to him, I was content just to watch. Trouble is, in the desert, it's not always easy to stay upwind of someone. It shifts direction constantly, and at the wrong moment…" di Ravello didn't finish the thought, but the image lived in Moonchild's mind for a long time afterwards.

"It's getting late," her partner told her eventually. "We need to find shelter."

"Yeah, I've been thinking about that. I haven't seen any suitable caves or anything for a long time. Maybe we should walk a little further, see if something turns up."

Di Ravello looked all around. The snowfall had eased up and visibility was greatly improved, although what they'd gained from clearer skies was lost in the gathering gloom. "No, I don't think we'll find anything now. Let's make camp here."
"In the open? We'll freeze!"
Di Ravello shook his head. "No, we dig a foxhole and get in. The snow will retain the heat and keep us warm. It's what the Eskimos of Earth do with their igloos, as well as the Vihansu, with their ice yurts, and various other races."
Moonchild followed his lead and together they made a cosy looking space from the snow. "Shall I take first watch?" she volunteered when they were finished.
"Not an option, tonight, I'm afraid. We have to get in there together and share body heat. The foxhole can only retain what we generate. At least we'll both get a good night's sleep. Take your shirt off."
Moonchild blinked. "Oh, changed your mind about me, have you?"
He laughed as he began opening his own shirt. "We have to put our bodies together, and have as much air in there with us as we can get. The warmer we can make it, the more toes and fingers we'll have when we wake up tomorrow."
She nodded her acknowledgement and removed her shirt. Di Ravello didn't even glance at her as he stepped up to her and began fastening his shirt to hers. Once the two shirts were together, and the jackets similarly fastened, they struggled into them and clumsily manoeuvered themselves into the foxhole. Moonchild could feel her heart pounding against his chest as their flesh connected. She wondered if he could feel it too. For that matter, she would be surprised if he couldn't hear it. He was so

incredibly sexy, despite three days worth of sweat, mixed with the combined odours of swamp, jungle and rain. She was aware of her own smell, more so now she was thinking about it, and she was itching under her breasts, where she couldn't reach because of di Ravello's chest pressing against them.
She tried to ignore it.
"You know," she said. "This would be a lot easier if you weren't gay."
He smiled at her. "This would be a lot easier if you were," he answered.

***

The night passed peacefully, and Moonchild knew she'd drifted off sometime, her weariness overwhelming her discomfort, as well as the torrent of hormones that threatened to burst her body apart like some kind of proximity bomb, wired to di Ravello's presence. She woke to find their arms entwined around each other. They could have been lovers, the easy way they held each other in their sleep. She realised his eyes were open and he was watching her. She blushed, and he smiled knowingly.
"Breakfast, darling?" he said, and the spell was broken. They shared a hug, one of pure friendship, and they started to squirm back out of the foxhole.
Then the beast charged them. The first they heard was a grunting snort and, their heads whirling to locate the source of the sound, they saw what seemed to be a white and grey pig-like creature hurtling across the tundra at them. In a ridiculous show of uncoordinated choreography, they both tried to step backwards out of its way. This merely meant neither of them moved, and both

simply fell sideways. Struggling to regain their feet, they tried to get the jackets and shirts off to give themselves room to manœuvre. As they did their unlikely dance, the beast was gaining ground on them. Glancing to the side, Moonchild could identify the wickedly curved tusks jutting from either side of its jaw, like pictures she'd seen of a warthog, only bigger. Whether or not this was the same creature that had killed Ballantyne and Vasquez, she knew without any doubt, it was aiming to kill her and di Ravello. At the last possible moment, she pushed herself against di Ravello, sending them both over in his direction. The beast was wrong footed and caught Moonchild a glancing blow on the right leg as she fell. Then as it turned and resumed its charge, they struggled to their feet and began a sideways dash in the opposite direction.

"This is so undignified," di Ravello managed to say, his voice a mix of anger and panic. Moonchild said nothing, but tried to help him remove their clothes as they galloped sidelong into the white wasteland. There was a jarring impact, and they were suddenly flying. Moonchild found herself free of the jackets and shirts, as she landed face down in the snow. For a moment she stayed there, expecting the beast to gore her exposed body at any moment. But it was quiet. She carefully raised her head. The beast lay half wrapped in the clothes she'd so recently abandoned, and di Ravello sat in the remaining tatters. Both lay together beside a rock that had been uncovered in their flurry. Di Ravello was watching her with a pained expression and his breath was quick and shallow, it was clearly agony for him to draw air into his lungs.

She stood and approached, peripherally aware of her nakedness, but unconcerned. He watched her, his expression telling her all she needed to know about his condition. She knelt beside him and looked into his eyes. He looked down, indicating with his gaze where the injury was. Carefully, Moonchild cleared the fabric from the area, tearing where it was necessary. The tusk was buried into his side. Again, their eyes met.

"I'm going to get this thing out of you," she promised him. He nodded, unable to speak, but his look told her he had no doubt he was dying. She was acutely aware that he was no longer the beautiful, ethereal, unreachable man she desired so much, and couldn't have, but a mere boy, just nineteen, facing his death in the snow, light years from home with just her for a witness to his passing. She looked all around her for inspiration. All she could do was gather snow in both hands and begin packing around the wound. If she froze it, she could stop it bleeding, and deaden the nerves to make it easier on him when she had to drag the beast out of him. He seemed to understand, and nodded to indicate she should carry on with her plan. Even though she did her best, he still hissed in anguish as she pulled the huge pig-like head away from him. Blood welled out over the snow and she immediately grabbed more snow, carefully placing it against the wound. As she worked, he gripped her hand. She looked up at his tear-filled eyes.

"You have to leave me here," he whispered.

"No, dammit! I'm getting you to base, or I'm staying here with you."

"Elise, don't be a fool. I'm not going anywhere. You have to get to base while you've got time. Don't be a martyr for me. Don't let my death be the cause of yours too."

"Hush," she admonished as she wrapped the tattered remains of the clothes around him to try and give him some warmth. "You're not going to die, I'm going to get us both to base, you'll see." Even though he nodded, she knew she wasn't convincing him. She wasn't even convincing herself.

"Elise," he whispered. "You need to keep warm. If you freeze here, you'll be no use to me. And if they find us both here half naked, they'll get the wrong idea about me." His laugh was forced and turned into a bubbling cough. A trickle of blood ran from the corner of his mouth. "Listen, Elise, you have to get some clothes. Ballantyne and Vasquez are only a few minutes in that direction," he tried to point, but hadn't the strength. "Go and get their clothes and put them on. Then we'll see about getting out of here, ok?" She wasn't going to go, but he locked his eyes on hers. "Elise, I mean it. With just these rags, neither of us has a chance. Go now, or we'll both die here debating it. Go on, I'm not going to run away."

Knowing her expression was as full of tears as his, Moonchild left him there and ran with all the speed she could muster to where Ballantyne and Vasquez had died. She took the shirts and jackets and ran back, without stopping to put anything on. She was gone from his side no more than ten minutes. He was sitting where she'd left him, his eyes closed, looking for all the world like he was asleep. He looked so peaceful, it almost burst her soul apart. Her wordless scream rushed across the snow, desperate to be heard. But there was only her.

***

As the snow began to fall again, Moonchild roused herself from her inactivity. She had to get to base, she knew that.

To stay here would be to destroy his faith in her. She pulled Vasquez's jacket tighter around her. It was too big for her, but Ballantyne's was bigger, so she'd settled for this. As she approached di Ravello's body, she became aware of the anomaly. A set of footprints in the snow that didn't belong to either of them. She didn't recognise the pattern of the tread. They seemed to begin in the middle of nowhere, as if the owner had been lowered into position, and then approached di Ravello. Too tired and too consumed by grief, she dismissed them from her mind. She wasn't in the right frame of mind to solve mysteries now. She gently eased di Ravello up into a position where she could haul him up over her shoulder. She laid him gently on the snow and turned to the place where he'd died. She dug another foxhole, and once finished, she placed di Ravello in it and covered his body as well as she was able with their ruined clothes, then buried him under more snow. She dragged the beast's corpse over the rock. Let that serve as his headstone, she thought, aware that the tears were coming again. She drew herself up and looked down at the grave.
"We still could have been great together, you know," she whispered. She lingered for a few seconds more, then turned and continued her journey alone.

***

As the mountain became foothills, so the snow became rain. Moonchild stumbled out from the wooded hillside, following the course of the river whose source she'd found on the upper slopes of the mountain. It was almost dusk of the fifth day. She reckoned she'd covered the required amount of ground to make it back to base in time. So she turned and went back into the woods, finding a suitable tree stump to rest against for the night. As she had done every time she rested since di Ravello had died, she wept bitterly for him. Even though she had always believed crying herself to sleep was a childish cliché, she knew she was still crying when her awareness faded.

11

"Wake up, Moonchild, you lazy piece of filth!"

She was instantly awake, and crouched in a position ready to attack. Sergeant Galloway glared down at her from ten yards away. What was he doing here? She considered she might be dreaming, but knew even as she thought it, she was really awake.

"What do you think you're doing, lying about when you should be moving, moving, moving!" Galloway bellowed at her. "Don't you think you need to reach your objective on time? Do you think we'll wait for you? Make an exception for you? No! You don't deserve to be in the army, you miserable cretin! You deserve to stay here and spend the rest of your pathetic little life considering what a complete and utter failure you are! Your second year's dead, and you can't be bothered to make the effort and tell his comrades how he died, you'd rather spend your precious time sleeping it off and feeling sorry for yourself! Well, damn you, Moonchild, didn't I always tell you it would come to this? Didn't I always know you'd fail? You're a disgrace to the army, you're a disgrace to yourself and, my God, girl, you're a disgrace to Giovanni di Ravello!"

Moonchild had got to her feet and was boiling away during the entire tirade. Eventually, Galloway fell silent and it was her turn. "You can say what you want, you arrogant bastard, but get this through your stupid head: I have not given up on anything! The more you push, the more I will resist you, and you will never beat me! Do you understand me? You will *never* beat me! I will not allow you to get in the way of my life, and I will reach my objective! You can try and stop me if you dare, but if I have to walk through you, so help me, that's what I'll do, and they can pick up the pieces afterwards, but di Ravello was my friend and I will do this for him. I have not disgraced anyone, and I will never disgrace di Ravello! You just said the wrong thing to me!" Without once thinking about due deference to a superior, Moonchild stormed out of his presence and continued her journey.

Galloway watched her with a satisfied smile. "Oh, no, Moonchild," he murmured as she disappeared. "I think I said exactly the right thing."

***

Moonchild arrived with three hours to spare. A little over three quarters of those who had set out had been there waiting for her. A few more rolled in after her. As the survivors exchanged testimonies about fallen comrades, she knew that she now faced a choice. Let it end like this, find her own way in the galaxy, or find some way to break Galloway, beat him at his own game. She considered di Ravello, and knew her choice was made. Sergeant Galloway had better be ready, because she was coming for him.

***

The figure stepped from the shadows. "Sergeant Galloway," his voice was dangerously low, the threat implicit in the dark tone. "I am very disappointed. I gave you an order to ease up on Private Washington, and instead you tightened your grip on her. That makes me very angry, Sergeant."

"Yes, sir. I understand, sir. However, there were extenuating circumstances."

The officer raised his eyebrows. "What circumstances?"

"Well, sir, firstly that having talked with you, I explored the imperial database for a lieutenant colonel fitting your description, and found no such lieutenant colonel exists. Secondly, I received a communication advising me to proceed with caution."

"A communication? From whom?"

"From me," said Magpie, stepping from the shadows behind the officer. "An admiral of our acquaintance furnished me with your name, Mister Oatey and told me what you were up to. Fancied a spell in the army did you? Oh, well, it can't last, you know. No, Mister Oatey, that would be unwise," Magpie admonished as he noticed the Balsari agent was reaching for his pistol. "Bouncer, Gunboy!"

Two others appeared from the gloom, rifles aimed squarely at the traitor's ribs. Oatey could see his escape vanishing into the realms of imagination.

"Sergeant, these men aren't in the database, either, don't listen to them."

"Yes, sir, I know they aren't. I know who they are and I know who you are. And I also know why I had to do the opposite of what you told me. Because despite everything, Elise Washington will become one of the finest soldiers the Empire has ever produced. And you would have had me prevent that coming to pass. You, sir, are a disgrace to the people that birthed you, and you deserve everything that's coming to you. Now, gentlemen, if that will be all…?"

"Yes, thank you, Sergeant," Magpie smiled gratefully at him.

Galloway saluted smartly, even though he figured the officer he had just acknowledged was probably just a kid somewhere in the galaxy right now. Then, he continued on his way back to his quarters, as if nothing out of the ordinary had occurred.

As his door scythed open, he was immediately aware of the presence in the house. Drawing his pistol, he cautiously made his way to his living area. The lights were on and he saw her sitting in his favourite chair.

"Hello, Sergeant," her face and voice were strangely familiar, but he couldn't place her. She wore the uniform of a full colonel.

Then he realised. "Moonchild," his vocal enhancers seemed to be struggling to function.

"I remember you telling me about this day after I graduated," she told him. "You must do me a favour, Sergeant. You must continue to treat me the way you always have. You made me the person I am today. When you broke the rules and found me that morning in the woods, you changed the course of history. I was so tired, I'd have slept all day, and I'd probably still be there, waiting on some crappy table or other. But you knew you'd sting me into defying you, didn't you? So thank you, Sergeant Galloway. You will always have my respect for what you did, even if I take a few years to show it."

Galloway smiled, unsure of his place. Moonchild stood. "I have to go, but please remember. You and I, at this point in history, are trying to kill each other. Make me hate you, but when I graduate, bring me here and explain why you did what you did."

"Yes, sir!" he barked, then saluted, but she wasn't there.

***

Di Ravello opened his eyes and slowly focussed on the new arrival. A colonel. He had the irrational instinct to stand to attention.
"At ease, trooper," the colonel told him. Her voice… he knew the voice from somewhere. She walked towards him and knelt in front of him, putting a gentle hand on his shoulder. "I haven't got long. I just wanted to see you."
"I know you," he said, weakly, his strength ebbing.
"Yes, you do," she said, her voice catching.
He looked at her face, familiar, but unfamiliar. He'd seen that face only recently, but the only thing he remembered was Moonchild. He saw the tears on the woman's face and realisation came. "Oh, God, but how…?"
"Long story, my friend. All that matters is I'm here now."
"I'm dying," he said.
"Yes, and I'll stay with you to the end."
"Do you really get to be a colonel?"
"I hope I go further, but the future isn't open to me, just the past. But yes, right now, I'm a colonel."
"I knew you'd make it back to base."
"I nearly didn't."
"No," di Ravello disagreed. "You were always going to get there, even when you didn't know it. I knew you would."
He winced as the pain lanced through him again.
"Easy there," Moonchild told him, squeezing his shoulder knowing even she did she couldn't change history.
He focussed again on her. "This morning," he whispered with effort. "When I woke up and we were holding each other like that… I thought… I thought you were so beautiful. I really did. I wanted… wanted…"

"But you said you were gay," she frowned. "You did say that. It's true isn't it?"

He smiled at her and the light faded from his eyes. For a long moment, she stared at him, unable to work out what he'd meant. What had he been trying to tell her? Or had he just been winding her up at the end?

"You son of a bitch, you got me good that time," she smiled through the tears and held him close. Then she let him back down to rest against the rock, smoothed his eyes closed and stood back.

She took out her communicator. "Colonel Washington to Control. I'm ready now, Iceman."

Then she was gone, leaving her footprints in the snow as the only sign she'd been there at all.

12

Tranquillity Base, Luna, 2487

Goldfish wiped the sweat from his face and continued working. A thin bead of the stuff had evaded his hand and found his left eye, making it sting. Cursing the heat, he tried to realign the cortex for the hundredth time.
"You'd better get out of here, folks, I'm running out of time here."
"Keep working," Moonchild instructed him. "If that thing goes off, there'll be no point to us surviving."
She glanced at Magpie to get his assessment. Her second in command just shrugged and continued his observation of Goldfish's efforts. She took that as total agreement.
Cursing again, and dropping his tools as a spark flew between the cortex and his hand, Goldfish stepped back briefly to suck his burnt fingers. Gingerly, Magpie prodded one of the tools to check it wasn't charged, then picked it up, handing it back to his colleague.
"I won't do that again," the demolitions expert grimaced, getting back to work. Magpie flashed him an encouraging grin, and he smiled back before becoming all business again.
Will.
Magpie whirled round to locate the source of the sound. Moonchild turned in response. "What's up, hon?"
Magpie frowned. "Sorry. I thought someone spoke to me."
"I didn't hear anyone," Moonchild shook her head. "Are you sure?"

"I suppose not," he concluded, and returned to his observation.

"Got it!" Goldfish sighed with evident relief. "Ah, it's a light sequence detonation principle. Magpie, do you still have that photonic replicator you never admitted to having?"

Magpie didn't hesitate, simply reached into one of his many hidden pockets and handed the device to Goldfish. "Of course not," he said. "They're highly illegal and no self-respecting officer of the Imperial Navy would stoop so low."

"Thought not," Goldfish commented, taking the device and fiddling with it behind the bomb. He handed it back. "Can you tell me the correct sequence of lights, based on the frequency of each one?"

"You mean the most common down to the least?"

"That's it, sir."

"Ok, wait… here we go… green… orange… white…"

Will.

Magpie turned again. There was still no-one there.

"Sir?" Goldfish said. "We're running out of time."

"What's wrong, Will?" Moonchild asked, moving closer.

"Someone called my name again. Are you sure you didn't hear anything?"

"Nothing. Are you sure you're ok?"

"Yeah, I'm fine…"

"Sir? Now would be a good time with that sequence. Do I go with red or blue?"

"Er…"

Will.

It was in his head. "Wait! There's another psi-operative in here. A woman's voice."

"Sir! Red or blue?"

"Blue!"
"A woman? Are you sure?"
"She's in here with us."
"Got it, thanks."
"Where?"
"Somewhere in the base, I can't be more specific at the moment."
"You need to find her, quickly. How's the bomb, Goldfish?"
"Sorted, but it was all a bit last minute," he said, looking questioningly at Magpie.
"Sorry, I got distracted. The thing is, now I think about it, there's something vaguely familiar about her."
"You got some dark secret you want to share, hon?"
For once, Magpie didn't rise to the bait. He frowned deeper. "I can't place her, but I know her, I'm sure of it."
"Well, our work's done here, the Empire and the Arajak can get on with their negotiations, and all's well with the universe. Do you want to stay here?"
"I need to find her, whoever she is."
Moonchild nodded and took out her communicator. "Be careful, Will, ok? Control, this is Colonel Washington, lock onto Lieutenant Warner and myself and bring us home."
Magpie watched as they shimmered out of existence. Pulling himself upright, he stretched to get the tension out of his body, then rubbed his still-aching knees. He knew he ought to be taking it easy, but events seemed to be conspiring against his ability to recover from breaking his legs.
Will.
"Where are you?" he demanded. "Who are you?"

Don't you remember me, Will?
"Should I? Why don't you show yourself?"
Soon. It's not time yet. Try and find me.
"I'm not playing games with you."
That's a pity, Will. You always used to play with me.
Magpie went cold. Who the hell was this? How did she know him? Who did he play with in the past? He began to search with his mind.
"If you won't show yourself, why should I believe anything you tell me?"
Because you know I'm telling you the truth, Will. You know in your heart that I'm not lying to you.
"If you know me as well as you think you do, you'd know I'm too cynical to listen to my heart."
You never were, though, Will. You always followed your heart. Even when it got you into trouble.
"Not since I was a child. Not since I found out who I was." He couldn't find her. He extended his search.
But there was a time before that. Do you remember, Will? Before you discovered your heritage?
"So you knew me as a child, did you? And you expect me to remember you? I remember lots of kids from then. You could be any one of them."
Oh, really? Any one of them? Were all your little friends psionically gifted, then? Or just a few?
Magpie frowned. Maybe that's why he wasn't finding her. If she was somehow blocking him, if she didn't want to be found, he could search forever and not find her. If that was the case, perhaps there was a clue in that fact. He began slowly walking from the cellar.
"I have no idea who you are. You'll need to give me a bit more to go on if this is a guessing game."

Very good, Will, that's the spirit. Now, think back to the beginning. You remember all the tests, don't you? You remember how Uncle Xavier used to check up on you?

"So, you were involved in Project Cyclone were you?" Magpie ghosted up the service stairs and halted at the top. Just around the corner, he could see a discrepancy in the shadows that should have been cast by the corridor lighting.

Now you're getting there, Will. Can you remember what else was there? In the room where the tests were conducted?

Magpie crept closer, inching his way to the junction. He stopped using his voice to speak to her.

How can I remember that? I was just a baby.

Oh, come on, Will, you were a special baby. You remember a lot further back than most babies. Think back. Look around that room. See where Uncle Xavier went after he finished with you.

Magpie remembered. There was a door that he used to come through to his left, and another he used to leave through to his right. There was another baby in each room.

Are you saying you're one of those babies?

Very good, Will, I knew you'd get there in the end.

There's only one problem with your claim.

Oh? And what's that?

"Those babies are dead," he said, turning the corner and putting his gun to the head of the young woman who was waiting there. She opened her eyes, surprised that he'd found her. Then her eyes widened.

"Oh! You're much older than I expected." Magpie knew the answer was that he was twenty years into his own past. The girl, who was expecting a twenty year old, was finally wrong-footed. But she recovered quickly. "But you're wrong. I didn't die."

Magpie knew she was telling the truth, that somehow she'd survived the destruction of the project's research centre. Because, as he looked at her, he saw his own eyes looking back at him.

13

Moonchild watched him as he heaved a weary sigh and tried to explain it all again. "No," he said, as patiently as he could. "Not my sister. She's another clone created from the splicing of William and Angel's genetic material."

R'sulek-Entah came to his rescue. "There is an Arajak term for such a relationship. We call it vel-dek'mor. It is a loose definition for one who is less than a twin, but more than a sibling."

Moonchild was none the wiser, and suspected the liaison officer was winding her up.

"There isn't an official designation within the Empire for the relationship between clones from the same parent-genes," Magpie continued, nodding his thanks to R'sulek-Entah. "But that just about sums us up. In the same way as identical twins are created from the same egg splitting in two, we were created from the same batch of genetic material, but we were always intended to be separate individuals. We were part of a big experiment into human engineering."

"The Arajak abandoned cloning centuries ago," R'sulek-Entah enlightened them. "With our caste system physiology being a natural consequence of our social rigidity, it was deemed to be a waste of resources. Instead, we redirected the funding into other research."

"Like how to wage war on the Empire?" Moonchild suggested innocently.

"Ara'Sayal was unaware of Earth at the time," she replied candidly. "There was no Empire, your home system was limited to one inhabited planet. At least one that you knew of," she added darkly. "No, we were funding research into how to wage war on the Vihansu at that time."

Moonchild narrowed her eyes, aware that the Arajak liaison officer had been deliberately provoking her, by not responding to her own provocation. She wasn't sure how much of what she'd just said was genuine. She decided to push a little further. "Maybe your caste-specific physiology is the result of ancient genetic tampering," she dropped the comment in as if it were of no consequence to her, but she knew the Arajak were intensely proud and protective of their social system. She accepted the victory when R'sulek-Entah failed to answer and simply glared at her nominal commander through cold blue orbs of ice.

"None of which is actually helping me resolve this problem," Magpie mentioned.

"Sorry, hon," Moonchild turned back to face him. "Please, carry on."

"The point really isn't who she is, or what our relationship is, the point is can I find her now? For that matter, is she even alive now? For all I know, she may not have lived beyond 2487, and she died shortly after we met."

"Ok, let's assume we understand the relationship issue, let's move on," Moonchild waved her hand, indicated she was brushing aside that aspect of the conversation. "How did she find you, and what did she want?"

"She said she'd been looking for me since the project was destroyed. She knew I'd survived, but had no idea where I'd gone. She left Mars soon afterwards, and lost all contact with me. She was working at Tranquillity Base in a civilian capacity at the time of the negotiations. It's funny, I assumed I was the only survivor, I assumed the other babies had died. If Legna survived, maybe the other one did, too."

R'sulek-Entah frowned. "I have a question. You took your name from the combination of your parents' forenames, yes?" She waited for his confirming nod before asking. "How did she arrive at Lenya?"

Magpie found a stylus and a notepad among the jumble on his desk. He quickly wrote the name. "It's only pronounced Lenya", he explained.

"Ah," realisation was somewhat anti-climactic. "It is the reverse of Angel."

"Yes, she calls herself Legna Williams, it's a variant on my rationale. Quite clever too, if you ask me."

"I did not," R'sulek-Entah told him. "If you will excuse me, I have to return to my children."

Magpie instructed the door to open, and with a nod to both human officers, she left.

Moonchild waited until she'd gone before saying her next carefully weighted words. "If you want to find her, I can give you as much leave as you need. I know it's a personal matter for you. You can take as much time as you need."

"Thanks. I appreciate it."

She nodded. "Well, I don't have kids, but it's late, and I ought to go."

"You know there's always a bed here for you if you need it," her host said, optimistically.

"Oh, but, hon, where would you sleep?"

He shrugged innocently, as if he hadn't considered that.

"Thanks for the offer, but the walk will do me good."

"Last chance to change your mind," he called as she moved to the door.

"Goodnight, hon," she blew him a kiss and was gone.

"Oh, well," he said to himself as the door closed. "One day, she'll come running, just wait and see."

***

When he entered the imperial database, he tried everything he could think of. He tried to search under Legna, Angel, Williams, Project Cyclone, Xavier, everything he could imagine, with even the most tenuous link to her. Yes, she had been employed at the base during the imperial negotiations with the Arajak. She had been involved in an administrative capacity, but although she was quite well placed in the civilian section, she left soon after the treaty had been signed. There was no record of where she'd gone. Maybe, he wondered, she'd left because she'd found him. How could he tell her why he was there? How could he explain to her the discrepancy in their ages? He'd listened as she told him about her ongoing quest to find him. How she'd spent nearly twenty years trying to find him, only to find an old man who was Will, but wasn't. Who vanished from her life again an hour later, presumably for at least another twenty years. And now he was trying to find her, he was experiencing the same problems. Where was she? Where had she gone after they'd met in 2487? Nothing he tried brought up any leads, despite the huge amount of red herrings the database through up at him. Coming back out, he decided to go home and try again in the morning, and see if anything occurred to him overnight.

***

Nothing did. Moonchild came to see him. "The rest of us are moving out in a couple of hours. Search and rescue operation. The *Starfarer*'s disappeared somewhere in the Granfelt Reaches."

"*Starfarer?*" Magpie searched his memory. "Captain Rivers, right?"

"That's right, you know anyone on that ship?"

"Benny Delgado, we were at the academy together. He went into Command while I followed Espionage, but our careers have been pretty similar with regard to promotion. What's the report?"

"A log buoy just came in. An unidentified vessel appeared and opened fire on them. There's data in the report to suggest some form of chronotech was used in the attack. So they're sending us in. Last report was that both ships were damaged and racing to bring weapons online. What we find when we get out there depends largely on who won that race. You don't have to come, Will."

"I know, thanks. But I want to find out if Benny's ok. I'll come."

***

The Imperial Battlecruiser *Traveller* approached her sister ship on an intercept vector suggestive of a galley at ramming speed. At the back of the command deck, Moonchild and her team watched on the science station monitors. The *Starfarer* hung in space, clearly damaged beyond her ability to be repaired with the resources available in deep space. The other vessel was about thirty kilometres away, equally damaged.

"Lifesigns?" Moonchild asked.

Iceman looked up from his instruments. "Fluctuating, Colonel. The human lifesigns are not enough to account for the entire crew, but there are other signs appearing at random all over the ship."

"What about the other ship?"

"There are no lifesigns aboard the other ship."

"Are they all teleporting onto the *Starfarer*?"

"Unlikely, Colonel, they are still appearing, but their point of origin does not appear to be the other vessel."

"Could there be a stealth vessel in the area?"

"Possibly, but the power source for their teleporter should show up, and it doesn't."

Moonchild turned to R'sulek-Entah, a question in her look.

"I am not aware of any species with technology that can hide and still carry out such operations."

"Ok, we need to get over there. We go in two teams. Bouncer, Goldfish, you're with me, in Engineering. Gunboy and R'sulek-Entah, you go with Magpie to the bridge. Iceman, you get to stay here, I need someone to coordinate the operation. You need to keep track of our movements, and the movements of the unknowns. We need to find as many *Starfarer* crew as we can and get them back over here. Also, you can be working on figuring out the nature of the chronotech that was used in the attack. Any questions? Good. Ok, people, let's go. Captain Ulanov, can you get us in teleport range, please."

***

Magpie's team arrived on the bridge to find a scene of calm chaos. The crew appeared to in a state of orderly panic. Magpie surveyed the members of the bridge crew who as yet hadn't noticed their arrival. Eventually he found his quarry, hunched over the helm controls.

"Captain Rivers?" The woman looked up and he noticed her face was scorched on the right side, a fresh burn. "Lieutenant Commander William Angel, Space-Time Axial Response Team, ma'am. This is Lieutenant Commander R'sulek-Entah, and Lieutenant John McCallum. We're here to offer what help we can."

Rivers returned Magpie's smart salute. "Good to see you, Commander. Thanks for coming. Have you assessed the enemy vessel?"

"Yes, ma'am, there's no lifesigns registering from it, but there are multiple unknown lifeforms appearing all over your ship. I've been instructed to assist with the evacuation of *Starfarer*. I'm sorry, ma'am."

Rivers was pragmatic, at least. "Very well, Commander, I suppose it's too much to hope we'll get home in this old girl." She patted the helm control fondly, looking round her ruined bridge. "I'll require all my bridge officers until I'm ready to leave, but I want to stay until everyone else has been taken."

"Understood, ma'am, I'll take all non-essential personnel from the bridge now, and make my way through the ship. My CO is in engineering and will be working her way towards us, doing much the same." He and the others began distributing homing patches to the bridge crew.

"Will you be requiring any of my security personnel?" Rivers asked.

"It would help if they were aware we were coming and be available if needed, but I think we'll let them help with the evacuation where possible, ma'am."

Rivers nodded. "One more thing, Commander. Why did they send S.T.A.R.T.?"

"Your ship's recorder registered the use of chronometric technology, ma'am. We need to establish to what extent it's involved and how it affects the situation."

"Good luck then, Commander. Keep me informed on your progress."

Magpie saluted again and turned to the others. "Ok?"

Gunboy hefted his rifle. "While you were talking, Iceman reported lifesigns appearing on the other side of these doors."

"Where does it go?"

R'sulek-Entah showed him the schematic on her handpad. "The corridor leads to a crossroads. There are three elevators leading to all decks."

"How many lifesigns?"

"About twenty," Gunboy reported.

Taking his rifle and motioning to R'sulek-Entah to do the same, Magpie approached the doors. They failed to open and he smacked his left knee against them. Biting back a pain-filled curse, he turned and looked for the manual handle. Turning the handle and slowly opening the doors, their ears were assaulted by the sound from the other side. A hideous keening choir, howling its hunger as it searched the corridor for food. Magpie took a moment to react to the last thing he was expecting to see beyond the doors. R'sulek-Entah and Gunboy took a similar length of time to assimilate the sight, before opening fire, blasting into the masses without aiming, intent solely on destroying indiscriminately. Magpie finally managed to get the doors closed without any of them getting onto the bridge.

As the trio of S.T.A.R.T. officers took advantage of the respite before they had to go back into the fray, Captain Rivers approached them. "What the hell was that, Commander?"

Magpie blew out his cheeks and thought of the implications of his next statement. "That, Captain, was what we call goblins."

14

Moonchild appeared in Engineering and immediately looked round for the ranking officer. "Who's in charge here?" she demanded, striding forward to the main engine panel.

A man in the uniform of a lieutenant commander turned to face her. "Who the… oh, sorry ma'am, Delgado. Lieutenant Commander Benjamin Delgado, ship's pilot. Are you with the rescue team?"

She returned his salute. "That's right, Commander, Colonel Washington, S.T.A.R.T., what's your status?" She was vaguely aware in the periphery of her vision Goldfish and Bouncer, as they began issuing the homing patches.

"Engines are offline and not looking good for a while yet, ma'am. We've got problems with the hyperdrive batteries, they were badly drained in the fight." All the time he was talking, Delgado was moving, adjusting control settings as he spoke, bringing people into the panel and pointing at what he wanted them to manage. Moonchild was impressed with the way he worked, clearly an efficient officer with a calm outlook. No wonder Magpie thought so highly of him.

"If you're the pilot, where's the chief engineer?"

"Dead, ma'am. There's very few of the engineering staff left. I'm doing what I can, but I could use any expertise you can provide."

"Not an option, I'm afraid, Commander, this is an evacuation scenario. There are hostiles aboard, and they're threatening to outnumber the crew at any point. We're teleporting survivors now before we secure the ship."

Delgado was clearly shattered that the ship was considered too damaged to repair, but hid his disappointment well. "Understood, ma'am, what's the nature of the hostiles? Can we help with security?"

"Glad you asked, Commander, you know the layout of the ship, you can help us get around. Magpie, Iceman, any sightings of the hostiles?"

"You're not going to like this, Colonel," Magpie's voice sounded tense. "The ship's full of goblins!"

"What? Magpie, repeat, did you say goblins?"

"Yep! Don't ask me how, but they're appearing all over the ship!"

"Iceman, how the hell is this possible?"

"Impossible to speculate, Colonel," the unhurried voice of the technical coordinator seemed unconcerned, totally at odds with the seriousness of the latest revelation. "However, it would appear to be linked in some way to the presence of chronotech."

"You don't say!" Moonchild realised there was little point in sarcasm when the intended recipient was incapable of recognising it. "Ok, any problems with the evacuation?"

"We are removing survivors at the optimum rate, Colonel, although some are requesting a return to the *Starfarer* in order to defend against the invaders."

"No, any such requests are denied. If we're dealing with goblins, the sooner the entire ship is abandoned, the better. Magpie, did you get that?"

"Got it. Captain Rivers is requesting she be last to leave, but I'll make sure the others get off as and when we get to them."

"Acknowledged. Right, let's move out. Magpie, we'll meet you somewhere around deck 10, I should think."

"Race you."

"With your knees? I haven't time to give you that kind of head start, hon!"

Magpie laughed and she closed the channel. She turned back to Delgado and saw he was the only remaining crewmember left in Engineering. "Are you armed, Commander? Good, we'll need all the firepower we can get."

"Excuse me, ma'am, but what are goblins?"

"At the moment, you only need to know this: they are extremely dangerous, and they shouldn't be here. Assuming we get off the ship alive, we'll give you a proper explanation then. Now, if you could open these doors and stand back, we've got some shooting to do."

***

To a crew not accustomed to the ravening mass that is the goblins, the new threat was terrible to behold as they teemed into areas already depleted of staff and began to feed. Already reeling from their recent brush with destruction, they were unprepared for the fresh assault which caught them all off guard. Moonchild and Magpie, however, led their teams into the fray and made good time sweeping through the *Starfarer*, tagging each crewmember they found with homing patches. Where they found armed security personnel, they added them to the teams, and the extra firepower was a bonus they hadn't factored in when originally sizing up the extent of the task ahead of them. Indeed, the additional weaponry combined with the fact that the goblins were only encountered in smaller groups, around twenty to thirty at a time, meant the S.T.A.R.T. members found it ludicrously easy to stem the tide. The goblins were, according to Iceman, still pouring into the ship at random locations, but never in large enough quantities to pose a serious threat to them, although the *Starfarer* crew were finding them too much to handle. In their favour, though, was the fact that with most of the internal power out, and all non-essential systems re-routed to weapons, the internal doors refused to open except manually, meaning any crewmembers who could seal themselves into areas were usually safe, unless the goblins began appearing in those areas before they were tagged and teleported. So it was that their minds began to turn elsewhere. R'sulek-Entah was the first to suggest they capture some goblins and study them. So far, due to the nature of the creatures and their existence which, until now, had been limited to the dead time zones in temporal refractions, it had never been possible to isolate even a dead goblin and bring it back. Now, R'sulek-Entah was considering the possibility of a live specimen and Magpie became caught up in the idea, giving it his full support. Their plan, once they'd had time to think of one simply needed the right circumstances to put into action.

"Iceman, stand by," Magpie told the technical coordinator. "Have a security team and a forcefield in place when I give the signal."

"May I enquire as to your intentions?" Iceman asked politely.

"We're going to try and catch a goblin."

"Is that wise?"

"No, but it's probably the only opportunity we'll ever have. Stand by."

"Acknowledged," Iceman responded, his voice betraying no sign that he approved or disapproved of the plan.

Magpie turned to Captain Rivers. "This is your ship, ma'am, it's your right to veto the plan. But this may help us more than we can imagine in the future."

Rivers appeared to give it serious consideration. Magpie and Gunboy tensed, afraid she would refuse. Her crew tensed, afraid she'd give the go ahead. R'sulek-Entah never gave the impression she cared one way or the other, although Gunboy could tell she was hoping for a positive response.

After what seemed like forever, Rivers looked at Magpie. "Proceed, Commander."

Restraining himself from his usual exuberance, Magpie merely nodded. "Thank you, ma'am. Positions, please, people."

***

The wall slowly opened and they could sense the arrival of food from the opening. The food began running away from them. They ran after the food, their unspeakable howl of hunger accompanying their hunt. There was only a solitary piece of food, but there were only a handful of them, so they all figured they had a good chance of being first to the kill. They hurtled onwards, aware only of the food they were closing on rapidly.

***

Gunboy charged headlong back towards the junction, images of the goblins catching him and running him down trying to insinuate themselves in his mind. He was already scared, he didn't need that making it worse. He'd only volunteered for decoy duty because he knew Magpie's knees wouldn't withstand the heavy pounding they'd take from the running, and he wasn't going to allow R'sulek-Entah to risk herself. It would be unfair to ask a *Starfarer* crewmember to do it, so he was the only realistic choice.

Now, though, he was questioning his reasoning. His only previous encounter with the goblins was a couple of months ago, right at the outset of his S.T.A.R.T. career, and it had scared him almost witless. But he'd been assured their appearance was a rarity due to the nature of their home environment and the conditions surrounding access to that environment. So how come he was now running from them down the corridor of an imperial battlecruiser in conventional space?

As he turned the corner, the sound of the goblins close behind, a lot closer than he liked, he grabbed his rifle from R'sulek-Entah and spun to face his pursuers, adding his fire to that laid down by the others. The goblins that followed him were mown down in a red haze, as their bodies exploded under the intensity of a dozen rifles and pistols. Most of the goblins at the back of the group stopped to take advantage of the easy meal. A few continued after the bigger prize, excited by the appearance of even more food. Those which weren't killed in the first wave were shot down by weapons reset to heavy stun. At the completion of the operation, upwards of forty goblin bodies littered the corridor. Separating the live ones from the dead, they selected three healthy specimens and tagged them. R'sulek-Entah then tagged three corpses.

"Because we have no idea how death affects their physiology, other than in the obvious way," she explained when Magpie questioned this. "Their bodies may respond differently to ours. If we have an opportunity to study this, it would be unwise to ignore it."

"Good point," Magpie agreed, impressed with the Arajak's thoroughness. "Iceman, six goblins to take when you're ready."

"Acknowledged," Iceman replied, and the goblins were gone.

Any remaining goblins that were still alive were killed by R'sulek-Entah who was taking no chances. As she stood, wiping the blade of an evil-looking Arajak battleknife on a goblin corpse, she looked around to see all the others, Gunboy included, staring with ill-disguised horror. She shrugged and replaced the knife in her belt.

"Ok, fun's over, let's go," Magpie said, and they continued their journey through the ship.

***

Deck 10 was deserted apart from Moonchild and her extended team. "What kept you?" she asked innocently.

"Just a little diversion to save the Empire from a horrible fate, why? You have a nice day too, dear?"

Moonchild just grinned her relief and pleasure that he was unharmed, and turned to the captain. "Captain Rivers? I'm Colonel Elise Washington, I'm pleased to see you're ok."

The captain took the colonel's hand and shook it warmly. "I wish I could say the same for all my crew, but I'm grateful for all the help you and your team have been able to give us, thanks."

"Iceman says all the crew are either here with us now or aboard the *Traveller*, so we'd better get going. I look forward to us becoming better acquainted later. Iceman, are you ready?"

"Stand by," Iceman instructed, shortly before the living occupants of the room were teleported back to the other ship.

***

They were back aboard the *Traveller* before Magpie had the chance to speak to Delgado. They shook hands and slapped each other's shoulders and grinned stupidly at each other for a long while before either actually spoke. Eventually Delgado broke the silence. "So, how's my favourite spy?"
"Not spying, these days, Benny, I've been reduced to a common thief. So much for a promising career, eh? What happened to you, though? Have you put on weight? Ship life obviously agrees with you, my friend."
"Not ship life, Will; marriage."
"You're kidding! Who's the poor sucker?"
"Her name's Tatiana." He waited for the penny to drop.
"Right, and she… Tatiana? As in Tatiana Romanova? The cute one from Navigation?"
"Oh, you remember? Yes, the same one. We always kept in touch after she was promoted to the Unbreakable. We finally did the deed two years ago."
"Really? Was that before or after you married her?"
Delgado punched him on the shoulder in mock indignation. "Should've seen that coming, huh?"
"Seriously, Benny, congratulations. Where's she posted now?"
"Until last month, she was second officer here. But, hey, someone's got to look after the baby."
"You're a dad? Man, it just gets worse! What've you got?"
"Little boy. Daniel, after my father. Looks like me, too."

"Good for you, Benny, I'm really impressed."
"Thanks, Will. That means a lot. So, how about you, any romances I ought to hear about?"
"None that involve me, I'm afraid."
"No? Pity. Anyone in mind for when it does happen?"
"Well, there's one very special lady I've got my eye on…"
"Oh?"
"So far she's managed to resist my charms, sadly."
"You're kidding, how does she manage that?"
"She keeps pulling rank."
The other penny dropped. "Oh… ah… right… you never did go for the easy target, did you?"
"I like a challenge," Magpie shrugged. "Although I have to admit, I'd prefer it if it wasn't quite such a challenge. A man can wear himself out chasing the unobtainable."
"Looks to me like we've got a lot of catching up to do, Will."
The two officers went to their quarters, with the promise of a long talk when the opportunity presented itself.

***

Moonchild and the two captains sat discussing the situation. Although of lower rank, R'sulek-Entah was sitting in on the discussion as the Arajak representative.
"I'm sorry, Colonel," Captain Ulanov was saying. "I'm not happy with these creatures on my ship. The dead ones came back to life within an hour of their arrival here. I'm uncomfortable with their proximity to my crew. And I've had to put acoustic dampeners in the holding cells. That hideous noise is unsettling my security people."
"I understand, and I sympathise completely, Captain," Moonchild hated diplomacy, but saw the need for it in

this situation. Ulanov had to take her team and the *Starfarer* survivors back to Earth, but he was quite within his rights to ditch the goblins if he chose to. "All I can say in favour of keeping them aboard is that getting them safely back to Earth so we can study them may be of great benefit to the Empire."

"Oh, please, Colonel, every time someone wants me to do something I'm not happy with, they roll out the old line about benefit to the Empire. I need solid reasons, not propaganda. I'm not a raw recruit with wide eyes and empty mind."

Moonchild would have thumped the man, except he would have put her in a cell next to the goblins had she done so. Her face, though, betrayed her instinct and Ulanov stared, an open challenge on his face, mocking her loss of power. Moonchild didn't know what worse: the fact that she wasn't in command, or the fact that he knew how she felt about it.

Captain Rivers stepped in. "If I may make an observation? I agree to an extent with Captain Ulanov. I wouldn't be happy with these creatures on my ship. However, they were on my ship, and in far greater numbers, which Colonel Washington and her team contained with incredible efficiency. And if we have a chance to find out what these creatures are, and how they came to be on my ship, I would take the risk. Forget the party line, forget the rhetoric, and just consider this. These goblins don't belong in normal space, but the fact remains they are here. Until we know why and how, we can't prevent them coming again. And the fact that they appeared on my ship in the middle of nowhere, and seemingly not connected with the other ship, suggests they can be sent with pinpoint accuracy to any location. Suppose whoever sent them chooses this ship next? Or a colony full of civilians and children? Or the Emperor's throne room? Can we afford not to take this risk with six of these creatures when there is so much potentially at stake?"

R'sulek-Entah observed the expressions on the faces of the two captains, as Rivers swung the argument in the colonel's favour. She still struggled to tell, but she thought the man looked trapped, and was trying to find a way to be happy with the situation. She thought Rivers had the calm look of one who has just reasoned that a mathematical impossibility is in fact a basic tenet by which the whole universe operates, and proven it. Colonel Washington simply looked annoyed, an expression she had come to recognise, largely due to the fact that it was the one she most often showed when dealing with her liaison officer. R'sulek-Entah couldn't care less what the colonel thought of her, but it was gratifying to know she was becoming more adept at recognising human facial expressions.

"Very well," Ulanov finally sighed. "But I want your team posted to the holding cells round the clock, Colonel. If there is any threat to anyone on this ship, I want your team to be the first ones in the firing line. I have no intention of putting my crew in any danger while I have the option."

"Thank you, Captain, that's a perfectly acceptable condition. As soon as they get back from their assignment, I'll have them posted on a rota basis. Now, as Commander R'sulek-Entah and I are the only ones here, will you excuse us while we take the first shift?"

They all stood, and the S.T.A.R.T. members left to make their way to relieve the security officers.

***

Bouncer switched through all the settings available to his ocular implants, but still couldn't find any sign of life. "It's weird, sir, it's like the entire ship was unmanned."
Magpie wasn't thrilled with the idea. It suggested too many potential complications. Like you wouldn't put your own people in a bomb and pilot it into space. "Thanks, Bouncer. Goldfish, you found anything?"
"Nothing down here," was the response from the ship's engineering deck. "But that's good, it means the place hasn't been wired to explode."
"Hmm… still doesn't mean I'm happy about it. Ok, I don't see that I have a choice." He sat at the helm and placed his hands on the controls, closing his eyes. Frowning, he began to concentrate.
The goblins were running amok. They swarmed onto the command deck and attacked the crew. The crew were overrun, taken by surprise as they tried to repair the damage, consumed by the goblins, as they tried in vain to halt their attack. Then, the automated defence system kicked in, destroying the goblins. It had been damaged and was slow to respond, sluggish when it finally did begin its task. But all the goblins had been evaporated because they were too stupid to take evasive action. Now, there was no-one left. How had they got on the ship in the first place? He went deeper. They didn't invade like they did on the *Starfarer*. They were already aboard. Were they being held in the ship's cells? Did they escape when the ship lost power? He went deeper still. And he saw her. Legna. She was calling his name, silently calling. *Will. Will.*

Magpie removed his hand and wiped at the sweat. How was he to interpret what he'd just seen? He looked up at Bouncer. "This is not good," he said.

Bouncer opened his mouth to ask, but was distracted by a noise. Looking for the source, they both saw the tiny nozzle in the ceiling struggling to get a lock on Magpie's position. Diving from his seat, Magpie managed to avoid the first shot as it streaked across the space between them. A tiny hole appeared in the back of the chair, where his chest had been a second before. A second shot scorched the floor where Magpie landed and immediately rolled away from. As he struggled to his feet, a third shot hit him, a graze on his left thigh. Waves of pain and nausea exploded all over his body as he tumbled to the deck clutching his wounded leg. He looked up and through the haze of agony, watched as the nozzle fixed its aim between his eyes. That was when Bouncer blasted it from its position.

He hurried to Magpie's side. "Are you badly hurt sir?"

The string of incoherent expletives answered his question. "Goldfish, Gunboy, Iceman, watch yourselves, there's an automated defence system up here, and there might be one down there too. Afzal to *Traveller*, teleport Commander Angel directly to sickbay, medical emergency." Bouncer watched as Magpie shimmered out of existence, and the air quietened down as his swearing went with him. Let him give the *Traveller* something to talk about, he decided. Checking for more such devices, he found none. Good; he didn't want the same thing happening to him. He left the command deck and went to find the others, checking all the time for similar devices.

As it turned out, there was one in the engineering section, but Goldfish had disabled it after the warning. They had assimilated the information about the crew's fate, but were none the wiser, largely due to missing the benefit of Magpie's insight.

It was Iceman who made the discovery. He'd been exploring the medical section, looking for records about the crew. Apparently, they were a lizardlike race called the Kalaszan. Iceman searched the imperial database for references to this race, but found none. He downloaded the details into his brain for further study later. Then, as he continued his search, he found the genebanks.

***

There were only five goblins, and had been for some time. Moonchild had produced a tiny hole in the forcefield, wide enough to shoot a pistol set to heavy disrupt into the goblins. One burst open, its chest utterly smashed by the shot, and the others immediately pounced. The cries of agony and the triumphant howls of the others were cut off when she closed the hole again. Now, she had determined that dead goblins don't come back to life if they've been at least partially eaten. There wasn't much left of it now, as two goblins squabbled over licking the blood from the floor.

Then the team returned and reported. Magpie was hurt again. He really didn't have a great deal of luck, especially where his legs were concerned. But crucially, they'd come back with a genebank. Magpie had been removed before this discovery, so Moonchild went to see him.

"I would imagine it's the genetic material needed to create goblins," he told her when she explained. "Whoever these Kalaszan are, they had the goblins aboard their ship long before they were wiped out by them. I wondered if they'd captured them, but now it looks like they were breeding them."

"Well, we'll find out more soon enough," Moonchild said from the edge of his bed, where she had perched. "Iceman's reviewing their species data and Goldfish has got Ulanov's people transferring the ship's logs to the *Traveller*. In the meantime, the *Indomitable* is being reassigned to the area, to bring the Kalaszan ship back to Earth. We'll get all its secrets, one way or another."

"There's something else," he seemed uncomfortable. "Legna is involved somehow. She's been aboard that ship at some time, at least once."

"Well, we'll figure out how later. Right now, we have to get this stuff to someone we can trust. And you are going to get your body sorted once and for all."

"You know," he tried. "If you were just to rub it better, it would do me the world of good."

"Oh, hon, you know I would but if I get too excited, I might start playing rough and, well, I wouldn't want to hurt you," she stood. "Get some rest, we'll be home soon. Goodnight, hon."

***

Doctor Joshua Hanson was usually far too busy to deal with visitors, but this one was special. Moonchild had come to make sure Magpie was settled in comfortably and had diverted herself away to see him.

"Colonel, how can I help you?"

"Hey, Hacksaw, how are you?"

"I can't complain. Hospital food is always better when you're on the staff. I trust Magpie's happy? I made sure he gets the staff menu, rather than the patients' one."

"He's fine. Just make sure you keep him in until he's fit for duty. I want you to take personal care of that, he can't intimidate you. The last lot let him out with his legs still too weak because he threatened to tell them how he'd personally seen them all die."

"He can't see the future, it's not possible."

"They didn't know that."

"Consider it done. Anything else?"

"Yes, I wanted to give you a chance to look at this. Chances are, as CMO for the navy, you'd get this anyway, eventually, but I want you to see it now."

"What is it?"

"Goblin DNA."

"You're joking! You're not joking... you really got some? Here, let's get it down to the lab."

They went to work. Moonchild explained the whole story. While S.T.A.R.T. activities were technically classified Top Secret, much of what they did came out in the wash eventually, if a little diluted sometimes. Also, as Hanson had been one of the team's original members, it wasn't like she was telling him something about which he previously knew nothing. He had experience with goblins himself. Hanson took a sample of the DNA and put it under the microscope. The screen showed a strand of DNA that Moonchild wouldn't have been able to distinguish from any other. Hanson, on the other hand, was clearly disturbed.

"What's wrong?" Moonchild asked.

"I don't know yet. I could be wrong."

"What?"

"Wait here, would you, please?"

He went to another office and was gone a few minutes. Moonchild looked at the goblin DNA for a while, trying to decide if there was anything about it she should be noticing. She concluded that even if it carried a sign declaring the truth, she wouldn't recognise it. Eventually, Doctor Hanson returned.

Setting up another sample, he placed it under the microscope. "Let's see if I'm right about this," he said, not really seeming as enthusiastic as he could be.

Moonchild looked at the screen. Another strand of DNA appeared. She couldn't really tell the difference.

"Now let's compare the two, shall we?" Hanson suggested, flicking a control on the microscope. The screen split, bringing up the picture from the sample Moonchild had brought in, next to the one Hanson had just placed there. The doctor adjusted the controls of Moonchild's sample until it was brought into alignment with Hanson's sample. The screen flickered as it highlighted sequences that were similar. Hanson looked at Moonchild.

"I'm not an expert," the colonel said, slowly, not sure where this was leading. "But I'd say those two strands of DNA were identical."

Hanson nodded, cautiously. "And you'd be right. It's an exact match."

"So somehow, someone's already found a sample of goblin DNA?" Moonchild could hardly believe the implications of that. "When? And how? And who?"

Hanson held up his hands. "Wait. It's not as simple as that. This one," he pointed to Moonchild's sample. "Is from the goblins you caught on the *Starfarer*."

"Ok, I'm following that," Moonchild said, warily.

Hanson indicated the other, identical strand. "And this one was taken from Magpie," he said.

15

The Great Tree, Ara'Sayal, 2507

Being a new father was somewhat more than Gunboy had been looking for when he joined S.T.A.R.T. He had been told his mission briefs would take him into previously uncharted territory. Parenthood was not expected to be one of those territories. However, he was determined to make the most of his new role. It had been disconcerting, to say the least, to discover that his offspring would first resemble blue caterpillars, but he was determined to love them just the same. So much so that when R'sulek-Entah was preparing to ship them back to Ara'Sayal for formal training as children of the royal line, he insisted that as the father, he should be allowed to rear them on Earth. R'sulek-Entah, being the perfect mother, consulted with her own mother, the Queen's sister, who allowed the break with tradition, although it created a minor scandal among the ruling caste. It hadn't been any easier when the first grubs were hatched within a week of their fertilisation, as Gunboy had been hoping for some time to adjust to his impending fatherhood. But, a month later, the first of them started settling into their cocoons. Now, a month further on, each one had broken free of the chrysalis and was playing with his or her siblings. Of course, having fifty-six newborn children running around at the same time was quite wearing. They'd been forced to move into new quarters and had hired several nannies, mostly from the Arajak teaching caste, whose pale yellow skin and canary yellow hair were in sharp contrast to the blue shades of R'sulek-Entah's caste. The children, however, shared their father's skin tones, although the cobalt-coloured blood gave it a pale blue hint. They all inherited their mother's antennae and wings, although there was some question over whether or not they would function as well as for a full-blood Arajak. None of this concerned Gunboy when compared to the immense difficulty he was facing remembering the names of all his children. R'sulek-Entah was having no trouble, but he assumed the Arajak were used to multiple births on that scale. Worse still, the news of the births was greeted with enthusiasm by the Empire's official press machine, and journalists were hounding the couple for their story. R'sulek-Entah was having none of it, and was claiming, of all things, diplomatic immunity, leaving Gunboy to field all questions. He did so with consummate ease, being from an aristocratic family and therefore schooled in such dying arts as public speaking, but he really struggled when they asked him to name them all. He found himself wishing he had something like Goldfish's mnemonics, but he had to make the best of it. When questioned about the discrepancies between lists of names, he claimed it was something to do with Arajak naming traditions meaning that children changed their names with alarming frequency until they reached adulthood, at which point they should ask him for the definitive list. By then, he reasoned, no-one would care anyway, leaving him free to learn them all at his leisure.

But when the call came from Moonchild, family matters had to take second place.

***

Magpie wasn't there, which they were expecting. He was still recovering from his injury sustained aboard the Kalaszan ship. Unlike last time he was hospitalised, he was staying there until he was told differently. Hacksaw was going to make sure of that.

Moonchild made use of this fact to bring the others up to date on a difficult and delicate subject. "We have a problem that needs a lot of consideration before we take any action," she told them. "It seems we have a match for the goblin DNA. It's identical to Magpie's."

The sudden vocal activity was as much as she expected, and she gave them time to settle down again before continuing. "Now, no-one is suggesting Magpie is in any way responsible for this. In fact, I've made sure he isn't told about this until I feel it's right to do so. And it should be me that tells him. Only one other person knows, and that's Hacksaw. So we have discretion on our side, but we need to secure the genebanks from the Kalaszan ship when the *Indomitable* gets back here with it, before the rest of the galaxy gets hold of this information. For Magpie's sake, this information must remain classified."

R'sulek-Entah raised an eyebrow. "Forgive my difficulty in interpreting your words, Colonel, but would your intentions not constitute treason?"

Moonchild met her look without flinching. "You may interpret my words any way you wish, Commander, I can't control that. Is the tone of this conversation causing you any discomfort?"

"None, Colonel, I merely requested clarification. I believe I understand perfectly now."

Bouncer seemed to have thought of something. "It makes sense now," he said. "When the defence system on the Kalaszan ship turned on Magpie, no-one else was in any danger. It wasn't looking for interlopers, it was looking for goblins."

"That's useful information," Iceman said calmly. "If the Kalaszan have a defence system that can isolate goblin DNA, we could adapt it to our purposes."

"Excellent," Moonchild enthused. "Smart thinking, Bouncer. Now, we need to figure out how to get past the *Indomitable* crew and get our hands on the goods. Any suggestions?"

R'sulek-Entah was the first to answer. "Perhaps it would be easier to approach this from a different angle. Rather than steal the incoming genebanks, why not simply alter Commander Angel's records?"

"Now who's having treasonous thoughts?" Gunboy whispered, not entirely cheerfully.

"I am merely attempting to be a team player. Besides, I would be acting against an alien government, rather than my own. That crime is covered under the term 'espionage', not 'treason'. Although, it is a moot difference, considering the penalty is the same for both."

"Are you saying you're in?" Moonchild was uncertain she'd heard correctly.

"My duty is to S.T.A.R.T., not your Emperor. You are my commanding officer until such time as I am told otherwise. Therefore, I am in. My only condition is that Ara'Sayal's interests are not hurt by this."

"I'll try and remember that," Moonchild smiled. "Thank you. Now, as R'sulek-Entah says, this action, whatever form it takes, will most likely be considered treasonous, so anyone who feels unable to follow through will be allowed to leave. No-one here will hold it against you, and all we ask is that you don't betray either us or Magpie."

"You can stop looking," Goldfish said. "Nobody's leaving."

Moonchild looked at each one of them and nodded her gratitude. "So. Let's plan treason."

***

Doctor Joshua Hanson couldn't believe what he was hearing. "Are you mad? That's treason!"

"Please, Hacksaw," Moonchild tried to calm him down. "I've had this discussion already, and it went along similar lines. Spare me the lecture and just tell me. Will you help us?"

"How do you know I won't just alert the authorities? That's what I should be doing now. They'd give me a medal for it."

"Yes, they would. They'd probably promote you as well. But poor Magpie would spend the rest of his life being torn apart by vindictive surgeons trying to be the first to discover his secrets. As his friend, you won't allow that to happen."

Hacksaw looked away. "No, I won't allow that to happen, you're right. But treason? That's too much to ask. Even if I'm the only one to ever see the comparison between Magpie and the goblins, not reporting it would raise questions, and I'm a terrible liar."

"But you wrote that fake post mortem for Magpie's trial, and that wasn't too long ago."

"I know, but if I'd been summoned to give evidence in person, I couldn't have gone through with it. I'd have blurted the truth, or been so unconvincing everyone would have guessed it anyway."

"It comes to this," Moonchild sighed. "Either help us, or turn us in. Here, take my communicator. You just need to flick the switch, and say the words. That's all it'll take. But don't leave us guessing. We need to know now if there's any point in attempting this, before we commit ourselves. Now, tell me: do I need to spend the next few minutes trying to break Magpie out of here, or can I go back and tell the others to get ready to take the genebanks?"

They spent some time staring into each other's eyes, waiting for some sign. Eventually, Hacksaw handed the communicator back to her. "As you say, I couldn't do that to Magpie. I should have reported it the instant we saw it when you brought it to me, but I didn't. The Hippocratic Oath doesn't answer to the Emperor. You realise we're all going to be executed for this?"

"Only if we get caught," Moonchild answered.

***

Iceman stood by Magpie's bed. His relaxed posture hadn't changed since he'd arrived several minutes earlier. "Download is complete from the *Traveller*," he said, the first thing he'd said since the request was made.

"Good, let's review it, then," Magpie leaned forward to look at his computer screen, which remained neutral. He glanced up at Iceman, who had not moved.

"I meant together, Mark," he gestured at his screen.

"That will take longer due to your organic processing speed," Iceman informed him. "I assumed it would quicker if I reviewed it at my normal speed."

"You don't know what you're looking for," Magpie told him. "This requires human intuition." He tapped the screen, reminding Iceman of the request.

"As you wish," Iceman complied. The computer screen came to life as he began downloading the Kalaszan logs from his brain.

Magpie sat straighter, leaned in closer, as if the nearer he got to the screen, the more answers he could get from it. "We're looking for any sign of Legna aboard that ship. She may have been located on a planet they visited, she may have been on a vessel that docked with it, she may have her name included on some kind of database they're holding..."

"I've found her."

"...she may have been in communication with them, she may have..."

"I said I've found her, Magpie."

"How? I don't see anything."

Iceman pointed at a name on the screen. A ship called *Firewood*. "This is her ship."

"You can't possibly know that," Magpie frowned. "There isn't even a crew manifest to go with it."

"Nonetheless, it is her ship."

"All right, tell me. How do you know it's her ship?"

"It's called *Firewood*," Iceman explained without a hint of triumphant crowing. "Legna da ardere is the Italian phrase for firewood. Hence, the *Firewood* is Legna's ship."

Magpie looked appraisingly at the technical coordinator. "That was very intuitive, Mark. Are you exceeding your programming parameters or are you just broken?"

Iceman's body language didn't change. "It just seemed obvious," was all he said.

Magpie cleared the screen and went into the imperial database. "Show me the vessel: *Firewood*", he instructed. The computer showed him a small cargo ship. Capable of long-range interstellar trips, it could spend years at a time in space without making planetfall to resupply. The model was listed as requiring only a crew of one, but no crew manifest was forthcoming. It was shown as being owned by the Firewood Foundation, with its headquarters on Mars.

"Perhaps we should visit these coordinates," Iceman suggested. "See if any of the administrative staff can help us locate her."

"Pointless," Magpie told him. "The company doesn't exist."

"Your gift for intuition is clearly greater than mine."

"Those coordinates are where Project Cyclone was. The project was destroyed more than thirty years ago. She's just using those coordinates to register a fictitious company so she doesn't have to name herself as sole proprietor. She's covered her tracks very well."

"Magpie, I have to go. I have an engagement elsewhere. If you require me again, I will return later."

"Thanks, Mark, I'll call you."

"Goodnight, sir."

"Goodnight."

16

Captain Verhaaren paced the command deck, trying to look like he had something to do, but in truth he knew it wasn't convincing his crew. More to the point, it was probably adding to the tension rather than dissipating it. No-one was happy that they were crawling through hyperspace, nursing an unknown quantity like the Kalaszan vessel. At least he could occasionally go over there and check the progress of the science officers and engineers he'd sent to dig around for clues about Kalaszan technology. But even that was difficult. The report had mentioned chronometric technology, but no-one on the *Indomitable* had the first idea about temporal science. Nor had they any experience with these so-called 'goblins' that were the main prize, locked away in their millions in the genebanks that had been discovered. So, he was limited to pacing his own ship looking bored, or pacing the captured ship looking equally bored.

"Captain," the voice of the relief science officer cut into the silence. "Something just showed up on the sensors. It was there for a second, and then it was gone. It could've been a sensor error, but I thought you should know."

At last, even a false alarm would be something. "Good thinking, let me see the data."

The young woman had never actually been on the command deck before and was clearly trying to make sure she wasn't overlooked again by keeping the captain informed of everything. Ordinarily, Verhaaren would have found such an attitude annoying, but right now he was glad of the distraction. The science officer replayed the incident. It was hardly anything at all, but something made Verhaaren edgy. "Run it again," he said. "Where was it?" he asked the science officer.

"Directly below the other ship, sir," she said. "Do you want an outside view?"

"Yes," he answered and looked at the monitor. There was nothing there. After all that, it was back to boredom. Was there no justice in the galaxy? "Thank you, ensign, carry on."

***

The ship travelled in stealth mode, sliding through the blackness of space until it found the *Indomitable*. The battlecruiser was moving at slightly higher than light speed in order to tow the Kalaszan vessel without distorting the hyperspace envelope. The stealth ship matched their trajectory and speed before settling under the Kalaszan hull.

"Are you ready, Iceman?" Moonchild asked.

"Ready, Colonel. The hatch must be closed without delay as the exposed interior will show up on any scans they may be running."

"Acknowledged. Good luck."

"Thank you, Colonel, I will endeavour to have nothing but good luck," answered the man who was incapable of accepting such an unscientific concept as luck. The hatch flicked open. With inhuman speed, Iceman burst from the airlock and the hatch flicked closed again.

Clinging to the outer hull of the Kalaszan ship, Iceman began his journey round to the nearest airlock on the ship. Moonchild and the others watched his progress on the monitor of their tiny vessel. They knew an organic life form would never be able to survive the stress of exposure to hyperspace, even suited up, but Iceman was free of such considerations. He found his target and signalled to the others. They lost his signal as soon as he'd opened the outer hatch and entered.

"Ok, get ready, boys," Moonchild nodded to Gunboy and Bouncer, who took their positions and waited.

Having established that the Kalaszan teleporter did not register on imperial sensors while in use, they realised that getting someone in to operate them was the only real problem, but having Iceman on the team was the best solution. The only complication was that they hadn't expected to lose the signal once he was inside.

***

Iceman paused momentarily to confirm the signal was gone. Then he dismissed the problem and continued towards his objective. It was pointless wasting time trying to fix it if it turned out to be a property of the ships' interaction with stealth systems in use. If it was in his nature to shrug, he would have done so. Instead, he just went straight for the teleport chamber nearest the genebanks. His first concern was avoiding the crew of the *Indomitable*, but this was relatively simple, as they weren't expecting anyone who didn't belong there. He was even able to walk past a couple of lab technicians, who saw his naval uniform and its lieutenant's insignia and saluted. Returning the salute, Iceman made it to the teleport chamber without major incident. That was when he made the first discovery that suggested the mission was compromised. A security officer lay in one corner, not immediately visible. Iceman's internal sensors swept over him, cataloguing the many and varied injuries sustained in what was undoubtedly a brutal but short assault. Whether or not the man had even known he was under attack, the assailant had made sure of his success. Ignoring the dead man, Iceman turned his attention to the controls, noting they had been used recently. Committing the coordinates to his memory, he reset them and began bringing his colleagues across. Gunboy and Bouncer took up sentry positions while Goldfish and Moonchild came next, followed by R'sulek-Entah. Moonchild gave the corpse a cursory glance, then looked questioningly to Iceman.

"I found him in this condition, Colonel. I believe there is, or was, a third party aboard this vessel."

"That's all we need," was Moonchild's only comment, before she nodded to the two tactical support men.

Gunboy and Bouncer were out quickly, taking up positions in the corridor. The others followed. Bouncer took point duty, while Gunboy watched the rear, and between them both, the others moved safely through the ship to the cold storage chamber where the genebanks were kept. Except they weren't. When they arrived, neatly avoiding the *Indomitable* crewmembers, they found the chamber empty.

"They must have transferred them to the *Indomitable*," Goldfish said.

"No," Moonchild shook her head. "They were under orders not to move anything, although I think they're stretching the definition of 'leave well alone' by having science and engineering techs here. They're probably too busy ripping the secrets from the propulsion systems to realise this lot's even gone. No, I think this just backs up Iceman's theory about a third party. Probably came in the same way we did and stole it from under their noses."

"Can I help you, Colonel?" the unfamiliar voice came from the doorway. "And may I please see some ID?"

They all turned to see a security officer with his pistol raised in one of the navy's favourite 'aimed unthreateningly' modes. Moonchild remembered Magpie expounding for about an hour on the subject while they were both blind drunk on Zeneb VI. She found him quite witty at the time, although when her head cleared, she couldn't recall any of the details from his actual main arguments. Now, faced with the situation in reality, she wasn't at all amused.

She took a step forward. "Certainly, ensign," she said, reaching for her ID. "Here you go."

Holding out the card, she suddenly flicked it right in his face. His instinctive flinch gave her the opportunity to close the gap and deliver a vicious thump to the side of his head. Reeling from the blow, he hit the wall, where Iceman covered his mouth with one hand while pressing a finger on his other hand to the man's temple. The young ensign went limp and slid to the floor, gently guided by Iceman.

Aware that the others were watching him, he held up the finger and said. "Electrical stimulation to the brain's sleep centre. May I suggest we leave now?"

Moonchild nodded. "Ok, everybody out. Back to our ship. We need to rethink our options."

***

Captain Verhaaren continued to pace the command deck. No-one noticed when the little stealth ship moved off, back in the direction of Earth.

17

Magpie opened his eyes. Someone had called his name. For a moment he wondered if it was Elise. His hospital room was empty. He glanced at the chronometer on the wall. 0316 hours. Probably just dreaming. He closed his eyes again.
Will.
He opened them again. It was her.
Legna.
I found you. It's been so long, Will.
Yes. Where are you?
Nearby. I'll come to you.
Then there was silence again, although there hadn't been any sound to begin with. Soon he heard a noise at the door. It slid open and she stepped cautiously into the room. In the dark, Magpie couldn't really tell, but he knew it was her.
"Come in," he said quietly.
She approached him and, fumbling in the dark, found a chair next to the bed and sat in it. She sat opposite the window, and as the moonlight spilled in from outside, he was taken aback by the difference. In his terms, she'd aged twenty years in a week. He saw her confused frown and understood from her perspective, he hadn't aged at all in twenty years.
"It's a long story," he offered, before she could find words for the question.
She nodded, accepting that at face value. "It's good to see you again, Will," she said, her voice deeper, richer, than a week ago. "I hope you stay a bit longer this time."

"It's good to see you too, Legna," he answered, but without feeling sure about that. "As you can see, I'm a captive audience. I tried to call you at the Firewood Foundation, but they said to leave a message."

"Will, I'm impressed," her shock changed to admiration as she tried to work out how he'd made the link.

"I just put two and two together," Magpie explained. "And got seventy nine. However, one of my best friends is a walking pub quiz and he told me all about it."

"Oh. I see. What's a pub quiz?"

"Ah… that's part of the long story. Don't worry about it. So, tell me, how did you find me again, and why?"

"I've spent my life looking for others who survived the destruction of Project Cyclone. I found a few, after our first meeting, but the one I really wanted to find again was you. You were the one I always saw when Uncle Xavier came into my room. You always looked at me with such compassion. We were too young to make a connection, but you always seemed to care what happened to me."

Magpie thought back. He remembered. He remembered what Xavier would do to him, knew that he was going next door to do the same things to the baby in that room. He felt such pity for that baby, and always looked in there, tried to make eye contact, to somehow convey the message of hope. It'll be all right. When he's gone, it'll be all right.

"You remember, don't you?" she said.

"Yes. I wanted to try and reassure you. I hadn't learned how to focus my mind enough to tell you."

"We were barely six months old, Will," she laughed. "Most babies wouldn't even realise I existed at that age."

"I hadn't realised there were other survivors," he said. "To be honest, I never really knew how many of us there were."

She looked down at the floor. "More than you think, Will. There was a lot of genetic material there."

"How many? I only saw you, and the one in the room to my left. Are you saying there were more? I suppose that shouldn't be a surprise, should it? How many?"

She met his eyes. He felt very cold. "How many?" he repeated, the foreboding in his voice suggesting he was prepared for a shock.

"Oh, Will," she whispered. "There were millions of us."

***

Moonchild came for him. Instead she found Hacksaw. "Where is he?"

He shook his head. "Gone. I'm sorry. I arrived and he wasn't here. One of the nurses said he left with a woman she took to be his sister. I'm guessing it was this Legna character."

"We have to find him. We have to find *them*. Did you review the security systems?"

"Yes, they left by a service entrance and disappeared into the city. They could be anywhere on the planet by now."

"Or off it. Damn!" She took out her communicator. "All S.T.A.R.T. members report to my quarters, immediately, we've got problems. Hacksaw, I need you there too."

Already in too deep, he knew it was pointless stalling. "I'll tell my deputies to expect me when they see me. I'll give you as long as you need."

She nodded her thanks and they left.

***

They gathered in Moonchild's living room. "I want any ideas, no matter how unlikely. They must have gone somewhere, and I need every suggestion you can make. Anyone got any to start us off?"

Iceman didn't hesitate. "Project Cyclone," he said. "Magpie and I discovered it was the address given for Legna's company."

"Project Cyclone?" Bouncer repeated. "Isn't that where they came from?"

"That is correct," Iceman glanced at him. "It was originally a play on words as the project was intended to produce so-called 'psi-clones', and required a designation that would hide its purpose from the public accidentally discovering the truth. Officially, it was a weather control research centre."

"But the Martian climate is controlled just as well as Earth's," Bouncer argued. "How could the people be so gullible?"

Moonchild coughed. "People tend to believe what the Empire tells them to believe. That way they stay healthy and the Imperial Thought Police don't come knocking in the early hours. Don't forget, I was born on Mars, and my parents told me that's what it was. It was only after I met Magpie that I learned the truth."

R'sulek-Entah spoke. "The history lesson is fascinating, not least because you are compounding your treasonous behaviour with treasonous allegations, but it is not bringing us any closer to Commander Angel. Nor does it answer the other important question."

"Which is?" Moonchild asked through gritted teeth.

"Which is," R'sulek-Entah continued without noticing the antagonism she was causing. "Is Legna Williams working in Commander Angel's best interests, or against them?"

***

The *Firewood* sailed into the asteroid field's periphery and opened its scoops. While refuelling, Legna shut down the engines and sat back. "We'll be here for a while. Why don't you go below and get some rest?"
Magpie stared straight ahead. His eyes stung with the grit of weariness and his entire body ached with the knotty tension that comes with lack of sleep. His knees cried out to be given respite, but he refused to give in to his body's demands. "I'll stay here," he told her. "I'm not tired."
"Well, if you're staying, do you think you could try and be a bit more sociable? It isn't often I have company, and when I do, I prefer conversation. Right now I think there's more atmosphere out there." She gestured to the cabin window, and the depths of space beyond.
"I'm sorry," he conceded. "I'm just worried that I've done the wrong thing. I should have left some word for the others. They should know about this."
"No, Will. How many times? No! They mustn't find out. It would be the end for us if they knew."
"But they're my friends. They would help us," he insisted.
"They are all members of the Imperial Armed Forces," she countered. "Their first duty is to the Empire, not you. Friendship doesn't count for anything when duty is involved. You know that more than anyone. Weren't you prepared to kill your precious colonel when you thought she'd betrayed the Empire? Don't you think she'd do the same to you?"

Magpie said nothing. He didn't trust himself. The memory was too fresh, too painful. And he knew she was right. If he'd been ready to do that, how could he expect her to do otherwise? Like it or not, he was now a fugitive from his own friends.

"Listen, Will, once we've refuelled, we'll go home. We'll be able to live our lives free from persecution."

"I wasn't being persecuted!"

"But we are being persecuted now. Your choices are simple, Will. Come with me, or die."

He glared at her. She hadn't wanted it to sound like a threat, but faced with such finality, it was hard to put an optimistic spin on the situation. "Maybe I'd rather die than live as a fugitive," he muttered, too darkly for her liking. Then he hauled himself out of his seat and went below. Maybe he did need to rest after all.

18

They arrived in the Martian orbit. Legna roused him from his sleep by gently stroking his forehead. When his eyes flicked open, they locked on hers, already focussed. For a second, she thought he was going to attack her. For a second, so did he, then he realised where he was and relaxed.

"We're here," she said, softly.

"Where's here?" he asked.

"Home. Our home. Project Cyclone."

"But that'll be the first thing they'll think of," Magpie climbed out of his bunk and reached for his boots. "They'll come straight here looking for us. Iceman may reconsider and decide the coordinates were right after all."

"Well in that case, we'll only stay to pick up some things, then we'll be going first thing in the morning."

Magpie looked doubtful, but said nothing. Legna took that as the closest she was getting to a positive sign and let go of the hand he'd been unaware she was holding.

A few minutes later, they were in an approach vector for the main starport at Olympus City, with a docking berth prepared for them. As they disembarked, Magpie looked round, breathing in the Martian air that he thought he'd left behind forever. Now, a woman he thought had been dead for over thirty years had appeared in his life and called this place home. What was happening to him?

"Come on, we need to move quickly," she touched his arm with an intimacy he found confusing. She clearly trusted him implicitly, despite knowing virtually nothing about him.

He found himself following her through the security gates as she placed her hand on the scanner. The computer recognised her DNA and matched it to the Firewood Foundation sample it had on file. "Please proceed, Firewood Foundation," the computer instructed. She went through, motioning for him to do the same. He hesitated. Logically, he reasoned, if it recognised her DNA, it should do likewise with his. If he was found to be on Mars, the computer would alert the authorities and his flight would be terminated before it had really even begun. The man behind him made an ill-concealed noise of impatience. Magpie glanced round, but anything he wanted to say was curtailed by the sight of a security guard approaching.

"Is there a problem, sir?"

Magpie shook his head, gave an easy smile. "Not at all," he said cheerfully, and placed his palm on the scanner. He waited for the sirens to begin, surreptitiously glanced round, checking the placement of the nearest guards, working out his chances, deciding if he would need to draw his pistol.

The computer beeped. "Please proceed, Firewood Foundation," it instructed.

Of course, he realised, the computer was only likely to have a record of his DNA if he'd passed through Martian security before. He hadn't, not for eighteen years. While it was unlikely the computer had forgotten, or ditched the file, it was probably only comparing the sample to the most recent one it had a record of. He vaguely wondered if Legna had had a problem the first time she'd come back here after he left, but it clearly hadn't been a big problem if she had. Either way, it had recognised him as her, rather than who he really was, and so he was safe.

They took a taxi through the city. Magpie watched the streets as they passed through, an uneasy mix of nostalgia and revulsion sitting in his gut. The place was little changed. Most of the difference was in the condition of the buildings. He'd been thrust into a world of violent upheaval, where property and lives were destroyed with equal callousness. He remembered these places as being dark, forbidding places, where rival gangs would spring from the shadows and attack everything they didn't recognise as their own. He'd learned to survive on these streets, honed his skills as a thief as well as his psionic abilities to give him an edge against those who would kill him if he didn't learn quickly enough. Now the same buildings shone like gold under the streetlights, calling out their prosperity like a war cry, demanding that the people take notice and give respect.
"Different, isn't it?" Legna said, close to his ear.
"But the same," he answered, cryptically.
"Yes," she laughed. "Different, but the same."
She had an easy laugh, and he wondered how real it was. He was trained in the art of simulating emotional states. But he'd been in the Imperial Espionage Division for a long time. What was her story?
"We're nearly there," she broke his concentration and pointed. He couldn't really see what she was trying to show him, but she seemed intent on doing so anyway.
He peered into the night, aware that the streetlights had thinned out. So, the ghetto was still the ghetto. He remembered there had been no outward indication that Project Cyclone was there, among the housing units of Olympus City's poorest residents. After the destruction, there had been nothing to hide, by whatever definition one chose to apply to the phrase. An unexplained

explosion, deep in the bowels of the research centre had destroyed it and damaged buildings for several blocks. Now those blocks had been replaced, with new, colourful, state of the art, but equally overcrowded blocks. And there, in amongst them, was the Firewood Foundation. A non-descript building, it sat in the midst of the housing units and got lost there. He would never have noticed it except for the fact that Legna pointed it out, and even then he nearly missed it.

They got out of the taxi and approached the building. The few people still on the streets noticed their arrival and called out to her, waving and smiling. Legna responded in kind, calling out names as she addressed individuals.

"You seem popular," Magpie observed.

"I know," she looked at him, and he didn't doubt her smile was genuine. "We've been providing for these people for a few years now."

"We?" Magpie's guard went up again.

"The Foundation," she explained. "We needed a cover for our operation, so we chose a charity to help the people of Mars get back on their feet again after the Galkasian war. No-one seemed to be interested, even though we're next door to the heart of the Empire, so we asked the people what they wanted."

"And what did they tell you?"

"They had no food, no water, they didn't even have power for their homes. They said they'd settle for a bundle of firewood, if that was all we could offer them. Hence the Firewood Foundation. What's so funny?"

Magpie managed to stop laughing long enough to tell her. "I never explained how my colleague figured out the connection between you and the Foundation. Legna is the Italian word for firewood."

"You're kidding! Really? Wow! You're not serious," she concluded.

"You have no idea," Magpie said. "This guy is a computer on legs. He knows everything, but he's got no sense of lateral thinking. So, you can imagine how impressed I was when he came up with that one. And you're saying it's not even something you thought about?"

"Until you said it, I'd never heard it. I don't speak Italian."

"This is too much," Magpie laughed. "Iceman's going to be so confused by this. Except he isn't, is he? I'm not going to see him again."

Again, she touched his arm. "Will. Don't torture yourself. Let's get you inside and see what we can work out."

They continued across the street, making detours to speak to neighbours. She introduced Will as a member of the team who had been working on Earth, trying to secure better funding for the Foundation, and was here to see what his work had resulted in on Mars. The neighbours accepted this information, and therefore him, with no difficulty and were universally pleased to meet him. Magpie naturally experienced no difficulty lying to them while smiling warmly and shaking hands as if these were his long-lost friends. As they got within a few yards of the front door of the Foundation, it slid open and a man appeared on the top step like some kind of sentinel.

He looked pleased to see Legna, then frowned at Will, before he seemed to recognise something about him. At about the same time, Magpie noticed the similarity between him and Legna, and therefore himself.

"Another clone?" he whispered.

"Yes," she replied, her whisper matching his. "Hello, Gabriel. This is Will."

Gabriel stepped forward. "You're one of us, aren't you?"

"I hope so," Magpie said, and offered his hand. Gabriel took it, though the shake was anything but warm. Making a mental note, Magpie withdrew the hand. They went inside.

"Legna, what are you doing? Do you realise who this is?" Gabriel hissed. With a shock, Magpie realised Gabriel must have used the contact to read him without him even noticing.

"It's ok, Gabriel, I know exactly who he is. He's William Angel, and he's the person who set me off on the road to finding you all. If we hadn't found each other at Tranquillity Base all those years ago, I'd have spent the rest of my life believing I was unique. None of us would be together now."

Magpie looked at her again. "Are you saying all of this," he gestured around the Foundation building, "is because of our chance meeting twenty years ago?"

"Don't be so surprised, Will, of course it is. Until that day, there was only me. After that day, there was a galaxy full of our kind, and I had to find them and bring them home."

Magpie's mind reeled with the implications. "For all my life I believed I was unique. Now I find a couple of weeks ago I set something in motion that changed your life forever."

"A couple of weeks ago?" Legna frowned. "No, it was twenty years ago. Oh, yes, of course, from your point of view."

"That's what I've been trying to tell you," Gabriel interrupted. "He can't be trusted, he's a time traveller."

Magpie had had enough. "You know, Gabriel, you're very rude. You read my mind without invitation and you're trying to find a reason for me to hit you. Now I don't know how good you are in a fight, and I don't like to resort to fisticuffs, but I can see where this is leading. Can you?"

"I don't like to be threatened, William," Gabriel said, smoothly, an undertone of menace creeping in.

"I'm not threatening, Gabriel," Magpie said, squaring up to the inevitable. He wondered if Gabriel had some kind of ability that could damage him without physical contact. Too late, he couldn't back down now.

"Have I come back to the Firewood Foundation or Testosterone Alley?" Legna demanded. "Stop it, both of you. I know full well who and what he is, stop being suspicious. And you, Will, stop being aggressive. I haven't brought you here to start fights. Where's Michelangelo?"

Gabriel had a look about him that Magpie would have called quietly smug. He clearly thought he'd come out best from the exchange. What worried Magpie was that he agreed. Gabriel would have to be watched. For now, though, Gabriel contented himself with answering the question. "He's in the back, checking the figures for this quarter."

"Ok, follow me, Will. Let's go and meet Michelangelo."

It turned out that Michelangelo was the bookish one. It amazed Magpie that all the clones had such radically different personalities. Aside from a few details, they were identical in looks, but their attitudes were so far apart and Magpie had the image in his head that here was the ultimate extreme in multiple personality disorders. Unlike Gabriel, Michelangelo offered his hand immediately and seemed genuinely pleased to see him.

"I've heard Legna talk about you so often, I wondered if I'd ever be able to meet you," he enthused.

"I've only just heard of you, but I'm glad we have met," Magpie answered, his broad grin matching Michelangelo's. "You were with S.T.A.R.T., weren't you? Magpie, as I recall. Do you prefer Magpie, Will or William?"

"Will is fine, thanks. Very few people call me Will, it's a nice change."

"Good. Will it is, then. Oh, Legna, that journalist has arrived. He's coming back in the morning, but he came to introduce himself this afternoon. Just thought you should know."

"Journalist?" Magpie said, aware that his ability to hide might be seriously compromised with a reporter in his face.

"Don't worry," Michelangelo reassured him. "He only gets to speak to the girls, and Seraph."

"Seraph was caught in the explosion," Legna explained. "His face was ruined. No-one really knows how he survived at all, he was caught pretty much at the lowest level. Anyway, the journalist is here to do a story on the Foundation, give us some Empire-wide publicity, make us seem even more legitimate while generating money at the same time."

"Can't be faulted," Magpie conceded, his fear dying down.

***

Gunboy and Bouncer came back from their brief excursion.

"It's the *Firewood*," Gunboy announced. "Just sitting there. No sign of anyone."

"Arrived last night, according to port security," Bouncer added.

Iceman returned from his assignment. "I've downloaded the scanner logs for the last 24 hours. Searching… two matching DNA patterns."

"They're both here then," Moonchild decided.

"What now, boss?" Goldfish asked.

"Now we go find him. R'sulek-Entah, did you locate the Firewood Foundation?"

"Yes, Colonel. I believe I can lead us to it."

"Good work, people. Let's go."

***

Legna had gone out into the streets to introduce the journalist to the people who lived in the neighbourhood by the time Magpie emerged from his room. She'd left word that she would be back in less than an hour and that they would be leaving as soon as she returned. He found Gabriel and Michelangelo in the dining room along with another male and female whose names he didn't know. He tried not to change his attitude when he noticed the man who could only have been Seraph. Ordinarily, he didn't react to the sight of facial disfigurement, but when it was your own face, it was hard not to be shocked. If he hadn't known Seraph was a clone, identical to himself, he would never have guessed, the face had been so completely destroyed. He reined in his shock quickly enough for the others not to see it, and he hoped none of them had the ability to read impulse thoughts.

Glancing up from where he sat at the table, Gabriel's eyes darkened and he stood up. "Excuse me," he muttered to Michelangelo, and left, glowering at Magpie as he went.

"Will, come on in," Michelangelo beckoned him over. "Don't mind Gabriel, he's in a bad mood this morning."

"He's in a bad mood most mornings," the woman observed. "Hello, Will. I'm Lucy."

"Pleased to meet you," Will responded, shaking the hand she offered. "All of you."

"Have a seat," Seraph waved him towards Gabriel's now vacant chair. "I'm Seraph. Don't be fooled by my stunning good looks, I'm just as ugly as the rest of them, deep down."

Relieved, Magpie laughed with the others. This was clearly some kind of in-joke, and he'd been included.

"So," Seraph continued. "Legna says you're the one who set her off on this quest to round us all up. How come it's only now you turned up?"

"Well, mainly because for me it wasn't twenty years ago. It was a couple of weeks. Up until I came here, I was a member of S.T.A.R.T., and I met Legna on a mission to the past. But then I got recalled and she spent the rest of the intervening time looking for us."

"I'm glad you were honest about your involvement in S.T.A.R.T.," Michelangelo nodded. "Gabriel thinks you're here to spy on us. He spent most of this morning telling us all about it."

"Well, there's one way to find the truth," Magpie said. "You could read me. After all, that's what he did."

Lucy laughed, not unkindly. "You're asking the wrong person, Will. Of all of us, Michelangelo's the only non-psi."

"Non-psi? How did that happen? I thought we were all created with it."

Michelangelo shrugged. "Apparently not. I don't know how many of us were created this way, but I'm the only one here. Maybe, for some reason, I rejected the psi-genes, or maybe I wasn't given them in the first place."

"That must be difficult for you," Magpie sympathised.

"Not at all," Michelangelo laughed. "If you never had it, you don't miss it. Do you miss having a prehensile tail? No, of course not. It actually frees me to use the rest of my mind, the parts none of the others seem to realise exist, like the thinking bit, concentrating on mundane things like running the company, which some people find too tedious. I worked for several years as computer instructor for the governors of Arboreous, the forest colony. I never needed to be particularly gifted, psionically, for that. And if I need quiet, and I can't find somewhere private, I make them all communicate telepathically, so it works out well for all of us. Besides, with psionics being the norm around here, I feel quite special."

"You have a point, there," Magpie conceded.

"And if you did have any kind of ability," Gabriel said from the door. "You'd have spotted him for the spy he is. Look who just came to visit." He switched on a monitor and called for a front door view.

Magpie immediately recognised Moonchild and the others, including Hacksaw. He turned to the others. "Let me say this now, once and for all. I have not, to the best of my knowledge, led them here. But as I explained to Legna, one of my former colleagues had already worked it out."

Michelangelo glanced at Gabriel. "We have to take him at face value. Why would he betray us? What have we done wrong anyway? Seraph, Lucy, please go and receive our visitors. Gabriel, let's listen to what they have to say before we judge them. Will, you should stay here until we can guarantee your safety."

***

Flanked by Gunboy and Bouncer, Moonchild ascended the short flight of steps and looked for some kind of calling mechanism. Even as she looked, the door opened and a man and woman emerged. Moonchild took a step back as she recognised Magpie in the eyes of both individuals, despite one being female and the other having a horribly disfigured face, in which only the eyes were unharmed.

For their part, the two surveyed the visitors. The woman was calm, serene, her hands clasped in front of her, but relaxed. The man seemed to react when he saw Bouncer, but recovered quickly.

"Welcome to the Firewood Foundation," the woman said. "My name is Lucy Williams. This is my colleague, Seraph. How may I help you?"

"I'm Colonel Elise Washington of the Space-Time Axial Response Team," Moonchild said. "We have reason to believe William Angel is here."

Lucy seemed to consider this possibility. "William Angel? I don't think I know the name. Are you sure?"

Moonchild gave a grunt. "I can see I have to do this the hard way," she shrugged, then lashed out her hand and grabbed Lucy's wrist. Unaccustomed to physical conflict, the clone had no chance to react. She cried out in shock, and the man took a step back in alarm. Again, he glanced at Bouncer, just for a second, but long enough for Bouncer to notice.

Meanwhile, Moonchild had brought Lucy's hand to her temple and held it there. "We don't have time for games, Lucy. Read my intentions and you'll know we're here to help Will. You can read my mind, can't you, Lucy? You are one of the psi-clones, aren't you?"

With a pleading look at Seraph, who simply stood looking terrified, Lucy realised she had no choice. She entered the colonel's mind. She didn't have to search; it was there for her to see as soon as she went in. Everything she felt for Will, all her emotions concerning the man were at the front of her mind. Their eyes locked. "Yes," she whispered. "You're here to help him. You'd better come in."

Lucy led them into the building, through the main reception and into the dining room. All the way, Seraph was staring at Bouncer, trying not to be obvious. Eventually, Bouncer couldn't take anymore. "Excuse me, sir, but do we know each other?"

Seraph gave a startled yelp, and took a step back. "No," he answered in a strangled voice.

Bouncer didn't make anything of it. There could have been any number of reasons the clone was singling him out, but he couldn't work out what they might be. So he chose to ignore the surveillance. Then they were in a large eating area facing several people, all of whom could easily have been Magpie. But the real Magpie was easily identified. He was the one who had the perpetual shadows under his eyes, the perpetual growth on his chin that should either be allowed to develop into a full beard or removed, but never seemed to go one way or the other. Now, though, he seemed more tired than usual, more unkempt than usual, haunted, even.

Moonchild moved to him and swept him up into a hug that seemed to take everyone by surprise, even him. After a couple of seconds, he recovered and returned the hug.

Then they broke and looked at each other for a moment. "You look awful, hon," she told him.

"And you're as beautiful as ever," he said, although the joviality seemed forced.

Gabriel sighed, heavily, obviously. "So are we all under arrest now? Have you got what you came for?"

Lucy held up her hand. "Hush, Gabriel, this isn't what you think it is. They're not here to hurt us, they're only here for Will."

Magpie took that as his cue. "I can't come back with you, Elise," he said quietly. "I can't go back to Earth."

Moonchild looked at him appraisingly. "So you know then?"

"About the DNA? Yes. That's why you're here isn't it?"

"Yeah, kinda," she winced. "We tried to control the problem, but it's gotten a bit more complicated. Someone else has the genebanks. That means until we can find them and secure them, you're not safe. In fact, if I'm right about who you people are, none of you are safe."

"Excuse me," Michelangelo said. "What do you mean by that? What genebanks?"

Magpie turned to him. "Some time ago, Legna discovered genebanks containing an alien species we call goblins. They're unintelligent, their only interest is finding food, and they are forever hungry. Except it turns out they're not aliens after all. They're versions of us."

"What? Impossible! How can that be possible?"

"Maybe Uncle Xavier had several experiments on the go at the same time," Magpie speculated.

The others watched in growing confusion, as their friend and colleague essentially conducted a conversation with himself. Magpie seemed to have it pretty much figured out, while the rest of them, especially the one who was speaking, seemed to be stricken with horror, but then, they'd just been told their very essence had been violated to make some kind of obscene monsters.

"That's horrible," Lucy moaned, tears appearing at the corners of her eyes.

"It gets worse," Magpie shrugged, apologetically. "I nearly got eaten by them. I looked right into their eyes, and saw nothing but bloodlust and hunger. And now it turns out they were our own eyes."

Gabriel snorted. "Are we expected to believe this? Why hasn't Legna mentioned finding these genebanks before now? You've come here and turned our lives upside down, you've led your little friends here to us, and you've given us the most ridiculous story I've ever heard. Do you think we're stupid, Will?"

Magpie met his accuser's gaze. "Of course not, Gabriel. Not all of you."

"Why don't we ask Legna?" Michelangelo seemed desperate to maintain the peace. "She's just come back. But let's not resort to violence and name-calling, at least not until we know what's going on."

The two clones continued staring at each other while the rest waited for Legna. She found them all in the dining room and, momentarily, looked ready to run before realising she had nowhere to go and no chance of getting there before someone caught her.

"It's ok," Lucy said. "They're not here to hurt us. They're on our side. At least," she qualified. "She's on Will's side, and he's on our side. Whatever Gabriel thinks."

"I know what I read when I touched him."

Magpie whirled on him again. "You read who I am and what I do for a living, Gabriel, that's all. None of that told you why I'm here. You just read the obvious and jumped feet first to a grossly inaccurate conclusion. So just stop being so bloody paranoid and listen to the others. You don't even have to take my word for it. You trust them, don't you? I'm surprised you haven't given yourself an ulcer."

Gabriel's reply was cut off before it formed as Legna interrupted. "He's right, Gabriel, you're being paranoid. But he's also right about the genebanks and the goblins. I docked with a Kalaszan vessel about a year ago, and discovered they had them. They were taking them to their paymasters, the Balsari. How they got them in the first place, I never found out, but they'd made many deliveries over the years. When I found them, I thought it was more of us in an undeveloped state. All I sensed was the instinct to feed. So I docked with them under a pretext of needing repair and when I got the chance, I investigated. I found the goblins, although I didn't know they were called that. I couldn't tell you, it was so heartbreaking, I couldn't put you through that."

She stopped, her eyes filling from the memory.

"Thank you, Legna," Michelangelo said quietly. "I think we all understand your reasons, and we appreciate your honesty now." He looked pointedly at Gabriel, who glowered back at him, but said nothing.

The conversation changed course when Moonchild noticed the monitor. "Who's that?" she asked, pointing at the man in the reception area.

"It's the journalist who's covering the Foundation," Legna said. "It's ok, he's staying there, he'll never know what's happening back here."

"He already knows," Moonchild cursed. "He's my ex-husband, Maek Newark. He lost his job after we exposed Admiral Chalk as a Balsari spy. I don't know why he's really here, but it's not for the benefit of your Foundation."

Magpie frowned and went to the door separating the reception from the rest of the building. He closed his eyes and concentrated. The man in the reception was not the open book he should have been. This sent warning bells through Magpie's mind immediately. Maek was just a human, he shouldn't be able to keep secrets. Instinctively, Magpie burst into the reception area and was upon the journalist before he'd turned round properly. He seemed shocked but not surprised at the sight of Magpie bearing down on him, which should have told him volumes. But Magpie was intent only on one thing. He grabbed Maek by the shoulders and forced him backwards. Maek struggled to gain purchase on the floor, but Magpie was too strong for him. As the others came out from the back, Magpie pinned him against the wall and, cupping one hand under his chin and the other over his forehead, thrust his mind into the hapless journalist's. He rampaged through half-formed defences, looking for the information he sought. Maek tried to plead with Moonchild, but couldn't move, couldn't make his vocal cords work. He felt Magpie running roughshod through his thoughts. Deeper and deeper Magpie burrowed, digging messily through the incomplete barriers that Maek was attempting to block him with. Eventually, he found it. What would normally be delicate tendrils and gentle fingers were more like clawed fists as he insinuated himself into the naked awareness, wrapping them around the information and then ripping it mercilessly from his mind. With a strangled cry, Maek slid down the wall and sat weeping where he landed.

Magpie turned to the others, his eyes ablaze with pure rage. "He's a Balsari spy!" he said. "And they know everything!"

19

Olympus City, Mars, 2507

Seraph moved quietly through the lower levels of the Foundation, into the part that was originally the research section of Project Cyclone. He knew where he had to go. A room that had been utterly destroyed in the blast over thirty years ago, a room which looked much the same as any other room, at least prior to the explosion. This had been Seraph's room, the one he'd grown up in. Uncle Xavier had always come through the door to his left, conducted his tests, and moved on through the door to his right, to carry out tests on the child in the next room. Seraph came back here often. His clone siblings thought he was a bit morbid, as though he couldn't get over the fact that it was here his face was destroyed. But that was not the reason. For Seraph, coming here was always a matter of honouring those others who hadn't survived. He would stand here, in this room and remember the dead, in silence, alone. It was his way of showing the universe he was grateful to have his life, and not bitter about losing his face. His face wasn't important. He saw his face every time he looked at Gabriel and Michelangelo, and even when he looked at the women. And now he saw it when he looked at Will. Why did he need a face, when he saw it on all the others every day? No, Seraph had no room in his heart for bitterness, not when so many had given so much so he could live. Today was different. Seraph didn't stand and remember the dead. He sat in a corner and wept for the dead.

***

Lucy found him. "Seraph, why are you crying?"
He looked up at her. "I can't tell you, Lucy," he sobbed. "I will, one day, but now I can't."
"I don't understand," she admitted.
"No. I didn't at first. But now I do, and that's why I'm crying."
"Do you want me to leave you for a few minutes?"
"No. Please stay, Lucy. I don't want to be alone right now."
She sat beside him, and they held hands. They didn't move until he was ready.

***

Maek Newark sat quietly in the dining room, squirming under the scrutiny of the clones, the S.T.A.R.T. members and, worst of all, his former wife. Moonchild was glaring down at him, although he wasn't meeting anyone's eyes.
"When did you sell your soul, Maek?" she hissed at him. "I knew you were low, but I never realised you were scum. What did the Balsari offer you that was worth betraying your own people?"
"You can stand there and ask me that?" His retort wasn't even strong enough to convince. "You two set me up and let me fall. I was a respected professional, and because of you, I became the laughing stock of galactic journalism. What did I have left to lose? When the Balsari came to me, I'd already lost everything."
"All of which was your own fault," Magpie pointed out. "You should never have been at the execution in the first

place. You knew it was classified, but you still broke the story. You got what you deserved. Besides, she didn't set you up, you weren't important enough to set up. She set me up. I'm far more important. You just chose the wrong time to draw attention to yourself."

Still unable to look up at anyone, he said. "Maybe so, but you're right, she set you up. She put you through it, didn't she? You wept like a child when you thought it was all real. And you still look at her as a friend. What kind of fool are you?"

"Not your kind, I'm pleased to say. When Elise put me through that, it hurt, you got that right, but let me tell you this, Maek. We serve a higher purpose than our own selves. Sometimes sacrifices are necessary. Are you even familiar with the word?"

"This is getting us nowhere," Gabriel huffed. "We've established he's a spy, and he's here to hurt us. Let's kill him now and be done with it."

Michelangelo laughed. "So, you finally believe Will, do you? See? Nothing's impossible!"

Gabriel glared at him. "If you had any psionic abilities at all, you'd know how unwise it would be to say anything else. I still say we kill him," he said to the wider group. Unseen by him, Michelangelo winked at Magpie, sharing the joke.

"No," Legna said. "That's not the way we do things. We can't solve all our problems by killing them. There has to be a better solution."

"There is," Moonchild agreed. "We take him back to Earth to stand trial for treason."

Maek laughed, a sharp, nasty sound. "Oh, Elise, you're not thinking about this. Take me back and I spill my story about these people. And the goblins. And you all join me in the dock. Kill me, and you never find the genebanks. Let me go, and your secret's safe."

"Unlikely," Iceman observed, calmly. "A proven traitor can't be trusted with information. There is another alternative."

"Lieutenant Vee is correct," R'sulek-Entah confirmed. "Ara'Sayal is allied to the Terran Empire, but is not required to divulge its secrets. I suggest we hand Mister Newark over to Arajak custody for the foreseeable future. We can decide what to do with him afterwards."

Maek realised where this argument was going. "Wait! If you do that, I'll never tell you where the genebanks are. Then it'll be too late to stop the Balsari."

Magpie turned to him, a vicious smile on his lips. "You don't seem to understand, Maek. I didn't just take what I needed from your mind. I took everything. I'll sort through it at my leisure and take what I want. I'll decide what's relevant as and when I find it. But don't imagine for one second you have any secrets from me. *Any* secrets! You don't. Your only chance of any kind of leniency is to save me the time and effort of going through all your embarrassing private moments. So this is the deal. You give us the truth right now, or I tell everyone here everything you don't want them to know."

R'sulek-Entah glanced sharply at him, but he cut her off with a raised finger. "Don't even consider explaining the ethics of this to me. I'm well aware of them, but this is too big an issue to get bogged down in psionic etiquette. Well, Maek, what do you say?"

Like a trapped animal, Maek searched for some means of escape, but knew it was pointless. He stared at the floor, weighing his options. "What do I get if I tell you?"

"The satisfaction of knowing I've ditched all the sordid details in your memory. That's all."

"No. I want to be on a shuttle off Mars within an hour. Or you can take your chances trying to sift through it in time."

Magpie looked at Moonchild who considered, then nodded. "Deal," he said.

"They're here," Maek told them, apparently satisfied that Moonchild's word was good. "Not now, in the past. The Kalaszan retrieved them and handed them over to the Balsari. They gave them to an agent and sent him to the past with them. And this much I'll give you for free. It's one of you."

"You want to tell us now, or wait for me to confirm it the slow way?" Magpie invited.

"Academic, I'm afraid," Maek's apology seemed anything but genuine. "I don't know who, I just know it's someone in this room. They told me that much, nothing else. Whoever it is they were supposed to leave with me when I'd finished the story. Then the authorities would be told about the clones and the goblins. That's all I know."

"Is he telling the truth?" Goldfish asked.

"I wouldn't know," Magpie admitted.

Maek realised with eye-popping fury what had just happened. Moonchild spoke first. "Thanks, Maek. And just to show we're keeping our side of the bargain, we'll make sure you're on that shuttle. R'sulek-Entah and Gunboy, you can use the time to visit your folks when you escort him to Ara'Sayal."

"Elise, you said…"

She rounded on him with unspent fury from the last twenty years. "I'm giving you a shuttle off Mars, like you asked for. I never agreed you could go free, don't be a naïve fool. You've sold out to the Balsari, now you're getting your dues. I don't care what happens to you, Maek, I just care about my people and my duty. And if I have to hurt you because I care for someone else, well, big damn deal, isn't that how you thought our marriage worked? You always thought you were the centre of the universe, and now you're finding out you're no more significant than a speck of cosmic dust. Like you made me feel. Goodbye, Maek, if we don't see each other again, it'll be way too soon."

Stepping back, she nodded to R'sulek-Entah and Gunboy, who moved to flank the journalist. Gunboy decided patience wasn't as much a virtue as a liability, especially as his commanding officer seemed offended by Maek's continued presence, so he roughly grabbed him and hauled him one handed to his feet. "Come on, Mr Newark, let's go and introduce you to some nice Arajak we know."

Moonchild turned her back on him, refused to look at him as he was hauled away. "So, what do we know, Will?" she asked quietly. "I mean really?"

Magpie closed his eyes and began sifting through what he had got. He hadn't been too careful, but that was because he'd had the sudden violent urge to seriously hurt Maek. He wasn't even sure why he'd done that. It wasn't in his nature, even though Maek had deserved it. But he'd brought out more than he went in for, and now he was exploring it. "He's right about the genebanks. They're in the past. We need to find out when, he didn't know. And he's right about someone here being in league with the Balsari."

"I thought you said you hadn't got any of that," Legna said.

Magpie smiled. "Nah, I just wanted him to feel even worse about it all. But someone in this room is a Balsari agent." He hadn't intended to look at Gabriel. It just happened that he did when he said it. Unfortunately, Gabriel was looking at him at the time and saw the implication. From somewhere, the knife appeared in Gabriel's hand and he lunged with a snarl that made him seem more animal than human. Taken by surprise, Magpie stepped back, but stumbled and watched in slow motion as the knife drove in at his chest.

The knife thumped into the outstretched hand, punctured the flesh, but went no further. Gabriel looked up in horror at Iceman, who stood with his arm placed between himself and Magpie, not a flicker of pain on his face. Then, as he tried to think of an explanation for what he'd just witnessed, Bouncer shot him. He flew across the room and the knife clattered to the floor where Michelangelo picked it up and replaced it in the knife block it had come from.

"Would someone like to explain what just happened?" he said quietly.

Legna stared at Gabriel, unconscious on the other side of the room, tears filling her eyes. "Oh, Gabriel, I never guessed you could do this."

"Well," Bouncer said, pragmatically, slinging his rifle. "That answers that question, what about the genebanks?"

"Ok, people, back to Earth," Moonchild announced. "I'm afraid that means you people too."

As one, the clones all looked to Magpie for his response. He nodded. "It's for the best. Just until we get this sorted out."

They made their preparations. Seraph and Lucy returned and were informed of the developments. They acknowledged the decision and went to get ready. Within the hour, they were on their way.

20

The temporal scanner was searching for anachronons, the telltale signs of something that belonged in another time period. Ordinarily, it was a passive search, simply keeping watch against temporal incursions. Now, it was hunting methodically, tracking down the goblin genebanks. The only place it was looking was Project Cyclone.

"I've found them," Iceman announced calmly. "They were installed at Project Cyclone on 17 June 2470."

Magpie and Legna exchanged glances. "The day before the explosion," Legna said.

"Do you think that could be a coincidence?" Moonchild asked, an eyebrow raised.

Michelangelo looked horrified. "Wait. Are you saying the genebanks and the explosion are linked?"

"It seems likely, although speculation is pointless," Iceman warned. "There are too many variables and unknown factors involved."

"Excuse me, but I remember it differently," Seraph said, frowning with his confusion. "It wasn't June."

"We measure everything in Earth Standard Time," Magpie explained. "Very arrogant, I know, but so much easier when working like this. Our computers immediately translate local dates and times into the temporal equator at the Greenwich Memorial."

"Why is it measured from there?" Lucy asked. "It's not like there's anything special there, is it?"

"It wasn't always under the sea," Iceman explained.

Moonchild interrupted the history lesson. "We have to go back and deal with the genebanks. My guess is that the

Balsari probably moved them again and destroyed the project. We have to make sure we know what happened."
"I've just realised," Bouncer said. "Magpie can't go. None of the clones can go. Neither can you, Colonel."
"Why not?" Magpie asked.
"Just in case," Bouncer answered, morosely. "Last thing we want is a repeat of what happened to Blade."
Magpie looked stunned. "Oh. I hadn't even thought of that. But you're right, we were all in the area at the time."
"I wasn't," Moonchild disagreed. "I was out in the streets."
"We've no way to guarantee we'll be able to stay within the confines of Project Cyclone," Iceman countered. "The risk would be too great if we were forced outside. For example, if we are delayed and need to escape the explosion."
"You're right," Moonchild sighed. "I was there, I remember the explosion. Don't worry, hon, I'll find something else for us to do," she assured Magpie. "Iceman, Bouncer, Goldfish, you three get ready for this one. Sorry, Goldfish, it's likely there'll be work for you. I can't afford to leave you here."
Goldfish nodded and went to prepare himself. He knew he was going to have to relive everything all over again as if for the first time. The team members watched with unconcealed sympathy as he left the room.
"I wish there was another way," Moonchild muttered.
Magpie came to stand beside her. "Hacksaw's still working on a treatment for it. One day we'll get it right."
She nodded. "Will, I'll need you to interrogate Gabriel while I coordinate their movements. Are you up to it?"
"What if he doesn't cooperate?"

"Sorry, Will, that's why it has to be you. We need his knowledge, whether or not he chooses to cooperate."

"You're the boss," he clearly wasn't happy about it, but knew better than to argue with her.

They shared a long look as if reassuring each other of their reliability, then he followed the others from the room.

***

Bouncer was intercepted by Seraph on his way to Control. He had the distinct impression the clone had been waiting for him. "Can I help you, sir?" he asked politely, a little jumpy.

Seraph looked at him, his eyes red, as if he'd been crying recently. The only part of his face that hadn't been scarred so horribly, they were the only things he recognised in the man. And they were disturbingly identical to Magpie's eyes. He couldn't shake the horrible feeling he was looking at his friend.

"I just want you to know," Seraph told him. "That whatever happens at Project Cyclone, you will always have my gratitude."

"I'm sorry, I don't want to appear rude, but am I missing something? You've been watching me ever since we first met, and I have no idea why. I'm guessing it's something to do with my future self meeting your past self, in which case it's against regulations for me to be discussing it."

"Ah. I see. Well, in that case, please forgive me, I meant no offence."

"None taken, it's just that armed with future knowledge, we can avoid situations and alter history by doing so, even unintentionally. It's an occupational hazard. Sorry."

"I understand."

"When I get back, I'll be free to discuss anything that's not classified information," Bouncer offered. "Perhaps then, we can have a proper talk, get to know each other a bit better. What do you say?"

"Yes," Seraph's smile seemed forced. "When you get back. Goodbye, then Bouncer."

Bouncer watched as the clone walked away, fresh tears in his eyes. He had a bad feeling about this conversation and where it might have led if he'd allowed it. But, he reminded himself, he had his duty, and that was the important thing. He turned and continued on his way.

***

Maek Newark sat alone in his cell. The ship was making steady progress towards Ara'Sayal and his life was once again hurtling towards its self-induced destruction. The Arajak were bound to make his life miserable, and he couldn't decide if that was better than the death he would face on Earth for his treason. He'd slept little, no great surprise. He wondered if he should have even gone to Mars at all. But the chance of revenge on Elise had spurred him on. He shouldn't have tried to save his reputation like that when they caught him. His instructions had been to expose the Firewood Foundation and S.T.A.R.T., take the information to Earth and have the clones destroyed as a threat to Imperial Security, and the others executed for treason. Without S.T.A.R.T. to police the timelines, the Balsari would be free to do untold damage to Earth's past. Maek became aware of the figure outside the cell. "What do you want?" he sneered, recognising his visitor. "I've nothing to say, you're wasting your time."

"Be silent if you want to live," the figure ordered, and he realised something was wrong. Taking a small device from a pocket, the figure did something to turn the forcefield off, then handed the device to Maek. "Go to airlock seven. There is a stealth ship docked there. They will take you away from here."

Maek tried to say thank you, but the figure was gone. The device was clearly of Balsari origin. He was amazed at the depth of their infiltration, considering his rescuer's identity. He didn't want to waste time thinking about it. Gathering his wits, he set off from the unguarded cells, heading for airlock seven.

***

On the command deck, the officer at the science station frowned. "Captain, there's an intruder on board. In the brig."

"Show me," Captain Talan demanded, as he crossed to the science station.

"Sorry, sir, it's gone," the officer seemed confused. "My lights came on, sir, there was someone there."

"Get me an interior view," Talan instructed.

The officer complied. There was no-one there. Not even in the cells.

Talan didn't hesitate. "Security, locate and apprehend Maek Newark. He's to be considered dangerous. Where's he headed?"

"Deck five, sir," the science officer said.

"What's on deck five? Just airlocks. Scan for anything that might be docked with us. Security, he's heading for the airlocks on deck five. Commander R'sulek-Entah, Lieutenant McCallum, your prisoner is at liberty on the ship and is heading for the airlocks on deck five. Please assist."

"Acknowledged," R'sulek-Entah responded.

The two S.T.A.R.T. officers looked at each other, then headed for the door of their quarters. They found the security detail standing by the interior door of airlock seven.

"What's going on?" Gunboy demanded, aware that he was technically the ranking officer until the security chief arrived, unless R'sulek-Entah decided to exercise her rank.

"The prisoner's in there, sir," a young ensign replied, snapping off a smart salute. "He's preparing the outer hatch."

R'sulek-Entah looked through the tiny porthole to see Maek glaring back at her. The disgraced journalist laughed at her. "You're too late, Arajak, I'm leaving now."

The intercom burst into life. "Newark, don't be a fool, there's nothing on the other side," he heard the human tell him.

"Don't be naïve, Lieutenant," he answered. "The Balsari look after their own."

The Arajak took her turn. "Mr Newark, it is true. If you are expecting a ship to be waiting for you, you are sadly mistaken. There is nothing there."

"It's in stealth mode, stupid," he sneered. The light changed on the panel. "Sorry, everyone. I'd love to stay and chat, but my lift's arrived. Bye-bye." He gave a cheery wave and pressed the button which opened the outer hatch onto the vacuum of space. Maek barely had time to register the betrayal before he was gone.

***

Project Cyclone, Mars, 2470

Bouncer was first to arrive. Quickly crouching, he swept his rifle around the room and ensured it was secure. Taking his communicator, he called the others, who arrived immediately after. Iceman gave a cursory glance to confirm Bouncer's opinion that they had teleported into a secure location. Then he handed the mnemonic card to Goldfish, as the demolitions expert began to panic. Iceman and Bouncer retreated to discrete distance to give Goldfish time to come to terms with his errant memory. They spent the time consulting over the layout of the project.

"No!" Goldfish fell to his knees. "No, no, no, Sarah!" he sobbed.

From her station thirty-seven years away, Moonchild monitored the movements of lifesigns around them. "Guys, there's some kind of elevator that leads to an even deeper level. I'm picking up some strange signals from there. I'm guessing it's probably the genebanks. I'm sending you the coordinates."

"Received," Iceman acknowledged. "These coordinates are not in the original design of the building. They've clearly been added since the project was started. Do we have any information concerning its construction?"

Moonchild turned to the clones who had stayed with her at Control. "Anybody?"

Legna, Michelangelo, Lucy and Seraph all looked at each other. Legna spoke. "Uncle Xavier built a massive subterranean gallery but he never explained it to us. I don't think he realised we were even aware of it. Many of us were taken to this gallery, but none came back."

"As near as any of us could work out," Seraph continued. "Some of the clones degenerated, lost genetic cohesion. Uncle Xavier took them away, but we lost contact with them and assumed they'd died."

"Maybe they did," Michelangelo mused, tapping his chin thoughtfully with one finger. "Or maybe they were somehow evolving into goblins."

"Interesting theory," Moonchild encouraged him. "Any evidence for that?"

"Possibly," he replied. "You three say you lost contact when they were taken away? Maybe that's part of it, as far as we've been able to deduce, the goblins aren't psionically gifted. Maybe that's part of the change. If they have their psionic impulses removed, maybe they really do degenerate into savages, cut off from their own kind."

"How would that account for the vast quantities?" Moonchild persisted.

Michelangelo shrugged. "Maybe the earliest ones were used to harvest genes. Maybe that also accounts for the degenerate status. However many of us there are, we're all first generation clones from the spliced genetic material of William and Angel. If the goblins were cloned from clones, especially defective clones, who knows what the results might be?"

"Unless," Lucy posited. "That was the plan all along."

Moonchild turned back to the communications array. "Any of that help you over there?"

"All information is helpful to some degree, Colonel," Iceman answered, and she heard someone in the background mutter something that sounded like 'creep', but she couldn't be sure.

"Ok, folks, be careful," she said and left them to their job.

***

Magpie dismissed the guards from the holding cells and moved to stand in front of Gabriel's cell. The clones stared at each other from either side of the forcefield.
"Come to gloat?" The bitterness was clear in Gabriel's voice.
"No. I've come to talk to you. That's all."
"Easy for you to say on that side of the cell."
"I could force this out of you. I don't want to do that. Don't make me."
"There's nothing to force. I'm not the one you're looking for."
"I know."
That statement of acknowledgement caught Gabriel off guard. "What?"
"I said I know. I know you're not the Balsari agent. You wouldn't have attacked me that way if you were. You'd have waited for a real opportunity and taken me out while no-one was looking. Then you'd make sure you had a watertight alibi. But, the question remains: why *did* you attack me?"
For the first time, Gabriel showed Magpie an expression other than intense dislike. "Honestly? I haven't the faintest idea. Maybe it was the way you looked at me when you said you were looking for the traitor. Maybe you had it coming anyway. Who knows?"
"Someone knows," Magpie said cryptically, a nasty suspicion forming in the darkness of his mind. "Why don't you explain what happened."

"Why? So you can tell everyone how you figured me out? Not a chance, Will, don't forget, I know how you think, because I am you."

"No, you're not, Gabriel. You're close enough, but you're not me. But I'll make a deal with you."

"Deal?" Gabriel narrowed his eyes. "What kind of deal?"

"You tell me what you felt when you tried to kill me, and I'll tell you what I felt when I tried to kill Maek Newark."

"You didn't. You just took information from him."

"I tore it from him. I didn't care how much damage I did to his mind in the process. That's unlike me. I try to at least maintain some sense of ethical protocol when dealing with non-psionics, even established enemy agents. But this time, I ignored everything I believed in and tried to kill him, at least mentally. How I managed to leave him intact is beyond me, but it wasn't due to any restraint on my part. I'm guessing someone else was controlling me, at least partially, and I think they did the same to you."

For a long moment, they looked into the crooked mirror, each weighing up the other. Then Gabriel looked away. "If I tell you the same thing happened to me, you'll think I'm just agreeing with you to get myself off the hook. So I'll end up in here, whatever I tell you."

Magpie grinned, disarmingly. "Oh, Gabriel, I beat you at your own game. While I was telling you all this, I was reading your surface thoughts. They told me the truth. You recognised everything I said as the same thing that happened to you. That's all I need to know."

"You... you read my thoughts? You bastard! You talk about ethics?"

"Hey, listen," Magpie spread his arms in mock surprise. "It's my job to adapt to cultural conditions. You live in a culture where it's ok to pry into people's minds. I merely adapted to your cultural mode. Don't take it too personally."

Gabriel said nothing for a few moments, then he looked up again. "You know, I feel like I've lost out to you, even though you've cleared me. You're a devious man, Will. We really should be better friends, you know."

"I hope from now on we will be. But for the time being, we need to establish who the real traitor is, and how he… or she… managed to coerce both of us into doing what we did."

"How are we going to do that?"

"I haven't a clue," Magpie admitted. "But I'm sure between the two of us, we can think of something. Until then, I think it's probably safer if whoever it is thinks we're still holding you for it. I'm afraid you'll have to stay here for a while longer. Sorry."

Gabriel nodded, but didn't comment. He'd already figured that out. Magpie looked at him for a moment longer, then left to find Moonchild.

***

Moonchild was less than thrilled by the prospect of it all. "So someone is running around making people do things they don't want to do? I don't like the sound of that, Will, it's too much of a 'could be anybody' scenario."

"I know," Magpie agreed. "But we can narrow it down with a little thinking. It's someone who was in the room at the time, someone who could force their way into our minds. I'm assuming you don't suspect me, and we've ruled out Gabriel, so who does that leave? Legna or Michelangelo."

Moonchild shook her head. "It's a lot of effort for Legna to go to, to get you all together, just to try killing you all off. She could have done that individually when she tracked you all down. And Michelangelo is the one clone among the lot of you who has no psionic ability whatsoever. Why does it have to be someone who was there?"

Magpie gave his answer some thought. "You know, it doesn't. You're right, it can't be either of those two, for the reasons you just gave. But if it wasn't either of those two, who was it?"

"When you went for Maek, Lucy and Seraph were there. They weren't there when Gabriel attacked you. Could that be significant?"

"I don't know. Maybe. If I was trying to set someone up, I'd want to make sure we counted only those who were there every time, or absent every time. But if they can control people from a distance…"

"Is that possible?"

"I don't know," Magpie shrugged. "I have no idea what everyone's capable of. Gabriel's abilities are limited to touch telepathy, but he can do it without being detected. I can do the same for surface thoughts at a distance, but digging for specifics would be detected by another psi-operative. If one of them has the ability to control others, and at range, it puts us all at risk, especially as both of us have been unaware of it at the time."

"So, Lucy or Seraph. Maybe Lucy and Seraph. What do you think?"

They both fell silent, considering the evidence. One of the clones had started acting strangely ever since S.T.A.R.T. had arrived, looking edgy, as if the life he'd carefully constructed had been exposed and was about to come crashing down. Their eyes met.

"Seraph," they both said.

21

Legna sat alone in her temporary quarters at S.T.A.R.T. Control and considered her options. Everything seemed to be spiralling out of her grasp. Meeting Will had been her life's goal, the one thing she had been aiming for since that first meeting twenty years ago, when his appearance had turned her world upside down. Now, he had turned her entire world upside down again, but life had changed to yet another course. She wasn't sure where it was going, but she knew she didn't like it. Her own little empire was crumbling around her. It wasn't Will's fault, she knew that, but he was certainly the catalyst both times. Now the Firewood Foundation had been closed down, and all the good works that were a side effect of her real work come to an end. There was no way they could go back to Mars, not with the Empire and the Balsari both aware of what the Foundation really was. She wasn't even sure which was the most dangerous for them, the one that had created them, or the one that had abused them.

The door announced a new arrival. She instructed the door to open. Seraph stood in the corridor.

"Come in, Seraph," she invited.

She examined the man's ruined face. He had been crying, something which had been happening regularly for a couple of days now. She knew he was haunted by some secret he would never speak about, but until Will appeared, he seemed to have it under control.

"Legna," he said, his voice unsteady. "I need to talk to you."

"I'm always here for you, Seraph, you know that. What's troubling you?"

He sat in the chair she indicated. For a long moment, he said nothing, simply stared at the floor. She could tell he was fighting against tears. She was itching to ask him, but she was unwilling to push. Finally, he seemed to draw strength from somewhere and took a deep, but ragged, breath and looked at her.

"Legna, I've got a secret. I can't go on without telling anyone anymore. I've decided to tell you."

As Seraph explained everything, Legna found herself going cold.

***

Goldfish looked at the equipment again. "I don't get it. I still can't find any hint of a bomb."

Bouncer leaned forward. "Is it possible it would kick in after someone tampered with it? Like a kind of delayed booby trap?"

"Smart thinking, Ibrahim," Goldfish nodded thoughtfully. "Trouble is, there's only one way to find out if that's the case."

"Ah," Bouncer realised the problem with the logic. "So, you want me to tamper with it?"

"Um... not yet," Goldfish cautioned.

"Is there a way to interrupt the power supply, then?" the Tactical Support Op persisted.

"No," said Iceman, returning from his investigation of the rest of the chamber. "It is self-contained. The battery that powers it is deep within the genebank itself. It appears likely that any booby trap will be connected to it, making it difficult to reach it in time to defuse it."

"Then we need to find another way in," Goldfish pondered. "What readings did you get?"

"The battery itself is constructed of an unknown alloy, presumably Kalaszan in origin. The liquid content of the battery is three parts solinium, three parts kovinium, two parts volatium and one part salzic acid."

"Oh," said Goldfish, ominously, and looked thoughtful.

"Oh?" Bouncer repeated. "That's a bad 'oh', isn't it?"

"Afraid so. It's a classic mix, if you happen to be a Balsari bomb maker. Did you find any coribium in the battery lining?"

"It's the only part of the alloy the analyser recognises," Iceman explained. "By which I infer the component parts of a bomb are present."

"Yes. My guess is that the whole thing is set up so delicately that the slightest movement will release everything into a central chamber. They'll react with each other and, even in the tiniest quantities, basically take half the city with them."

"That's a problem," Bouncer agreed.

"More than that," Iceman mentioned. "It is inconsistent with history. This building was almost destroyed, and several blocks were damaged, but nothing consistent with the damage this would cause."

"That's good, then," Goldfish smiled. "It means we defused it."

"But it raises the question," Iceman continued, as if Goldfish hadn't interrupted. "If the explosion wasn't caused by the genebanks, what did cause it?"

Bouncer and Goldfish looked uncomfortably at each other. Neither had an answer.

"What's going on, guys?" Moonchild's voice cut in.

"Tactical discussion, Colonel," Goldfish answered. "We're becoming aware of complications."

"Is the mission being compromised?"

"Don't really know, Colonel, there seems to be an extraneous explosion lurking in the shadows. Do we proceed?"

By way of an answer, Moonchild asked. "Iceman, analysis. How do you see it?"

"We should proceed with caution, Colonel. I believe Goldfish can contain the booby trap, but we should be aware of the possibility of unseen elements."

Knowing that was the best she would get from her technical coordinator, Moonchild weighed the evidence.

"Ok, guys, it's your call. If you agree, then proceed. First sign of trouble, pull out. Good luck."

Goldfish began by removing a small section from the front of the genebank with his laser wrench. He looked into the gap he'd made and, using various tools as a means to clear objects from his field of vision, made a brief study of the task ahead of him. "I can see the battery," he told the others. "It's kind of egg-shaped. I can't quite reach it."

Something crackled and Goldfish whipped his hand out from the machinery with a stifled yelp. Bouncer moved quickly to his side, half expecting to see a goblin attached to Goldfish's fingers. "Forcefield," the demolitions expert said between expletives.

"The device has been triggered," Iceman stated with the same calm as he might have announced lunch was ready.

"We've got to get it out of there now," Goldfish reached back inside.

"Did anyone hear that?" Bouncer said, turning his head to try and locate the source of the sound.

"Yes," Iceman confirmed. "It came from behind this wall."

Bouncer followed Iceman's finger and focused on the wall in question. Flicking through to x-ray, he searched for a clue. And saw the goblins massing on the other side. "Time's up, folks, we've got to move out. That wall's going to go at any moment."

"Do you need to evacuate?" Moonchild asked.

"No," Iceman said. "If we leave now, the goblins will be free to invade the project. If they attack the clones, they could do untold damage to the timeline."

There was another crackle, Goldfish swore again, then came out from the machine's innards clutching the battery. The lights on the genebanks died. "Got it, let's move!"

Iceman turned to the others. "Evacuate the clones, Bouncer. Goldfish, find somewhere safe to defuse the bomb. I'll stay here and hold off the goblins as long as I can. Go now."

The others knew better than to argue, and they also knew delay might cost more lives than the timeline would cope with. They fled the chamber, heading for the upper levels.

Goldfish went for the higher levels and lost Bouncer at some point. He began bursting through doors and suddenly he was meeting the children. It was like running from a room and finding yourself back in it, the exit door linked by some kind of perverse teleporter to the entry door. Every time Goldfish entered a room, a three year old identical in almost every way to the last looked up at him. To every child, he gave a variant of the same warning. "Come on, we're leaving here."

None of them asked who he was, none of them questioned his presence, or why he was there. It was as if

they all knew their time had come. He ushered them all from the rooms, and loaded them into the elevator, recalling it several times, and loading more children into it.
"Where's Uncle Xavier?" one little boy asked him.
"I don't know," he answered. "But you have to be brave, and go without him. Can you do that?"
The boy nodded, seriously.
"Good boy," Goldfish grinned at him to encourage him and ruffled his hair. "There are other people who will look after you when you get outside." He ushered the boy into the elevator with the last load. Then he went to one of the now empty rooms and set about dismantling the bomb.

***

Iceman waited with his customary patience for the wall to collapse. Clearly, the goblins were being bred beyond this wall and were exceeding the limitations of their captivity. He took up his position halfway along the corridor between the genebank chamber and the elevator to the regular levels of Project Cyclone.
He could hear the elevator returning. Was one of the others returning? He turned to face the elevator doors. They opened to reveal a man in a white lab coat. Immediately, Iceman's recognition database told him this was Doctor Xavier da Silva. He was clearly expecting to see Iceman, because of the gun in his right hand.
Iceman looked impassively at him as he aimed and fired without a word. The shot fizzed into Iceman's chest, searing away the flesh around the wound. Iceman glanced down at the hole, then back up at da Silva. "That was unnecessary, Doctor. Your weapon cannot harm me."

Blinking in astonishment, da Silva fired again, with the same result. "Mechanoid?" he guessed.

"I am a Mark V Sentient Mobile Unit, constructed by Kayanaga CyberSystems on Xeran IX."

"Impossible. Kayanaga is still conducting researching into the Mark II."

"Your failure to accept the fact is based more on your inability to believe the truth than on my inability to lie convincingly," Iceman told him, conversationally.

"I see," da Silva nodded. "Then the Balsari were right. Someone from the future is trying to stop us." He began adjusting the setting on his gun.

Iceman knew he didn't have time to close the space before da Silva got another shot off, but he had to try. As he started moving, the scientist fired again, this time catching him above the left hip. Momentarily puzzled, Iceman realised his motion was compromised. Momentum carried him a couple of metres, but his legs refused to respond. He crashed heavily to the floor.

***

Bouncer got separated from Goldfish early in the evacuation procedure. He began his search on the lower levels, while he assumed Goldfish was doing the same above him. There were very few children down here, and he found himself making good time through the various rooms. He found an elevator and ushered his new charges into it. "Up," he instructed and the elevator responded. At street level, he began ushering the clones out into the Martian evening. He was careful not to leave the building himself, for fear of someone recognising him from here when he reappeared in 2507. Making sure of himself, he took out his communicator and called for Goldfish.

"I'm still here, Bouncer, I've got this bomb sorted, but it's a bit delicate and it'll take a while yet. You'd better get out while you can. I'll follow you as soon as I make sure it's safe here."

"Acknowledged, sir. Afzal to Control. I'm ready to come home, Colonel."

"Ok, stand by, Bouncer," Moonchild told him, the relief evident in her voice. He grinned, knowing she always worried about her people when she wasn't there with them. He waited for the teleporter to take him.

Help me!

He shook his head, unsure of what had just happened.

Help me!

"Colonel, belay that! Someone's still here. Don't ask how I know, I just do. I'm going to find them."

"Bouncer, be careful. Don't do anything dumb, ok? And don't stay too long down there, I can't get a good enough fix on your signal to bring you back from down there."

"Got that, Colonel. Thanks." Bouncer went back to the elevator and got in. "Down," he said, and readied his rifle, in case this was a trap. When the elevator came to a halt, he stepped out and looked up and down the corridor.

Help me!

He wasn't sure why he chose the direction he did. He just went. He checked every room on his way, his optical enhancers set to detect lifesigns, until he found the right one. A little boy who looked exactly like every other little boy in the building sat in a corner, a terrified expression all over his face.

"Help me," the boy whimpered.

"It's ok, son," Bouncer shouldered his rifle and held out his hand, as he crossed the room. "I'm going to get you out of here. My name's Ibrahim. What's yours?"

"Seraph," the boy said, and Bouncer's blood ran cold.

***

From his position on the floor, Iceman observed Doctor da Silva's actions. The scientist was standing before the wall separating them from the goblins. "Come, my children," he whispered.

Iceman felt obliged to point out the problem. "Doctor da Silva, are you aware of the nature of the goblins?"

"Oh, yes, machine, I'm aware. I created them. I also created this," he indicated the buckle on his belt. "This is a mask, of sorts. The goblins will only be vaguely aware of my guiding presence, but they won't recognise me as food. They will follow me onto the streets of Olympus City and devour the population. From there, they will be delivered to Earth, and they will eat your precious Emperor."

Iceman considered this. "What of the children? Why are you prepared to destroy what you've spent your life creating?"

"Things change, machine," da Silva shrugged, philosophically. "We must adapt. The Balsari found out about Project Cyclone and made me an offer. I decided to accept their offer. After all, I had the genetic material, all it needed was a little tweaking here and there."

"You will be stopped," Iceman said. "That much is an established fact."

"You seem to believe that as you're from the future, you have information I don't. However, I doubt that very much. You have no weapons, and there is no-one here to help you."

The wall gave way, and the goblins poured into the chamber. They hovered around da Silva, clearly aware of his presence, but unsure of his nature. Iceman was fascinated by the fact that they were silent, without their usual keening wails. Perhaps they were the original goblins, still possessing psionic communicative abilities. As they swarmed towards him, Iceman reported back to Control. "Colonel Washington, my drivetrain is damaged and my mobility has been compromised. Doctor da Silva is a Balsari agent. They have supplied him with weapons and technology. He intends to release the goblins into the city."

"Can you stop him?" Moonchild was sounding anxious.

"Yes, Colonel. I have that under control. I have activated my self-destruct circuit. It has a four minute countdown."

Hearing Iceman's side of the conversation, da Silva laughed. "Four minutes won't help you, machine, I'll be out of here with the goblins in less than two minutes."

"You are failing to take into consideration, Doctor, that I activated the circuit as soon as you damaged my drivetrain. That was three minutes ago."

Moonchild heard that. "Iceman, no! Stop the countdown, now! That's an order!"

"I'm sorry, Colonel, that's not possible," Iceman's response was so calm, he sounded almost bored. "The countdown can't be stopped with less than sixty seconds to go. Goodbye, Colonel. It has been a privilege to serve with you all. Please express my regrets to the others."

"Oh, Iceman," Moonchild said sadly, realising his fate was sealed and there was nothing anyone could do about it. "Thanks for everything. We'll all miss you."

"Acknowledged," he said.
By now, the goblins were tearing the flesh from his adamantium frame. Doctor da Silva, realising he was never going to escape in time, nonetheless made the attempt. He tried to circle round the stricken mechanoid. At the closest point, a fleshless hand shot out from the pile of silently frenzying clones and grabbed his belt, yanking it off in one fluid motion. Suddenly, all the goblins turned to face him. Aware of his predicament, he made a break for the elevator, but he knew even then he wasn't going to make it. The first goblins hurled themselves at him, knocking the breath from his body and pushing him to the floor. He disappeared, screaming, under the heaving mass as they ripped him apart without mercy. Iceman watched impassively as the seconds ticked away.
"Goodbye," he repeated, and detonated.

***

Goldfish put the last part of the bomb carefully in the temporal flask. Now, the city was safe. "Control, I'm ready. The bomb's been dealt with."
Unusually, there wasn't even an acknowledgement. As soon as the words were out of his mouth, the teleporter took him. Then the rumble from below began coursing through the building.

***

Bouncer reached his hand even further towards Seraph. "Come on, son, take my hand. I won't hurt you."

The terrified boy began to move his hand in the direction of his rescuer, his eyes never leaving his face. As their fingers touched, they heard the blast and felt the tremor. Bouncer leapt to his feet and went quickly to the door. He switched to thermal x-ray imaging and cursed as he saw the huge ball of fire and destruction rushing headlong from the lower level. He also knew what he had to do. He had to save Seraph at any cost. A stab of fear pinned him momentarily to the spot as he realised what that cost would have to be. Resigned to the fact, he removed his jacket and wrapped the boy in it. That would protect him from much of the fire damage, but he already knew what it would do to his face. Thinking quickly, he took his rifle and blew the door out of its moorings. Collecting the fallen door from the where it had landed in the next room, he glanced down the corridor created by the open doors, to where the rushing, roiling firewall was screaming towards him. He clenched his jaw and leapt back into the room. "Stay behind here, Seraph, and keep yourself covered up," he said as calmly as he could, even though he was almost as scared as the boy. "And don't be afraid, it'll all be over soon."
Bouncer placed the door over Seraph, using his rifle to weld it in place, giving the boy the best chance he could. Then he turned to meet his destiny.

***

Moonchild gave a strangled cry as the screen monitoring Bouncer's lifesigns went blank. Hacksaw leaned over and placed a gentle hand on her shoulder, squeezing softly. He had no words to say to her. She sat in silence for a moment, her head in her hands. Then she looked up at him, her eyes full of tears. "I couldn't reach him," she said in a broken voice. "He was too deep."

"I know," Hacksaw said, solemnly. "I know, Elise. You couldn't have prevented it."

She didn't answer, just turned back to the now blank monitors. "Get Magpie up here," she said.

***

Seraph walked into Control between Magpie and Legna. All three looked serious.

"Will…" Moonchild couldn't bring herself to say the words.

Magpie came to her and gave her a wordless hug. When she was able to pull away, she met his eyes. He was suffering too.

"I know," he whispered. "Seraph told us everything."

She looked from him to Seraph. The other clone was tearful. "I'm sorry, Colonel. I couldn't tell anyone, in case I changed something. He saved me, Colonel. He sacrificed himself for me. He knew what he was doing. He was very brave."

"You saw him die?" she asked, knowing even as she said it she was clutching at straws.

"He told me to stay covered up, and I was too scared not to. But when the fire had stopped I found these."

She looked down at his hand, which was outstretched, offering her what was held there. She picked up the objects.

"I kept them safe all these years. They're yours now."

Moonchild turned the scarred and fire-damaged ocular implants over in her hand. She shook her head and handed them back. "No," she told the clone. "They're yours. They always have been. He'd want you to keep them."

Seraph closed his eyes, then nodded. "Thank you," he said.

Goldfish, who had regained his memory by the time Magpie appeared, stepped forward. "I don't know if this is what anyone needs to hear right now," he said, quietly. "But what just happened is how history remembers it. Bouncer was always meant to save Seraph. The explosion was always meant to be Iceman. We were always part of the history of the place. It doesn't make it any easier, but now we know we've ensured history followed the path it was meant to."

Moonchild looked at him. He was, of course, right. Knowing that they were part of the timeline wasn't any consolation, how could it be? But they'd both died doing their duty, and that was all they could ask.

***

The meeting room was solemn. Moonchild, clothed like the others, in dress uniform stood at the dais and surveyed her colleagues. Admiral Saastemoinen and General N'Komo sat at the front, along with Magpie, R'sulek-Entah, Gunboy and Hacksaw. Apart from Blade, all surviving former members of the team were present, as well as several former colleagues. All the clones were there. Members of the Kayanaga CyberSystems board had been invited, and she had been surprised to see Mister Kayanaga himself. The old man had clearly been moved by the success of his creation to come all the way from Xeran IX. She looked out at all those faces, making eye contact with every one of them. She finally settled her gaze on Magpie, who nodded encouragement.

She took a breath. "Friends," she began. "We are here to honour two of our fallen comrades. Lieutenant Mark Vee and Trooper Ibrahim Afzal. Iceman and Bouncer. They are what we all aspire to: heroes, in the real sense of the word. They both knew that their deaths could have been avoided, had they chosen to avoid it. But they were both dedicated to their duty, and that dedication has required of them the ultimate price. But they did not die alone. Iceman spoke to me throughout, and expressed, in his own way, his sense of joy at having been a member of the team." She waited a second for the muted ripple of understanding laughter, then continued. "Bouncer died saving a small child, and that child is with us today, to bear witness to his bravery." She nodded in Seraph's direction, and those who didn't previously know, turned to him. "Of Iceman and Bouncer, we can say this much: they are a shining example to those of us who remain. They light our way and show us the path we must follow. They were our colleagues, yes, and they were our friends. But more than that, they were…" her voice caught in her throat. "…they were our brothers."

Moonchild left the dais and took her place next to Magpie. He took her hand and squeezed. She squeezed back and they shared an encouraging look as the admiral and the general took their turns.

***

The street shook. People ran in all directions, panic-stricken. Was it an earthquake? A lone little boy found himself wandering the alleys of a strange place. He'd never

been outside of the project before. He saw a door, and some lights. There were people standing outside, talking in raised voices. He sent his mind forward. They were trying to decide if they dared to risk investigating the tremors and the screaming, or if they should stay here, or even head in the opposite direction. A few people began to notice him as he approached, but no-one took more notice of him than a cursory glance. He began to cry. A girl who was about the same age as him saw his tears and came towards him, holding out her hands to show she wasn't a threat, but he read her mind and knew she wasn't.
"Hey, don't cry," she said, holding up a small cloth and wiping away his tears. "My name's Elise. What's your name?"
"Will," the boy said.

22

The Great Tree, Ara'Sayal, 2507

R'sulek-Entah stood in the great throne room of Ara'Sayal and bowed her head before the eminence that was her mother's sister, the queen. Her eyes fixed upon a point on the floor and refused to shift their focus. She would not look up. She didn't speak. Such an error would be unforgivable. One did not speak in the presence of the queen unless one was instructed to do so.
"Thou hast performed thy duties well, child," the great one addressed her in the formal tongue, as she always did. "Thou hast brought honour upon thyself and upon Ara'Sayal. Thou art to be commended. It is our will that thou shalt be awarded the Faith of Ara'Nas. Speak."
"My queen," R'sulek-Entah replied in reverent tones, her head still bowed. "I have upheld the honour of Ara'Sayal to the best of my ability. That you deem this worthy of your attention is honour enough for me. I ask only that I may continue to serve while it pleases your majesty."
"Granted, child," the queen replied. "Thou hast proven thyself a capable ambassador in the presence of the Terrans. Thy new task is well suited to thee. It is our hope that thou dost conduct thyself with equal honour."
For a moment, she wasn't sure she'd heard right. Instantly reviewing the queen's words, she realised she had. She was being reassigned. She almost asked why, but stopped herself. She hadn't been instructed to speak. Therefore, the audience was over. She bowed low, backed away two steps, and turned, marching from the great hall without

faltering. She knew all the males in the hall were watching her, their uncomplicated minds unable to grasp the finer points of what had just taken place. R'sulek-Entah, the daughter of the queen's sister, had been given one of the highest awards possible but, at the same time, been stripped of her role as liaison officer to S.T.A.R.T., the role for which she had received the award. She couldn't think of anything she'd done to displease the queen. The queen was not in the habit of handing out such prizes if she doubted they had been earned. So this was no subtle plot to discredit her. In fact the only thing she had done that had been outside of Arajak parameters was the mating with Lieutenant McCallum, but even that had been done in direct consultation with her mother, one of the queen's chief advisors, and with the blessing of the queen herself. No, there was something else happening, and she could only think of one possibility that would fit the facts. Ara'Sayal was severing its ties with the Terran Empire. Uncertain of how to proceed, R'sulek-Entah first returned to her quarters where her new family were waiting for her.
"How did it go?" Gunboy asked, as she landed on their branch.
"I am not certain, John," she told him. "But I think it went badly."
Gunboy listened in growing alarm as she explained what had happened and what had been said. He couldn't find any way to fault her reasoning. "What do we do?" he asked.
"I must wait for this session to finish and speak with my mother. I have left word that I wish to speak, and she will send for me when it is convenient. Until then, we can do nothing."

Gunboy nodded, but said nothing. He couldn't find the words. He still didn't understand the Arajak way, and besides, he'd spent all his time and energy trying to keep track of fifty-six children as they leapt from the branches of the Great Tree, and tested their ability to fly. Gunboy was scared witless about the half-Arajak, half-human hybrids that, while possessing the wings of their mother's people, were not as gifted as full-blood Arajak. However, in his failed attempts to keep them grounded he had several times come close to falling from their branch himself. He had noted every time what a long way down it was. In the end, some of the neighbouring children had taken it upon themselves to fly with his children and he'd been somewhat reassured, but even at such a young age, the full-blood Arajak were very much aware of their status, and they knew that the skin colouring of these new children meant they were different somehow. They just weren't sure what caste laid claim to such a strange hue.

***

As the day gave way to evening twilight, Gunboy sat on the branch looking up through the upper branches and leaves at the stars, reflecting on his life. He'd once harboured thoughts of marriage to any one of the many eligible women among the Empire's elite. Maybe settle down on his own estate, have a couple of children. Become an imperial senator, maybe, and be famous for his political speeches. Then he'd found himself betrothed to that girl, what was her name? The daughter of the merchant from Volaris Secundus. He'd argued with his parents over that one for weeks. Now, he was involved in a relationship that wasn't quite marriage, to a member of a species the Empire had been at war with when he was born, and had more children than he'd ever imagined was possible. And he was a member of the Empire's elite military unit. He wished his parents had survived long enough to see him now. He wondered what they'd make of it all.

Of course, they hadn't survived. When the Balsari flattened Toronto, they'd been there. It was what had driven him to join up in the first place. Now, he was on leave, assuming a mission didn't come up. Moonchild and Magpie had been called in to find replacements for Iceman and Bouncer, and he didn't envy them that task. Both were sorely missed, and the tragedy hung about the survivors like a rain cloud. The atmosphere at S.T.A.R.T. Control was not healthy right now. He was glad not to be there at the moment, but felt guilty about his emotions. He wasn't sure why, but he did.

So here he was, watching the unfamiliar constellations as they hovered above his head. He was there until R'sulek-Entah returned from her audience with her mother. She did not look pleased, although he still found it hard to tell the difference between the facial expressions of an overjoyed Arajak and a depressed Arajak.

"John," she said, her voice unnaturally quiet, even for her. "The news is grave. The queen has indeed decided to sever our ties with the Empire. She has received an ambassador from Balsar and has decided to ally with the Balsari."

"What?" Gunboy's shout of disbelief echoed through the neighbouring branches, and he immediately lowered his voice to a hoarse whisper. "Why? What possible reason could she have for that?"

"It is not for me to question the queen, but my mother has explained to me that the Balsari are preparing a temporal assault on strategic points in Earth's history. They have advised the queen to join with them or share Earth's fate. The queen has decided to join with them."

"Then we've no time to lose," Gunboy began moving. "We have to warn the Empire."

"No, John," R'sulek-Entah shook her head, her wings fluttering in agitation and her antennae swaying with dismay. "I am not permitted to leave here. You must go alone."

"But I can't leave you and the children…"

"Go. Do not allow foolish sentiment to impede your thinking. You are a member of S.T.A.R.T. and therefore you are in the best position to warn the others, because you understand the nature of the threat. If you waste time and resources trying to make the impossible happen, we will both be trapped here, and Earth will be left defenceless. Go now, John."

23

He could see her as she approached the door. "Sarah, don't do it," he called, but she couldn't hear him. She just checked her pistol and continued her journey. He moved to the other side of the door, his pistol ready. "Keep away, Sarah, please!" he was begging, but when she looked at him for confirmation that he was ready, he simply nodded. They moved into position and he gave the hand signal for the countdown. Three. Two. One. She swung round, shooting the door mechanism, which exploded with a disappointing pop. The door slid open and she rolled in, coming up ready, her pistol swinging in a controlled arc as she searched quickly for targets. He followed, adopting the same tactic, but covering her back. There was no-one there still standing. She moved to the back of the room.
"The bomb's here, James," she said.
"Don't go anywhere near it!" he screamed at her, but she still didn't hear. Instead, she stayed where she was while he joined her to examine it. He looked at her, meeting her eyes. "Please just leave. Let me take care of it," he pleaded.
She took out her scanner and began studying the device. "Seems fairly straight forward," she commented. She put the scanner away and took out her tools.
"Please, Sarah, leave it. Just get up and walk away." He was in tears now, but he could still see every minute detail clearly. They both reacted to the noise out in the corridor. He moved to the exposed doorway.

He swung into the corridor, his pistol trained dead centre, but no-one was there. No-one ever was. He should go back in, take over from her, but he knew he wouldn't. Instead he told her he was going to investigate. As she always did, she looked up and said. "I love you." It was what she called their 'just in case' policy. If something should go wrong, the last words between them would be 'I love you'.

"I love you," he told her, and knew the words were real. They smiled their understanding to each other, and he went back out into the corridor to find the source of the noise. Which was what saved him when the device exploded. The gout of flame that knocked him off his feet seared his back. He could feel the heat and knew he was on fire. But, as soon as he regained his footing, he ran back to the doorway, unable to fight the heat and enter the room, knowing there was no way he could save her. Every time he returned to that room, he knew his wife's remains would be burning where they'd landed, but he would never be able to pierce the flames and see her. Then the building would begin its slow collapse, and another officer would grab him and pull him from the danger zone. Outside, he would stand and watch as the old and grand building was reduced to rubble and dust, becoming Sarah's tomb, and know that he was always powerless to prevent it.

His fellow police officers would do everything they could to offer their support, but they were also stunned at the loss of a colleague. He would just stand in a daze until eventually someone would come and take him away.

Only it never got that far in the dream before he woke. He would be staring into the flames when reality punched itself back into his awareness, just as had happened now.

He rarely dreamed of it at all, these days. He was glad of that, but recently, it had started returning to him. Now, he would wake up most nights, sweating, realising with a relieved shock that it was all in his mind. Goldfish knew it was the loss of Iceman and Bouncer, in similar circumstances that had brought it all back to him, and knew he was doomed to live with it resurfacing more often than before.

Hacksaw had suggested it was what had caused the memory loss in the first place, knowing that he could travel into the past but could never affect the outcome of that incident. He believed it was this additional trauma that caused him to unconsciously wipe his memory clean every time he made a temporal shift. Maybe there was a cure, maybe not. But always having to read the mnemonics Hacksaw had prepared for him, always discovering as though for the first time about Sarah, was wearing him down. Little by little, Goldfish was being eroded inside. The only thing that kept him going was the one thing that resulted in the memory loss. He knew if things didn't change soon, he would have to make a very difficult choice. His duty or his sanity.

***

Moonchild sat down heavily next to Magpie and rested her head in her hands. For a while she sat motionless and he just let her be, waiting for her to stir. When she finally did, she looked at him. "Give me a good reason not to quit," she said.
"You've contributed too much to the pension scheme?" he suggested.
"Give me a better reason."

"You'll miss me."

"I said a better reason, not more incentive to quit."

"Ok, what if I said we know where Admiral Chalk is?"

"That might help. Is it true?"

"Almost. He's in the past, we're just trying to figure out when."

"How soon will you know?"

"I'm waiting for the answer as we speak. Want some coffee?"

Moonchild nodded, gratefully, wearily. "What about the clone agent?"

"Haven't got any closer with that one, I'm afraid. I'm stumped as to who would have that level of ability. Now we know what's been eating Seraph, it eliminates him."

She took the coffee he was holding out to her, smiling her thanks. She took a sip and grimaced. "You make lousy coffee, Will."

"It's synthesised," he objected. "I never went near it."

"Even so…"

They sat some more in silence.

"Could Michelangelo be lying?" Moonchild said, eventually.

"What, about not being psionic?"

"Yeah. Could it be a front to throw us off the scent?"

"He'd have to have planned it from the beginning. If anyone had ever witnessed him using his abilities, he'd be found out."

"Maybe he did plan it. Maybe he's a criminal genius."

"Nah. That's my job."

They shared a laugh, but it was hollow. There was more silence.

"Watch him anyway," Moonchild said.

If Magpie had any doubts, he didn't share them. They were two friends keeping each other company in the midst of tragedy, but he recognised an order when he heard one. He chose not to acknowledge it. She would know he understood.
Magpie's communicator sounded. "Angel," he said into thin air.
"Commander," a voice came from nowhere. "You wanted to be informed when we'd traced Admiral Chalk."
"You've got him?"
"Yes, sir. Certainly to the correct year, probably the location too."
"I'm coming in. Good work, Lieutenant. Angel out." He turned to Moonchild. "You want to come too?"
"Try and stop me," she said through gritted teeth.

***

Goldfish checked his sidearm for the last time and holstered it. Then he hefted his kitbag and looked round the apartment to make sure he hadn't forgotten anything. "Power down," he instructed. "Security system online."
He watched as the apartment's lighting became dim, and the windows became opaque. Then he left, the door locking itself behind him. The short journey to the lunar surface was one he'd taken many times before, but rarely in such a dark mood. As he stepped out onto the permanently floodlit street, he was aware of the sights and sounds of Armstrong City. He took a deep breath of the filtered oxygen and decided, like he did every time he did this, it was time he moved away from the moon. The fake atmosphere, the lack of natural daylight, the permanently seedy appearance of the shop signs, advertising their

wares in a variety of languages, very few of which actually originated on Earth. As a member of S.T.A.R.T., he had no lack of resources, he really ought to get himself organised and move to one of the more appealing colonies. Trouble was, he needed to be within reach of Control, so it realistically had to be Earth, and he really didn't want to be there. It was no problem working there, especially as much of his work was in a different timezone, but living there again, without Sarah, was not something he was prepared to consider.

As he walked to the teleport terminal, he became aware of the figure at his side. He glanced up, but the man seemed to be ignoring him, looking straight ahead, simply keeping pace. He looked to the other side, and there was someone there too. He stopped. The two shadows continued a couple of paces, then recovered themselves, stopped and turned to him.

"You got a problem, gentlemen?" Goldfish asked, reaching with as much subtlety as possible for his sidearm.

"Lieutenant James Warner?" one of them asked.

"And if I am?"

"Forgive us, Lieutenant," the second man said. "We mean you no harm. There is someone who would like to meet you. Would you please follow us?"

"Follow you? I don't think so, gents. I wasn't born yesterday."

"That's very wise, Lieutenant," the first man conceded. "However, this is not a cheap assassination attempt, or a street robbery. I assure you, we mean you no harm, and our client has taken a lot of trouble to come here to meet you. Please, will you come with us?"

Despite his common sense telling him not to, Goldfish found his curiosity too strong to resist. He knew it was pointless threatening dire retribution if it turned out to be a trap. If that was what it was, he would most likely be dead before he could carry out any threat, and he'd deserve it too, and he didn't want to die with them laughing at him. So he just let them lead him where they wanted him to go.

The vehicle that sat at the far end of the alley was sleek, modern and obviously expensive. He wondered who would own one of these cars and still want to speak to him. When the door opened and the blackness of the interior beckoned him in, he felt like he was trapped in one of those classic holovids he and Bouncer used to watch. The thought made his chest tighten. He'd be watching them alone from now on. Against his better judgement, Goldfish climbed in. He noticed, and was impressed, that the antigravs cushioned the motion without unbalancing him. He sat in the nearest seat and the door closed on him, without waiting for the two men that had accompanied him. He became aware that the car was lifting away from the ground, and he settled back to wait. If he was expecting someone to be waiting for him in the car, he was disappointed. Apart from him, the rear compartment was empty. He wasn't even sure there was anyone in the front compartment. The windows had been blacked out, so he had no way of telling where he was going, or at what altitude.

Finally, the car came to rest. The door opened, and he figured that was his cue to get out. As he stepped into the light, he was aware of two other men waiting for him. He seemed to be standing in some kind of private parking lot, small but well maintained. A door stood in the far wall, and it was towards this that the two men gestured, allowing him to take the lead. The door slid open and he found himself entering the kind of apartment he wished he lived in. A large reception hall with a double staircase leading to an upper level greeted him. Doors stood to either side of the lower stairs, as well as between them. It was through the door to the left that the men ushered him. Goldfish entered as the door slid open, and took the seat offered, a grand chair, upholstered in materials he suspected weren't synthesised. He was aware that at no point since getting into the car had anyone spoken. He wondered what he'd got himself into. The room was huge, opulent, like some kind of stately home on Earth. He was reminded of his excursion to the White House, once the home of the political leader of the United States of America, when the team had prevented the Balsari from assassinating President Kennedy in 1962. Kennedy had been assassinated eighteen months later, but had survived long enough to negotiate a settlement during what became known as the Cuban Missile Crisis. Of course, now the White House was a nothing more than a tourist attraction, a remnant of the quaint practice of democracy, when leaders were elected to office to carry out the will of the majority.

Goldfish was brought out of his reminiscences by the arrival of the person who could only be his host. He leapt to his feet in disbelief.

"Please sit down, James," the new arrival smiled warmly and waved to the chair.

"But…" he tried to say.

"Please, James, don't even try to find an explanation," his host told him. "Just accept it. If you try and figure out how I can be in two places at one time, you'll give yourself a headache, and I wouldn't want that. I want you to have a clear head because I'm about to make a proposal that I think will interest you."

Goldfish tried to control his confusion. "What proposal?"

His host smiled, sympathetically, and handed him a mini-holodisc. Goldfish took it and activated it. The image that appeared was the last thing he expected.

"Sarah," he whispered, his throat tightening with the shock.

He watched as Sarah turned to him from where she knelt by the bomb. "I love you," she mouthed silently. Then she turned and set to work. Unable to tear his attention away from her, but knowing how the scene would end, he just stared impotently.

"Why are you doing this?" he demanded, with no strength to make it sound threatening.

"Please keep watching," his host said, apologetically.

The image continued to work, then reacted to something. He knew it must be the detonation sequence, as she realised she was going to die. Then she looked round and seemed to see something. With a last look at the bomb, she clambered to her feet and moved to the side of the room. He watched as she was enveloped in some kind of shimmering effect, then vanished. A teleporter, he realised, with a shock. A Balsari teleporter. The image faded.

"To answer your questions," his host anticipated him. "Yes, she is alive, and she is well. Yes, you can be reunited without changing the timeline, but there is a small price. However, I believe it's a price you will be willing to pay. And yes, I am an agent for the Balsari. Please don't look at me like that, James, when faced with the choice I was, it was an easy enough decision. Work for a corrupt empire for little reward, or work for another government for greater reward than I could imagine. I know I'm taking a huge risk letting you see me, James, but I believe the risk is worth it. I believe you will do what we ask of you for Sarah."

Goldfish held the disc in his hand. Could this really be the end to it all? To wake up beside her again, to be free of the constant nightmare? He looked his host in the eye and made the most difficult decision of his life.

"Let's talk," he said.

24

Gunboy reported for duty before he was expected. When the call went to Ara'Sayal, it went unanswered. This was in itself cause for concern. The Imperial Embassy was out of touch, even through its more covert channels. The total information blackout was unexplained, and Moonchild's worry was that two of her team were there. Then Gunboy turned up with the news that the Arajak had switched loyalties. Moonchild was stunned by it all, but it was all incidental at the moment. Right now, they had a bead on Admiral Chalk and he was their priority. She relayed the news back to Admiral Saastemoinen then promptly dismissed it as irrelevant. As soon as Goldfish reported in, the team as it stood would go in after him.

"Do we even need Goldfish?" Gunboy was as eager as the Moonchild and Magpie to get on with it. "We don't know that there's any ordnance involved."

"I'm afraid so," Magpie told him. "Even if there isn't, we may still need him as tactical support. It's nothing personal, but we always have operated with two."

"I understand," Gunboy wasn't offended. It was simply standard procedure for the team.

***

When Goldfish arrived, he went straight to Control for briefing. As he sat listening, his fingers strayed to the disc he'd been allowed to keep. He closed his hand around it gently, as if afraid to let go in case it turned to smoke and slipped away.

"Are you ok?" Moonchild hesitated in her presentation when she noticed he seemed distracted.

He was startled into awareness. Everyone was looking in his direction. "Um... I'm fine, boss. Really."

Moonchild nodded warily and continued. "Weapons will be limited to what was appropriate to the period. We can't afford to lose any equipment and change history ourselves by supplying them with directed energy weapons. Bear in mind, though, that Admiral Chalk probably has no such compunctions, and will use any means possible to avoid capture. Questions?"

Gunboy raised his hand. "Sorry to be the only one that ever asks," he said. "But did we get anyone new on the team?"

Moonchild and Magpie exchanged glances. "We have our eye on a few candidates, but nothing definite. I'm afraid we're on our own this time."

***

Ekaterinberg was quiet in the summer twilight. The figure stole quietly through the village towards the house of Ipatiev, the engineer. He knew there would be Bolshevik soldiers guarding the house, but he'd seen to that already. He activated his personal shield and continued on his way. Had anyone been watching, it would seem that he had simply vanished like a ghost into the evening air. He reached the house and, stepping between the two soldiers outside, hammered on the door. As the guards reacted with puzzled, almost frightened glances at each other, the door opened and another guard appeared.

"What do you want?" he demanded.

"We didn't knock," one of the others answered, which was greeted with a scornful snort.

The figure slipped beyond the guard and into the house. He was looking for the cellar. Another guard stood at the door at the top of the cellar steps, looking with interest at what was happening up front, but not expecting any action this deep into the house. Putting one invisible hand over the astonished guard's mouth, he used the other to slip a blade into his back. The guard stiffened then went limp. The invader eased open the cellar door and dragged the guard's body in with him. At the bottom was a set of three doors. Deactivating his shield, he opened the first, onto an empty room. He shoved the guard inside and closed it again. The second door opened onto a larger room and he recognised his targets. Stepping inside he approached the Tsar. "Your highness, I'm Admiral Chalk, British Intelligence. I'm here to rescue you, sir."

"Thank providence," Nicholas sagged gratefully against the wall. "Come, my children, we are delivered."

Between them, Chalk and the Tsar ushered the rest of the family and servants out and up the stairs. They escaped through the door at the back of the house, which was less well defended than the front. One guard stood at the back door, and put up at least a token resistance, wounding Chalk with his bayonet, he was quickly overpowered and killed, and the fugitives were on their way.

"We must leave Ekaterinberg," Alix, the Tsaritsa urged. "There must be no delay if we are to be free."

"Forgive me, highness," Chalk told her. "If you are to be truly free, you must leave Russia altogether. You will be made welcome by… in Britain." He cursed his lax approach, knowing he'd almost given himself away because he had no idea who was the British monarch. But the Russian family were too desperate to escape to have noticed the mistake.

Chalk was directing them towards the station where a train would be arriving within an hour. Once on that, the Trans-Siberian Express would take them all to Vladivostok, from where a ship would take them to England. As long as they were on the train, and the train moving before their absence was noted, they were in the clear.

***

The carriage was nothing grand, not what they would have enjoyed during their reign, but neither Nicholas nor Alix were of a mind to complain. Admiral Chalk, their British saviour, had secured the entire carriage, and split them into separate compartments, the Tsar and Tsaritsa in one, the Tsarevitch Alexei in the next, he and the royal doctor shared another, while the four Tsarevnas were placed in the next two compartments to them, with the three serving women in the end compartment.

As the train pulled out from Ekaterinberg, Nicholas reached wordlessly for Alix's hand. They needed no words. They were safe. That was all that mattered.

Admiral Chalk knocked and entered. "You should get some rest, Highnesses," he suggested. "It's a long journey, and we may have to change our plans at short notice. I'm doing everything I can to prevent anyone coming into this carriage, but if someone investigates, we may have trouble."

"Thank you, Admiral," Alix replied with as much dignity as she could muster in the circumstances. "You have done us a great service, and we... indeed, Russia... will never forget your actions this night."

Suppressing a smile, Chalk bowed and backed out of the compartment. Returning to his own compartment, he sat opposite the fool that called himself a doctor. He forced a smile as he watched the man babble and tuned out the sound as he removed a surgical stick from his coat pocket and applied it to the wound in his arm. After a while, even the background noise became too much. "Excuse me," he apologised, still smiling. "I must check on my equipment." The doctor, oblivious to the effect he was having on the admiral, truly believed he was being entertaining and felt sorry that the admiral had to attend to his duty, and not have the benefit of his voice to accompany him. "Oh, please, don't let me detain you, Admiral, but once you have fulfilled your obligation, you must hurry back. I have so much more to tell you. Like the time I was able to diagnose the Duke's bladder problem. That, let me tell you, is a fascinating tale."

"I'm salivating with anticipation," Chalk muttered through clenched teeth, and left the compartment.

At the end of the carriage, he opened the door which led to a tiny platform where it joined the rest of the train. Stepping over the link, onto the other platform, Chalk knelt to examine the shield he'd constructed against the door into the next carriage. It was still working perfectly. Everything was going to plan. Already, agents were in London, trying to persuade the powers there to reconsider the decision not to grant the Romanovs asylum. If they could just get them out of Russia, where they went made little difference. The alteration to the timeline would be enough to give the Balsari the upper hand. They were masters of historical engineering, they knew what they were doing. They couldn't just go back and destroy without inhibition, they couldn't afford to change their own timeline along with that of Earth. This way, the difference would be so slight, it would only alter the approach Earth took in its journey to Empire, resulting in certain strategic weaknesses, paving the way for Balsari victory in the future. And Chalk, like the other humans working for the Balsari cause, would benefit from the rewards offered. They hadn't promised him unbelievable things like rulership of Earth, or some such folly. Merely great respect and a life of peace in luxury. That was good enough for people like Chalk. He didn't want power, or the responsibility that went with it. He just wanted to live his life without wanting for anything. The Empire was corrupt; the Emperor was a galactic despot who'd done nothing to earn his place. He'd merely been born into the role, and strengthened his claim by continuing his predecessors' warmongering, conquering other races, cowing the undefeated into uneven alliances, stealing their technology and developing it for his own purposes. Of the few races that possessed temporal technology, the Empire had made peace with the Arajak, and within a few years had developed a temporal programme to rival the Balsari. Now the Space-Time Axial Response Team, as they were known, was pretty much dedicated to preventing the Balsari defending themselves from imperial aggression. Well, soon that would end. And he was going to be instrumental in bringing about that change.

But part of that action, unfortunately, required that he should suffer the doctor's attempts to regale him with tales of medical heroism. He made a last check on his charges and returned to his compartment.

25

The passengers in other carriages were reading, sleeping or talking with no concept of who they shared the train with. A man who had got on at Irkutsk found himself sitting in a compartment beside a woman who'd been on board since Krasnoyarsk. Opposite them sat two men who had boarded at Omsk. Now the train would head through the wilderness, not stopping until it reached Khabarovsk. But these four passengers had no intention of still being there by the time it arrived at that station.

The most recent arrival stood up and left the compartment, walking along the gangway towards the rear of the carriage, his body swaying with the motion of the train. He didn't look at anybody in the other compartments as he went. He didn't need to. The others had already told him that none of them were the ones they were looking for. Magpie moved through the door at the back of the carriage, across the platforms linking it to the next one, and looked along the gangway of the new carriage. The same as before. He continued to the far end. The door he found there led to the rear of the train. He could see through the glass panel the track as it got left behind in the train's wake. Magpie leant on the shifting wall and wondered about it. They couldn't have got it wrong. History never recorded this escape, but they were aware of it. But what if Chalk wasn't on the train? There was certainly no sign of him, and they'd all been the whole length of it. The only place left was the engine, and he couldn't see him fitting the entire royal family in the engine. He looked one last time at the receding track and turned away.

From the other side of the glass, Admiral Chalk watched him go, and laughed softly to himself.

***

Goldfish opened the door into the carriage at the end of the train. As he looked up the gangway, he caught sight of Magpie coming back towards him. His appearance seemed to catch Magpie by surprise, and for some reason, the acquisitions officer began making himself conspicuously large in the gangway.

As he closed the door into the carriage, he turned to his colleague. "Magpie, I need…"

"James, listen," Magpie whispered, as if he were trying not to draw attention to himself. "This really isn't a good time."

"But…"

Magpie opened a compartment door and ushered him inside. "I really wish I could stop and talk, James, but I'm on a knife edge at the moment and I can't wait. I'll tell you what though. In about sixty seconds, if you open the door, I'm going to be back and you can tell me all about it. Ok? I promise, open the door in a minute and I'll be there."

Wide eyed with something Goldfish considered to be almost terror, Magpie opened the door, looked up the gangway and dashed out, pulling the door closed behind him. Clearly, something was bothering him. Shrugging, Goldfish decided to let the matter drop. He waited for a moment, then opened the door.

***

As Magpie passed the compartment, the door opened. "Magpie," Goldfish called.
Turning to the demolitions expert, Magpie asked. "What's going on, James?"
"Come on in, please," he could tell Goldfish was being evasive. "We need to talk about this."
Magpie entered the compartment and Goldfish closed the door.

***

They both returned to Moonchild and Gunboy, sitting in their seats. Neither looked at the other.
"Everything ok?" Moonchild asked, noting the tension that seemed to exist between them.
"Everything's fine," Magpie told her. "Really. Don't worry about it." He flashed her a grin, but she noted in his eyes something much darker that wasn't smiling.
"Ok, hon," she said, resolving to get an explanation from him later. "Any sign of them?"
"Nothing," Magpie answered. "I'm beginning to wonder if we've been set up again."
"You mean like he was never here to start with?" Gunboy said.
"Exactly. Like there was never a bomb in John Gray's shop. Just a plot to get rid of us."
"So what are you suggesting?" Moonchild asked. "That we return to Control?"
"No," Goldfish seemed decisive. "He's here, on this train, somewhere. They all are."

"And how come you're so sure about that?" Moonchild wondered.

"You're just going to have to trust him, I'm afraid," Magpie intervened.

"Ok, that's enough," she made a chopping motion with her hand. "This isn't a game of trust, it's a military operation. For it to work, I need to in the loop, so does Gunboy. So, tell me, what's going on?"

Magpie and Goldfish looked at each other. Goldfish nodded, resigned, and at Magpie's signal, left the compartment. Magpie took the small disc from a pocket in his overcoat. "Goldfish was intercepted on his way here by the Balsari, who gave him certain information in return for his cooperation. They also gave him some very strong incentives for switching sides."

"What incentives?" the colonel demanded.

For an answer, Magpie activated the holodisc. He studied his comrades while Moonchild and Gunboy watched in horrified fascination. When the image faded, there was a stunned silence in the compartment, broken only by the sound of the train rattling along the track.

"Right," Gunboy whispered, eventually.

"Quite," Magpie replied, pocketing the device. "Now you see what the problem is. If Goldfish completes his mission for the Balsari, he gets his wife back. If he fails, he loses her again."

"But now we know about this, he can't succeed," Moonchild pointed out. "Unless I'm missing something."

"That's the whole point," Magpie agreed. "He came to me because he needed to tell someone. He is not a traitor, and much as he's struggling with himself over this, he can't bring himself to betray us for his own personal gain. So the real question is, how do we help him out of this?"

Moonchild and Gunboy glanced at each other, then back at Magpie. No-one spoke. No-one had an answer.

***

Goldfish walked as far as he could before he simply ran out of train. As he stood looking through the door at the end, he briefly pondered his options. One was to throw himself wholeheartedly into S.T.A.R.T.'s mission, and abandon any hope of being reunited with Sarah. Another was to throw himself wholeheartedly into the Balsari mission and turn on his comrades when they least expected it. A third option was simply to throw himself wholeheartedly through the door and off the train, and all his suffering would be over. Despite the temptation to follow this latter option, Goldfish finally turned and wandered back to see what decisions had been made in his absence. He passed an elderly woman on the woman and had to turn sideways and squeeze himself against the window so she could pass. She mumbled something in Russian that his forced learning hadn't quite covered, but he suspected it wasn't undying gratitude. He bit back on the desire to reply with something that wasn't 'you're welcome', and continued on his way. As he reached the door between carriages, he heard the woman scream, a piercing cry of terror that had him running back the way he'd come. He found her surrounded by several other passengers, gibbering about something in a loud and uncontrolled voice. He wasn't sure, but he thought the word she was using was 'ghost'. Some of the passengers were dismissing her as old and, possibly, drunk. Others were treating her with superstitious suspicion, believing that associating with her was a bad omen, and moving

away, back to minding their own business. As they left her, one by one, he went back to her. "Show me," he said, gently.
So she did.

***

Admiral Chalk was furious. "You idiot! Did I not insist everyone stay in this carriage?" He hauled the doctor up by the throat and dragged him to the far end of the carriage. "You have been seen, and you may have brought doom upon the Tsar and his family. And why? Because you were hungry! You are a complete fool with no thought for anyone other than your own stupid self. Do you think my superiors have planned this operation to the last detail just for you to ruin everything because of your rumbling stomach? No! You have driven me to the edge of insanity with your pathetic drivel about how you single-handedly rescued Russian medicine from the depths of barbarism, and now you've exposed us to others, and in all likelihood to enemies of the Tsar. Now you find what price is expected of you, and believe me, doctor, you've earned this in full."
With a savage punch, Chalk ran his knife into the doctor's midriff. The doctor, already choking, attempted to cry out with the sudden pain, but couldn't. He slumped in Chalk's grip, and the Balsari agent let him drop to the floor. He opened the door at the back of the train and hauled the doctor up and out. The body landed on the track, rolling as it did so. Chalk closed the door and dismissed the fool from his thoughts. He was pleased that no-one had decided to investigate the situation. He didn't particularly want to have to explain what he'd just done, especially as,

on reflection, he probably should have just pummelled the man into unconsciousness and thrown him back into his compartment. Now, he would try and protect the rest of them from their enemies.

***

Goldfish came back into the compartment. "I know where they are," he said without preamble.
They were immediately on their feet. "Where?" Moonchild asked.
"There's another carriage at the back of the train. It's shielded."
"Is this Balsari information?" Moonchild tried to make it sound like wasn't an accusation.
"No, boss," he tried to ignore the tone, understanding her doubts. "An old lady told me."
They went straight there. As they stared at the door leading out onto the track, Gunboy said. "Maybe he's using a repellent. Maybe that's why nobody thought to open the door and check."
"I agree," Magpie nodded. "Even now, knowing what I know, my every instinct is telling me to ignore it."
"I'd keep ignoring it for the time being," Goldfish warned. "My scan shows it's been wired up since last time we were here."
"Can you unwire it?" Moonchild asked him.
"I doubt it, if I can't get direct access to it," the demolitions expert said, putting away the scanner he wasn't even supposed to have. "But I'll give it a go anyway."

Magpie beckoned to Moonchild. "Listen, I've got a confession to make. I asked Lieutenant Stone to send some equipment through after we'd arrived."

"You did what? Will, I don't believe you, of all people, could do that. You know what that could do to our security."

Magpie shrugged. "It's my job to cheat. Besides, if Goldfish can't do anything about that booby trap, we'll still be here when the train gets to Vladivostok. Unless someone gets to them, the Balsari are going to win this by default."

Moonchild's anger subsided slightly. "What did she send?"

"Oh, just some train stopping stuff Legna packed for me while we were waiting for the others to arrive. It pays to think ahead."

"Go on," she said. "Get outta here before I have you court-martialled. And Will?"

He turned back to her.

"Don't do anything dumb, ok, hon?"

"Do I ever?" he answered, and was gone before she could say anything.

***

Magpie now realised he had a problem. He hadn't really had time to arrange where to drop his equipment. All he knew was it would be somewhere on the train. It had to be somewhere obvious, or it would be pointless even looking. He figured the most obvious would be in their compartment, but they hadn't been able to determine where they would be until Gunboy and Goldfish arrived and had chosen the first one that was empty. So, barring that, where was the next most obvious place to look? Probably the engine, he decided. He made his way forward, passing through several carriages until he reached the door at the front of the train. The sound of the engine was almost deafening, even this far behind it. The rear wall of the fuel storage was in his way and he found a ladder to one side which allowed him access to the top. There was a low upwardly curved roof which he climbed onto and took stock of his surroundings. A few metres ahead, he could see right into the engine. Two men, presumably the driver and engineer, stood with their backs to him. He edged forwards on his hands and knees, the motion of the engine from side to side somewhat less than in the carriages, but offset by the rushing Siberian wind which threatened to pluck him from his perch and hurl him from the train. As he reached the engine, he noticed a painted sign on the roof in front of him:

Дровá

Something clicked in his mind, as his forced learning surfaced. This was the Russian word for firewood.
"Well done, Legna," he murmured. "And what a clever boy you are, Will, for realising."
That was when the engineer saw him. "What are you doing?" he demanded, his voice barely carrying over the sound of the engine.
"Oh, don't mind me," Magpie smiled, cheerfully. "I'm just picking something up and I'll be on my way."
But the engineer didn't appear convinced. He hefted his large shovel and began to climb up to where Magpie knelt. Magpie made an instant assessment. Here was a man who was most likely quite happy to kill to defend his territory,

especially when the only witness was probably his best friend, or his brother-in-law, or some equally close relation. But that thought, in itself, gave him an idea.

As the engineer came closer, he tried to make eye contact, a task made easier by the fact that the Russian was staring right at him anyway.

"Hey, you don't want to hit me," he called out, his hands spread wide. "It's me, your friend. I'm your friend. Your friend. You don't want to hit me. I'm your friend."

The engineer paused as if considering this. His eyes cleared momentarily as he looked at Magpie. Then he charged at him. Magpie rolled to the side, cursing his failure to hypnotise the man. It would have worked, but the noise of the engine meant he'd had to shout, hardly the relaxing tone of voice he normally needed for such an action. As he struggled to regain his feet, the shovel swung in an arc and connected with his head. With a cry that was cut off as he landed heavily, Magpie fell and, dazed, began to slide with the camber of the roof. Scrabbling manically for purchase, he tried to grab the low rail on the edge of the roof, but the savage kick from the engineer sent him sprawling again. This time he rolled over the rail and only by accident managed to hook a few fingers round it and save himself. It seemed he was only postponing the inevitable, though, as the engineer appeared above him. Dangling there by one hand, with a man and his shovel bearing down on him, and the solid ground rushing by below him, Magpie conceded his options weren't looking too healthy. He'd be lucky to get out of this one with broken legs.

He didn't see what happened next, he was just aware of a shouted warning, followed by the engineer disappearing from his field of vision. Then he realised the train was slowly decelerating. As it finally came to a halt, he noticed a hand was extending down towards him. A blue hand.

"You appear to require assistance, Commander Angel," R'sulek-Entah called to him, her voice just carrying above the remnant of the engine sound.

"I don't know, I thought I'd just hang around here for a while."

"Suit yourself," she shrugged and retracted her hand.

"I'm kidding!" Magpie panicked.

Puzzled, she held the hand out again, and he took it. Between the two of them, they managed to haul him onto the roof. The engineer lay in a crumpled heap beside them, the driver was leaning over his controls, not moving.

"You didn't kill them?" Magpie's horrified question hung between them.

"Of course not," she seemed unimpressed with the idea. "I would not risk so much damage to the timeline. You are welcome, by the way."

"Oh. Sorry. Thanks. Why are you here? How did you get here?"

"I am here because I could not stand by and watch as the Balsari destroyed everything Ara'Sayal and the Terran Empire have achieved since the treaty was signed. I decided to help in any way I could to prevent their plan from coming to fruition. When I arrived on Earth and learned of your mission, I followed you. Also, Legna said you needed this, and she had no idea where to put it so you would find it." She held out the bag with his equipment. "Now, I suggest we leave before these two wake up and realise they were not dreaming me."

"Good idea," Magpie agreed, taking the bag. "Of course, I don't need this, now you've stopped the train. Pointless even coming out here in the first place."
She narrowed her eyes and glared after him as he stood up and made his way back to where he'd come from.

***

As the train slowed and finally stopped, Goldfish looked up from his work. "That's better," he said to no-one in particular. At least now the side to side motion wasn't going to hamper his progress.
"Magpie must have gotten through," Moonchild surmised.
Gunboy didn't offer any comment. He was too busy trying to keep the passengers in their compartments. The train's slowing and stopping made his job harder as people were now trying to find out what the problem was. He was popping his head into each compartment with a few words of basic Russian, hoping they understood enough, and believed him.
Beyond the door, Admiral Chalk watched from inside the shield as the S.T.A.R.T. members worked on getting through the door. He turned as he heard a sound behind him. It was Nicholas.
"Please take cover, your highness," he advised. "This will require all my efforts and I don't want any of you caught in the crossfire."
The Tsar approached him, ignoring the advice. "Let me help you, Admiral. I will gladly risk my own life for the safety of my family. It is every man's duty to protect his wife and children."

Chalk decided not to argue. He didn't want to anger this proud man. That would be counter-productive. He'd already failed the Balsari once. He knew he wouldn't survive a second such failure. So he contented himself with letting the fallen ruler stand by his side and waited to see what would happen. He silently fingered his sidearm, wondering if he would have to use it, and how Nicholas would react. Maybe he should have carried a more appropriate weapon.

That was when the idea struck him. "Your highness, why don't you keep watch at the back? Now the train is not moving, our enemies may attack from the rear."

"Good strategy, Admiral," Nicholas acknowledged, moving away, vaguely wondering how a naval officer became so well versed in land tactics.

Alone again, Chalk took out the energy weapon and waited.

***

Magpie and R'sulek-Entah made their way along the roof of the final carriage. "Get down," Magpie hissed to the Arajak. "There are people over there."

R'sulek-Entah ducked and looked in the direction Magpie was pointing. A couple of horses with maybe two or three riders between them were heading towards the train. That could be a complication if the riders, who were no doubt coming to investigate the train's lack of motion, saw her.

"We must hurry, Commander," she hissed in reply.

"I'd noticed," he replied, drily. "Shall we?"

As quickly and quietly as they could, they lowered themselves down the service ladder, trying to make certain R'sulek-Entah's wings were hidden from view as much as was possible. By the time they were on the platform, the riders had disappeared from view.

***

Nicholas looked in on Alix. "My love, please go and be with the children."

"Are we in danger?" she asked, anxiously.

He took a deep breath, and told her the truth. "Yes. Our enemies are almost upon us. Please go and reassure them. The admiral and I will try and hold them off."

"How will two men keep them all at bay? We are going nowhere, and help is not coming."

"My sweet Alix," Nicholas stroked her face, and she held his hand there. "We must try." He wiped away a tear with his thumb and smiled sadly at her. "If it must be that our flight has ended, well, we at least did what we could. Let us have no regrets. Let us only know that we still have our love, and that will never perish. Now, go."

Alix nodded and hurried to gather the children. Nicholas took a moment to gather his resolve, then went to his post. When he got there, he saw the man coming in through the door. He was dressed as an average commoner, nothing in his clothing or appearance marking him out as anything other than one of his former subjects. But it was his companion who stopped Nicholas in his tracks.

"Your highness," the man said with an almost apologetic tone in his voice. "It's over. I'm sorry."

Nicholas looked from the man to the gun in his hand to the angelic apparition next to him and knew he was telling the truth. He turned to go back to his family, the sense of utter defeat evident from his expression.

That was when the flash of light seared his shoulder and he fell to the deck, in more pain than he thought possible. Through his agony, he saw Admiral Chalk in a compartment doorway, holding some kind of gun he didn't recognise. "You can't take me down, Angel!" the admiral seemed crazy. "You can't have them!"

Nicholas rolled into cover, perversely relying on his assailants to protect him from his rescuer.

Again, the admiral screamed up the gangway. "I'm going to kill you, Angel! Do you hear me? I'll kill you!" All the time he was screaming, he was shooting up the gangway, taking great chunks from the rear of the train.

Nicholas could hardly believe his ears. Admiral Chalk was trying to kill the angel. The angel, meanwhile, was bending to him, and touching some kind of object to his wounded shoulder. Immediately, the pain eased, then went altogether. The angel looked into his eyes.

"Thank you," he said, not knowing how else to respond.

"You must stay here until Admiral Chalk has been stopped," the angel told him.

"Yes, of course," he whispered.

While they were talking, the man, who seemed to be just a normal Russian mortal man, was taking the occasional shot at the admiral but not making any real progress. Nicholas watched his attempts and wondered how he'd become involved with an angel, and how he managed to behave like there was nothing out of the ordinary here.

***

In his doorway, Chalk cursed as one of Angel's bullets found its target. A spray of blood burst from his right arm, almost exactly the same place as his earlier wound.

He struggled to maintain a grip on his sidearm, but the bullet had done more damage than Angel could possibly have aimed to achieve. The gun clattered on the carriage floor. He locked eyes with Angel, then the two men were in a race for the fallen weapon. Even as Angel charged headlong towards him, Chalk closed his left hand around it. Angel skidded to a halt as he realised he was too late. Chalk raised the weapon and aimed his head.

"I wouldn't if I were you," Moonchild said, her gun nuzzling behind his ear. While Magpie had been keeping him occupied, Goldfish had defused the booby trap and opened the door. Gunboy reached round and took the admiral's weapon, glancing up the gangway towards R'sulek-Entah, the relief and lack of understanding clear in equal measure on his face. By now the compartment doors were open and the Tsaritsa and her children were aware of what had just transpired. Magpie and R'sulek-Entah escorted Nicholas into the compartment amid the wondering stares of his family. Magpie nodded to Moonchild. He'd handle this. She in turn pushed Chalk into his compartment. Goldfish and Gunboy followed, their revolvers trained on the admiral.

"At least let me heal this wound," he pleaded, indicating the blood that was pooling between his fingers, and running down his arm. "There's a surgical stick in my coat pocket."

Moonchild glanced at the coat, laid over a chair, and nodded to Goldfish to get it. She and Gunboy maintained their careful watch on him, weapons never wavering from his chest. The admiral, to his credit, made no effort to escape.

"It's not here, boss," Goldfish shrugged, having turned out all the pockets.

Chalk glared, as if expecting a trick, then realisation hit him. "The thieving bastard! He stole it."

"Who?" Moonchild asked.

"The bloody doctor!"

Goldfish frowned and pulled a piece of fabric from the window where it seemed to have become lodged. Examining it, he shrugged, dismissed it and dropped it out through the window.

Magpie entered the compartment. "There appears to have been a misunderstanding," he said. "They think R'sulek-Entah's an angel…"

"She is," Gunboy smiled.

"…an opinion reinforced by Admiral Chalk's use of my name," Magpie continued. "They've interpreted that as a sign that they should return to Ekaterinberg. They seem to think it's the divine will that they face whatever awaits them in Ipatiev's cellar."

"That's very brave of them," Moonchild acknowledged. "Is everyone accounted for?"

"The doctor's missing," Magpie said. "We can't find him anywhere."

Chalk laughed. "That's because I threw the thief off the train. Of course I didn't realise he was a thief as well as a fool. He got what he deserved. And now you've got a problem, haven't you, Colonel Washington? No doctor, no timeline."

Moonchild went cold. "We have to find the body and bring it back, Will. They were all shot in that cellar, including the doctor."

"But that's the problem, isn't it, Colonel?" Chalk was still happily laughing, despite his situation. "He can't be shot in the cellar if he's already dead, can he? You've lost."

Then they became aware of Nicholas in the doorway. There was an uncomfortable silence as they all tried to review the conversation and decide at what point he'd arrived. He saved them the trouble.

"We will all be shot then," he said, not so much a question, but an acknowledgement. "All of us? Will none be spared?"

Moonchild finally dared to meet his gaze. "I'm sorry," she muttered. "I honestly am."

Nicholas nodded. "I cannot be surprised that you know the future. This day I have seen an angel, and I now know it is decreed. We will not resist you. If our deaths will serve the greater good, then so it must be. But I ask of you one thing."

Moonchild nodded cautiously.

Nicholas pointed at Chalk. "I insist on being accompanied by my doctor."

***

Moonchild handed them over to a man named Yurovsky.

"Treat them with dignity," she instructed. "They returned of their own free will."

Yurovsky promised he would do that, but insisted they must still be executed. Moonchild agreed that was the case, and took her leave.

In the early hours of the next morning, Yurovsky led his firing squad into the basement of Ipatiev's house and carried out his orders. The visitors from the future watched from a safe distance as the bodies were taken into the forest and thrown down a mine shaft.

"History will record only that they were held here until they were killed," Moonchild said, glumly. "Only we will ever know of the courage they showed in returning here. Let's go home."

They arrived to confusion. The Arajak who surrounded them in the unfamiliar control centre were mostly the mottled brown of the technical caste. A few were the jet black of the warrior caste, and these swung their weapons immediately to cover the new arrivals. Taking the initiative, R'sulek-Entah stepped forward.
"What is the meaning of this?" she demanded of the nearest one.
One of the warriors, the only caste completely made up of males, recognised who had spoken. "Your Excellency, we thought you were still on Ara'Sayal. Had we known you were coming, we would have prepared."
Moonchild stepped forward. "What's going on? Where are the regular staff?"
"Silence, slave!" the warrior shouted, viciously clubbing her down with the butt of his weapon. "You are not permitted to speak."
There was a stunned silence as they absorbed that last statement. Magpie bent to help Moonchild. R'sulek-Entah reacted quickest. "Do not presume to discipline my slaves, warrior. I have given these favourites of mine permission to speak freely. It is not your place to say differently."
The warrior went stiff with the admonishment. "Forgive me, Excellency, I meant no offence. My life is yours."
"Be thou more discerning from this day," R'sulek-Entah slipped easily into formal mode. "Thy lesson is learned. Let all here see and mark this. These are our favoured ones. They are free to speak and act on our behalf. If thou dost harm any of them, thy death is assured."

All of the assembled Arajak bowed low. As if she knew exactly where she was going, R'sulek-Entah swept from the room, the others trailing her.

Once they were alone, Moonchild called a halt. "What the hell just happened there?" she demanded.

R'sulek-Entah turned to face her. "I would have thought that was obvious. The history of Earth has been altered. The Arajak are the masters of Earth, and the entire human race has been enslaved."

26

Bavaria, Earth, 2507(alt.)

After a few moments, it became clear to all of them that R'sulek-Entah had no more idea of where they were going than they did. They didn't want to arouse suspicion by wandering aimlessly until someone decided they were behaving oddly.
"Any suggestions will be most welcome," she told them, as they continued what was rapidly becoming a tour of the facility.
For some reason everyone turned to Magpie. "What?" he asked, defensively.
"You're the one who's supposed to adapt well to these situations," Moonchild said, reasonably. "What do you suggest we do?"
Magpie gave it a moment's thought and then told them. So, when they crossed paths with the next warrior, R'sulek-Entah hailed him. "We have concerns regarding security. Thou art required to escort us to our quarters."
The warrior bowed low and set off immediately. R'sulek-Entah fell into step behind him while the others followed. Moonchild glanced at Magpie and grinned her appreciation. He winked back at her, but otherwise didn't react. Eventually, the warrior stopped by a door, waiting for his next instructions. Pausing before she entered, R'sulek-Entah dismissed him. Again bowing low, the warrior returned to where they had first encountered him. Then, experimentally, R'sulek-Entah stood before the door. It opened soundlessly. She cocked her head,

impressed. "It is coded to recognise my pheromonal signal," she observed.

"Great," Goldfish grunted. "That probably means we can't get in or out without you."

"Can I recommend we continue this discussion inside?" Moonchild said.

Once they were inside and safe, it was time to start planning. Magpie gave it some thought. "Can we access the historical database from here?" He indicated the computer terminal on the desk.

"I do not know," R'sulek-Entah admitted. "I believe the situation may be more complicated than it appears."

"How so?" Moonchild asked.

"This is not Arajak technology. Our technological advances took a more organic path. This is clearly another race's development that we have moved into. Whether or not we are in partnership with that other race, or have subsequently dominated it, is not obvious."

"It doesn't look like human technology," Gunboy noted, his gaze taking in the design of the small office and its appliances. "None of the writing is in Imperial Standard, for a start. It's more like…"

"Oh, dammit," Moonchild sighed.

"Russian," Magpie finished the sentence.

"We fouled up," Goldfish said, sitting in a corner and taking out the holodisc.

"Big time," Gunboy agreed.

They all stared at one another, as if they were all waiting for someone else to say something. Magpie watched Moonchild. R'sulek-Entah and Gunboy looked at each other. Goldfish focussed on the holodisc and the image of Sarah's rescue by the Balsari.

"We have to go back," Moonchild took responsibility.

"But we need to know what we're looking for," R'sulek-Entah argued.

"I know what we're looking for," the colonel grimaced. "A surgical stick. It's the one item that got left behind. The doctor stole it from Chalk's coat pocket, and then Chalk threw him off the train. We have to locate it and bring it back. Otherwise, we stay here and live as slaves to the Arajak."

***

Magpie eased his way along the corridor, his psionic senses guiding him. He had advance warning of any Arajak that were in his path. Sometimes he had to backtrack and signal to the others to turn around and find cover. Usually it meant waiting for them to move on. Occasionally they had to find an alternative route.

The computer had given them a layout of the base, signed both in Russian words and Arajak pheromones, so they all knew where they were headed. The shared human-Arajak technology was a novelty to them, but the new timeline was based on an alliance between Ara'Sayal and the Soviet Republic of Earth, an alliance which had in recent years been increasingly one sided until, within the last decade, Ara'Sayal had systematically struck at key worlds, including Earth, and the Republic had fallen. Now the Earth was simply another conquered world. It had been noted that despite the change of management, life was relatively unaltered for most humans who were little more than slaves under the old regime. At least with the Arajak in charge, they weren't constantly being told to smile and be happy as they gave their blood, sweat and lives to the glorious Soviet machine. At least the Arajak had the decency to call them slaves, and make all humans truly equal, a factor missing from the last six centuries of the previous system.

As they made their way by a circuitous route to the temporal transfer control centre, these humans had two distinct advantages over the rest of their species: they were not conditioned to accept their lot as slaves, and so were in a position to plan their own little rebellion; and they had the patronage of one of the highest placed Arajak. That particular advantage, however, was quickly negated in somewhat spectacular fashion.

***

When the warriors began thundering down the passage towards him, Magpie did the only thing he could to alert the others. He sent his warning directly into Moonchild's mind. Then he had to quickly run down the nearest corridor and hope the others knew where they were going.

Moonchild, for her part, looked up in surprise when she got the message. She took a moment to register what had happened, then immediately gave the order to find cover. She, Gunboy and R'sulek-Entah headed down the corridor to their right, while Goldfish, caught slightly behind them was forced down the one to their left. He knew that his main objective was now to circle round and join up with the others, but the question was how. He reviewed what he'd remembered of the layout of the base. Cursing quietly to himself, he realised he wasn't confident enough of his ability to navigate the corridors and instead decided on a simple strategy of bearing right whenever possible. He wondered if it was really that simple, or if he was deluding himself. But the strategy seemed to pay off quickly. He soon arrived in the control chamber and settled himself to wait for the others. He didn't have long to wait. Within minutes, R'sulek-Entah joined him. He stepped from the shadows as she entered the chamber. She flinched slightly as he suddenly appeared, but recovered quickly, coming to join him.

"Where are the others?" she asked.

"No idea," he admitted. "I thought they were with you. I haven't a clue where Magpie got to."

"I was with the others, but we were separated," she said. "I thought they might have come here before me."

"No, for some reason I'm the first. Must be lucky, I guess."

"Yes," R'sulek-Entah agreed. "You must be lucky."

She turned to him and made a quick motion, which was just outside his field of vision. The breath was punched from his lungs and replaced with a hot agony that sat deep within him. He managed to tear his gaze from her eyes and looked down to where her hand clasped the battleknife that was buried in his chest. He raised his eyes again to meet hers, trying to form words, but unable to convert the movement of his lips into something coherent.

"You are wondering why I have done this," R'sulek-Entah said, almost conversationally. "Let me explain. I have no desire to encourage slaves to express thoughts of independence. Slaves are without rights, without hope, without future. All slaves have to look forward to is death. Yours is now. Be happy. Now you are truly free."

Goldfish tried to say something, to scream a curse at her, but all that came was a ghastly rattle as his remaining breath escaped and his life slipped away. R'sulek-Entah slid the battleknife from his body and watched with a sense of achievement as he fell soundlessly to the chamber floor. She wiped the blade on his Russian greatcoat and sheathed her battleknife. As she straightened, she heard someone enter the chamber.

Magpie looked round, as he arrived. The first thing he noticed was R'sulek-Entah straightening up. The second thing was Goldfish, his staring eyes and open mouth making his condition all too clear.

"What in the name of…" he hissed, rushing over to his fallen comrade. "What happened?"

"I do not know," R'sulek-Entah said. "I found him like this."

Magpie knelt by the corpse, impractically trying to administer life saving treatment to a man who was beyond it. Behind him, R'sulek-Entah drew her battleknife.

27

When R'sulek-Entah arrived, the confusion was almost at the level of panic. The warriors didn't know how to react, and some suspected they were being tested. For her part, R'sulek-Entah was immediately aware of the variety of reactions, and demanded an explanation. The response, being a totally preposterous suggestion that she had already arrived with her favoured slaves, was so ludicrous she killed the fool who uttered the lie instantly. However, when another warrior bowed low before her and offered the same story in more reverent tones, she began to wonder if it might be true.
"Hunt them down and kill them," she instructed the soldier, on the off chance he was right. "Bring the impostor to me alive, but kill the humans. Kill all the humans in the base, in case they have been getting ideas about preferred status. I want no insurrection, nor any rumours of one, while I am here."
"As you command," the warrior responded, and went to do her bidding.

***

Maybe it was because he was naturally suspicious, maybe it was because something about her answer didn't feel right. He never knew. But Magpie knelt by the body and, under the pretence of trying to revive him, searched his recent history. He reacted slightly slower than he would have wished for, but faster than he might otherwise have done. Either way, he rolled to one side as the battleknife ripped into his right sleeve, digging into his flesh. The weight of the coat tore the blade from R'sulek-Entah's grip and even as he rolled away, howling in pain, she chased him, trying to regain her advantage. Unable to think straight with the pain, Magpie did the worst thing possible under the circumstances. He pulled the knife free and, rather than turning it on his assailant, he flung it into the furthest corner he could reach. R'sulek-Entah watched it go, turned to follow. As she reached it, Magpie was struggling to regain his feet, his left hand clutching his injured arm. She raised it up, her murderous intent obvious as Magpie struggled to find a means of escape. But backed into the corner as he was, he was too far from the passages that led from the chamber, and that was even before he considered how he'd get past her.

In the end, it was R'sulek-Entah who saved him. The arrival of the others from another corridor meant his would-be killer had to make good her own escape, which she did, giving him a last look of pure hatred. He hadn't seen such raw emotion from any Arajak before. When R'sulek-Entah arrived with Moonchild and Gunboy, Magpie did a quick double take, before he realised what had happened. Before he could say anything, Gunboy had barged past and knelt in front of Goldfish.

"What the hell happened here?" he demanded, the devastation in his voice telling them all how badly he was taking this revelation.

"It's not Goldfish," Moonchild called across the chamber, as she approached Magpie. "Are you ok?"

"I'm fine," Magpie told her. "I'm also very impressed. How did you know?"

"About him?" she shrugged. "Female intuition."

"No, seriously. How?"

"You still got that holodisc he gave you?"

Magpie nodded, reaching into his pocket and retrieving it.

"Thought so," Moonchild nodded, taking the same holodisc from the corpse's coat. "When he produced it from his own pocket in R'sulek-Entah's quarters, it made me wonder when you gave it back. I realised you hadn't."

"Hell of a leap, though. I could've given it back when you weren't looking."

"I suppose so, but add to that what happened when we arrived."

Everyone looked blankly at her.

"Who gave him his mnemonics?"

"No-one, only you have them," Gunboy supplied the answer.

"Precisely, hon," Moonchild crowed. "But he kept his memories intact."

Enlightenment showed in all their eyes, even R'sulek-Entah's.

"But where is Lieutenant Warner, if that isn't him?" the Arajak asked warily.

"Presumably, he's still in twentieth century Russia," the colonel told her. "Or else he was taken by the Balsari before he was replaced."

"I take it no-one's suggesting *our* Goldfish is dead?" Magpie said in a low voice.

"No," Moonchild looked at her second in command. "Because that would make the whole idea of a rescue pointless. And that is our other objective. Find the surgical stick and rescue Goldfish. If we can do both, we've succeeded. If we only manage one, we've failed."

The others all gave their support to the new mission statement.

"So," Moonchild said. "How did you know? Or did you wait till he attacked you?"

"Nah, he was already dead when I got here. But psychometry is a wonderful skill if you have it. Oh, you mean this?" he noticed the others looking at his wound. "That wasn't him, it was her."

R'sulek-Entah's expression didn't visibly alter, but her confusion was obvious, as was that of the others.

"She's been with us all the time," Gunboy argued, a little too defensively.

"I know. What I meant was the R'sulek-Entah that belongs in this timeline is also here. They're impossible to tell apart, physically, but she has a very nasty violent streak, and her sense of humour isn't as highly developed."

R'sulek-Entah opened her mouth to take issue with Magpie's last comment, but Gunboy caught her eye and almost imperceptibly shook his head. She let it go.

"So, all we need to do now is find a way back to 1918," Moonchild said, studying the teleportation system. It bore little resemblance to the one she was used to, not least because the controls were labelled in Cyrillic script and the machine had a very organic feel to it. It had the appearance of having been grown rather than built, consistent with Arajak technology as a whole.

"Perhaps I will have a better chance of deciphering this," R'sulek-Entah offered. "Its pheromone output may be able to guide me through its programming."

Moonchild stepped away. "Be my guest."

R'sulek-Entah began her work as the others settled in for an uncomfortable wait.

***

Eventually, she looked up. "I believe I have done it," she commented.

Moonchild thought that sounded as unconvinced as an Arajak could get. "How much do you believe?" she asked, trying to be gentle but not prepared to consider failure.

"Belief is absolute, Colonel," R'sulek-Entah replied archly. "Otherwise it is merely hope. Shall we?"

Moonchild and Magpie exchanged glances and weary smiles. Then all hell broke loose.

R'sulek-Entah yelled. "Kill the humans!"

She appeared just as shocked as the humans, but soon located her doppelganger as she entered the chamber, flanked by several warriors. It was an uneven fight from the beginning. The S.T.A.R.T. members were limited to archaic weaponry and were out of uniform, encumbered by bulky Russian winter clothing. The Arajak, who outnumbered them, were armed with state of the art technology.

Therefore they ran for their lives, including R'sulek-Entah.

The Arajak warriors took flight and followed, the other R'sulek-Entah following at the rear. She clearly wanted to be in on the kill, but wasn't prepared to put herself in the firing line. Moonchild noticed this as she herded her troops down the other corridor. Gunboy hung back, drawing his revolver.

"Don't stop," Moonchild ordered. "Just run, keep running, and when you've done that, run some more!"

Gunboy nodded his understanding and kept moving. Moonchild followed him.

The crazy sound of butterfly wings flapping behind them kept them all going. With Magpie in the lead, they took every corner they could, although Moonchild was worried about the apparently random nature of his course. It was a good strategy: don't give them a clear shot, and make them slow down to navigate the corners as often as possible. Give yourself as much time and space as possible. She nearly grinned at the irony. Their job was all about time and space, and here they were trying to get just a little bit of each, to survive. As they came to a T-junction, Magpie took them left. Moonchild spun to the right and immediately right again, waiting.

***

R'sulek-Entah was keeping pace with Magpie quite easily, and he wondered if she was built for speed or if her wings were helping her. Then their luck ran out and they reached a dead end. The first obvious point was that Moonchild was no longer with them. But there was no time to consider the implications now. They looked round for inspiration, drawing weapons. Magpie unslung the bag he'd brought with him. Then the idea hit him.
"All the warriors are males, right?"
"That is correct," she said. She wasn't even struggling for breath.
"How's their intelligence?"
"They are males!" she snorted, as if that were all the answer that was necessary.
"Good," he huffed, and stood up.

***

When the warriors came hurtling round the corner, they pulled up short, confused by what they saw. Their leader was standing at the end of the corridor with the humans pointing their primitive weapons at her head. The question of how she'd got there before them was superseded by the more pressing question of how to deal with it.

"Stand back and let us pass," one of the humans ordered, in a reasonable tone. They weren't sure, but he might have been smiling at them.

They looked to R'sulek-Entah. "Do as he says," she told them.

The warriors began to move back and the humans and their captive stepped forward.

Which was when the other R'sulek-Entah arrived. "Don't be fools," she spat. "Kill them. Now!"

"That wouldn't be a good thing," Moonchild's voice, behind her, was calm and quiet but her words were emphasised by the muzzle of the revolver that sat behind the Arajak duchess's ear. "One of these is your leader and if you make any move against us, one of them is going to die. Care to guess which one?"

Confused and uncertain of their next move, the warriors shuffled back to make it clear they would rather let them go than risk harm coming to their precious leader.

As the S.T.A.R.T. people began making their way forward, the R'sulek-Entah held by Moonchild turned as far as she dared to face her captor. "You can never hide from me," she sounded confident.

"I've no intention of hiding from you," Moonchild sounded equally confident. "I'm taking you along with us. Come on. Move."

"I am going nowhere with you," the Arajak drew herself up and tried to look indignant.

"Fine," the human shrugged, and began squeezing the trigger.

Trying to look as though she was only going because she was doing them a favour, and because she couldn't think of anything better to do, R'sulek-Entah began moving in the direction of the others. The warriors hung back. Moonchild gave them a last look.

"Count to five thousand before you make any move to follow us, or she dies," she told them. "And count all multiples of seventeen twice." She slapped a bug against the wall. "I'll be listening," she warned them.

By the time they were in the control chamber, she'd got bored of listening to the slow methodical working of the males' lack of mathematical prowess. "Forty nine... fifty... fifty one... fifty one again... fifty two..."

She closed off the communicator with her free hand, keeping her revolver trained on the prisoner. Turning to 'her' R'sulek-Entah, she said. "Can you get us back to 1918?"

R'sulek-Entah glanced at her, but without the caustic remarks that question would otherwise have earned. "The coordinates are unchanged from when I last set them," she said. "We may leave when you give the order."

The other R'sulek-Entah made a surprised sound. "You take orders from slaves?"

"I take orders from superior officers," she answered. "And Ara'Sayal has no need to make slaves of any race. At least, *my* Ara'Sayal has no need of slaves. What has become of the servitor caste?"

"They serve in positions more appropriate to their heritage. They may be servitors, but they are still Arajak." This last comment was aimed at the humans.

Infuriatingly, none of them rose to the challenge, instead choosing to shrug or smirk or simply ignore the comment. "Ok, folks, let's go," Moonchild said, turning to her liaison officer. "Would you do the honours?"

R'sulek-Entah placed the teleporter on a short delay before joining the others. The other R'sulek-Entah stood to one side under threat from the revolver. Then, as the teleport sequence kicked in, she made a lightning fast lunge for the departing group. Caught in the transfer effect, Moonchild couldn't bring her revolver to bear in time.

Then they were on the train.

28

They arrived in a heap in an empty compartment. Something thumped into Magpie and they all fell to the floor. It took them a moment to get their bearings and realise why. Both R'sulek-Entahs were locked in combat on the floor.

Moonchild regained her feet first. She quickly pulled down the blinds on the compartment's interior windows in case anyone passed them and looked in, then turned on the others. "That's enough!" she bellowed.

Everyone stopped what they were doing, even the two Arajak. Magpie and Gunboy struggled up and joined her. The Arajak also stood and faced them. For a while no-one spoke. They simply swayed slightly, as the rocking of the train set their bodies into the strange rhythm.

Magpie leaned across to Moonchild. "What now?" he whispered.

"I don't know," she whispered back, her eyes and aim never wavering. "You have any suggestions?"

"Why don't we just ask them?" Gunboy's comment was a lot more tense than he meant it to sound.

"Good idea," Moonchild agreed. She turned to the pair of humanoid butterflies. "Basics, then. Why are we here? You first," she gestured to the one on the left, the one she was beginning to think of as R'sulek-Entah One.

"We are here to repair the damage to the timeline following the death of the Tsar's personal physician," the Arajak said, turning to R'sulek-Entah Two.

For her part, R'sulek-Entah Two glanced sideways for a second, then turned back to Moonchild. "We also need to discover the fate of Lieutenant Warner," she said. Then by way of explanation, she continued. "We appear to have access to each other's memories, Colonel. I would suggest this line of reasoning will reveal nothing about who is real and who is not. On the positive side, I now possess intimate knowledge of the alternative timeline, and can extrapolate where and how it diverged."

"You already possessed that knowledge," R'sulek-Entah One countered. "And would seek to mislead. I, on the other hand, have recently gained this knowledge and will attempt to decipher it."

"Ok, stop it," Moonchild grumbled impatiently, turning to Magpie. "Can you figure them out?"

He shook his head. "Their brains are just too alien for me to get inside. Sorry."

"What about our children?" Gunboy said. "Can you name them all?"

"We both can, John," R'sulek-Entah One said, something close to an apology.

"Although we both suspect you cannot name all of them," R'sulek-Entah Two commented.

"We're wasting time," Magpie grunted. "With or without her, we need to get to the doctor before he loses the surgical stick."

"You're right, hon," Moonchild admitted. "You go see what you can do about that, we'll stay here until we can figure something out."

"You're sure?"

"Go on, Will, you're best qualified for the job anyway. If we have to stay here until you get back, so be it. We're not going to compromise the timeline any further than we already have done, just to stretch our legs."

He glanced at the two Arajak, then at Moonchild. Then he nodded and left.

In the gangway, he began moving towards the back of the train, towards where he knew Admiral Chalk had set up his shield. He just hoped he'd got the timing right. He was through the door to the last visible carriage when he saw a figure with his back to him looking through the window in the door at the far end. He knew that the view of the track receding in the distance was an illusion and that there was another carriage hidden beyond it, but he couldn't get in there while someone was in the way. That was when he recognised the man. It was him! Caught in a sudden panic, Magpie began looking round. He had to find cover before his earlier self turned and saw him. As he couldn't recall seeing himself before, he knew being seen now could be potentially disastrous for the timeline. As he looked behind him, he caught sight of Goldfish coming towards him. And Goldfish had seen him. This situation was rapidly descending into a nightmare. Filling as much of the gangway as possible, to block the view of the earlier Magpie, he approached his colleague and let him come through the connecting door.

"Magpie, I need…"

"James, listen," Magpie said as quietly as possible. "This really isn't a good time."

"But…"

Magpie opened a compartment door and ushered him inside. "I really wish I could stop and talk, James, but I'm on a knife edge at the moment and I can't wait. I'll tell you what though. In about sixty seconds, if you open the door, I'm going to be back and you can tell me all about it. Ok? I promise, open the door in a minute and I'll be there."

Wide eyed with near terror, Magpie opened the door, looked up the gangway and dashed out and into the next compartment. "Oh, pardon me, madam," he said to the middle aged lady who was staring aghast at him. "I seem to have come back to the wrong compartment. In fact, I'm probably in the wrong carriage altogether. I'm really not good on trains, I seem to be all over the place."

"Young man, I must insist you leave at once," the woman's tone was severe and even without the forced learning still fresh in his mind, he would never have mistaken her meaning.

"Yes, yes, of course, I must leave," he agreed, making no such move.

"I demand that you leave this instant," the woman insisted. "Or I shall call the guard and have you removed."

"Absolutely, quite right too," Magpie nodded enthusiastically. "I'd probably say the same thing in your position."

Again, he stood his ground.

"I shall have you thrown from the train!" the woman screeched at him.

"Ah," Magpie appeared to consider this threat more serious than the previous ones. "In that case, I'd better leave. So sorry to have inconvenienced you."

With a nod and an embarrassed smile, he quickly and quietly left the compartment before the woman could say anything further. Instead she moved to the door and locked it, pulling down the blinds.

In the gangway, Magpie quietly passed the compartment where his earlier self was now in deep discussion with Goldfish, and continued up towards the door at the end.

He tried to ignore the itching in his head that told him not to bother. The repellent was trying to convince him it was pointless proceeding. He would have to work quickly if he was going to get beyond it before his earlier self came out from the compartment. He smoothly removed his lockpicks from the bag and set their frequency to work the tumblers. Within seconds, he was outside the carriage, facing the door to the now extremely visible rear carriage. Glancing backwards through the glass, he watched himself and Goldfish coming into the gangway. Both glanced up towards him, and he could swear he'd just made eye contact with himself. Shaking with a reflex of fear, he turned round and set to work on the next door, again making short work of it. As he stepped inside and closed the door, he became aware that a compartment door was opening. Biting back on a curse, he realised he couldn't hide in a compartment this time, as they were all occupied. And, of course, he'd met all the occupants, and one of them would surely give him away. He was the enemy at this point, so Chalk would be told he was in there, and afterwards, if he wasn't turned over to Chalk, someone would recognise him when he arrived with R'sulek-Entah. The only option he had was the water closet. He pushed open the door and quickly went inside. The closet was just that, a tiny space with a bucket-like contraption in the middle, which led to the track below. He was assaulted by the smell of countless users who had somehow failed to position themselves correctly and instead smeared the sides of the bucket. He struggled with this idea. The gap was almost wide enough for a person to climb through, so how could so many get it so badly wrong? And this was what the royal family was reduced to using!

Then the door began to rattle. His heart almost stopping, Magpie quickly looked for somewhere to hide, but short of total invisibility, his options were extremely limited. Then he looked down at the bucket.

***

Outside, the doctor began to open the door to the water closet. As he pushed, he heard a sound. Pausing, he turned round. The Tsarevitch was looking down the gangway towards him.
"Forgive me, Highness, do you require the first use?" he gestured to the door, now slightly ajar.
The boy curled his lip, remembering the last time he'd been in there. "I would rather piss in my own pants," he told the doctor, and returned to his compartment.
The doctor smiled and pushed the door fully open. Stepping inside, he examined the rim of the bucket before deciding it would suffice. Dropping his trousers and undergarments, he sat. The metal bucket echoed like a gatling gun in a cathedral, a sound and a simile he appreciated and regretted in equal measure. He began whistling to himself, a traditional ditty he'd learned at his mother's knee. He was aware the tune as he rendered it wasn't quite the one he'd learned, but there was no-one in here with him to complain. Which was a good job, really, he was very much aware that he was contributing to the already unpleasant odour in the closet. But the simple food he'd been forced to eat for the past few months really hadn't agreed with him. Maybe now that Admiral Chalk had set them on their way to freedom, he would experience the high life once again. After a few more minutes, just to be certain he'd finished, the doctor stood

up. He made a couple of attempts at using the paper that was lying around for cleaning purposes, throwing the discarded tear offs into the bucket. Then he left.

From his position jammed up against the ceiling, Magpie blew his breath out in disgust. His hiding place had been easy to reach, but he hadn't counted on being there for so long. His legs were beginning to hurt again. Slowly, carefully, he eased his way back down to the floor. He pulled the door open the slightest crack and glanced out. The doctor was hastily returning from his aborted foray for food, coming back into the carriage with a frightened look. Then he went back to his compartment. Magpie realised now was the time. He stepped into the gangway, ready to go to the back of the carriage and wait for the body to be thrown out. That was when he glanced through the window and saw the scene beyond. Goldfish was trying to get past a large woman who was crushing him up against the windows. Magpie suddenly realised what had happened. The doctor had been out, seen people coming and come back again. Without being seen. His mind raced. History had been altered already. He watched as Goldfish disappeared to the far end. Now he wasn't going to return to his compartment and tell everyone where Chalk and the royal family were.

That was when he made his decision. Magpie opened the door and stepped into the carriage in front of the astonished woman.

"Boo!" he said, in a quiet voice, barely more than a whisper. As the woman stared with ever-widening eyes, and began to scream, Magpie closed the door again. This time, rather than returning inside the rear carriage, he used the service ladder on one side of the door to climb onto the roof. Very much aware that in a few minutes, an earlier version of himself would be hanging from the front of the train, he manœuvered along the roof with as quickly as he could without endangering himself. He was also sickeningly aware that he had just condemned the doctor to death by his actions. The thought left him cold, a cold that had nothing to do with the freezing Siberian wind that tried to pull him from his perch as the train rattled obliviously on to its destination. But then the thought struck him that if that was the case, then he was responsible for creating this entire alternative timeline in the first place. There was so much theory he'd had to plough through and make sense of when S.T.A.R.T. had been formed concerning cause and effect, and predestination and an alternate timeline becoming what was effectively a self-fulfilling prophecy, but he had never imagined that the first one he'd experience would be one of his own making.

"What have I done?" he whispered to himself, and his words were whipped away the instant he uttered them.

Cursing his own stupidity, he set about the only option left to him. He had to retrieve the situation by first retrieving the surgical stick. Then he would have no alternative than to turn himself over for court martial. At least this time the penalty would only be imprisonment for a predetermined period, followed by dishonourable discharge. He could live with that, if he could set time back on its original course. He crawled over to the edge of the carriage roof and waited. He didn't have to wait for too long. The door opened within minutes and Admiral Chalk stepped out, with the doctor in his grip. Magpie felt a wrench of guilt at the sight of the doctor, blood on his shirt presumably from some kind of knife wound. He appeared to be dead or unconscious. Chalk wasted no time with niceties. He just hauled the doctor off the platform and onto the tracks, where he rolled with the forward momentum in the direction of the train for a couple of turns before coming to rest and receding into the distance at an alarming rate. Fortunately, Chalk went back inside quickly, giving Magpie the chance to climb down the service ladder and time his leap.

It took him a moment to gather the courage to do it, and he knew if he landed badly his legs could well be smashed to pieces again. No job and no legs wasn't a pleasant prospect, but no job, no legs and a timeline shot to hell was even less pleasant, and it was this that finally convinced him to jump. He landed with a remarkably well executed, if completely accidental, roll. He lay in the dust at the side of the track and finally gave in to the cry of pain that, on reflection, could have been much worse. He pulled himself to his feet and watched the train as it disappeared on its way. Surprised that he didn't seem to have broken any bones this time, he set off back the way he'd come.

It took him longer than he expected to find the doctor's body. Magpie saw it in the distance, but couldn't say how far. The flat landscape offered little in the way of clues and, contrary to what he'd always believed about Siberia, there was a heat haze. Unconsciously, he began removing his greatcoat, but caught himself. He didn't know what the temperature would be like tonight, and if he needed the warmth, it would be suicide to drop the coat. Besides, although it was now quite badly torn and absolutely filthy, it was probably what had stopped him being horribly injured, or worse, as he jumped from the train, so there was even a kind of sentimental attachment to it.

Finally, he reached the body. If the wound that Chalk had inflicted on it hadn't killed him, the fall from train had done. He grimaced at the sight of the face, caved in as it was. Shards of bone mingled with matter that could only have been the man's brain, the entire sight accentuated with blood that had not yet dried. Magpie shook his head mournfully. Like the others, he'd been so accustomed to death, almost immune to the sight, but this was no combatant. The doctor had been dedicated to saving lives, not taking them. He was simply in the wrong place at the wrong time. Magpie was aware of what a cliché that was, but he could think of no other way to look at the corpse. He was as much his victim as he was Chalk's, perhaps more so.

It occurred to him that if he hadn't died here, like this, he would have died by firing squad a few days from now. That proved little comfort to Magpie, who knew at least that much was historically accurate, and by replacing him with Chalk, they'd at least preserved the timeline from that perspective.

Pulling himself back to the here and now, Magpie attended to his duty. Kneeling before the body, he began a methodical search for the surgical stick. But when he didn't find it, he knew they were in deeper trouble than he'd first realised.

29

R'sulek-Entah One turned to R'sulek-Entah Two. "If we are to remain here until such time as one of us is deemed to be an interloper, would it not be wise to determine to what extent we share memories, and why?"
R'sulek-Entah Two cocked her head. "I have no interest in satisfying your curiosity," she remarked, and continued to level her gaze in Moonchild's direction.
"Why not?" Moonchild asked.
"Because her knowledge of my history is already impressive, Colonel. I have no wish to make it complete."
"Ok, why are you so keen to do it?" Moonchild turned to R'sulek-Entah One.
"Because I suspect there is some kind of psionic connection here, Colonel. We have access to each other's memories because we have access to each other's thoughts. I can sense this one's abhorrence at the fact that my children are half human. This is not a memory, it is an opinion she holds since discovering the truth."
"That attempt to deflect the focus of the investigation was beneath a true daughter of Ara'Sayal," R'sulek-Entah Two said derisively. "You clearly believe the humans of this timeline are as gullible as your slaves."
R'sulek-Entah One narrowed her eyes, but did not comment. Moonchild couldn't decide if this was because she had none or because she considered it unworthy of one.
Beside her, Gunboy was clearly fretting. His revolver was parked in one of those 'non-threatening' positions the navy was so proud of. Her own was aimed at the space

between the two Arajak, ready to cover whichever one she deemed the greater threat.

"Hand me your revolver, please, Lieutenant," she said.

Gunboy complied without question. Moonchild pocketed the weapon then turned on him. "I just realised what happened," she explained. "It was you all along, wasn't it? You're the Balsari agent. The one who sprung Chalk from prison, the one who gave Goldfish the holodisc. Stand over there, traitor, with them."

Shocked beyond words, Gunboy moved towards the two Arajak. They parted for him and he took his position between them.

"Colonel," he finally managed to say. "I don't know how you came to that conclusion, but please, you have to believe me, it's not me."

"Shut up! You were supposedly on your way from Ara'Sayal when Goldfish was intercepted. There's no-one here who can tell me differently. As your commanding officer, it's my job to pronounce a field sentence. The penalty for treason is death." She raised the revolver and aimed squarely at his heart.

R'sulek-Entah Two stepped in front of him. "No, Colonel," she said. "I cannot allow this."

Moonchild shot her. The bullet impacted with the leather of her tunic and dropped to the floor. She stumbled back under the pressure of the shot but retained her footing. She stood, her breath short and ragged. Before anyone could react, R'sulek-Entah One stepped in and punched her battleknife into R'sulek-Entah Two's back, between her wings. R'sulek-Entah Two's eyes widened with pain before losing their light, and she slipped off the end of the battleknife, slumping on the floor.

Moonchild nodded, apparently satisfied. "Here," she said, handing Gunboy his revolver.

Gunboy, clearly relieved, took it without hesitation. "You don't really think it's me, do you?"

"Never did," she admitted. "But I had to do something to figure out which of these two was ours."

"How did you know?" R'sulek-Entah asked, cleaning her blade on the corpse. "Placing herself in the way should have been enough to convince you."

"No chance, hon," Moonchild confided. "She did that because she knew you were about to and she beat you to it. She wasn't at all concerned for Gunboy's safety, and she knew she'd withstand any bullet that wasn't a head shot, so the gesture was a good gamble. She just never took body language into account. When I first threatened him, your wings and antennae started going like you'd had a power surge. Hers didn't move."

Leaving R'sulek-Entah to try and decide if she should be grateful or embarrassed, she turned to Gunboy. "You ok?"

"Bit shaken, but I'm ok," his breathing was back to normal. "Next time, can you at least try and warn me beforehand?"

They both smiled, then she turned away, leaving the pair to tend to each other. Then the train stopped.

***

Magpie trudged along the line, knowing at some point the train would have stopped. He had absolutely no idea how long he'd have to walk to reach it, but he couldn't afford not to keep going. All he could think was that the surgical stick was still somewhere on the train. Maybe the doctor had dropped it, or perhaps Chalk had mislaid it and the doctor never had it at all.

Trying to work out the many variables was hard enough, but factoring in his guilt over the doctor's death was taking its toll on him. His body hurt all over, and he was further punishing it with this walk through the heat of the Siberian day. He doggedly kept his coat on. If he got out of this alive, he'd keep it as a souvenir. But right now, that was a very big if.

He became aware of something behind him. A couple of horsemen were galloping hard along the line in his direction. He glanced round for cover but, aside from a few trees, there was nothing worthy of the name, and he'd never make it without being seen. Besides, the way they were coming at him suggested he'd been seen already. He decided to take the gamble and wait for them. He realised that if they intended to kill him, there was little he could do about it anyway. Making sure his revolver was to hand, he raised his other hand in greeting.

"Hello, friends," he tried, hopefully.

The two horsemen slowed as they approached, weighing him up, but saying nothing.

"I fell off the train," he said, lamely. "Would you allow me to ride with you?"

The horsemen glanced at each other, uncertainly.

"Do you speak Russian?" Magpie tried again.

Neither of them spoke. He began making gestures, trying to sign to them what he intended. He realised how pathetic he must appear to them.

"Well, what bloody language *do* you speak, then?" he exclaimed, inadvertently reverting to Terran standard.

That got a reaction. "What's an Englishman doing walking along the track on the Trans-Siberian Express?" the nearest one asked.

"English? No, I'm from…," he realised what he was about to say would be considered crazy by the two horsemen. "Um… I'm from Wales."

The two conferred and nodded, coming to a decision. "I'm Colonel Charles Carter," the one who'd spoken told him. "This is Captain Edward Smith. British Army. We're looking for the train."

That was the point at Magpie realised what was going on. "Oh, you'll be Admiral Chalk's people," he said in passable Balsari, pushing his mind into Carter's.

Their reaction was exactly what he expected. They both pulled Balsari energy weapons on him.

"Who are you?" Carter demanded in Balsari.

Magpie smiled and spread his arms, leaving his revolver in his pocket. "I'm with you," he told them. "I'm supposed to be facilitating the transfer of the Tsar and his family."

"Admiral Chalk never mentioned you in his last report," Smith said, clearly suspicious.

Magpie knew he had to be careful with this one. While Carter was as human as he was, Smith was Balsari.

"That's right, his plans changed when S.T.A.R.T. showed up."

"S.T.A.R.T. are here?" Smith was surprised, and Carter glanced at him, alarm evident in his eyes.

"I'm afraid so," Magpie acknowledged. "Chalk wants one of them capturing for questioning, to find out how they knew he was here. That was supposed to be my job. Unfortunately, the Tsar's doctor got cold feet about the whole thing and I had to deal with him, which is why I'm trying to catch up with the train now."

The Balsari and his agent conferred again, and eventually Carter put away his weapon. "You'd better ride up here with me." He extended his hand. Magpie wanted nothing more than to pull him from his horse and bludgeon him to death for betraying his own people, but instead he grasped the offered hand and hauled himself up into the saddle behind Carter. By now he had a fairly good grasp of Chalk's plan. As it worked out, Chalk was going to stop the train anyway, to allow these two to catch up and remove the royal family to a safe place and from there transport them out of Russia. As he held on to Carter, he probed his mind for the location of that safe place.

"I'll explain everything on the way there," Magpie said. "I've arranged for the train to stop, so it won't be too far from here. I know you won't like it, but I'm afraid my orders now take precedence over yours."

He was right. They didn't like it. Especially Smith, but what could he do? It grated that a Balsari had to defer to a human agent, but they were nothing if not strictly regimented. Smith would follow his orders, as long as he didn't push him too far.

***

With the approach to the train, Magpie motioned to Carter. "We need to get me into one of those windows," he said, trying to draw attention away from the two figures trying to climb surreptitiously off the roof. He knew it was himself and R'sulek-Entah on their way for the final showdown with Chalk, but it wouldn't do to point that out to Carter and Smith.

Smith, whose Balsari senses allowed him to hear what Magpie had said to Carter, turned in his saddle. "Why do we need to get you in there?"

"Look, stop treating me like your enemy," Magpie told him, exasperated. "I need to retrieve a piece of technology if the plan is going to work, ok?"

Smith looked nothing like as convinced as Magpie would have liked. "Well, you have two choices. You can trust me, or you can watch the entire operation crumble around you. It's up to you. But I have to get in there now or not at all."

Smith glanced at Carter and nodded. Magpie wondered why the chain of command here was the exact opposite of their assumed military rank. Perhaps because the Balsari wanted to present lower profile targets if the operation was compromised? Maybe he'd never know. Whatever the truth was, Carter manœuvered his horse to the window that Magpie indicated, as Magpie finally did remove his coat, handing it to Carter.

"You will retrieve this technology and pass it straight to me," Smith ordered.

"Of course," Magpie acknowledged, and raised himself up to the window. The small window at the top was slightly open, to allow for ventilation. He pushed it to its full extent and, climbing up on Carter's unwilling shoulders, began to haul himself up and slide through into the compartment beyond. Halfway in through the window, he became caught on the latch. He stopped there for a moment, trying to work out why he wasn't able to move. Then, as he hung suspended from the window, the door to the compartment burst open and he heard Admiral Chalk's voice.

"You can't take me down, Angel! You can't have them!"

For a wild moment, he expected his life to end ignominiously there and then. Then he looked and saw the admiral only partly in the compartment. He realised he was currently occupied with trying to kill the earlier Magpie. With renewed determination, he continued his struggle to enter the compartment. His only salvation seemed to be in the fact that the blinds were down and Chalk would have to actually fully enter the compartment to see him.
"I'm going to kill you, Angel! Do you hear me? I'll kill you!" the admiral shouted in such rage that it drowned the surprised grunt of Magpie finding himself in freefall, landing with a muffled whumpf! on the seat. He quickly got to his feet and glanced round, looking for the coat. Finding it, he rooted through the pockets until he found the surgical stick. Then he began his attempts to get out again.
He heard Chalk curse, knowing it was the bullet hitting his arm that caused the outcry. He knew he was running out of time, and reached up to haul himself back out of the window.
He was vaguely aware of Chalk bending, he knew to retrieve his fallen gun. Then he realised he was stuck again.
"I wouldn't if I were you," Moonchild said, and he twisted his head to look back into the compartment and try and bluff some kind of explanation. Then he remembered, she had said that to Chalk as he prepared to shoot the earlier Magpie. He renewed his struggle. Any second now, they'd be in here and he couldn't let them find him, especially not like this, hanging from the window like a hooked fish drying in the sun.

Carter reached up impatiently and lent his weight to Magpie's struggle. With an ominous rip, something gave way, and Magpie fell on top of the Balsari agent, knocking him from his horse. As Carter and Smith seemed about to comment vociferously about this, Magpie made wild shushing motions and backed up against the train's wheels, beckoning for the others to do likewise. When they joined him, he pointed further along the train then made walking gestures with his fingers, clearly intending that they should follow him. Something landed on his shoulder and he realised it was a piece of fabric, from his trousers. Then he realised his trousers were a lot looser than they had been. Indignantly, he began slowly moving along the carriage.

When they were at a safe distance, he turned to Smith. "These are our orders. We need to capture one of them, but you need to replace him to avoid arousing suspicion. This is the technology I was after," he said, handing the Balsari Goldfish's holodisc. "You'll need it to convince them you're him. Activate it when they're all looking, and look sad. It's his wife. Let's go and get him."

30

Goldfish came out from the water closet and glanced back along the carriage. For some reason, he could see Magpie at the other end, beckoning. Unsure what was happening, he went to find out what he wanted. As he reached the end, he saw Magpie was on the platform between carriages, looking at the linking mechanism.

"Do you think you could set some kind of device to break this?" the acquisitions officer asked him.

Frowning, Goldfish knelt to examine the link. "Well, I'd need…"

He fell unconscious onto the deck. Magpie looked up at Carter and Smith as they stood over the body. Smith knelt down and spread his hand over Goldfish's face. Magpie watched, fascinated, as Smith began to change. His facial features softened, blurred, dissolved, then reformed into the familiar features of his friend. Clearly, he realised, this was how they infiltrated into human society when their agents were not the appropriate choice. He filed the information away for later use.

"You will be rewarded," the voice of Goldfish came from Goldfish's face on the head of the Balsari.

Magpie nodded. "Just remember, when you see me in there, you mustn't give me any indication that you aren't him. I can't afford for my cover to be compromised. From this point onwards, our missions are separate."

The false Goldfish nodded his acknowledgement and went back inside the carriage.

"Let's get him onto the horse," Carter said, hefting the body.

"Wait," Magpie said. "I need his trousers first."
Removing Goldfish's trousers, Magpie replaced his own with them. Then he helped Carter get the unconscious man across the saddle of his horse.
"I have to go back inside," he told Carter. "My mission was just to secure the prisoner, not stay with him. Once I'm in a position to do so, I'll have relief sent for you. Keep him under observation, don't answer any questions, don't ask him any. Do not harm him. I can't stress that enough. Admiral Chalk's mission may be compromised, but my orders stand. There are highly placed people who want to talk to him."
The two humans looked at each other, then without a word Carter turned his horse around and sped off into the distance. Magpie watched him go, his head spinning with the temporal juggling he was doing. Then, stirring himself to motion, he went back to find the others.

***

Moonchild raised the revolver to cover the door as the handle turned. R'sulek-Entah moved to a position that would place her behind the door as it opened. Gunboy stood the other side, ready to pounce on whoever came through.
"Tickets please," Magpie grinned, as he poked his head through the door.
"You idiot," Moonchild let out a long breath. "You could've gotten yourself shot."
"Nice to see you too," Magpie said. He looked round, took in the fact that only one Arajak was in evidence.
"Don't worry, sir," Gunboy explained. "That was pretty easy in the end."

"Oh, good," Magpie entered fully and closed the door, dropping the surgical stick onto the table where they could all see it. "So did I miss any excitement?"
"It was eventful," R'sulek-Entah said, enigmatically.
"What about you?" Moonchild said.
"Well, funny you should ask," he grinned. "I've had quite a long walk and it gave me time to do some thinking. So I figured out where Goldfish is."
"You did? Great! Where?"
"He's at a secret Balsari hideout nearby. Don't worry, he hasn't switched sides, he's being held prisoner."
"How do you know all this?" Moonchild asked.
Magpie seemed embarrassed. "I'd better start at the beginning, hadn't I?"

***

Goldfish wasn't sure what was worse. The fact that his captor was treating him well but refusing to speak to him, or the fact that somewhere along the line he'd lost his trousers. The village he found himself in was apparently deserted, and the base seemed to have been set up at a moment's notice, and could be taken down in the same kind of time if necessary. He was sitting on a packed earth floor against a wall in a small cellar, his arms and legs bound with rope. The rope seemed to be soaked in some kind of liquid, in order to make it harder to escape. He'd given up trying. His captor sat against the opposite wall, covering him with a gun in one hand and munching something with his other hand.
"So, if you aren't allowed to talk to me, how about feeding me?" he attempted another means of communication, having failed with all previous efforts.

Carter, by now tired of the constant tirade of questions and taunts, stood up and took a chunk of something from his rations. Bringing it to Goldfish, he held it out for the demolitions officer to take like a newborn bird waiting for its mother to feed it.

Chewing thoughtfully, Goldfish nodded slowly, understanding. "Balsari food. You're holding me so your superiors can question me about my apparent change of loyalties. Because I wouldn't betray my colleagues."

"So that's why he said you weren't to be harmed," Carter finally spoke. "You tried to double cross us." He laughed. "Oh, I wish I could be there when you get what you deserve."

"I'm afraid that's not going to happen," said Moonchild as she entered the damaged cellar.

"Are you my relief?" Carter demanded, impatiently.

"No, I'm his," she replied and smoothly shot Carter in the stomach.

The Balsari agent fell to the floor, wordlessly gasping for breath. Moonchild picked up his weapon and turned to Goldfish. "Are you hurt?"

"Just my dignity, boss," he glanced down at his bare legs.

"Hmm, well, you need to speak to Magpie about that."

"Magpie? He's got my trousers?"

"You just can't keep a good thief down, hon," she replied, and turned back to Carter, who was still writhing silently. "You'll live, you treacherous bastard," she spat at him. "But by the time we've finished with you, you'll be glad of your death penalty."

Her communicator sparked into life. "Colonel Washington, are you receiving this message? Please respond."

"I'm here," she answered. "Talk to me."

"Colonel, this is Control, we thought we'd lost you for a moment. What's your status, ma'am?"
"Um, yeah, we lost power a little while back, but we seem to have it back now. Have you got a lock on all the team?"
"Yes, ma'am, though there appears to be another lifesign in your immediate vicinity."
"That's right, Control, we're bringing a prisoner in. And an Arajak corpse. And some Balsari technology, too. Bring us home."
"Acknowledged," Control responded, and she felt the grip of the teleporter as it pulled her back into the twenty sixth century.

***

They stood looking at each other. Control was as it should be. The S.T.A.R.T. support staff buzzed around Control as they should, swooping upon the Balsari equipment and the corpse of the alternative R'sulek-Entah as soon as they saw it.
"What's happening?" Goldfish yelled in panic. "Who are you? Why am I tied up?"
Moonchild knelt to help him, taking out the mnemonics as she did so.
"Excuse me, ma'am," Lieutenant Stone frowned, looking at her panel. "I couldn't bring the prisoner through."
"Why not?" Moonchild handed the mnemonics to Gunboy and went to see what Stone was looking at.
The panel was showing Carter was where he'd fallen, in the cellar in 1918.
"The teleporter wouldn't bring him through," Stone had no explanation. "It recognised him, but wouldn't bring him."

"How's that possible?" Moonchild asked. "It only ever refuses when it's something that belongs in the past. It should have brought Carter through if he belongs here."

By now Magpie had joined them. Looking at the readouts, he frowned. "Have the Balsari developed some kind of anti-teleport technology?" he wondered.

Moonchild moved to another panel and started issuing instructions to it. "Will, you'd better look at this." Her tone was grave. Magpie, Stone and R'sulek-Entah joined her. The readout was showing a picture of the man she'd shot, the same man Magpie had followed on the back of the horse. It also showed a contemporary news report about him:

CARTER, CHARLES; COLONEL (BRITISH ARMY [INTELLIGENCE])
BORN: ENGLAND 8 NOVEMBER 1875; DIED: RUSSIA 16 JULY 1918.
COLONEL CARTER WAS FOUND IN A CELLAR IN THE DESERTED VILLAGE OF MARETSK WITH A SINGLE BULLET WOUND TO HIS ABDOMEN. THE BULLET WAS FIRED FROM A RUSSIAN REVOLVER. COLONEL CARTER'S MISSION IN MARETSK REMAINS CLASSIFIED INFORMATION. THE RUSSIAN AUTHORITIES CONSIDER IT UNLIKELY, IN THESE TROUBLED TIMES, THE ASSASSIN WILL BE FOUND.

"Oh," Magpie groaned, the full horror of the situation becoming apparent.

"They're recruiting people from the past," Moonchild announced.

***

Later, in Magpie's quarters, Moonchild looked at Goldfish. "Are you sure you want to do this?"

He swallowed hard, then nodded. "I'm sure, boss. I need to know."

She turned to Magpie and handed him the holodisc. Magpie took it without a word. He closed his eyes and began concentrating. Moonchild waited, knowing he couldn't be hurried. She glanced at Goldfish. The poor man was really going through it right now. She reached out, squeezed his shoulder. He looked at her, and she smiled encouragement. He wasn't able to smile back.

Eventually, Magpie opened his eyes.

"It's a fake," he mumbled. "The Balsari never rescued her. This is not a genuine record. I'm sorry, James."

Goldfish heaved a heavy sigh. "No, it's ok. I suppose in a way I'm glad. At least now I can lay her to rest. Thank you. Both of you. You should know that the Balsari agent who gave it to me was you, Magpie. At least, he looked like you. I know that probably doesn't help much, but there it is."

"Thanks, James, it does help," Magpie encouraged him. "Chances are it's one of the clones. Maybe even one we don't know about yet."

"Well, if you're sure it'll help, that's fine."

Magpie offered him the holodisc.

"No, please, it's not her," Goldfish waved it away, though they could tell it was a difficult decision. "I'd rather remember her as she was. You know the last thing she said to me? 'I love you'. I'll always have that."

He made his excuses and left, still visibly suffering.

Moonchild turned to Magpie. "Is it really a fake?"

He looked at her for a long moment before answering. "Sarah Warner died six years ago in that explosion, and that's the end of the matter, Elise. What would you have him believe? That she's alive and recruiting for the enemy? You heard him. He can lay her to rest now."

She stared intently at him, trying to decide if her question had upset him. "Sorry," she conceded with a resigned shrug. "It just seemed so real, I guess I should have been prepared for another Balsari trick. I didn't mean anything by it. Goodnight, Will."

"Goodnight Elise," he said, and she was acutely aware that there was none of the usual overt flirting from him. She left him, wondering what to make of the whole episode.

He stood by his window for a long time, watching as her car took to the night sky and became lost among the many other lights that filled the darkness. Then he turned his attention to the holodisc and activated it, watching the image again and again, his soul becoming darker and emptier with each viewing.

31

Munich, Bavaria, 2507

When Lieutenant Commander William Angel was recruited for the Space-Time Axial Response Team, he had no idea what it would involve. Maybe a bit of travel, see the universe, visit different time zones, kill a few bad guys. If someone had told him he'd end up being recruited by the Balsari as well, the very enemy he was supposed to be fighting, he'd have laughed. Then arrested the person making the comment for treason. But here he was, doing exactly that.
Of course, it helped that as time had passed he had been made aware of the truth. That the Emperor and, indeed, his entire Empire were corrupt. The Balsari only wanted to live in peace with their neighbours, but certain neighbours had no such intentions. The Terran Empire was intent on conflict. There was a succession of other races that bore testimony to the Empire's belligerence. The Vihansu, the Galkasians, the Arajak, among others, all bore the brunt of imperial expansion. The Vihansu had made peace, while the Arajak had forged an alliance. The Galkasians had been practically wiped out, the survivors no more than a servitor race forced into hard labour, mining the remains of their planet's mineral wealth to fuel the Emperor's war machine as it rolled on towards Balsar.
When the Balsari agent had first approached him, his first instinct was to kill the traitor, but then he'd been shown something. A holodisc. The image on the holodisc was of the woman he loved, the woman he thought was dead.

She hadn't died. The Balsari had gone back for her, rescued her, brought her to Balsar. Now, they were together, both agents of the Balsari. Their lifestyle was nothing extravagant, but she was comfortable, better by far than the life she'd led before she'd been pronounced dead. His was one of similar comfort, although he was still required to undergo field missions. Will didn't complain. He had his one great love back, and he was grateful. He would now do anything for the Balsari.

All he had left to do on this mission was one simple assassination, then he could go home. To Elise.

***

They stared at the new guy.

Admiral Saastemoinen coughed loudly, clearly embarrassed, when the silence became too much for him to bear. "Colonel, I'm really sorry you weren't involved in the selection process. But Lieutenant Veçescu has come with the highest recommendation."

Moonchild and Magpie exchanged glances. "With all due respect, sir, I was promised faithfully that we would be part of the selection committee," Moonchild tried to keep the anger out of her voice, aware she wasn't being entirely successful.

"I know, Colonel," Saastemoinen sounded apologetic. "But when I say the highest recommendation, I mean it. The Marquis of New Transylvania has put Lieutenant Veçescu's name forward to the Emperor's top advisors. They've recommended him to me and General N'Komo, and so here he is. I trust he will be made welcome as a member of the team."

"Of course, sir," she replied, as if she couldn't believe there was any doubt. "It's nothing personal, Lieutenant, it's just a bit of a shock to the system."

"As you're probably aware," Magpie expanded, "we lost two very good friends recently, and it's taking a while to adjust."

"I understand, sir," Veçescu snapped easily to attention. "I'm sorry to hear that. I hope I'll be able to live up to their reputation."

"Let's give you time to settle in first," Magpie smiled, more with sadness than humour. "Come on, I'll introduce you to the rest of the team."

He shared another look with Moonchild before taking the young lieutenant in hand and escorting him from the office. Saastemoinen was all too aware that Moonchild hadn't moved.

"Is there something else I can help you with, Colonel?"

"Yes, sir, there is. Is it now our policy to accept people on the basis of someone else's recommendation?"

"When the recommendation comes from such lofty heights, yes, Colonel, it is our policy. To be truthful, I'm as unhappy about it as you are."

"Really?" she sounded unconvinced.

Saastemoinen looked away and sighed. "You'd better look at this." He invited her to join him on his side of the desk. "Computer, show biography of Veçescu, Daniel, Lieutenant junior grade."

Moonchild stared at the screen as the information appeared. Veçescu was born 15 January 2478, New Transylvania to Daniel (senior) and Maria, a couple of planetologists. New Transylvania had been colonised by Romanian settlers in 2179 looking for a forest world similar to the original region on Earth. Veçescu was the descendant of some of the first colonists. His parents had died in 2489, killed in a rockfall while researching the structure of one of the planet's moons, leaving him and a sister, four years his junior, to be raised by relatives. He'd enlisted in 2492, in the Medical branch. He was a qualified field medic.

"So, he's a doctor," Moonchild commented. "That's good, we need one. Gunboy's good, but he's really Tactical Support, not a doctor like Hacksaw."

"Keep reading," Saastemoinen warned.

She did. "What the hell is this? He's personally responsible for the deaths of eighty-nine troops under his command? My God, in two separate incidents?" She read further. "He killed the Balsari field commander on Varius VIII? What kind of medic is he? He's supplying his own patients!"

"That's exactly right," Saastemoinen confirmed. "So you can see why I'm not happy. To be honest, our hands are tied. This one really has come from the top, and General N'Komo's as unhappy as I am. You need to keep an eye on Veçescu. For the record, he seems very much on the level. He had a psych profile as soon as we met him, and he has a burning hatred of all things Balsari, which he readily admits."

"I'll be sure to bear that in mind, sir," Moonchild mumbled.

"One other thing, Colonel," the admiral mentioned. "Despite his medical prowess, he's assigned primarily as Tactical Support."

She frowned. "This gets crazier by the minute. Anything else I should know?"

"If I think of something, I'll let you know."

Moonchild knew then that she'd been dismissed. She nodded at Saastemoinen and left the office.

***

When she met Magpie later that day in her quarters, she told him everything. Magpie didn't seem surprised.
"I spoke to Hacksaw," the acquisitions officer explained. "He'd never heard of him. And before S.T.A.R.T. was formed, he had a spell teaching at the medical academy. Veçescu should have passed through his hands at some point, but he didn't. He even checked his own records in case his memory was faulty, but it's true. Wherever this guy learned medicine, it wasn't where other naval doctors learn it. So, I thought I'd have a look around my old haunts to see if I could turn anything up."
"You mean the Espionage division records?" Moonchild said.
"Exactly. And what was very interesting was the new codes that have been inserted to prevent me getting in."
"They updated the codes? That shouldn't be a problem for you, they've always done that, it's never stopped you before."
"No, Elise, what I mean is they inserted the new codes to prevent *me* getting in. Specifically. As of yesterday. There's something they don't want me accessing, and that makes me suspicious. I'm willing to bet it's connected with Veçescu in some way."
"How do we get round it?"
"I have a number of options open to me, but I need to consider each one carefully. Espionage Division is, by definition, the one branch that you don't want to mess with when it comes to hacking into their systems."

"There's another option," she said quietly. "You could go straight to Veçescu."

"But if we're wrong about him, I'll have violated his rights without cause. I can't do that."

"You use that excuse a lot, but you know, when we stood outside that shop you checked everyone."

"Surface thoughts, Elise, that's all. I didn't go deeper than that. But if Veçescu's working against us, I may need to go deeper into his mind."

"So you won't do it?"

"I can't, Elise," he shook his head firmly, then brightened up. "But I know someone who can."

***

Gabriel smiled warmly as he shook hands with Veçescu. "Very pleased to meet you, Lieutenant Veçescu," he enthused. "Please don't let my appearance fool you, I'm much smarter than Will. I managed to avoid military service, for one thing. So, how did you get dragged into S.T.A.R.T.?"

"Um… isn't that classified information, sir?" Veçescu glanced at Magpie for help, but he just smiled.

"Don't let Gabriel get to you," he grinned. "He just likes to live in his own little delusions. He's perfectly harmless, but he is very much aware of what we do, and why. You can treat him the same way as you treat me, just don't feed his ego by calling him sir."

"You don't have to tell me anything if you feel uncomfortable, Lieutenant," Gabriel apologised, finally taking his hand back and breaking the contact. "Here, let me introduce you to Michelangelo, he's worse than Will, he lives for his computers."

Michelangelo stood to introduce himself formally, while Gabriel glanced at Magpie, nodding slightly. Magpie nodded back. Now it just remained for the two to find a moment's privacy.

"I can tell you're all related," Veçescu was relaxing in Michelangelo's presence. "You all look so alike."

"Quite," Michelangelo laughed with good humour. "We were the result of an interesting multiple birth. This is Seraph, by the way."

"You've been brought in to replace Bouncer, haven't you?" Seraph's voice was as nervous as his handshake, which Veçescu, to his credit, accepted without reaction to the clone's appearance.

"Yes, I have. Were you friends?"

"I wish we had been," Seraph looked down at the floor.

Michelangelo put a hand on Seraph's shoulder. "It's bit complicated, but essentially, yes, they were friends," he told Veçescu. "Tell you what, why don't we go meet the girls?"

Seraph looked up and his eyes were full of gratitude that Michelangelo had suggested the distraction. Between them they led Veçescu from the room in search of Legna and Lucy.

Alone, Magpie and Gabriel faced each other. "What do you think?" Magpie asked.

"He's a bunch of contradictions," Gabriel told him. "He's an open book, but there are areas I couldn't touch. That's a surprise for a start, there's usually very little I can't get through."

"Is it a psionic block?"

"No, he hasn't any psionic ability. It's more like a natural ability. On the other hand, the things that I did read were very clear. He has an absolute hatred for the Balsari and everything they represent. But you might find this interesting. He has very good memories his father, but he doesn't like to think about his mother. Or his sister. It's like he's closed off that area of his life."

"Fascinating," Magpie wondered if that was significant. "Thanks, Gabriel."

***

On the way back, Veçescu asked him about the women.

"I understand you were all named for angels, or there's some connection, but I don't get your sisters. What does Lenya mean?"

"The way it's spelt, it's Angel, backwards," Magpie explained.

"Ah," Veçescu nodded, visualising the name and realising. "What about Lucy? There never was an angel called Lucy, was there?"

Magpie looked at him and smiled. "It's short for Lucifer. I guess dad was running out of ideas by the time she arrived."

He was aware that Veçescu, for all he was probably a man with an ulterior motive, had no idea about Project Cyclone, or that with the single exception of Michelangelo they all had psionic abilities. Magpie was perfectly happy for the situation to remain that way, and easily adapted his approach to Veçescu. He'd have to make sure he spoke to the rest of the team before the truth became apparent.

"We need to find a codename for you," he said, changing the subject.

"Excuse me?"

"Everyone in the team has a codename. You need one."

"Do I get to choose my own?"

"Not a chance, I'm afraid. Moonchild started the tradition a long time ago, and it's a fact none of us has ever chosen our own codename, not even her. Give me a while, I'll think of something. You're from New Transylvania, right?"

"Um… yes, sir."

"Ok, give me a couple of hours, I'll give you a codename."

The rest of the journey back to Control was silent.

***

Lieutenant Commander William Angel squeezed himself into the shadows on the rooftop. He waited, his rifle resting in his lap. He was in no hurry. His target would be here in his own good time. Will just sat, knowing it was just a matter of being patient.

32

R'sulek-Entah faced a dilemma. Because the Arajak had formally broken contact with the Empire, she was viewed with suspicion on Earth. Because she had disobeyed the explicit directive of the Queen herself, she was not going to be welcome on Ara'Sayal. Her position in S.T.A.R.T. was as liaison officer. Without anyone to liaise on behalf of, what role did she have? And where did she go now? It had not escaped her notice that her children were now beyond her reach. She couldn't help wondering what was happening to them. It was not the Arajak way to be so concerned for offspring, but she had, she realised, become used to the human way of things. Her mother would say she was tainted. But her mother was prepared to stand by and allow the Balsari to overrun her world. In R'sulek-Entah's view, that was the greater taint.

She paced the confines of their quarters, an uncharacteristic action, she admitted, but her exposure to humanity was affecting her in a variety of ways, not all of which she found unpleasant. Since she had been asked to remain here, something she considered not far removed from house arrest, she'd done a lot of pacing. And very little else. Her access to the communications array had been restricted. Not that she believed anyone on Ara'Sayal would speak with her anyway, unless it was to threaten dire reprisals should she show her face there again.

The door to their quarters scythed open, and he was there.

"John," she said, unfamiliar feelings of relief evident in her voice.

"Are you ok?" Gunboy asked, aware of the difference in her attitude.

She did something she had never done in all her life. She stepped into his personal space and put her arms round him, pulling him close and holding him. Dazed, he responded.

"I'm so alone, John," she whispered. "And you are the only one I feel safe with."

"Are you ok?" he repeated, not daring to let go, for fear that she might revert to her usual detached self.

"No, I am not ok. I am scared. I have no home, no people, and I am trapped among a people who view me as their enemy."

"You're not the enemy," he tried to reassure her. "You're not my enemy. You're my friend. I'm here for you, R'sulek-Entah, and I don't care what the diplomatic status happens to be between our peoples. You and I are who we are. Nothing will change that."

"You have always wanted to mate with me, haven't you, John?"

"I thought I had done," he answered, uncertain where the conversation was going.

"No, I mean the way humans mate. The messy way."

He tried not to laugh. "Don't worry, I've accepted it now."

"I want to," she pulled away, looked into his eyes. "You are my friend, and it is not fair."

"I didn't think you could," he said.

"Of course we can, we just choose not to. Recreational sex is not the Arajak way."

"So… have you ever…?"

"No. I will require instruction."

"Instruction?"

"Yes. I am not familiar with the technical aspects of human mating activities. I will require instruction before I am able to commence with confidence."

He reached out and took her hand. "Follow me," he smiled, gently. "There's really only one to learn. You'll be fine. Trust me."

He led her to the bedroom.

***

Veçescu was fuming. What kind of a name was Creepshow? The idiot was simply dispensing with the traditional concept of Transylvania and replacing it with the stupid notion that vampires and all manner of supernatural menaces originated there. But what could he do? Magpie had announced to the others that he was called Creepshow and the others had accepted this without question. On reflection, it wasn't as bad as Goldfish, although for the life of him, he couldn't work out where that name came from. And what was Moonchild about? Wasn't she from Mars? What kind of name was that for a team leader anyway? At least Gunboy, basic as it seemed, summed up his job. Creepshow, indeed!

He paused briefly as his door opened to admit him into his quarters. He went straight to the food processor.

"Nutrition supplement Veçescu six," he demanded. As the processor supplied his order, he picked up the container and made his way into the living room. He took a sip and grimaced. Making a disgusted noise, he turned back to the processor to change his order. The switch in direction saved his life.

The window burst inwards and the wall opposite flared and blistered as the beam began boiling it away. He threw himself to the floor, rolling and getting back to his feet in an instant. A second shot followed, but it was more a hopeful attempt from the marksman than a serious one. He sprinted across the room, slamming against the wall next to the ruined window. He glanced out, judging where the shot must have come from. There, on the roof opposite, was his would be assassin. His eyes widened. Magpie! What was going on? The man was giving him an unacceptably stupid name one minute, trying to kill him the next. He watched him as he made his way across the roof. He narrowed his eyes. There was something about him. Literally. A kind of aura. Creepshow had no idea what that meant, but he was sure it wasn't a good thing. He activated his communicator. "Veçescu to Commander Angel."
"Go ahead," Magpie responded immediately. Clearly the person speaking to him was not on the roof opposite.
"Sir, may I recommend you come over here as soon as you can? There's something you need to see."
"On my way."
With the link broken, Creepshow was free to act. He bolted for the door.

***

Will cursed. For some reason, the target had turned round, and the shot had missed. He'd fired again, but he wasn't really a marksman. He pulled himself from his hiding place and began making his way across the roof. He was almost at his escape door when Veçescu appeared. Damn, how had he found him, and how had he got here so quickly. He brought the rifle up, but Veçescu was quicker. His shot missed but Will had to dodge and he lost the initiative. Trying not to panic, he searched for another way off the roof. In the background, he could hear teleporters operating. But they weren't Balsari teleporters. Veçescu had alerted others, probably S.T.A.R.T. people, and they were converging on his position now. Realising he couldn't allow himself to be caught, he swallowed hard. All he'd wanted was to be able to go home to Elise. Now, he wouldn't be going home at all. Looking for the nearest edge of the roof, Will began running. He was aware of Veçescu closing on one side, but he wouldn't reach him in time to stop him. Then his legs were blown out from under him. Crashing to the deck, he tried to crawl the two or three yards left to the edge. Veçescu moved closer, but Will knew all he needed was one last push. He heaved with all his strength, and disappeared over the edge.

Creepshow and Magpie came to the edge and looked down. They looked at each other. Then they slowly turned and retraced their steps. A few moments later, they had retrieved him from the balcony where he'd landed and had him in custody.

***

Lieutenant Stone waved the scanner over the prisoner. "Ah," she said, then fell silent, as the scanner continued its work.

"What?" Magpie tried to keep the exasperation out of his voice.

"Oh, sorry, sir," Stone looked up, as if surprised to see her commanding officer in the same room. "He doesn't belong here. He's actually temporally displaced."
"Meaning what?" Creepshow asked.
"Meaning," Moonchild explained, entering the room with Hacksaw in tow. "It's Magpie, but from an alternate timeline. Correct?"
"Uh, yes ma'am," Stone confirmed.
The effect on the prisoner was electrifying. He sat bolt upright, his eyes wide. "Elise," he whispered.
"Oh, no," Moonchild stopped him, pointing at Magpie. "He gets to call me Elise, because he's still loyal to the Empire, and me. Whatever happened in your timeline to turn you, it took away your right to use my name."
"You don't understand," he continued whispering, with almost zealous urgency. "It was you who turned me. After the mine collapse on Hermitage, we all thought you were dead, but the Balsari went back and rescued you just before the collapse. They brought you back to me. That's why I did it. For you, Elise."
Moonchild stepped forward with alarming speed and hauled him up by his collar.
"You stupid bastard," she spat. "Magpie dug through those ruins for days, by himself, using nothing more than his hands. He dug until his fingers bled, and then he carried on till his hands bled, and he didn't stop even when his arms bled. He found me in that mine, and he got me out. That's why he can call me Elise and you can't. You are so pathetic, you couldn't even bring yourself to look for me, could you? That's where our timelines split. Over *your* decision to leave me to die. That's how the Balsari got hold of *your* Elise. But he came looking for me,

and that's why… that's why he's a better man than you'll ever be."

She let him drop back into his chair then. She was acutely aware how lame her last statement sounded, but she was equally aware how revelatory it would have been had she not stopped herself in time. Everyone stared at someone else for the next few seconds.

"Well," Hacksaw finally said. "Pointless me being here. I was going to look at his physiology and try and figure out where the timeline split based on that. Now we know, I'll just get on with being a doctor again. Oh, hello, you must be Creepshow, I'm delighted to meet you."

Hacksaw and Creepshow shook hands. Then Hacksaw took his leave and Moonchild left with him, not even giving the prisoner another look.

"No," Hacksaw admitted. "I still don't recognise him. I thought if I saw him in the flesh, as it were, I might remember, but I can honestly say I have never seen that young man before."

"Thanks," Moonchild nodded. "That pretty much sums up how we feel about it. Something's going on behind our backs, something at the highest levels, and I hate being the dumb ass in the middle of it all."

Unsure he could contribute any more, Hacksaw patted her on the arm and moved away. Moonchild waited for the others to come out. When they did, she dismissed them all except Magpie.

"I know what you're going to say," he told her. "And in this instance, I agree."

"You been reading my mind, hon?"

"No, just your face. Trouble is, obviously, he's going to be an exact match for me. I won't get in any further than he lets me. It's stalemate before we've even started."

"Not necessarily. You have a few aces up your sleeve."
"I do?"
"Sure. They're called Legna, Lucy, Seraph and Gabriel."

***

Moonchild watched Creepshow from across her desk. The new guy looked fairly relaxed despite the assassination attempt. "Anything you'd like to ask about any of this?" she offered.
Creepshow gave it a few seconds before answering. "No, ma'am, I think I have it all worked out."
"Really?" she resisted the temptation to snort her disbelief. "I envy your certainty. How come you figured it out so quick?"
"The way I see it, ma'am, my attitude to the Balsari is well documented. Now I'm on the team that does more damage to their plans than any battlefield defeat. It's fairly straightforward they'd target me."
"You realise they've targeted every member of the team, past and present, you're not unique."
"I would never suggest I was, ma'am," he conceded. "I'm just thinking the amount of damage I intend to do them must give them cause for immediate concern."
"Does it surprise you that the guy they sent to kill you was an alternate?"
"Alternate? That's the technical name for someone from an alternate timeline?"
"It's what we call them, whatever the technical name is. Our job is to deal with it, not find legally accurate or politically correct names for it."

"It's a surprise, but not entirely unexpected. The Balsari are masters of temporal manipulation. It can't be beyond their abilities to access other timelines."

"You seem very knowledgeable about the Balsari."

Creepshow shrugged. "It serves to know your enemy, ma'am."

"Yes, it does," she agreed, although the alarm bells were ringing loud and clear in her head. "As long as you're happy that you're ok. Dismissed."

She watched him go, and wondered.

33

Michelangelo frowned. "What exactly are you going to do?"
"We're going to see if between the five of us we can get into his mind and get at the information he's holding in there," Magpie explained.
"Will that be safe?"
"I don't see why it wouldn't be," Magpie shrugged. "There's five of us, plus you to watch our backs, against him. And he only has the same abilities I have. I don't see what could go wrong."
"So often are they the last words of the overconfident, Will," Michelangelo warned. "But if you're determined, I'll be there for you. But, the first sign of a problem, I'm going to stop it, ok?"
"That's exactly why I want you there," Magpie grinned. "Come on, the others are waiting."

***

They entered the cell one by one. The prisoner, expecting Magpie, had no worries. He was a total match in every way and, as far as he knew, they were the only psionically rated humans with their level of ability. After the destruction of Project Cyclone, he was the only one left.
So he was not expecting the others. In his timeline, he'd never met Legna, never found the Firewood Foundation, and never discovered the truth about the others. He was caught completely by surprise when they all ranged themselves in front of him.

"Who are you? What's going on?"

"Hello, Will," Legna said, not in a friendly manner. "You probably don't remember me, do you? But we grew up next door to each other."

"That's not possible," the prisoner shook his head, desperate not to believe. "You were all killed."

"You wish," Lucy answered, her expression and tone identical to Legna's.

"You have something we want," Seraph said. The prisoner gaped at the ruined face whose voice was his own voice.

"We've come to get it," Gabriel said, the same voice behind him as he placed his hands firmly on the prisoner's shoulders.

"Ok, everyone," Magpie glanced at each one in turn. "Let's get this over with."

The prisoner met Magpie's eyes. They became locked, neither willing, neither able to look elsewhere. He could feel Magpie rooting around in his mind, but his defences were easily able to fend him off. He knew anything Magpie tried would be dealt with before it caused any problems. Then he felt someone else in there, and he knew it was the man behind him, Gabriel. From either side came the women, Legna and Lucy. Then Seraph, the man with no face, whose power was clearly way beyond his own, even though it was being held in check, came in and began his assault from the front. All the time, Magpie merely held station, taking all his attention, demanding he put up barriers to hold him off, leaving himself wide open for the others to move in and take what they wanted. The prisoner was aware of the other occupant of the cell, presumably another clone who did nothing but stand out of his line of sight.

Now he could feel them all surging forward into the darkest recesses of his psyche, threatening to strip his soul bare and expose every secret he held.

"He gave Lieutenant Warner the holodisc," Gabriel murmured.

"Please, stop," he whispered.

"He tricked Maek Newark into killing himself," Lucy said, quietly.

"Stop," he pleaded.

"He released Admiral Chalk," Seraph commented.

"Help me," he sobbed.

"We're closing on something big," Legna said. "I think it's his contact in our timeline."

Magpie noticed Gabriel frowning. The prisoner, under his hands, was starting to writhe and moan.

"Gabriel, step back, we've almost got what we need," he said gently, without taking his eyes from the prisoner's.

"I can't," Gabriel gasped, the effort clearly hurting him.

"Neither can I," Lucy reported through gritted teeth.

Magpie tried to let go, but found he was locked into the contact. He couldn't break it. The prisoner was staring wildly, clearly in pain. Blood welled up from his eyes, red tears of agony.

"Will!" he heard Michelangelo call. "Will! Stop it, now, you're hurting him!"

"I can't!" Magpie heard a rushing in his ears as the power surged through him, into the prisoner.

Seraph began to growl with pain. Magpie watched as blood began to seep onto the prisoner's face, as thousands of capillaries burst.

"Will, for God's sake, stop it!" Michelangelo moved forward and tried to haul Magpie away.

Magpie didn't move, couldn't move. He didn't even break eye contact with the prisoner. The prisoner was now screaming in dire agony, as blood covered every exposed area of flesh. Gabriel held him in a death grip but couldn't release him.

It was like an explosion, a soundless blast that flung them all away from the prisoner. Magpie recovered first, hauling himself to his feet to assess the situation. Gabriel sat against the wall behind the prisoner, the women lay on the floor where they had fallen. None of them moved. Seraph groaned and attempted to sit up. Michelangelo stood where he had been trying to pull Magpie away, his eyes wide as he stared around himself at the sight of everyone on the floor. The prisoner still sat in the chair, his face fallen onto the desk. Magpie cautiously approached him and reached out. There was no response, no movement. He gently eased his hand beneath the forehead, placing the other hand around the chin, and lifted. Seeing the destruction on his own face was shock enough, but the fact that the bloody, destroyed eyes stared straight into his own was too much to take. He lowered the head back to the table and lowered his own head into his hands. He felt a hand on his shoulder.

"Will?" It was Michelangelo. "Will, what happened?"

He couldn't answer. He knelt there, lost in the barren wasteland that was his soul. How many more would he kill and destroy before he was finished?

"Psychic backlash," he heard Legna hiss, as she regained her senses. "He must have induced it to stop us getting to his big secret."

"What big secret?" Michelangelo helped her to her feet.

"We were close to finding out who the top Balsari agent is," Legna explained.

"Did you find out?" Michelangelo asked.

"No, he killed himself first. If we'd just had another minute, we'd have got it."

Michelangelo winced. "So close? Can you still get it? Is there some way?"

"No," Seraph said sadly. "That was our best hope. Whoever it is, he's taken the name to hell with him. And he nearly killed us all doing it."

While the others checked Lucy and Gabriel to determine if they needed medical attention, Magpie stood up. "Thank you, all of you, for doing this. I'm just sorry it didn't work."

"Are you ok, Will?" Michelangelo looked long and hard at him.

He nodded his thanks at his concern. "I'll be fine. I just need to figure out how to tell Elise what's happened."

"Will you be going via sickbay?" Legna asked, rubbing her right elbow.

"I can do," he said. "It'll give me more time to think about it."

After calling security to deal with the removal of the prisoner's body to the morgue, the clones dispersed, Michelangelo, Seraph and Gabriel to their quarters, with Lucy joining them, while Magpie and Legna went to sickbay. Once they were a safe distance from the others, Legna let go of her elbow and turned to Magpie.

"Will, what just happened in there, it wasn't what it looked like," she said.

"In what way?"

"It wasn't a psychic backlash. The other Will was helpless, he was concentrating on keeping you out. He wasn't capable of doing that."

"So, what are you saying?" Magpie didn't like the direction of the conversation.

"I'm saying someone else locked us into that spiral, someone made us all kill him, before we could get the name of the agent he reported to. He was murdered, Will. By one of us."

"Who?"

"I don't know, but whoever it was wasn't quick enough. I got this much from his mind: the Balsari agent is a clone. A male clone."

"So you mean one of us four?"

"I'm afraid so."

"Why are you telling me this when it could be me?"

"It isn't you," she smiled. "Don't ask me to explain, I just know it isn't you. But whoever it is has the power to control us all and kill someone right under our noses, to protect his identity."

Magpie spent a long moment letting it all sink in. "Thank you, Legna, you've just confirmed something Elise and I discussed recently. For the record, it isn't Gabriel, and I don't believe it's Seraph."

"You think it's Michelangelo?" She couldn't believe what he was saying. "He doesn't even have any psionic ability."

"None that anyone's ever witnessed," Magpie corrected, his tone dark and warning.

Legna considered this. "You really do believe it's Michelangelo, don't you?"

"He's my main candidate, let's say that much," Magpie confirmed. "And if it is him, he's a very dangerous opponent. Think about it. He can control any number of us without even breaking sweat. And he's working against us. He can do what he wants, when he wants, and none of us are any the wiser. How do you stop an enemy like that?"

They looked at each other for several seconds, each considering the implications of what they were saying.

Then they resumed their walk in silence.

***

Legna went into sickbay and walked straight out again. "I never said I needed to go, I just asked where you were going. See you later."

Their eyes met.

"Be careful," Magpie told her.

"Always," she assured him.

He turned away and made his way to the morgue. He breezed in and went straight to the young attendant.

"Where's the body that was just brought in? The prisoner?"

"This way, sir," the girl said.

Magpie followed her into the storage area. She looked so young to be down in the morgue. Or maybe I'm getting too old, he grimaced to himself.

"Here, sir," the attendant indicated the drawer.

"Thank you, er…"

"Krakowiak, sir. Med-tech, second class.

"Thank you, Krakowiak," he smiled, the dismissal implicit.

As she left him to his work, he instructed the drawer to open. The body had been cleaned up since it was brought in, but that just served to highlight the level of damage that had been done. The skin was mottled and bruised, slightly misshapen due to the capillary bursts. Looking at the corpse, Magpie tried not to think about what he was looking at. This was even closer to him than the clones. This wasn't even a sharing of DNA, this was someone who, until he'd made a different decision, had been him. Literally.

Magpie remembered the incident as if it was yesterday. Moonchild was still coming out from the depths of the mine when it had fallen in. He'd stood there for a brief moment, thinking she'd been killed, that there was no hope of her getting out. At that moment, he'd gone into frenzy. Hope was only lost when they produced a body; until then he was focussed on one thing, and that was finding her alive. The search nearly killed him, initially through his own recklessness and desperation to reach her, then through exhaustion, as four days and three nights of relentless backbreaking effort finally paid off. Another few hours and she would have finally given up and died. But she'd clung to life, knowing he'd come for her. He knew what had happened to this one. He'd stood there for that moment and decided she was beyond him. And he left her there to die. In that moment time had taken two different paths, the one he lived in, where the two of them had lived, and this other path, where she'd died. The Balsari had gone back for her. He couldn't work that out. If they'd gone back, she shouldn't have been there when he reached the point where she'd fallen. There were so many theories about that, but none had ever had a practical application. It had never been an issue. Maybe they waited for a point between when he found her in his timeline, and when she died in the other. He shook his head to clear the memory. All that mattered was the here and now. He looked down again at his dead self, and gently caressed the broken face. He closed his eyes and began the real search.

34

Admiral Saastemoinen was waiting for Moonchild when she returned to her office.

"Admiral," she said, uncertainly. "Can I help you?"

"Yes, Colonel, you can," the admiral answered. "The joint chiefs have decided to launch an all out assault on the Balsari homeworld. They want S.T.A.R.T. to be involved."

"I don't understand, sir," she said, cautiously. "We're not strictly a battlefield unit, we're special ops. Why do they want us involved?"

"Because it's generally recognised you and your team are the best there is."

"I'm too old and cynical to fall for lines like that, sir."

"Nonetheless, it's the truth. I made the same objections you will, and it fell on deaf ears. They want you in first, to clear the way for the main force. And they don't want anyone screwing up. Which is why they want you rather than anyone else."

"I see. What's brought this on? I mean, why have they now decided to go straight for the heart, rather than taking the long term strategic aim?"

"Because of the shift in galactic politics. The loss of Ara'Sayal has hurt the Emperor. He wants the reprisals to be swift and brutal. He wants Balsar to suffer. And that's why he wants you in at the beginning."

"Wait! This came from the Emperor himself?"

"Yes it did, Colonel. And, believe me, I'm as unhappy about it as you are. S.T.A.R.T. was set up to deal with temporal incursions, not standard warfare situations. But the Emperor feels you and Commander Angel are two of the best soldiers the Empire has available right now, and he wants you in there. I'm sorry, I'm repeating myself."

"Ok, but I need to establish a few things first."

"Of course."

"What's the official status of R'sulek-Entah?"

"Officially, she's a citizen of a foreign power, and to be treated with all the rights and privileges that entails."

"Ok, what about her unofficial status?"

"She's essentially a prisoner of war, but until war is officially declared, she can come and go as she pleases. As long as she doesn't enter restricted areas."

"What constitutes restricted?"

"Anywhere outside her quarters, or Lieutenant McCallum's quarters. They're watching her. She can travel between the two, but any deviation and they'll arrest her."

"Will war be declared?"

"It's inevitable."

"So, she's going to be in an internment camp before too long?"

"I'm afraid so."

"Not acceptable. She's a member of my team, and I want her reinstating."

"She was assigned by the Arajak as liaison officer, she has no official status, especially not now the alliance is ended."

"Sir, I have total faith in your ability to see that she is reinstated," Moonchild leaned forward to get as close as she could. "She's a sel'ved-ar in the Arajak Defence Force, she can be officially enrolled in the navy as a Lieutenant Commander. It's not impossible. Not for an admiral of your skill and intelligence."

Saastemoinen raised an eyebrow. "I'm too old and cynical to fall for lines like that, Colonel," he said.

"Then we have an understanding, I take it, sir?"

"No promises. But I'll do my best."

Moonchild sat back. "That's good enough for me," she said.

***

Magpie lifted his hands from the face of his alternate. He slowly let his discovery sink in, standing for a moment to gather his thoughts.

"So now you know," a voice said from the doorway.

He didn't even turn. He'd been somehow expecting him to show up.

"Hello, Michelangelo."

"You don't seem surprised. Why is that?"

"I've suspected for some time. To be honest, I had my doubts, and you threw me off the scent a couple of times, but in the end it had to be you. I couldn't see why Uncle Xavier would deliberately produce a clone with no psionic ability. It defeated the object of the project. But for you to pass yourself off as non-psionic, you had to have massive discipline, and incredible power. And you killed this one, because he knew your identity. Am I right?"

"That's just about the top and tail of it, Will," Michelangelo agreed. "And I must say I'm impressed with your reasoning. I couldn't have said it better myself."

"I suppose now the next step is that you'll have to kill me," Magpie seemed resigned to his fate.

"I'm afraid so, Will. It's nothing personal. If it's any consolation, I actually quite like you. But I can't let sentiment get in my way."

"I have one question," Magpie said.
"This had better not be some kind of stalling tactic, Will. Although I suppose you'd be the expert in that."
"Thanks," Magpie grinned, in spite of his predicament. "But seriously, I'd like to know why?"
"Why I've done all this?"
"Yes," he'd thought that was obvious, but then realised despite his power, despite his ability to control others, he clearly couldn't read them. It was a shame it was too late to capitalise on that information.
"Simple," Michelangelo was saying. "It's all about power. I work for the Balsari, they keep me well stocked in resources. I'm becoming very wealthy, and all I'm doing is what I'd be doing for my own personal amusement anyway. Why do something for a hobby, if someone's prepared to pay you to do it?"
"Good point," Magpie accepted the logic of it all, and brought his pistol to bear.
"How disappointing," Michelangelo sighed, as if bored.
Magpie tried but failed to fire on him.
"I'm controlling your trigger finger," Michelangelo told him, in easy conversational tones. "That's why you can't shoot me."
Then he pushed with his mind. Magpie was hurled backwards against the wall. The breath was slammed out of him as he slumped to the floor. As he struggled to get up, he felt himself being lifted up again. Michelangelo was laughing at him as his mind reached out and threw Magpie across the room into the far wall. Magpie cried out with the force of the impact. He heard something snap, and his left hand went numb. He finally let go of the pistol, now his gun hand was useless. He clutched the wounded hand, but Michelangelo hadn't finished.

"See what I can do, Will?" he taunted. "Let's see what else I can break."

Magpie shouted in pain as he heard and felt the snap of something in his wrist. Michelangelo was breaking his bones by his mind alone.

"Make no mistake, Will, I'm going to kill you. But I'm going to do it slowly. I'm going to cause you great pain, and I'm going to take great delight in it. I had hoped I could just snap your neck, or make you jump from a great height, but you've really annoyed me with your pathetic attempt to shoot me. I can't believe you thought you could get away with that. It's because I can't read minds, isn't it? You discovered my one blind spot. That's not good for you, Will. It just drags it all out horribly for you. How are your legs, by the way?"

Magpie screamed as his legs shattered all over again. Not just the bones he'd previously broken, but all of them. He felt the wave of black nausea wash over him as consciousness fell away. Then he was ripped back into full awareness.

"Oh, no," Michelangelo admonished. "I can't allow you to go to sleep just yet, that won't do. I want you to be aware of everything I do to you, feel it all, know the moment you die."

Magpie writhed in abject agony, the full horror of his fate plain before him. A ragged screech was ripped from him as, one by one, Michelangelo broke his ribs.

"Stop it," someone said.

Through his tears of terror and pain, he could see Seraph in the morgue. Michelangelo looked a little put out.

"Oh, Seraph, not you as well," he groaned, theatrically. Turning to Magpie, he said. "Don't go away," then wrenched Seraph across the room against the wall opposite.

Seraph crashed against the wall and crumbled to the floor. Michelangelo watched his progress. Then Seraph stood up, apparently unharmed.

"You should have known, Michelangelo," Seraph told him. "The universal rule: it doesn't matter how big you are, there's always someone bigger than you."

"Maybe so, Seraph, but that someone isn't you." Michelangelo locked his mind on Seraph and began forcing him to his knees.

Seraph gave a strangled cry, and forced himself back to his feet. Magpie watched, helpless as the two of them struggled in psychic combat. It was always going to be a one-sided contest. For all Seraph's sudden revelation, Michelangelo was stronger. He'd controlled all of them earlier and, even with the combined psionic strength of all of them, he hadn't broken sweat while he held them all and killed the prisoner. Seraph hadn't been able to break him then, he wasn't able to do it now. The end was inevitable.

Michelangelo forced Seraph back to his knees. Magpie watched in horror as Seraph's eyes started bleeding the way the prisoner's eyes had done. Michelangelo pressed his advantage, but then the bloody tears started running back up Seraph's face and his eyes took on a more determined focus. Michelangelo stumbled backwards briefly, before he steadied himself. With a clearly gargantuan effort, grunting with the strain, he flung Seraph back into the wall. Seraph cried out as the impact smashed the air from his lungs. He looked up, a spent force, the fear in his eyes mirroring what Magpie knew to be in his own eyes. Recognising his victory, Michelangelo took a step forward and thrust his mind forward. Seraph was flattened against the wall, as he struggled to retain some kind of control of himself. Slowly, oh so slowly, like a malfunctioning holovid, Seraph was lowered to the floor, the life being squeezed from him.

From somewhere there was a flash and the back of Michelangelo's head exploded in a frenzy of blood. With wide, shocked eyes, he looked round, trying to find the source of the flash, and the reason he could no longer control Seraph. Then, apparently realising half his head was missing, he flopped bonelessly to the floor.

"Medical emergency, morgue!" Moonchild screamed into the air. "Get me someone here now!"

She dashed over to where Magpie lay. "Hang in there, hon, I'm getting help, ok?"

Magpie's lips moved, but no sound came. He managed to move his eyes to where Seraph lay. She glanced at the other clone, then turned back to Magpie. "It's ok, Will, you hear me? It's ok. Help's coming."

As the blackness at the edge of his vision began closing in, and he found he was no longer concerned that he couldn't breathe, he focussed on her face, her wonderful face, as she looked helplessly at him.

"I love you," he tried to say, but the words wouldn't come.

Blackness took him.

35

Hacksaw came out into the waiting room where they were all waiting with as little patience as it was possible for a group of people to demonstrate.
Moonchild had to forcibly hold herself in to keep herself from grabbing him. "Tell me," she demanded, her voice hoarse beyond the ability to express the fear that was eating her.
"Magpie's condition is more stable, but he's still in serious danger. We've got a long night ahead of us," Hacksaw looked so tired, and clearly was only able to contemplate the following hours because it was his friend on the operating table."
"What about Seraph?" Lucy asked, her voice just as hoarse, her face filled with tears.
Hacksaw looked at her for a few seconds, then took a deep breath. "I'm sorry. We did what we could. But the extent of his injuries was too much. He never regained consciousness. I'm truly sorry. I have to get back in there," he said to Moonchild.
"Go," she told him, too distraught to say any more.
She watched him go back into the theatre before turning to the others. Legna and Lucy held each other, sobbing together, while Gabriel had pulled them both to himself and laid his head on theirs. She saw he was crying too. She caught Gabriel's eye. He nodded, and she nodded back.
She moved away, leaving them to their grief.

***

She found a quiet room and sat down, her head in her hands. How long she sat there, she had no idea, but she was still there when she realised she wasn't alone. R'sulek-Entah stood before her. Moonchild looked up. "How long have you been there?"

"I have only just arrived," the Arajak said. "How is Commander Angel?"

"He's in a bad way. They're trying to save him now. We lost Seraph."

"I heard," R'sulek-Entah said. "His loss is a great shame. I understand he saved Commander Angel."

"Yes, he did. He distracted Michelangelo long enough for me to get there. He knew I was coming. He fought him for so long, put up such a struggle, just to give me time to get there. He knew Michelangelo would kill him, but he still did it."

"Then Bouncer's sacrifice was not in vain," R'sulek-Entah observed.

"No, it wasn't," Moonchild agreed. "Not if Magpie survives this. I think Seraph was probably thinking about that at the time."

R'sulek-Entah said nothing for a while.

"I just realised," Moonchild said. "You called him Bouncer. You've never called any of us by our codenames before, always our rank and real names."

"Well, it seems I have to adapt, now I have been drafted. I believe I have you to thank for that, Colonel."

"So they managed to get you in? Good. Welcome to the Imperial Armed Forces, Commander. How do you feel?"

"Well," R'sulek-Entah raised an eyebrow. "I like the pay, but the uniform does not suit my hair colour."

Moonchild blinked. Had R'sulek-Entah just made a joke? She laughed, the first thing she'd found funny all day.

***

Magpie died in the early hours of the morning. Hacksaw and his team wearily put down their tools and closed down the computers that were breathing for him. Hacksaw personally recorded his time of death. He dismissed the doctors, nurses and other theatre staff so he could spend a few minutes alone with him.

"Well, my friend, I've patched you up a number of times over the years," he whispered sadly. "I guess it was bound to happen one day I'd be unable to fix you. I'm sorry."

He called the morgue and asked for someone to come up and see to Magpie. Then he went to find Moonchild. This was the worst thing he'd ever had to do.

He found her in a darkened room, with R'sulek-Entah. They were getting on a lot better than he thought they were capable. The only other time he'd seen them together, they were on each other's back. This just made it worse. Moonchild was even laughing. She looked up as he knocked and walked in. She was smiling, but then she saw his face.

"Oh, no," she said, her smile faltering.

"I'm sorry," he said again. It seemed to be the only phrase he was capable of at the moment. "He didn't suffer at the end. Once he was unconscious, he was out of pain."

She nodded, unable to trust her voice to remain level if she tried to speak. She held her breath for a long time, long enough for Hacksaw to wonder when she was ever going to let it out again. Finally, she sighed the deepest sigh, all her grief communicated in that one breath. R'sulek-Entah reached out and drew her into a hug. The two of them stayed like that long after Hacksaw left them.

36

R'sulek-Entah met the remnants of the team at Control. She told them what she had understood from the previous night. The grief that emanated from Gunboy and Goldfish was awful to behold, especially coming so soon after Iceman and Bouncer had died. Creepshow held his peace, allowing them to grieve for their friend. It was humbling to know the man had such a deep friendship with these people.
When Moonchild appeared, she looked rough. She clearly hadn't slept, and the time she'd spent awake had been spent in mourning for her best friend. She looked them all in the eye as she passed them, and knew how they'd all taken the news.
"We haven't much time to really say goodbye," she said, quietly. "We've got our new orders and we ship out today. Anyone who wants to do anything about Magpie has to do it this morning, because there won't be another chance. And it may be we won't be coming back from this one ourselves."
"What's happening, boss?" Goldfish asked, equally quietly.
"We hit Balsar," she answered, noticing how Creepshow absently nodded, as if this wasn't news to him. "We're being sent in to open the way for the main force to attack. We get in, take down their planetary defence grid, and try and get out before our people start the bombardment."
Gunboy frowned. "That's not what I understood to be S.T.A.R.T.'s prime objective."
"It isn't," Moonchild acknowledged. "And believe me, I've had this conversation with Admiral Saastemoinen,

and he's had it with his superiors. This has come all the way down from the Emperor himself. So we don't get to argue about it. On the plus side, R'sulek-Entah has been given an official rank and position in the navy and is now our Technical Coordinator."

"Congratulations," Goldfish offered, but it sounded understandably hollow.

R'sulek-Entah accepted it in the spirit it was intended. Gunboy smiled encouragingly at her. She almost smiled back, but it was still an alien gesture that she couldn't quite manage.

"Any questions?" Moonchild looked round at each of them. When no-one spoke, she nodded, satisfied. "We meet back here at 1400 hours for a full briefing. Make sure you have any non-regulation items you feel you will require. Don't worry, Creepshow, you'll find we usually operate outside of regulations, that's why we're as good as we are. Ok, folks. Dismissed."

***

As the time approached, Creepshow found it increasingly difficult to contain his mounting excitement. This was what he'd been waiting for, what he'd been preparing all his life for. Now the day had come, and he was ready. Vengeance would no longer be just a dream, it would be a reality. He hefted his kit bag and checked his mental list one final time. Nothing had been left to chance. This day had been planned for, the Emperor himself had made sure it would come to pass. Creepshow set off back for Control, happier than any of his new colleagues at what lay ahead of him.

Moonchild met with the clones.

"I don't know what will happen now," she admitted. "But if you can leave Earth and go as far from here as possible, you should. I don't know how long you'll be safe here."

"Thank you," Legna said, genuinely grateful. "The *Firewood* is ready to leave at any time. We may not be here when you get back."

"I understand. If you can get a message to me, I'd like that. In a way, you're all I have left of Will."

"No," Lucy said, a sad smile playing on her lips. She reached up and touched the side of Moonchild's head. "What you carry in here is far more than we could represent. I've seen it, remember? I know the truth. You loved him."

Moonchild made her excuses and left as soon as she could, trying to hold back the tears. The clones watched her go.

"It's just a shame she never told him how she felt," Lucy said sadly.

"She was his commanding officer," Gabriel said, with an air of practicality.

"Yes," Lucy sighed. "But even so…"

***

They met at the appointed time and went straight to meet the shuttle waiting to ferry them to the transport that would take them to Balsar. The *Imperial Hammer* was a stealth ship, designed to take them straight there. No-one was prepared to risk them being seen once they were off the planet. Admiral Saastemoinen and General N'Komo were there to send them on their way. They both shared a long look with Moonchild, knowing they were being sent, most likely to their deaths, on a mission that they shouldn't even be given. As they settled in their seats, Moonchild noticed R'sulek-Entah and Gunboy were holding hands. Some things had really changed recently. She was very much aware of what Lucy had told her before she'd left. How she wanted Will to be there right now. The team needed him, but more than that, she needed him. She turned away from the others in case she started crying again. If she could just hold out until they were aboard the stealth ship, she could retreat to her quarters and let it all out. But right now, she was a colonel in the Imperial Army and had to behave like one. So she turned her thoughts to the mission.

***

The shuttle left the atmosphere and docked with the stealth ship. The S.T.A.R.T. members boarded the ship that would be their home for the next few days and went about the business of settling into their new quarters. Goldfish was somewhat surprised to hear Gunboy's request that he swap with R'sulek-Entah. He couldn't work out what was happening with her, but she seemed to be less Arajak and more human as the days passed. But Goldfish wasn't complaining, if it meant he got a room to himself, rather than sharing with Gunboy. It seemed a little odd that Creepshow was assigned a room of his own, but Moonchild put that down to him being the Emperor's little pet, and thought no more of it. As long as he did his job when she needed him, she didn't care whose backside he kissed.

Finally, they were just waiting for a last minute cargo shipment to arrive. Moonchild was summoned to the cargo hold to supervise the unloading and storage of the team's equipment. The transport shuttle docked and the airlock opened, admitting the crew, who were already carrying crates. Then, as she turned to watch them place the crates carefully in their designated bays, she did a double take. Someone else was standing in the airlock.

"Room for one more?" said Magpie.

37

<u>*Munich, Bavaria, 2507*</u>

When he opened his eyes and found himself in the storage drawer, he felt a surge of panic. Where was he? How had he got there? Then memory came back, and with it the terror of his ordeal. That was when he guessed he was in storage.

"Drawer, open," he said, his voice higher than it should be, which he put down, quite accurately, to fear.

Fortunately the drawer, unaccustomed to receiving instruction from within, nonetheless obliged and he hastily, if somewhat clumsily, clambered out. His chest hurt as he struggled to fill his lungs. That was when the full realisation of his predicament first hit him.

He was dead. Or, at least, he had been until recently. Why had that changed? He had been given to understand that, even with modern medical technology, death was generally a permanent condition. He wasn't entirely comfortable with his current status. Would it be temporary? Was it just a brief respite? Or was he in fact immortal? Or had what had happened been so similar to death that no-one had noticed, and he'd been put in the morgue by mistake?

"Somebody help me, please," he called out.

A young man came running. When he saw who had called, he went pale but, admirably, kept coming.

"Sir? Are you ok?"

"No, I'm not ok! I've woken up in the morgue and it's scared the hell out of me! I'd like to go home now."

The attendant helped him from the storage area and led him to a seat in the outer office.
"Do you feel better now, sir?"
"A bit, thanks. I need a shower, though."
"You do look rough, sir," the attendant agreed, before realising who he was talking to. "Oh, I mean…"
"It's ok," Magpie grinned. "As it happens I think I smell pretty bad too. Give me a few minutes and I'll be ok."
He closed his eyes for a moment and the attendant thought he'd drifted back into his original state, but after a while, they snapped open again. "Right!" he said, jumping to his feet and rubbing his hands together. "I'm off for that shower. Thanks for all your help."
The attendant watched him go, unable to decide what he'd just witnessed.

***

Back in his own quarters, Magpie took his shower and changed into a fresh uniform. He then grabbed something from the food processor and checked on the status of the others. When he realised where they were, he quickly finished his food and hurried out.
He managed to talk the pilot of the cargo shuttle into letting him tag along, and eventually found himself on the stealth ship, facing Elise.
"Room for one more?" he asked, hopefully.

***

Moonchild stared for a few seconds, her mind unable to take in the fact that he was there.
"Will," she finally whispered.

"Hello, Elise," he said, quietly.
She took hold of him and hugged him tightly.
"Not so hard, please," he complained. "I ache all over."
She stared into his eyes. "How did you…?"
"Before you say anything, I have absolutely no idea," he cut her off. He pulled away from her. "I ought to go stow my things."
"You're right," she accepted. "I'll show you to your quarters. How are we going to explain this to the others?"
"Do me a favour," he asked. "Don't tell them. Not yet."
She nodded. "Ok, I won't, but…" she took a deep breath. "There's something I need to say. Here we are."
They entered the cabin that would now serve as his quarters.
"What did you want to say?" Magpie asked as he put his bag on the single bunk.
"Something I should have said a long time ago, and never did. Until last night, I thought I'd eventually say it, one day a long time from now, but then I thought I'd lost my chance and I realised how much I really wanted to tell you. So here goes. I love you, Will. I have done for a long time, but I was too scared to say it. I've always known you've felt the same way, but that kinda made it harder for me to say it. And I want to say it now because I've been given a second chance, and I'm not going to miss it again. There," she let out a breath. "I've finally told you."
She looked at him. He was just looking at her.
"Well? Aren't you going to say something?"
"Elise," he said finally. "I love you too. I want you to know that. I've felt this way for a long time, as well."
She looked at the floor.
"Come to my quarters tonight," she told him. "I don't want to be alone. You understand what I'm saying, right?"

"Of course," Magpie said. "I never thought you'd get around to asking."

She turned and left, retreating to her own quarters. Magpie watched her go, then turned his attention to unpacking his things. He smiled slightly to himself.

38

He became aware of a voice, tugging him back to awareness.
Will. Can you hear me?
He opened his eyes. He couldn't see anything. Was he blind? Or just in some dark place?
Will?
The voice, which was in his head, was weak, struggling to heard.
Seraph?
Will, I'm here, but I haven't much time.
Then the pain hit him. All his broken bones. He remembered. A scream of fear ripped its way out of him, but the sound was strangled by his inability to breathe properly.
Will, it's ok. You're alive. But you must listen to me. I haven't much time left.
What's happening, Seraph?
This is what I must do, Will. I have to help you.
As he listened to Seraph, he became aware of the pain easing all over his body.
What are you doing, Seraph?
This is the ability I was given, Will. I'm a healer.
You're a what?
Please, listen. As I heal you, my own life is fading. You have to relax and let me heal you.
Seraph, are you saying you're killing yourself to heal me? Stop, now!
I can't, Will, your injuries were too great for you to heal on your own. Michelangelo damaged so much of your body, you can't recover without help. Listen, this is what Bouncer gave his life for. So I

could give mine for you. Accept my gift, Will, accept Bouncer's gift to you.
Seraph, why?
Because we all have choices to make in our lives. Sometimes those choices are trivial, sometimes they are momentous. This is my choice. Goodbye, Will. Be worthy of this gift.
Seraph? Seraph!
There was no answer. Magpie began hammering at the inside of what he now knew was a storage drawer.
"Seraph?" he called, suddenly aware his voice was working normally. "Seraph! Answer me!"
Then the drawer began to slide open. He squeezed his eyes closed in the sudden relatively bright light of the morgue. A young man stood looking down at him, his eyes wide with wonder.
"Don't just stand there," Magpie ordered. "Help me out."
"Yes, sir," the attendant complied immediately.
"Where's Seraph?" he demanded.
The attendant opened the relevant drawer. Magpie looked in at the clone. He looked so peaceful. Magpie leaned over and kissed his forehead. "Thank you, Seraph," he whispered. "I'll try and be worthy."
Then he closed the drawer. "Show me Michelangelo," he ordered.
The attendant took him to another drawer. His killer lay in a less peaceful pose. Magpie looked at him for a moment, trying to decide what was odd about him. Then he realised that much of Michelangelo's skull was missing. A number of very nasty suspicions were forming in his mind. "Has he recovered at all?"
The attendant laughed, nervously. "Most of his head's missing, sir. I think he's staying there."

Magpie snapped an impatient look in his direction. "I'm serious. I was dead, but I'm here now. Where's the alternate?"

"In here, sir," the attendant told him, opening the drawer. It was empty.

"How long have you been on duty?" Magpie demanded.

"About an hour, sir, I relieved Med Tech Sewell at 1500 hours."

"Get Sewell back in here, now!"

When he was in the office, Magpie put a call through to Control.

"Control, Stone speaking," the young woman answered.

"Lieutenant Stone, this is Commander Angel, I need to speak to Colonel Washington. Where is she?"

"Commander?" Stone was clearly shocked beyond her ability to comprehend. "But..."

"Never mind, Lieutenant, I'm coming up."

Sewell arrived. He came to attention when he saw Magpie. "You look better, sir," he ventured.

"Ah, Mr Sewell," Magpie turned on him. "I'm assuming from your words you saw me earlier. When?"

"About 1300 hours, sir," Sewell frowned. "Is there a problem?"

"That wasn't me," Magpie hissed, his eyes like hot bolts driving into Sewell's soul. "It was the alternate. Did you think to check? Don't bother answering that, it's obvious you didn't. So because of you, he's out there, free to act. Do you have any idea where he went?"

"To get a shower, sir," Sewell replied, miserably. "He said he was going home."

"The bastard's been in my quarters. Sewell, you're on report. You," he turned to the other attendant. "What's your name?"

"Uh, Painter, sir."
"Painter, what happened to Krakowiak?"
"She's in sickbay, sir, she had massive haemorrhaging of her internal organs."
"Will she be ok?"
"As far as I know, she's out of danger, sir."
"Good," he said, apparently satisfied, and left.

***

Lieutenant Stone had called security, so by the time Magpie arrived, he was surrounded by weapons. He came all the way into the chamber, and raised his hands cautiously.
"Sorry, sir," Stone told him, as she brought her temporal scanner to bear. "I need to be sure."
"Of course you do," Magpie granted. "Good thinking."
The scanner obviously gave Stone the information she was looking for.
"It's ok, people, he's ours," she told the security officers, who were relieved to be able to holster their weapons.
She was still troubled.
"What's the problem, Lieutenant?"
"Sir, we had word from the cargo pilot who resupplied the stealth ship. He said he'd taken you up there."
"Wait a minute, Lieutenant," Magpie held his hands up. "I've been out of the loop for nearly twenty four hours. What stealth ship?"
Stone took a deep breath and began to put him in the picture.

***

Admiral Saastemoinen wasn't expecting his office door to open without his authorisation. And when he looked up, the last person he expected to see abusing his privacy was standing in the doorway, looking like he was ready to murder someone.
"Commander? But you're…"
"No, I'm not, sir, but it'll take too long to explain, and besides I'm not really sure myself yet."
Aware of the surreal quality of the situation, the admiral invited him in. "How can I help you, Commander?"
"I need to know all the details of the mission they've gone on. There's at least one traitor on that ship, and I want to find out how to deal with them."
He listened in growing disbelief as Saastemoinen explained the mission to him.
"Who the hell authorised this mission?" he demanded.
"It came from the Emperor himself," the admiral told him. "I had this conversation with Colonel Washington, and she feels the same way you do about it. But we all realise there's very little we can do about it."
"Yes, sir," Magpie conceded, realising he was pushing his luck speaking to an admiral this way. "Sorry, sir. I don't know what I was thinking. I'm going to make a strange request, sir, but I hope you'll grant it without asking too many awkward questions."
"If I refuse your request, will you carry on anyway?"
"Very likely, sir."
"In that case, name it, and I'll try and accommodate you."
"Thank you sir. First of all, I'm going to need Lieutenant Stone to pull some overtime."
"Agreed."
"And I'll need to get inside Espionage Division's record centre."

"What? Are you mad?"

"Very likely, sir," he repeated.

"Why do you need to do that?"

"Because I don't trust Creepshow. I think he's hiding too much, and I think it's all a bit too much of a coincidence that a Balsari killer like him gets transferred to S.T.A.R.T. on the eve of their actual arrival on Balsar, which we all know they shouldn't be doing in the first place."

"Ok, here's the deal, Commander," Saastemoinen said. "I'm prepared to let you do this. I'm prepared to give you access to any resources you need, either material or personnel, but this is not an officially sanctioned operation. If you are caught, you are just a rogue agent up to no good. Is that clear?"

"That's what I was trained to be, sir. I guess it's time to see how good a rogue agent I can be."

***

Moonchild summoned them all, including Magpie, to her briefing. Magpie was clearly unhappy about his presence being broadcast, but had no choice in the matter. So he sat in the conference room as Moonchild explained the plan to them, knowing that Creepshow could tell who he was. Which made his job harder, because he was only there to kill Creepshow anyway. At least Creepshow couldn't act against him in public, unless he was prepared to explain himself and his insights.

So he sat and did his best to look interested, all the time thinking how he was on his way home to Elise. He'd worry about how to deal with Creepshow later.

Moonchild was explaining her theory about his sudden reappearance. "I believe it's the goblin DNA. When

R'sulek-Entah and I were on the *Traveller*, we found that even dead goblins made a complete recovery within an hour, although it was possible to do sufficient damage to prevent this. It's seems that this was built into the clones' DNA from the beginning, meaning that Magpie is back with us. Magpie, anything you want to add to that?"

"I don't think so," he replied. "Except to say I had no idea until I woke up today that this was the case."

Moonchild continued her briefing, keeping it professional. But to the others that knew them, it was obvious something had changed between them. And they didn't like it.

After she finished the briefing, she dismissed them all. As they left, she called Magpie back.

"Listen, Will, are we still good for tonight?" she sounded embarrassed. "I didn't want to put you on the spot. I'm sorry if I backed you into a corner. You can back out if you want. I won't be angry."

"Don't be ridiculous, Elise," he said to her. "Like I said at the time, I feel the same way. You know I want this as much as you do."

"I know," she smiled. "I just wanted to be sure. I'll see you later."

Magpie smiled and turned to leave.

"Oh, Will?" she called after him, as he reached the door.

He turned back to her, and she drilled him in the stomach with her pistol. With the searing heat evaporating most of his lower digestive tract, he fell to the deck in uncomprehending agony. With what mental control remained, he searched her for a clue.

"Let's have a little chat about how things are," her voice was as cold as a glacier, as she moved closer to him, kneeling beside him as he writhed, clutching his ruined gut. "My Will, the real Will, knows I love him, the same as I know he loves me. But we would never act on it because we're professionals. If I'd said what I said to him, and not you, he'd wonder why I was suddenly allowing him in like that. But you… you never even blinked. You never questioned me, you just said yes, straight from the off. So the only question really is why are you here? You're obviously a Balsari alternate. But I want to know what your mission is."

"You won't get much out of me, you fool," he managed to gasp. "I'm going to be dead again before you get a chance."

"I know. But later, you might be alive again, and I can hurt you again, you piece of filth. And keep hurting you, and keep killing you until I'm satisfied I've gotten as much out of you as I can squeeze. Then you can say hello to the airlock, like you did to Maek Newark."

Her eyes were like ice as he tried to focus on her. The pain overtook him, and he lost consciousness. Moonchild stood. She looked down at him, a sneer working its way onto her face. Then, for good measure, she kicked him.

39

Imperial Espionage Offices, Europa, 2507

Magpie glanced around the office.
"Ok, I'm in," he said to the communicator attached to his throat.
"Acknowledged," Stone's voice sounded in his ear.
It had been many years since Magpie had last walked these halls, and back then he didn't need to do it quite so covertly. The irony hadn't been lost on him. But he had no time for irony right now. Instead, he made his way towards the computers at the heart of the building by a more circuitous route than he wanted to take, placing markers in random locations as he went.
Finally, he reached his destination. The interface cowls formed part of the headrest on the chairs at each station. Unlike conventional computers, Espionage Division computers interacted with the user completely. Rather than showing plans of buildings to break into, for instance, they allowed the user to act as if he was actually inside the building. It made sense to give the agent the experience of the locations they were going into. Now, Magpie wanted to get into the records pertaining to Creepshow. He sat in one of the seats, and the cowl moulded itself to his head.

***

Security officer Paranteau glanced at his monitor as it began to light up. He double-checked the reading. It was reporting a total of seventeen intruders in various locations around the building. With a curse, he abandoned his sweep of the building, and decided this was a drill. After all, the building was probably the most secure building in the entire Empire outside of the Emperor's palace. Which was why even the single guard on duty was often deemed the most redundant person in the Empire. But, every now and then, they made the guard earn his keep. Tonight was Paranteau's turn. He checked his sidearm and stood up, taking his tracker and setting off for the nearest lifesign.

After neutralising the first few markers, he'd become bored. This was not the usual high standard of drill they made them go through. Usually, he'd be up against a few actual humans trying to penetrate the buildings defences. Maybe there was something else going on here. On a hunch, he returned to his post at the main security desk.

"Computer, show me the computer chamber," he instructed.

The chamber was in semi-darkness, lit mainly by the working lights of the computer itself, as well as the emergency lighting strips along the walls. He couldn't see anything amiss. He turned away. Then he turned back to the monitor, frowning. One of the cowls wasn't in its correct position. That suggested it was in use, but he couldn't see anyone. He leaned closer.

"Computer, switch to thermal scan."

Immediately, the view switched, but still nothing showed up.

"Switch to sonic location," Paranteau ordered.

This time, a model of the room was constructed on the monitor. And this time, there was very obviously someone sitting beneath the cowl.

"Computer, show me what station 3 is accessing."

"That information is not available," a disembodied voice informed him.

"Oh, you're good," he nodded appreciatively. "But I'm pleased to say, I'm better."

He set off for the computer chamber.

***

Magpie had tried all the tricks he knew, and was still struggling. If he didn't get somewhere soon, he'd have to bludgeon his way in with an obviously stolen code. That wasn't what he wanted, but he was running out of options. He knew the markers had gone off, as they were set to do as soon as the security guard tried to do a sweep with the surveillance equipment. He figured he had anything up to fifteen minutes, but possibly less than ten, depending on how good the guard was. He decided he had to aim for the lower end of the estimate. He tried not to vent his frustration at being unable to access the files. He appeared to be standing in front of a door, an old-fashioned one that opened manually and swung into the room. He was used to these rooms, as they were commonly encountered in his line of work. Unfortunately, this one wouldn't open, and he was well aware that his lockpicking skills were redundant here. The sign on the door read:

**ESPIONAGE DIVISION (PERSONNEL FILES)
STRICTLY NO UNAUTHORISED ADMITTANCE
THIS MEANS YOU TOO, COMMANDER ANGEL!**

In a way, he was flattered that they'd thought to single him out, but it also meant they were expecting him to try. But placing a locked door in front of a thief was like putting honey before a bear. There was no chance it was going to be ignored. Especially if you tell the bear not to eat the honey.

"Commander," Stone's voice cut through his activity. "Someone's just done a sonic scan of the chamber. They know you're in there."

"Acknowledged," he said.

There had to be some other way. Think laterally, he told himself. And there was.

He stood in the hospital lobby on New Transylvania. Grinning to himself, he looked for the filing department. A sign helpfully pointed him in the right direction. Walking towards the door as if he belonged there, he congratulated himself on his own cleverness. The door swushed open and he walked straight in. The filing cabinets were also old-fashioned. He wondered if the new commandant of Espionage was a history buff, or simply lacked imagination. He wondered what this place would like if he was actually there, and not in a cyberspace representation of it. He searched for the correct cabinet, and found it labelled "Births, 2478: T-Z". He pulled open the drawer and began rummaging for Veçescu.

He found the card he was looking for. Veçescu, Daniel. But it was blank. He cursed. Had they thought of everything?

"Commander, the guard's on his way," Stone warned him.

"Ok, I won't be long."

He closed his eyes, thought about what his next option should be. There was a sister. That's what Gabriel had told him. But what was her name? And was she older or younger? And by how much? This was impossible. He needed a central system that could tell him what year any named child was born. So when he opened his eyes, he was standing in front of a filing cabinet labelled. "All Births".

He pulled open the drawer labelled T-Z, wondering if everything in here was labelled the same way. There was the card. Veçescu, Maria, born 7 May 2482. Perfect. He looked round for the 2482 cabinet. There it was. Again finding the T-Z drawer, he found her card.

"Commander, he's almost there, do you want me to get you out?" Stone sounded frantic.

"Not yet," he told her, trying to remain calm as he read the details on the card. Parents' names, Daniel and Maria, home address, inconsequential, important details concerning the birth.

He almost dropped the card in shock. Then he read it twice more to make sure he'd understood what he had seen.

"Oh, you must be kidding me," he whispered, as everything fell into place.

***

Paranteau entered the chamber. Station 3's cowl was still in place. He crept as quietly as he could towards the intruder. He couldn't see him, but he knew he was there. A swift chop to the groin would cause immense pain and also disorient him as he was pulled forcibly back into the real world. Paranteau prepared his chop, and delivered it with stunning force. He fell straight through the gap between cowl and seat. Then the invisible fist connected with his temple and he fell to the floor. He rolled with the punch, coming back up and letting his vision settle from the impact. That took a few seconds, but he still had his sidearm and tracker. The intruder was only just out in the corridor, but making good time. Paranteau leapt to his feet again and began his pursuit.

When he reached the corridor, the signal broke into six separate lines. Whoever it was, he was *very* good. But Paranteau only lost a few seconds deciphering them. Only one was still moving. He followed it. The intruder was entering the lower levels, presumably trying to lose him in the service conduits. Well, let him try, Paranteau grinned to himself. Then, as the intruder got to the lowest part of the building, the signal stopped moving. Trapped, he realised. Paranteau picked up the pace. With luck, he'd catch him before he could retrace his steps. He was in a small room with only one exit. When he reached the room, the tracker said the intruder was still inside. Something wasn't right about that. He approached the room with caution and dropped into a defensive stance. As the door opened, he let off a volley of shots that covered every angle. Anyone in there should have been dropped by at least one of the shots. Then he saw the marker lying in the corner and knew he'd been tricked.

An unseen foot connected with his arm, knocking him over, making him drop his sidearm. Quickly regaining it, he swung in the direction of the retreating footsteps and fired off another shot. A cry of muted pain was accompanied by an electronic crackling sound as the stealth circuits fused and lost power. A man, now clutching the wound in his side, was suddenly visible. The man was staggering slowly up the corridor, aware of his plight. Paranteau stood and followed at nothing more than a leisurely walking pace, as it was obvious the intruder wasn't going to outrun him.

Then the intruder did a strange thing. Knowing he was effectively trapping himself, he went through another door, into a similar small room. Paranteau followed. The intruder was desperately trying to whisper and shout at the same time. "Get me out of here, Control. Please! Now would be good!"

Then he looked up and saw Paranteau in the doorway. And he realised he was lost. Paranteau smiled at him, and pulled the trigger, shooting the intruder's legs out from under him.

He scanned the intruder with his tracker and waited for it to identify him. As it did so, a smile spread across his face. The intruder, gasping hoarsely with pain, squeezed his eyes shut in defeat.

"Well, well," Paranteau crouched, cruel satisfaction edging into his voice. "Welcome home, Commander Angel."

40

The others crowded round the sickbay bed. Moonchild studied them all as they looked at the man they thought was Magpie.

"Bloody hell, boss," Goldfish said, but that was the only comment any of them made.

"I have a theory," Moonchild began. "I'm having a day full of theories, and this is one of them. Whenever Magpie has been injured in some way, assuming his injuries aren't too serious, his DNA has certain sequences which trigger a healing process. We've seen this in the goblins, and their DNA is identical. Here's the theory: actual medical attention interferes with the body's natural healing, which is why one clone, our Magpie, can have so much trouble with his broken legs, while another clone, identical in every way, can be killed and get up again within twenty four hours. Now, to test this theory, we're going to observe this sack of dirt here until he regenerates the damage I've done to him."

They all stared at the corpse on the bed.

"Now, observe," she said, taking a medical scanner and waving it across the bed. "This readout says he's dead." They all looked at the readout and confirmed that he was, as they all knew anyway, dead. "If my theory is correct, it won't be long before he's demanding to be fed."

"Who will be observing him?" R'sulek-Entah asked.

"All of us, in shifts. There'll be medical staff on hand at all times, but we take main responsibility for this."

"If this is true," Goldfish mused "then is it possible Magpie might be alive?"

Moonchild was quiet as she mulled the words over. "I've asked myself that question a few times since I realised what he was. I can hope Magpie is ok, but I can't allow myself to think too much about that. None of us can. Until we get back and see him, Magpie is..."
She couldn't get the word out, and the others understood.

***

They found Paranteau sitting smugly in his seat. When the chief retracted the cowl, the security guard was suddenly wrenched from his desk and found himself back in the computer chamber.
"Having fun, are we?" the chief asked, humourlessly.
That was the point at which Paranteau realised the truth.
"Sir, it was Commander Angel, he was here last night. He accessed the computer."
"I doubt that, Paranteau," the chief sighed. "We've covered all our tracks. If Angel had accessed anything, we'd have known about it. But he couldn't have, because he's been dead a day and a half already!"
The chief's voice rose steadily into a high pitched crescendo until it threatened to do physical damage to the hapless Paranteau. For his part, Paranteau sat meekly and accepted the tirade, his mind beginning to concentrate on where he might find gainful employment, because his prospects here were looking bleak.
The chief, meanwhile, was accessing the records for last night's computer activity. "Oh, Paranteau, whoever it was, he really did lead you a merry dance, didn't he? And you fell for it all. And look, all the time you thought you were chasing him through the bowels of the complex, he was sitting beside you, with free access to the computer. How

stupid can you be, man? Anyway," he turned to one of his colleagues, and indicated the record. "It seems that our mystery visitor was trying to get into the restricted areas, but didn't manage it. It can't have been Angel, but it must have been someone with a connection to S.T.A.R.T., because of the nature of his enquiry. Look, he's been trying to get at Veçescu's file."

"Did he get in?" the colleague asked.

"No, look. The locks are still in place. What else was he looking at? Oh, no. Oh, that's very bad. I think we might have overlooked something."

"What?"

"The sister."

The two of them looked at each other, their faces mirroring each other's growing horror. They'd been exposed. And at such a critical time. They both hurried from the chamber, leaving Paranteau to sit and wonder what the problem was.

***

Creepshow watched the aura around the prisoner and wondered about it. Was this some inherent skill he possessed, the ability to see someone from an alternate timeline? Maybe it was, maybe it wasn't. He really couldn't care less. Although it provided him with some thoughtful contemplation, in the end it made no difference. The mission was everything. It was too late to start thinking of what else he was capable of.

"What do you think?"

He jumped, startled by Moonchild's voice. That was careless, he chided himself. He turned to face the woman who believed she was his commanding officer.

"About what, ma'am?"
"About him? You've been staring at him for several minutes now. Are you expecting something to happen?"
"You said yourself, he's coming back."
"I said I thought he might, but not for a while yet. Is he spooking you?"
Creepshow shook his head, irritated by her line of questioning. "No, ma'am. I'm just studying my enemy."
"*Our* enemy," she corrected.
"Of course. That's what I meant."
She nodded. There was a silence.
"Have you been there long?" he finally asked.
"Long enough to notice how you were staring, but no, not long."
He didn't respond.
"What are you thinking?" she said suddenly.
"I'm wondering what he'll feel when he goes out the airlock," he didn't hesitate. "I'm wondering if, once he's dead, his body'll regenerate the damage and he'll come back to life to find himself floating in a vacuum. I'm wondering how many times he'll go through that before he stops coming back."
"Is that your medical interest taking over?"
"No, ma'am," he turned his dark eyes on her. "I'm just enjoying the idea."
She held his gaze without flinching. "What did the Balsari do to you? What is it that drives you to this level of hate?"
"With all due respect, ma'am, that's personal." He looked away.
"I understand. But I'd like to know anyway. I don't want the mission compromising, or even screwing up completely, because someone on my team is so blinded by total hatred of the Balsari that he can't remain focussed.

This mission depends on professional objectivity from everyone."

"The mission will succeed," he answered, with a quiet fervour that made her wonder.

"Whose mission, Creepshow? Yours or mine?"

He looked at her again. There seemed to be a slight smile playing on his lips, but she couldn't be sure.

"I'm a loyal servant of the Empire," he told her. "And I obey my Emperor without question."

Moonchild nodded as if his response was the one she was waiting for. In a way, it was.

41

Magpie went back to Stone. "Lieutenant, I need some more help," he said, as he breezed into Control.
Stone, he noted, was looking tired, shadows just starting to appear under her eyes. She looked like she'd just pulled a very long shift and was near the end of it. This was, of course, because she had, and he was aware of it, largely because he'd requested it in the first place.
"I'll do my best, sir," she tried very hard to keep the weariness from her voice.
"Thank you, Lieutenant," he smiled, encouragingly, genuinely grateful. "I need you to help me find someone. Her name is Maria Veçescu."
"That name's familiar, sir," she commented, dryly. "You're going to tell me there's a connection next, aren't you?"
"Very astute, Lieutenant," he enthused. "Yes, she's his sister. Can you find her? She was born 7 May 2482 on New Transylvania, but where she went after her parents died, I don't know. That was sometime back in '89. I'm afraid there's not much else I give you."
"Don't worry, sir, I should be able to work with that," Stone assured him.
She began manipulating the temporal scanner. Magpie watched for a few minutes.
"It might take a while, sir," she warned him.
"Oh. Right. Well, why don't you call me when you find something?"
"Right, sir," she acknowledged, and turned back to her work.

Magpie left and went to find something to eat. He hadn't even got halfway into his meal when the call came through.

"Stone to Commander Angel."

His first reply was muffled by the mouthful of food, but after the second acknowledgement, Stone had called him back to Control.

"She's actually left New Transylvania," she told him as he entered the chamber.

"Where is she?"

"Irwin City, Luna."

"Really? That close? Excellent. Tell me, have you ever considered a field assignment?"

"What? Me? A field assignment?" She laughed at the notion. "Sir, I'm strictly a number cruncher. I'm better here keeping an eye on the real field operatives."

"Maybe so, but you have a unique position within S.T.A.R.T.," Magpie persisted. "And I think that might just sway her if need be."

***

Goldfish contemplated his position. The Balsari agent in their custody had given him the holodisc of Sarah, claiming it was genuine. Magpie, the real Magpie, had declared it to be a fake. But the prisoner himself had insisted he had switched sides because of a similar holodisc he'd been given, one which he claimed was genuine. This led Goldfish to a quandary of sorts. Who did he believe? Who did he want to believe? Was it possible, now he'd finally found some peace, that she was alive? The idea brought him to some more very difficult questions. If she was, what was her outlook on life? Was she now a Balsari agent? Or was she looking for an opportunity to get off their accursed planet, back to Earth? Back to him? How much time had passed for her? Was she taken to a contemporary Balsar, or was the holovid presented to him as soon as it was produced?

He lay back on his bunk. Too many damned questions. And he'd just began accepting that she really was dead, all over again. The real question was which of the two did he trust? The traitor, or the man he'd called his friend all this time?

The more he thought about it, the less he liked the answer.

He left his cabin and made his way to sickbay. Moonchild was there. She looked up as he came in.

"Hey, Goldfish," she greeted him. "What's on your mind?"

"Is it that obvious?" he snorted, upset that he must be broadcasting his troubles.

"It is to me, hon. Come on in, tell me about it."

She waved him into the seat opposite. He sat and stared at the corpse for a while before speaking.

"I've been thinking about Sarah," he said, his voice little more than a whisper.

Moonchild decided the best thing she could do was let him talk, and say nothing until an opinion was sought.

"I can't help wondering if Magpie was wrong about the holodisc. Or if he was trying to keep me from learning the truth. That Sarah's on their side now. I don't know what to believe."

She didn't speak. What could she say? She had her doubts as well. And when she'd challenged Magpie over it, his answer was so ambiguous, it wasn't really an answer at all. In fact, she was veering towards the holodisc being

genuine, based largely on Magpie's not-quite-an-answer. If he'd just said to her, yes, it's a fake, she'd have been satisfied. But he hadn't said one way or the other. She knew he'd never lied to her before, and he'd probably said that because he couldn't bring himself to actually lie then. So she just watched as Goldfish agonised over it, knowing she couldn't help him, because she knew they shared the same doubts. And now, she knew, he was struggling to find peace because if she really was alive, he was going to the place where she was and he was going to be instrumental in its eventual defeat. In a way, he was actually desperate to find out she really had been dead six years.
"How do I go on with the mission?" he said, eventually. "Knowing she might be there?"
Now he'd asked a question. Now, she was free to speak. "You go on with the mission because completing the mission is what's in your heart," she reached over the bed and squeezed his hand. "And I promise you, if she's somehow alive, and on Balsar, we'll find her and get her out. Ok? I promise you that."
She looked intently into his eyes. He finally met her gaze and whatever he saw there must have reassured him. He nodded.
"Thanks, boss," he said, a little life returning to his haunted eyes.
She let go of his hand, but maintained the eye contact. "Good man. Now, your shift's about to start, so you may as well stay here, ok? But if you need to talk to me again about this, you know where I am, right?"
She kept looking at him until he smiled and nodded. She nodded back, satisfied that he was ok, then she left. And as she went back to her cabin, she wondered how she

would ever find out if Sarah was on Balsar and, more importantly, how she was going to be able to keep her promise if she found that to be the case.

***

Irwin City was named for the eighth man to set foot on the moon. Back in the twentieth century, when this had happened, this place was a barren dustbowl, sitting in the shadow of Mount Bradley. Now, it was a sprawling metropolis that spread across the Palus Putredinis, the huge dome that stretched above it providing artificial sunlight, even its own weather system. It was home to several million people, not all of whom were human, remotely or otherwise. Had James Irwin been alive nearly five and a half centuries after he had stood on this very spot, he would have wondered if someone were playing a trick on him. The city looked, to the casual observer, like any city on Earth, only the slight sheen of the dome spoiled the effect, and even then you had to know it was there, and be looking for it.

Magpie and Stone stepped off the shuttle into the shuttleport. Magpie looked for the check-in desk, while Stone took in the surroundings.

"Never been on the moon before?" Magpie asked, noticing her childlike attention to everything she saw.

"No, sir," she admitted. "How about you?"

"Mmm," he answered absently. "A long time ago, fairly recently."

She processed that statement for a moment before she realised what he meant, then continued her survey of the shuttleport. Magpie checked them in at arrivals, and then hailed a taxi to take them to their destination.

"She should be at home by the time we get there," he told her, but she wasn't really listening.

She was staring out of the window at the variety of people and buildings that they passed.

"Lieutenant," he whispered, gently, bringing her back to his world.

"Sorry, sir," she apologised, her cheeks turning a deeper shade of green.

"That's ok," he smiled, disarmingly. "I remember the first time I went exploring Olympus City. I was only four blocks from where I was staying, but I'd never been so far from my home turf. I just lost myself looking at all the buildings and people. The gang were sent to look for me." He leaned closer, his voice taking on a conspiratorial tone. "I took a real kicking when they brought me back."

"It must have been hard being homeless," Stone sympathised. "Especially so young."

Magpie shrugged, but she could see the memory still hurt. "It was all I ever knew. Same with Moonchild. We had nothing to compare it with, so we thought it was normal. What hurt most was when she enlisted and I was alone. But I managed. Someone told me recently, you don't miss what you never had." He frowned, remembering. "But he had it in abundance, and he was lying. Anyway, that's history. I think the moral of the story is you should get out more."

"Yes, sir," Stone said, as if she would treat it like an order.

The taxi stopped outside the apartment block. They got out and headed for the main entrance. Once the DNA analysis had been processed and they'd been registered and cleared for entry, they took the lift to the ninety eighth floor. They found the door labelled with Maria's name and waited for the door to announce their presence to the occupant. After a moment, the door slid open and a young woman, about Stone's age, looked out at them.

"Can I help you?" she asked.

"Maria Veçescu?" the man asked, but didn't wait for confirmation. "My name is William Angel, this is my associate, Kahrena Stone. We're from the Office of Ethnic Studies. May we take a moment of your time, please?"

The woman looked frightened for a moment. But she nevertheless stepped aside and let them in. The pair smiled at her as they entered her apartment, and she decided his smile was more practiced than hers. She seemed uncomfortable being there, while he seemed to be in his element.

"The Office of Ethnic Studies?" she said, uncertainly. "Am I in trouble?"

"Not at all," the man answered, with a shake of the head and a smile that seemed to put her at ease. "No, no, no, we're simply getting round to calling on all the citizens of Irwin City who've recently come from other colonies. We're especially interested in citizens of mixed species origin."

She felt her pulse increasing and her throat seemed to tick in time with her heartbeat. "Mixed species origin?"

"Yes," the man smiled his charming smile. "It's actually my favourite subject, I've made a study of all the different races that can interbreed without medical intervention, and it's surprising what you learn. Take Kahrena here. As you can see, she's of human and Vihansu descent. There's recently been a case a multiple birth between a human and an Arajak. It seems there's no end of species humans will mate with. But please forgive me, I'm sure you already know this. Right now, we're very interested in following up on a few unconfirmed rumours of children being born to human fathers and Oriveen dwarftroll mothers."

He laughed slightly, not in an offensive way, but in an easy, friendly way. She found herself laughing with him. Which was when he hit her with the sucker punch.

"Of course, you and your brother are the only known cases of successful mating between humans and Balsari."

Her fear was quite apparent. "What do you want with me?"

The man turned to the woman. Maria thought she was very pretty, her green skin tones accentuating her youthful beauty, as she raised her catlike eyes to her own. "Please Ms Veçescu, we're not trying to trap you, we're just carrying out our survey. My grandparents met and married while the Empire was still at war with Vihan. We know how difficult it can be to be descended from people who are considered the enemy, believe me, but we aren't trying to get a confession from you. Your birth details are on record, that's how we found you. If we wanted to cause you trouble, we wouldn't have come here, we'd have sent Imperial Security instead."

Maria looked from Stone to Angel. Both smiled sweetly at her.

"We only have a few questions," Angel prompted. "And then we'll be out of your way. Please?"

"Ok," she finally relaxed. "Come and sit down."

They sat in the chairs she indicated.

"Ask away," she told them.

"Thank you," Angel seemed genuinely glad that she'd eased up. "We know that you and... Daniel, is it?"

"Yes, Daniel."

"Right, Daniel. We know you were originally from New Transylvania, but you've been here on Luna since last year, is that right?"
"Yes, August, I arrived."
"And your brother?"
It was an innocent sounding question, and Maria fell for it. "Oh, no, he's in the Imperial Navy."
"Really?" Angel's face lit up with interest. "You must be very proud of him. What does he do?"
"I don't really have a lot of contact with him," she confessed. "In fact, I haven't had any contact with him for a long time. I assume he's found an outlet for his medical expertise, but I wouldn't really know."
"He's a doctor?" Stone interjected, settling into her role.
"Not really, he studied pathology on New Transylvania, then the Marquis took him in and I haven't seen him since."
"Fascinating," Angel told her. "Now, what about you? Tell us a bit about yourself."

***

When they left, they didn't say anything. They were in the taxi before either of them spoke.
"What did you make of that?" Magpie asked.
"You mean the pathology thing?" Stone clarified.
"Yes."
"I'm not sure. How does a pathologist wind up getting assigned to S.T.A.R.T. as Tactical Support? It doesn't make sense."
Magpie sat for a few moments, silently wrapped up in his own thoughts.

"Yes it does," he said suddenly, startling her. "Oh, crap. It makes perfect sense."

"You've lost me, sir," Stone admitted.

He looked straight at her. "Think about it. An expert on diseases and how they work, with a psychotic hatred of the Balsari, gets assigned to S.T.A.R.T., who then get assigned to attack Balsar. This is not a S.T.A.R.T. mission, but they got assigned anyway. Why? Because of orders from above."

"Sir, you're saying…"

"That's right, Stone, I'm saying Creepshow's a time bomb. He's somehow developed a pathogen and he plans to release it once he's on Balsar. He's nothing more than a galactic terrorist."

"But, sir, the order to attack Balsar came from the Emperor himself," Stone protested.

Magpie's eyes seemed to go dark as a shadow crossed his face. "I know," he said. "Frightening, isn't it?"

42

The captain of the stealth ship reported directly to Moonchild's quarters.
"We've arrived in orbit, Colonel," he told her.
"Thank you, Captain," she rose from her bunk. "Any indication they know we're here?"
"None. They're carrying on as normal. They seem to be aware of significant fleet movements, but they're putting that down to bravado on our part. They don't realise we're about to hit them with the same fleet."
"Ok, thanks. I'm going to speak to my people and I'll want to be on the surface in fifteen minutes. Please have the defensive grid located and analysed for an insertion."
"I'll get onto it," the captain nodded. "Good luck."
He left her to get ready. She waited a few minutes then contacted the others.

***

Within a minute, they were all gathered at the shuttle.
"When we set down, I want Gunboy and Creepshow deployed in standard watch pattern. R'sulek-Entah and Goldfish will work on bringing the defensive grid down. I'll be piloting us there and back again. Any questions?"
No-one had any. "Let's go, people."
As they entered the shuttle, Moonchild's private communicator sounded.
"Colonel Washington, this is Doctor Ratcliffe, you wanted to be informed if the prisoner regained consciousness."

"Ah, thank you, Doctor," she said. "I'm on my way. Wait here for me, I'll be a few minutes," she told the others, and left for sickbay.

***

He wasn't looking good, but that was no great surprise. She stared with what she hoped was a dispassionate expression, but she knew he could probably see her sneer. "Tell me," he whispered, his voice a ragged echo of Magpie's. "What do you know about Veçescu?"
She smiled her sarcasm. "If you mean have I figured out he's not really on my team, yes I have. I don't need you to point that out. Was there anything of use to me that you wanted to say?"
"Do you know what he is?" he croaked.
"Do I care? His agenda is different to mine, that makes him my enemy. But hearing it from you doesn't make you my friend. It just means I've got two enemies."
"He's Balsari."
Moonchild considered this revelation. "Big deal," she dismissed it.
"You don't know why I was sent to kill him, do you?"
"I bet it's something to do with him being Balsari but hating them all, hasn't it?"
"Listen very carefully to me," the prisoner suddenly sounded as if everything depended on his ability to say the next few words. "If you let him get on the planet's surface, the Balsari are doomed."
"They're doomed anyway."
"No, I mean it. Every Balsari man, woman and child will be endangered."

"War is hell, you know that. Was that all?" She began to turn away.

"Think about it, please, I beg you." He was becoming more desperate as he sensed he was losing her attention. "It's not about war, it's about hatred, all-consuming racial hatred. It has nothing to do with the war. We're not dealing with soldiers in battle, we're dealing with genocidal maniacs. Veçescu has the power to wipe the Balsari from existence, single-handedly. Please, I know you don't care about the Balsari, and you don't care about me, but you always had compassion. There are millions of innocent children on Balsar and he is going to kill them too."

"How is he going to kill them?" Despite herself, she felt compelled to hear him out.

"He's a pathologist. He's carrying a virus within his own system. Once on the planet's surface, he'll release it into the atmosphere. Eventually, if it goes unchecked, every person with Balsari genes will be exposed and contract the virus. It'll kill Veçescu, for sure, but he considers that a fair price for the betrayal he feels at the Balsari's hands."

"Do you expect me to believe this?" she tested him, but her mind was pretty much already made up.

"You have no reason to trust me, but you are still my only hope. I have friends on Balsar. I'm a soldier, I know the risks of war, and I always accepted that if Balsar lost, our future would be determined by the Empire. But if Veçescu succeeds, Balsar will have no future. Please!"

She considered him as he lay on his bed pleading with her. Without a word, she left him there. She knew what she had to do, but she wasn't going to give him the satisfaction of thinking he'd reached her.

***

When she reappeared in the shuttlebay, it was with two armed guards to arrest Creepshow.

They led him away without protest. A few minutes later, as she was explaining it all to the others, one of the guards came back.

"With all due respect, ma'am, I was wondering if you needed a replacement," he offered. "I'm also rated as a pilot, so I can pretty much do anything you need. My name's Fulton, by the way."

"You understand the nature of the mission, Fulton?" Moonchild asked him.

"Yes, ma'am. I cleared it with the captain, he said if you could use me, I was free to go."

"Welcome aboard, Fulton," she answered, and ushered him onto the shuttle. "You can take the co-pilot's seat."

With a full crew, they departed, in stealth mode, their target locked. Moonchild quickly briefed Fulton on the plan, giving him Creepshow's job.

Silent and lethal, the shuttle pierced the defensive grid using technology they could only guess at, although they had a fair idea where it came from, and set down close enough to the control centre to cover the ground quickly on foot. Espionage Division had obviously done its research.

"Remember, folks," Moonchild said. "As soon as the hatch opens, they'll know we're here. Stealth suits activated, everyone."

The members of the crew began fading from view as the suits were enabled one by one. Then their own scanners kicked in and they could see each other with perfect clarity. Then the hatch opened for the briefest of periods and they dashed out to put as much ground between themselves and the shuttle as they could. When Moonchild turned round, they were all there except Fulton. He was hanging back by the now concealed shuttle, actually removing his stealth suit.

"What the hell are you doing, Fulton?" she screamed into her communicator. But when he turned to face her, she saw his face melting and reforming into the unmistakeable features of Creepshow.

"Thank you, Colonel," he laughed. "You've done the Empire a great service today."

43

Balsar Military Command, 2507

Moonchild had already drawn her pistol when she saw what was happening. As soon as Creepshow had finished his victory speech, she drilled him in the chest with a shot set to light disrupt. Still laughing as his chest exploded in red blossom, Creepshow fell backwards.

She rushed to where he'd fallen. He was still smiling when she reached him, although it was a rictus-like grin of something consisting of equal measures of ecstasy and agony. He watched her through half closed eyes. His breath bubbled from his mouth in bloody gasps, the blood not quite human red, not quite Balsari orange.

"Don't be upset," he gurgled at her. "Today our names will go down in history as the people who defeated the Balsari once and for all."

"Yours won't, you evil bastard," she spat. "You'll be reviled forever for the sick monster you are."

He chuckled, an ugly sound that was almost a death rattle. She denied him that pleasure, blowing a hole in his face on the highest setting she could get to without looking.

She turned to the others who were all looking right at her. "What?" she challenged.

"I believe the correct response is 'he had it coming'," R'sulek-Entah said after a while.

"Not soon enough, I'm afraid," Moonchild replied. "He's just released a pathogen into the atmosphere that could kill every Balsari on the planet. What we do next is largely academic, our mission was always just an excuse to get

him here. So the question now is do we continue with the mission, or do we abort and go back? Or do we try and warn the Balsari about this?"
Everyone looked at each other.
Goldfish spoke first. "I need access to a scanner, boss."
She understood. "Ok, so we go back to the ship."
As everyone resigned themselves to the new course of action, they heard the whine of a Balsari atmospheric craft approaching. Their initial response was to look for cover, but then they all realised they were invisible to most forms of detection and stood their ground. They watched as the odd-looking craft came to a halt above where they'd left their shuttle. Then a bolt of some kind of energy hit the ground, ripping up a great chunk of the paved area they'd landed on. The craft hovered a moment longer, then moved away, returning to where it had come from.
They stood for a long time, absorbing what had happened.
"That settles that then," Gunboy said. "We're trapped here now."

***

The scanning equipment that S.T.A.R.T. used was, by its very nature, far more sophisticated than anything the regular military possessed. From their base on Earth, Lieutenant Stone was able to spot the anomaly when it appeared on Balsar.
"Commander?" she called to Magpie. "The stealth shuttle just registered. They opened the hatch briefly."
"Good work, Lieutenant," Magpie hurried over.
"I only had it for a few seconds, but I've locked onto the coordinates. Do you want me to insert you there?"

"Yes, put me right into the shuttle. If we saw it, it's a certainty the Balsari saw it. If I can get in and move it before they come and investigate, it should give us a few more options. Can you get me through the defensive grid?"
"Not exactly, sir, but I've thought of that. I can insert you into the exact spot, but before they invented the grid. Then I just piggy back a secondary signal and move you forward in time."
"That's brilliant, Stone, how did you come up with that?"
"Oh, I just followed your example, sir," she deadpanned. "It sounds good if you say it fast enough and with enough conviction to stop the victim thinking too hard about the science of it."
Magpie's grin froze. "It'll work, though?"
"To be honest, I really have just come up with the idea. You'll be a kind of guinea pig. Do you want to risk it?"
He thought about it. About what would happen if it didn't work. And about what would happen if he didn't at least try it.
"I'm in your hands, Lieutenant," he said.
Stone grimaced, but turned it into a smile for his benefit. Then she began manipulating her control panel and he felt the familiar pull of the teleporter as it thrust him through time and space towards Balsar. When his vision cleared, he was standing in what seemed to be some kind of primeval jungle.
"Bloody hell, Stone, how far back did they invent this grid?" he asked, not really expecting an answer.
Then with an unexpected wrench, he was yanked forwards and, this time, found himself standing in an operational imperial shuttle. Quickly checking its status, he settled himself in the pilot's seat and silently took off,

landing at the other side of the complex which, he assumed, was where the defensive grid was situated. He watched as the Balsari craft arrived and realised he'd found a way out of the shuttle. Timing the opening and closing of the hatch, he waited for the Balsari to deploy their weapon. If it showed at all on any scanners, they would probably read it as an echo from the blast.

Congratulating himself on his cleverness, he emerged from the shuttle and began looking for his comrades. Which was when he realised he'd never see them if they were wearing stealth suits. Oh, well, he'd just have to find the powerhouse and let them come to him.

He found the right building on his first attempt. Again patting himself on the back, while realising it was nothing but pure luck that had brought him here, he began his descent into the depths of possibly the most sophisticated machine in the known galaxy.

As far as anyone could ascertain from the Espionage Division, and he'd contributed much of the known information himself in his earlier incarnation as a spy, the defensive grid operated as a temporal barrier which prevented temporally inert material penetrating it. This included vessels, weapons, space dust, anything at all that didn't shift into temporal phase. He had been transferred out from Espionage to S.T.A.R.T. before he learned what had been made of his discoveries. At first he'd thought it had been this very information that had brought him to the attention of the chiefs of the new project, but then he'd found out the field commander had already specified whom she wanted for her second in command. So he'd been reunited with his best friend and found that nepotism wasn't such a bad thing after all.

Although it was the first time he'd set foot on Balsar, and therefore the first time he'd been anywhere near this building, he'd made himself familiar with the original layout when he'd borrowed the blueprints for a quick photo opportunity on the moon of a Balsari colony world. Now he was wondering if he could remember that far back, and even if his memory was reliable, had the layout remained unaltered?

What he needed was someone he could ask, although he figured the predominantly orange tinge the Balsari had to their skin in their normal form would be so obviously missing from his own complexion that he really needed a blind Balsari. The chances of that occurring here, he conceded, were minimal, so he settled for keeping to the shadows and finding his own way.

As it was, the first person he saw was human. She appeared in the corridor as he was halfway down it, and he knew immediately the game was up. But even as he reached for his weapon, recognition dawned.

"Elise?" he said.

"Will!" she cried, and ran to meet him.

She swept him into a fierce hug. "Oh, Will, I thought you were dead."

"Ah, yes, well I can explain that, you see..."

She cut him off as she kissed him with such a passion he nearly passed out. He pulled away slightly, to her consternation.

"Elise... you've changed your hair."

"What?"

They both realised the truth at the same time. He was quicker. He put one hand over her mouth and hauled her to the floor.

"Don't make a sound, don't make me kill you, because I will if I have to. The situation's changed, Elise. Your Will and my Elise are both here, and we all have the same problem. This planet has been infected with a pathogen that's going to kill every living thing with Balsari DNA. This has gone beyond petty parochial disputes between the Empire and Balsar. I'm trying to prevent genocide, and I can't do that if you're going to give me away. So you need to get me to someone with enough authority to listen to me and do something about it. Do you understand me?"
She nodded, wide eyed.

***

Moonchild led them into the nearest building. They rested for a few minutes while they assessed their new circumstances.
"We have to make a decision," she told them. "We have to decide if we're going to try and stop the pathogen wiping out the Balsari, or if we're going to stay hidden until it's all over. I, for one am going to try and stop it. I will not think badly of anyone who feels they can't do that, nor will I give them away to the Balsari. All I ask is that you don't try and stop me. Please will you all indicate which course of action you intend to take?"
"I don't see how there's much of a choice," Gunboy sighed. "As soldiers we're trained to fight an enemy. Right now, the enemy is the pathogen. To hide from it is cowardice. I'm with you."
R'sulek-Entah moved to stand with him. "Aside from any ethical debate, I have been assigned to the team and my future is with the team. However long that future may be.

My duty is clear. Besides, I cannot stand by and watch an entire species die like this, either."

Goldfish stood a moment, thinking. "I have an ulterior motive, you know that, boss," he said. "But let's be clear about this. My first duty right now is also to the team, whatever else happens."

"You're all good people," Moonchild said. "But be under no illusions about this decision. Whatever happened before with Magpie, when we were just talking about it, this is not ambiguous in any way. The Emperor himself ordered this pathogen. What we do from this point on *is* treason, and we have no future in the Empire. Last chance to back out."

"With respect, ma'am," Gunboy said, gently. "We're wasting time."

"You're all good people," she repeated. "Ok, let's do it properly, stealth suits off. We need to be seen."

***

They moved out into the open. Unbelievably, having now done everything they could to get themselves noticed, it seemed no-one was about to see them. So they found another building and entered, making no attempt to mask the sound of their presence. Even then, no-one came running to arrest them. Finally, they ran into a lone guard who immediately flung himself at the mercy of the superior force.

"No, you don't understand," Moonchild insisted. "We surrender."

It was clear her grasp of the Balsari tongue was loose at best, and the guard seemed to have difficulty understanding why they were still insisting he surrendered when he so obviously had. In frustration, Moonchild turned to R'sulek-Entah. The Arajak stepped forward and explained their odd position in flawless Balsari. The guard looked doubtful, but the fact that he wasn't being threatened seemed to go some way to convincing him. In the end, he insisted on taking out his sidearm and taking them at gunpoint to see the commandant. They complied, letting the bewildered guard have his moment of glory.

As they were herded into the command chamber, they saw the most bizarre sight. Another Moonchild and Magpie were already there, talking earnestly with the commandant. Moonchild drew alongside Magpie. He glanced at her, did a double take, and smiled.

"How the hell did you get off the ship?" she hissed.

"I was never on it," he whispered. "Hello Elise."

Before she could say anything, the commandant barked something, to which the guard made some form of proud reply.

"So," the commandant said, in passable Terran Standard. "One guard single-handedly captures the entire Space-Time Axial Response Team? How very skilful. And are you coming to me with the same tale of a plague that is about to destroy my world?"

"I'm afraid so, sir," Moonchild answered, not entirely certain how to address the commandant, or even if his rank was above or below her own. On the face of it, she decided diplomacy was the way forward until she discovered otherwise.

"And why do the Terran Empire's elite warriors come to me now, on the eve of my destruction, and offer to help me fight this plague?" the commandant sounded scornful.

"That's exactly what we've been asking ourselves," Moonchild told him. "And you've answered the question yourself. Because we're warriors, not cowards. So. Do you want our help or not?"

"I require more proof than the word of my enemies," he snorted.

"Then you'll have it," she replied, taking out her communicator. "Colonel Washington to *Imperial Hammer*. Please send the prisoner to these coordinates."

There was no response, but she wasn't expecting one. However, within a minute, the prisoner was in their midst, the very fact he'd traversed the defensive grid proof that he was temporally out of phase with the rest of the universe. He seemed shocked to be there, but when he saw 'his' Elise, he went to her and held her like they were lovers. Which, Moonchild reflected, they were. Which made the wrench she felt now, in Magpie's presence, all the more painful.

The commandant, who was somehow able to tell that this was the same Magpie who'd sworn loyalty to him, spoke to him in the Balsari tongue. Magpie, who'd spoken Balsari since he'd studied languages in Espionage Division, spoke with passion and remorse, but she could only guess about what. It wouldn't surprise her if he was badmouthing her and arranging for her slow torture when this was all finished. She glanced at the other Magpie. To her surprise, he was looking at her, as if he'd never taken his eyes from her since he first saw her. Could it be possible that this really was her Magpie?

The commandant turned back to her and spoke in Terran Standard. "I have been told I should trust you. So this is what I choose to do. I will need your doctors from the stealth ship in orbit to assist. I have no wish for my doctors to die of plague and leave us without hope."

"I'll try and arrange it," Moonchild sounded doubtful.

"No," the commandant warned. "You *will* arrange it. The Empire has brought this on us, if the Empire does not reverse the damage, the reprisals will be more severe than you can contemplate."

44

They were left to wonder about the commandant's dark warning as they were shown to a large stateroom which was effectively a communal cell. Moonchild and Magpie found the closest thing to a quiet corner.

"What happened?" she whispered. "How come you're alive?"

His eyes clouded over. "Seraph," he said. "My DNA was wired to revive me, but I was too badly damaged to survive. Seraph could have, but he sacrificed himself for me."

"I'm sorry," she sympathised. "Michelangelo?"

"No, you sorted him out properly."

"How come you wound up here?"

"Long story, but essentially, I did a little digging in Espionage central computer and found the bit they missed. That led me to Creepshow's plan. I got here as quickly as I could."

"Pointless really, I'm afraid, we lost our shuttle, and with the ship practically held hostage in orbit, we're stuck here."

"No we're not, I sorted that out. The shuttle's safe."

"So, we can leave if we want?"

"Just say the word."

She sat quietly for a moment. "There's something I need to tell you, Will."

He looked at her, expectantly.

She took a deep breath. "But not right now," she backed down. "It'll wait."

She stood up and went to see how the others were doing. He watched her, his heart heavy with the disappointment. Maybe now really wasn't the best place. When he thought he was dying – when he *was* dying – he'd tried to say it, but she hadn't heard him. Now the moment had passed.

***

They were transferred to the central palace that night. The news seemed to be that the imperial fleet was gathering for its assault, but the defensive grid was still in place. S.T.A.R.T. had failed, but the *Imperial Hammer* was holding station. But when asked, the captain maintained he was waiting for contact from Colonel Washington. He never mentioned the fact that most of his medical staff was on Balsar. He was aware that if that came out, he would be executed for treason. He just had to sit tight and hope he wasn't ordered to return to Earth.

Then the Balsari began dying. First, there were a few deaths, isolated cases in the vicinity of the grid complex, then dotted all around the continent, as people who had travelled while incubating the pathogen succumbed to it. As dawn approached in the palace, the horrifying facts were becoming known. Within those few hours of Creepshow releasing the pathogen, ten percent of the planet's native population was dead. By the time dusk fell again on the palace, ten percent of the planet's native population remained alive. It had been indiscriminate in its killing. The victims were of all social classes, all nationalities, all ages, both genders. There was only one factor common to them all, and that was their Balsari blood.

And that was when the reprisals began. All over the Empire, responding to a signal sent from Balsar, the hidden genebanks began forcegrowing hordes of goblins. On thousands of imperial colonies, people were waking up to what was possibly going to be their final day.

When Moonchild first heard this, she went straight to Magpie. "We need to get out. Now."

Magpie nodded without comment and immediately produced his lockpicks and began working on the door. Within seconds, he had eased it open and peered out to find the guards slumped in the corridor outside. He beckoned to the others. Then, as they all hurried from the room, they ran straight into the alternate Magpie and Moonchild. For a moment there was a standoff, as each side weighed up the other. Then the alternate Magpie spoke.

"Please come with us," he said. "It's time to put aside our differences and work together."

With an obvious lack of trust, Moonchild glanced at the others and nodded, stepping forward. "This had better not be a trick," she told him. "You might come back to life, but she won't."

The alternates looked at each other, then back at her.

"This isn't a trick," she said.

They led them down into what looked like a classic dungeon. As it turned out, that was exactly what it was. The alternate Magpie took a specific route which his counterpart memorised in case it became necessary to backtrack. But eventually they stopped by a door. It looked no different to any other cell door, but they seemed to think it was significant. The alternates produced some form of electronic key which obviously unlocked the door.

As the door swung open, Elise said. "You can come out now."

The occupant groaned, a heartfelt weariness born of long confinement.

"Sarah?" Goldfish immediately reacted.

The woman in the cell came forward, squinting in the light. "James? James? Is it really… is this another trick?"

She shuffled forwards, and he saw her in the light. She was a bit older than he remembered, and her hair was dirty and matted and flecked with grey. He stared, hardly able to comprehend what the alternates had done. Then he stepped hesitantly towards her and reached a trembling hand to touch her face. She flinched, but let him touch her. It was like some kind of spell had been broken. As soon as he touched her, she fell into his arms and he gripped her tightly. They were both sobbing with all manner of emotions.

Moonchild was acutely aware of her surroundings. This couple had just been reunited after six years believing each other to be dead, or somehow unreachable, R'sulek-Entah and Gunboy stood behind her, clearly a lot closer than they'd been before, even the alternates were holding hands, proving they were in love. And beside her, a million miles away, was Will, poor Will who'd walk through fire for her, who'd rip his own heart out if she asked him to. Will, who was so close, but she was holding him so far away.

"You have to go, now," the alternate Magpie said. "Follow this corridor. It will take you out through the side of the hill. There is a shuttle waiting. Take it."

"What about you two?" Moonchild asked.

"We'll make the best of it here, if you'll let us," he said.

"There's nothing else for us, nowhere else we can go," Elise added.

"Please," he urged. "Just go. Your shuttle can pierce the grid. There's little point to shutting down the grid. There's nothing left worth protecting."

They all looked at each other. "Come on," Moonchild said quietly. She looked at the alternates one final time, and then she left them to find their own fate.

***

The journey back to Earth was much shorter than the outward trip, largely due to Moonchild requesting an emergency teleport back, once they were beyond the grid. Once they were back in Control, they reported the entire scenario to Admiral Saastemoinen and General N'Komo. The two of them listened in silent horror as Moonchild and her team revealed the full extent of the pathogen's progress. But they had no time to react before the news began filtering through that the first of the colonies were being overrun by goblins.

Moonchild immediately called for a scan of Earth, to locate the genebank she was convinced was hidden somewhere on the planet. The answer was paradoxically both shocking and predictable. Beneath the imperial palace.

"What do we do?" Magpie asked quietly, beside her.

"We've no choice, Will," she answered, as he knew she would. "We have to go and save the Emperor."

45

The Emperor's palace sat on top of a hill overlooking what used to be Salt Lake City in the old United States of America. Deep inside the palace, the Emperor surrounded himself with loyal advisors who did nothing but encourage his decisions, and agree that he was a genius for arriving at the astounding conclusions he did. If he said war, they all called for blood, if he said peace, they all rushed to find their olive branches. Either way, they congratulated his astuteness. When the Emperor had listened to the Marquis of New Transylvania tell him about the half-breed with the interest in diseases and the hatred of Balsari, he had agreed to put the half-breed to use. The zealot had been all too willing to lay down his own life to destroy the object of his hatred, and the Emperor saw an opportunity that he couldn't waste. When he had put the idea to his advisors, they had all enthused about his strategic ingenuity. And because they kept him happy, he kept them in luxury. They wanted for nothing. They had wealth, in material terms, social terms, sexual terms, if that was what they desired; they had everything they could wish for.
Of course, most of them believed the Emperor was mad. They would give anything to be able to flee the palace and never come to his attention again. But their decadent lifestyle came at a price. They were always in his orbit, and he was always aware of them. If anyone crossed him, he had him or her removed. Fatally. He would not tolerate anyone who argued, disagreed, disapproved, or even hesitated to shower praise upon him. Thus it was that

while every single one of his advisors was appalled and sickened to the soul with the plan, they all congratulated him for his tactical acumen. And none of them would ever let their mask slip in front of the others, because betrayal by one's colleagues for expressing treasonous thoughts was always uppermost in their minds.

So when the guards in the lower levels began shrieking and crying out for help, the advisors rushed to the Emperor for his wisdom, knowing that he probably had less of an idea what was happening than they did. When the captain of the guard checked the monitors to find out what was happening, and saw the hideous cartoonish monsters bursting from the deepest dungeons, he wondered what they were. As he watched them overpower his men, he wondered how many there were and how they'd got into the palace. When he saw they were an unstoppable force, moving up the levels and sweeping over his men without hesitating, he wondered if today was the day he was going to die.

***

Then S.T.A.R.T. arrived. Moonchild presented herself to the Emperor's personal guard, who in turn presented her to the Emperor himself. She and her team bowed obsequiously, feigning the stomach-churning attitude that all in the Emperor's presence displayed. Magpie, naturally, excelled when it came to fawning and offering platitudes as if it were his long held belief the Emperor was infallible. R'sulek-Entah was inscrutable and mysterious and had no trouble hiding her thoughts. The others struggled to keep their faces from betraying them.

Moonchild asserted their belief that they were equipped to deal with the goblin threat, and the Emperor gave them complete charge over the defence of the palace. Not once did he ask how the afflicted colonies would fare under similar siege conditions. Moonchild bowed again when he'd finished with his commands, then the team was dismissed and expected to willingly and lovingly sacrifice themselves for their Emperor.

The Emperor watched them leave the great hall, then called to his bodyguards.

"Let them make their plans, follow their instructions but, when you have an opportunity, kill the Arajak. I will not have aliens in my presence, they offend me. In fact, once safety is assured, kill them all. They associate with aliens. I will not tolerate that."

***

R'sulek-Entah, oblivious to her peril, was stationed in the palace security chamber, with access to all the monitoring equipment for the entire palace complex, inside and out. It didn't surprise her that the level of sophistication was better than was generally available, nor was it surprising that the Emperor felt paranoid enough to need to monitor the activity on both sides of the palace walls. The city beyond the palace was swarming with citizens, and he clearly trusted none of them. She reminded herself that paranoia only existed when the conspiracy didn't. She sat down to coordinate the operation that Moonchild had outlined to them in their brief conference after the audience with the Emperor. All the internal doors in the palace had been closed, making it difficult for the goblins to move from sector to sector.

The initial plan was to open each door individually, then move into the sector before closing the door and opening the next one in a kind of airlock system. It would be easier to deal with the relatively small number of goblins in each sector than to let them come at them in one huge mass. So, backed up with the palace guards, Moonchild, Magpie, Gunboy and Goldfish began the fight back.

It went well to begin with. With R'sulek-Entah keeping them informed about where the goblins were, and what they were doing, they made good progress. They lost a handful of guards to injuries, but no fatalities among the humans. The goblins were dying in their droves, though, and R'sulek-Entah was settling into her role, discovering a talent for logistics she had been previously unaware of.

Then she realised something was going on behind her. The overeager assassin who was drawing his pistol had no real experience of the Arajak, didn't realise their antennae gave them the equivalent of all round vision, among other things. So when he aimed at her head, he didn't expect her to move. She whipped to the right as he fired his pistol, drawing her battleknife as she whirled to face him. The look of surprise on his face was replaced by the look of fear, then agony, then a blank mask as she plunged the blade deep into his chest. She turned to face the others in the chamber who were all drawing weapons, and her predicament was clear. R'sulek-Entah knew she had no chance of running or flying to safety. She judged her only chance to be in her ability to avoid their shots as best she could and hope she was quick enough. She hauled the corpse of the first guard round in front of her, using him as a shield just as the first shots came in. The body was torn to shreds under the combined firepower and she soon abandoned it and flipped sideways, the battleknife slicing a throat as she did so, then ducked and rammed the blade into another man's side in one fluid motion.

By now, three men remained. There was no chance for her to reach any of them before the next shot came in. She ducked again, this time to retrieve the nearest corpse's weapon. In the same manœuvre, she flung the battleknife at the furthest one, pinning him against the far wall. Amidst his sharp, terminal cry of pain, she brought the pistol up to bear, sliding to the left. Finally, one of them got a shot on target. It slammed her backwards onto the floor. She realised her tunic, while designed to withstand certain types of damage, would never stop another shot like that. That was her last chance. She fired rapidly, three times at the man who'd shot her. Her second and third shots took him down with a grunt, which somewhat anticlimactically signalled the end of his life. All the time, she was moving, faster than a human would be able to manage, faster than many humans would be able to respond to. But her next shot was simultaneous with the final guard's connecting effort. As the guard fell backwards, dead, she felt the fire in her side. Struggling to hold in a howl of agony, she stumbled and staggered to the monitors. The first shot fired, the one that she had avoided, had instead hit the monitors, most of which were now dead.

As the full significance of that fact became apparent, she realised Moonchild no longer had any information about what was behind the next door, or what might be coming up behind her. Even as she tried to see some way that she might be able to jury rig a repair and at least offer the others some assistance, she felt the waves of pain overwhelming her, followed by the darkness.

***

Magpie gave a sharp cry of pain as the static burst into his ear. Moonchild, at the same time, cursed and instinctively removed her helmet to check the equipment before noticing her comrades' reactions.

Goldfish cocked his head. "This has got to be bad," he muttered.

Gunboy's reaction was the most extreme. "R'sulek-Entah!" he knew his voice was pitched higher than it should be, but he didn't care. "Something's happened to her!"

"Stow it, soldier," Moonchild warned, aware the palace guards were waiting for their next move. "We both know she's resourceful enough to deal with it."

Gunboy was clearly struggling to put his duty before his private life, but she said no more, just held his gaze long enough to be sure he would.

Satisfied, she turned to the others. "From this point, we're operating blind. Stay tight, people, we'll get through this. Retreat isn't an option; if even one goblin gets out of here, the operation's a failure, ok?" No argument was forthcoming, so she nodded and turned to Magpie. "Can you tell us anything?"

He looked pained. "It'll tire me out, but if you need me to, I'll do it."

"I'm sorry, Will," she grimaced sympathetically. "I'm afraid I do need you. Do you need to be in front, or can you manage in the middle."

"Doesn't matter, for the distance involved. I'll take point anyway and retreat if I need to."

"Go for it, hon," she patted his arm and stepped back.

With an expression that said all she needed to know, Magpie took a deep, steadying breath and took the lead. At every door they approached, he stepped up and closed his eyes, concentrating on the other side. A few were pleasantly free of goblins, but most were hiding varying quantities of the aberrant clones.

As they progressed, Moonchild could see Magpie's face becoming greyer with each door negotiated. A couple of times she caught him blinking, as if to force himself to stay awake.

"What's happening, Will?" she whispered when she had the chance.

"I don't know," he admitted. "I'm finding this more exhausting than I expected. Maybe it's a side effect of being dead." He laughed at the absurdity of the comment. "I guess I should be grateful to feel the side effects. But I honestly don't know."

She kept her concerned eyes on him. "You tell me the moment this gets too much, ok? No heroics, I mean you tell me."

"Yes, ma'am," he mock-saluted and grinned crookedly to suggest he had more energy than he actually did.

She wasn't fooled for an instant. "Make sure you do, Will," she said sternly.

And so they continued. They finally arrived in a huge chamber that appeared to be empty. Cautiously entering, they were aware there was no sound from the goblins.

"What's in here?" Moonchild asked the captain of the guard.

He pointed at the doors in the north and south walls. "They lead back into the palace," he said, then pointed straight across to the door in the west wall. "That leads to the dungeons. There's a bridge over the chasm. It was guarded at both ends, but I saw those creatures take out the guards. They came from inside the dungeons. I imagine they ate all the prisoners before they started coming up here."

Moonchild frowned. The man seemed to care little for the fate of the prisoners, most of whom were probably there because the colour of their clothes clashed with the Emperor's choice on that day. She turned her attention to the door before she said something she might regret.

"Can you tell if anything's behind the door?" she asked Magpie.

He stood, concentrating for a moment. He wavered slightly on his feet, then opened his eyes.

"Nothing," he told her.

Opening the door, they stepped through onto the ledge that held the bridge. Although the chasm was lit from above, they couldn't see the bottom. The bridge was, Moonchild estimated, some thirty metres in length, straddling the chasm, which looked natural. She didn't think for a second that the cavern system beyond was any more natural than the underground levels of the palace that they were leaving, but the effect was quite claustrophobic, even despite the lights.

"Goldfish, I've got a job for you," she turned to the demolitions officer. "If the genebanks are down there, we need to have a failsafe in case we don't manage to destroy them. I need you to wire this bridge up."

"Consider it done, boss," Goldfish acknowledged, and immediately knelt to study the structure for weak points.

"Everyone else, let's go," Moonchild ordered. "No, not you, Will. You're not in any shape to deal with this. Stay and guard the bridge, we might need you on the way back."

"Elise…"

"No, Will," she placed a firm hand on his chest. "If anything goes wrong in there, I want to know you're here and ok. Please, Will."

For a moment she thought he might lead a one-man mutiny, but in the end he just nodded and slumped against the wall. She reached out and put her hand back on his chest.

"Thank you," she whispered. "See you soon."

Then they were gone, across the bridge and into the darkness.

Goldfish was only peripherally aware that they were gone. As he worked on making and setting the charges, he glanced up at Magpie who was apparently asleep as he hunched into the corner. He watched his superior officer for a few moments.

"What's on your mind, James?" Magpie asked, suddenly, startling him.

"I was just thinking about when we were in your quarters," he answered quietly. "You told me the holodisc was a fake."

Magpie said nothing. He didn't know what he could say. He'd taken a gamble and been proven a liar.

"I just wanted to say," Goldfish continued. "That I understand why you said what you did. I'd have done the same thing in your position."

Magpie looked appraisingly at the demolitions officer. "Thank you," he said. "That decision has weighed heavily since I made it. I didn't enjoy lying to you like that."

"I know. But like I said, I'd have done the same, and I've felt as bad about it as you do. Just do me a favour, ok? Don't feel bad on my account. If I'd never seen Sarah again, I'd rather think she was dead than stuck in a Balsari cell for the rest of her life. But we're back together and it's all history. Ok?"

"I don't know what to say, James. I'm humbled."

The two shared a look, then Goldfish turned back to his work. Magpie closed his eyes again, but he didn't rest.

46

Moonchild and Gunboy led the others into the dungeons. They encountered nothing, which the guards seemed to consider a good thing, but which made the two S.T.A.R.T. members nervous. Where were they? They came across the remains of several prisoners, mostly just skeletons stripped of all the meat. The goblins hadn't been too careful and many of the bones were broken and scattered, showing signs of gnawing. The stench was overpowering and more than one guard was forced to cover his mouth and nose to avoid retching. Finally, they reached the very last cell. It was empty. Moonchild turned to the captain.

"Is there anywhere we haven't seen? Any secret passages, or anything of that sort?"

"No," the captain shook his head. "I know every inch of this place. There's no other way in or out."

"They must have teleported in," Gunboy said.

"Not possible," the captain countered. "The shielding round the palace won't allow it. And even if they could penetrate the shields, we'd have detected any teleporter use."

"If that's true," Moonchild raised an eyebrow, clearly giving the captain's argument little credence, "then we'd have found the genebanks down here. We haven't. Therefore, there must be another explanation, and I personally like Gunboy's suggestion."

"I'm sorry, Colonel, I can't believe anyone can do that," the captain stood his ground.

"What do you know of the Kalaszan?" she asked him.

"Who?"

"Precisely!" she said, curtly, turning to Gunboy. "Would that be your assessment?"

"Yes, ma'am," he replied. "I think they probably have the genebanks on a stealth vessel, somewhere in the palace grounds, certainly inside the shield."

Taking his agreement to mean the argument was settled, she took out her communicator to inform Control. It wasn't working.

"We're too deep," the captain said.

"No," she disagreed. "You won't like this, but our technology's better than even yours. Something's jamming the signal. Which means the Kalaszan know we're here. They've probably been monitoring this entire operation."

Almost as if that was a signal, a slow, undulating chorus arose, discordant wailing from outside the cell. They all turned to the door. Moonchild and Gunboy glanced apprehensively at each other. The guards, including the captain, found it impossible to conceal their fear. Two of them couldn't hold it in check and made a break for freedom.

"Get back here!" Moonchild bellowed, but they were gone. Within seconds, their terrified screams echoed back through the corridor towards the others, cut off with agonised croaks.

"Well, that settles it," Moonchild said quietly, stepping forward to the door and looking out. "We're in trouble."

***

Magpie's eyes snapped open.

"That doesn't sound good," he whispered, fearful of the implications for Elise.

"I've finished setting the charges," Goldfish told him, quietly. "We can blow the bridge as soon as the others get back."

"Good work," Magpie stood, obviously still very tired. "Get ready to do it."

They both stared across the bridge, waiting for some sign of the others, praying they'd appear before the goblins did.

***

Moonchild did a quick head count. As well as herself, Gunboy and the captain of the guard, there were nine palace guards. On one level, it was comforting: they had always previously dealt with goblins with fewer people. On the other hand, she was aware that none of them had the experience or expertise that S.T.A.R.T. possessed.

"Ok, listen up, people," she raised her voice slightly, not trying to give the goblins any more clues about their location than necessary. "We have to move quickly and keep moving. We can't afford to be forced into making a stand, if we stop moving, they've got us. If anyone falls, I'm sorry, but you're going to be left behind. If you can't follow, your job is to hold them off for as long as you can to give the rest of us more time to get away. We will not be able to come back for anyone, we will not be able to stop and help you get up again. Any questions?"

"With respect," the captain said, with less respect in his tone than his words suggested. "These are my men, and I'll decide whether or not we leave them behind. You just look to yourself and your own man."

He drew himself up to his full height and looked down at her, clearly not prepared to back down. She took the bait.

"Listen, Captain, I don't much care who owns who round here, but I do care about people following orders. I accept you're not under my direct command, and for that reason you can decide the fate of your own people. But let me make this clear. One of you falls and can't get up, that's one dead man. Someone stops to help him, that's two dead men. These goblins don't consider tactics, don't applaud heroism, and they don't believe in fair play. They just eat, and you've seen the results of that. So you decide how many people stay behind to help the first man down, but remember when you do that, none of them will be coming back. Now, can we get on with trying to survive?" Without waiting for his reply, she turned and nodded to Gunboy. Despite her obvious dislike of the captain, they were still taking point and putting themselves in between the guards and the goblins. This clearly had an effect on the guards, who seemed to appreciate the gesture. With a quick look behind her at the captain, Moonchild nodded and began moving at a jog back the way they'd come.

As soon as they left the cell and entered the corridor, the howling rose in pitch. They'd been spotted. As they headed along the corridor to the junction at the end, they all made a final, unnecessary check on their weapon status. Then, with metres to go before they got there, the goblins appeared at the corner. Like a rushing tide, they swept into the corridor, their screams and shrieks tearing at the eardrums of the humans.

"This is it!" Moonchild shouted above the din, dropping to one knee to get a steady aim. Gunboy did likewise, and between them they began blasting the foremost goblins. As expected, some hesitated to enjoy the nourishment provided by their fallen kin, but most continued towards the object of their desire.

Moonchild began considering their options. The plan to keep moving was no longer viable. The goblins were already in front of them and retreat now seemed the only possibility, but even as she contemplated this, she wondered where they could go. They'd come from a dead end and if they holed up again in a dead end, they'd only be prolonging the inevitable. And if they did hole up, the only thing that would happen before they came out again would be the arrival of even more goblins. Retreating was suicide. Going forward was suicide. Staying where they were was suicide. She thought of Iceman and what he must have been thinking in this position. And that was when she realised they weren't defeated yet.

"Everyone, listen!" she commanded. "Set your weapons to overload, detonate on my mark!"

"Are you mad?" the captain spluttered. "We'll be defenceless!"

"One overloaded weapon can take out more goblins than a charge full of shots," she replied, still firing. "There's no other way to get past them. You can die with your gun in your hand, or you can give yourself a chance to survive without one. You decide, but we need to coordinate this precisely!"

The captain looked like he was about to explode, but finally he turned to his men.

"On her mark," he told them.

"Set weapons now," she called. "Three second timer."

She threw her pistol over the heads of the first few rows of goblins. A number of them leaped upwards, trying to catch it, to see if it was edible. She knew there was a risk involved, but she figured the dungeon was, by its very nature, made of sterner stuff than John Gray's shop. She unshouldered her rifle and counted.

The blast evaporated most of the goblins in the immediate vicinity. As soon as the blast died down, they were moving forwards towards the junction again.

"Gunboy, now!" she ordered.

Gunboy responded by throwing his pistol into the space where the corridors met, before taking up his rifle. By now the goblins were boiling into the corner and advancing with terrifying speed. Then the pistol detonated and again cleared the area. Immediately, they hurried on to the junction. The goblins appeared to be regrouping in both directions. Quickly deciding which group was smaller, Moonchild amended her instructions.

"You," she said to the nearest man, a nervous looking youth. "Detonate that way. Everyone else, fire towards the rear."

And so it continued. By keeping those who were still armed to the rear to shoot at their pursuers, Moonchild managed to direct their progress back to safety. Eventually, they reached the long flight of stairs that led up from the dungeons back to the bridge.

As she turned to begin the ascent, the captain called to her.

"Colonel!"

She turned and saw he was holding his own weapon, which he had managed to hold onto, against Gunboy's head.

"You will both now hand your rifles to my men or I'll kill the Lieutenant," he said, a sly smile playing on his lips.

"Don't, ma'am, he'll kill us both if you do," Gunboy argued.

Moonchild nodded and brought her rifle to bear on the captain, knowing that her shot would probably take out

Gunboy as well, and aware that a couple of guards also had pistols drawn on her.

She flicked her rifle onto overload.

"I'll make sure you all die with us," she stated calmly, moving her thumb towards the detonator.

The shot that took her down made her lose her grip on the rifle and she dropped it as she fell. It clattered to the floor just out of her reach and was scooped up by one of the guards, who disabled the overload. Another guard took Gunboy's rifle. He immediately dropped to her side and began frantically examining her injury. From further into the dungeon, the sound of the goblins rose anew. The captain looked down at the S.T.A.R.T. members and decided it wasn't worth killing them both. They needed to get over the bridge without delay, and besides, it would be more fun leaving them to the goblins.

"It's nothing personal," he grinned at Gunboy, as they moved up the stairs. "I'm just following orders."

Gunboy ripped open the side of Moonchild's shirt and studied the wound. It wasn't immediately fatal, but it was bad. If she didn't get proper medical attention soon, she would die. In the corridor, he could hear the goblins searching for them. His mind drifted back to his first mission, when he was in a similar position with Magpie. He was dying as well, and the goblins were closing in on them then. He knew this time, though, he had a chance to save himself. All he had to do was follow the others up the stairs, leave her here. No-one would know. He glanced up the stairs. Then back at Moonchild.

"Don't worry, ma'am,' he said, as he reached for his med-pac. "I'm here."

Her eyes flickered open. She focussed with effort on him, and gripped his arm.

"Don't let the goblins take me," she hissed. "Kill me and go."

"No chance, ma'am, I'm not leaving without you."

"Don't be an idiot," she forced the breath through clenched teeth. "Save yourself. That's an order."

"Really? So court-martial me," he continued to administer what aid he could to her wound.

"Does no-one follow orders round here?" Moonchild cursed and let her head drop to the floor.

Together they listened to the approaching goblins.

47

As the captain and his remaining guards appeared at the far end of the bridge, Magpie's overwrought emotions twisted his gut again. He stood with an effort.

"What happened?" he demanded, as the captain approached him.

"Sorry, Commander, they were overrun by goblins," the captain told him. "They died bravely."

"Where?" Magpie had gone numb.

"Bottom of the stairs," the captain gestured redundantly.

Magpie turned to Goldfish. "If you see a single goblin on the other side before you see me, blow the bridge. That's an order." He set off over the bridge.

"Yes, sir," Goldfish knew better than to argue with Magpie once he had set himself on a course of action.

He heard the door behind him closing and realised the palace guards had left them. Shrugging, he watched as Magpie disappeared into the darkness, and settled himself to wait.

***

Magpie reached the bottom of the stairs and found them both alive. He wasn't sure whether to be relieved they weren't dead or furious they'd been betrayed.

"Will!" Moonchild whispered, painfully. "Why can't any of you do as you're told?"

"Can we move her?" he asked Gunboy, ignoring her.

"Not far, if at all," the Tactical Support officer offered his best medical opinion. "We don't have time to get her across the bridge, if that's what you're thinking."

"Let's get her into this cell," Magpie nodded in the direction of the small room.

"We'll be trapped if we go in there," Moonchild objected.

"We'll all die for sure if we stay here," Magpie answered. "At least if we hole up in the cell, we can choose to kill ourselves with dignity if it comes to it."

Even as he spoke, he was hauling her up. She hissed with the pain, but didn't argue. Gunboy added his strength to Magpie's efforts and, between them, they manhandled their commanding officer into the cell. Magpie closed the door.

"Is that a good idea, sir?" Gunboy asked, too late.

"If I can't get it open again, then I don't deserve my reputation," he replied, cheerfully, before turning back to Moonchild. "How bad is it?"

"Well," she answered. "If the goblins don't get us, I don't think I'll last long enough to starve to death."

"That's the spirit," Magpie's forced cheer wasn't convincing anyone.

Everyone looked at each other for a few minutes. Then the first goblins began slamming into the other side of the cell door.

***

Goldfish cursed as the first goblins appeared on the other side of the bridge. Despite his orders, he wanted to make sure he gave Magpie every chance to get back. So he resigned himself to shooting the goblins as they began to cross the bridge. Finally realising he had no other option, and in danger of being overrun, he detonated the charges. The near end of the bridge sparked and broke away, swinging in a downward arc. Screeching with uncomprehending alarm, the goblins on the bridge lost their purchase and fell into the chasm. The bridge smashed into the far side of the chasm, bouncing out again a couple of times, before settling in its final position, hanging from the far side. A few more goblins dropped off as it did so, and the rest gathered at the far side, gauging Goldfish and trying to decide if it was worth attempting the jump. A few clearly decided it was, their efforts pitifully short of the requirement, joining their predecessors at the bottom.

After watching for a while, Goldfish realised there was little point in remaining there. There was no way the goblins could get across, but in the same way, there was no way anyone else was coming back. The presence of the goblins testified to that. Miserably, he turned away, and wondered if spending the rest of his life with Sarah would in any way ease the grief of losing all his comrades to the goblins.

But the door wouldn't respond to him. Realisation came instantly. The palace guards had locked the door behind them and left him to die here. He was trapped on this little ledge with nowhere to go. And he knew he didn't have enough charge to damage it enough to open it. Surprisingly philosophical, he sat down to wait and consider his fate.

***

Darkness swirled and coalesced into light. The rustling of leaves as the wind stirred the Great Tree went through subtle changes, gradually transforming into the song of the chanters' caste. As she listened, and let the song bring her to awareness, she began to wonder what had brought her to this condition. She lay on her front, against a hard surface. Not her usual sleeping position, that was certain. Then R'sulek-Entah felt the pain in her side, where the shot had penetrated her armour. She was instantly back in the real world. She knew where she was, and why, and her awareness was focussed on the song, which she now realised was not a song at all, but the hunting cry of thousands of goblins swarming through the palace corridors.

R'sulek-Entah stood unsteadily and took stock of her surroundings. Since the battle with the palace guards, it seemed no-one had been in here. She made sure she had her sidearm and battleknife and stumbled from the chamber. Her antennae wavered with alarm as she understood her predicament. She could hear the goblins charging down the corridor towards her position long before she saw them. Looking up, she gauged the clearance she would gain if she was able to take flight. She decided it was sufficient, and flapped her wings experimentally. She was still weak and disoriented, but it should be possible. She had to find the others if they were still alive. She had to find them, whether or not they were still alive, she corrected herself, then felt an unfamiliar stab of something she couldn't identify as she considered the possibility that John might not have survived. Fighting against the instinct that told her to surrender to her fate, R'sulek-Entah took a few steps forwards, towards the goblins to give herself some momentum, then took off. She soared with a distinct lack of grace over the heads of the foremost goblins, flapping her wings to maintain height. The goblins, naturally, did all they could in order to bring her down, but they had neither the physical prowess to reach that high, or the intelligence to work together towards that end.

In the end, it was her own weakness that curtailed her flight. Hampered by her injury, and disoriented with the pain, she lost altitude and, although she struggled as hard as she could, she couldn't delay the inevitable. She dropped like a brick into the seething mass, which bubbled up and over her.

***

The captain of the guard led his troops into the throne room. The Emperor sat, surrounded by his advisors, looking for all the world like it was just another day, and nothing untoward was happening. For a man in danger of losing his home and, by the same means, his entire empire, he appeared remarkably casual.

"Ah, Captain, I trust our guests have been dealt with?" he asked in extremely conversational tones.

"They have, your majesty," the captain reported, bowing low with pleasure. "Both the invaders and S.T.A.R.T. have ceased to be an inconvenience."

"Excellent, Captain, I know I can always rely on you. You may name your own reward."

The captain bowed again. He wouldn't fall into this trap, like so many of his predecessors had.

"Serving you is all the reward I seek, your majesty," he fawned.

The Emperor didn't bother responding. The captain had merely given the correct answer. Then the undulating wail of the goblins cut through the air and the smile vanished.

From the doorways all around the throne room they appeared. Two of the Emperor's advisors couldn't control their terror and made a break for safety, through one of the few doors that the goblins hadn't appeared from. But their hope was cruelly taken from them as the monsters began to gather there anyway. The Emperor and the others watched with a variety of reactions as the hordes pounced on the two hapless advisors and began ripping them to shreds. The screams of the advisors were lost in the howls of delight.

But the rest of the goblins were not waiting for their comrades. They began closing at speed on the central dais and those who occupied it. The guards who still held weapons began their last desperate defence of their Emperor, who seemed mostly unfazed by all the activity.

"They will not attack me," he asserted. "They would not dare. I am the Emperor!"

His advisors didn't hear. They were too busy screaming their fear. Some lost control of their bowels in those final moments, some vomited with the terror. One died on the spot from sheer fright. He was the lucky one. The others crowded up to the top of the dais, surrounding the throne, almost feverishly trying to convince themselves that if they could just survive a few more seconds, someone would come and rescue them.

They were wrong. The writhing mass of revulsion poured upwards at frightening velocity, slamming into the humans and knocking them down. Flesh was torn from bones as they fed, as they devoured their victims without mercy. The captain of the guard tried to set his weapon to overload, to try and give himself a swift and painless death, the best he could hope for, he realised with fear and frustration. But, as he was jostled by a dying advisor, he dropped his weapon. He dropped to his knees in a vain attempt to retrieve it and knew, too late, that he'd made a mistake. The weight of the goblins as they leapt onto his back pushed him down the steps into the carpet of life that welcomed him with gleeful, bloody jaws and claws. His last thought before they savagely ripped his throat out was that he might have survived if he hadn't killed the S.T.A.R.T. people.

The Emperor was screaming with rage.

"Bow before me, you scum!" he shrieked in red-faced rage at the goblins. "I am your Emperor, and I demand you pay me homage!"

The goblins ignored his assertions and closed on him. They began by clawing their way up his legs, and climbing the back of the throne. Between screams of agony, his enraged demands for respect echoed above the howling. The fact they weren't obeying him finally registered when they gouged out his eyes with such a lack of finesse that they pulled most of the flesh from the top half of his face at the same time. His scream was muffled by the claw that plunged into his mouth and severed his tongue. As he struggled to make himself heard above the noise, and to try and control his agony, he could only gurgle from a blood-filled mouth, unintelligible words that carried neither the strength nor the conviction of an imperial directive. The Emperor fell, senseless and insane, into the seething horde and was swallowed up.

Moments later, the goblins went to seek more food, leaving the remains of their latest meal scattered across the throne room floor.

***

Goldfish had finally conceded defeat against the door. He had realised some time ago he really needed Magpie to get it open. But, he realised, that was not an option. He had to consider himself to be the last survivor of the team and act accordingly. He was trying to decide what his chances were of scaling the chasm wall and what he might find at the bottom, should he make it in one piece.

Then the door opened and he braced himself for one of two things. It might be the guards coming back to finish the job, or the goblins coming back to start the job. He turned to discover his fate, ready to hurl himself into the chasm and take his chances there. He raised his eyebrows and smiled with relief.

"Am I glad to see you!" he sighed.

***

Gunboy stood close to the door, listening to the undiminished noise outside. In the far corner of the cell, Moonchild tried to prop herself up but Magpie put a gentle hand on her shoulder.

"Don't move, Elise, you're in no condition and you'll only make it worse."

She smiled grimly through the pain. "Don't try giving me orders, Will, I can't follow them any better than you can."

He laughed despite himself. Their eyes met and locked. There was silence between them, broken only by the constant muffled howl of the goblins outside, and the intermittent thumping as they tried to open the door by brute force alone.

Moonchild glanced away briefly, but then, with an effort, sought his eyes again. It was now or never, she knew. She had so little time left.

"Will, I have to tell you something."

"Shhh," he told her, stroking her sweat soaked forehead. "You don't need to say anything."

"I do, Will. It's important. Please."

"Ok," he said.

She reached out and gripped his hand.

"Will, I…"

"I think they're going!" Gunboy shouted, his disbelief clear.

Magpie immediately leapt to his feet and joined him at the door. It was true; the sound of the goblins had abated. The only way to be sure, though was to see what was on the other side of the door. He reached out and touched the door, closing his eyes. He looked through the door, extending his awareness beyond it. The goblins were actually retreating back the way they had come, from what, he wasn't sure. He turned to look up the stairs and saw the reason, but didn't understand. He removed his hand from the door and went back to Moonchild.

"We're going to get out now," he assured her. "Hold tight, we'll get you the help you need. Then you can tell me what you were going to say."

She nodded and smiled encouragingly at him but, as he turned away, she let a single tear slip from the corner of her eye and down her cheek.

A voice called out from beyond the door. "Is anyone in this cell?"

Gunboy snapped to full awareness. "R'sulek-Entah? We're in here! Hold on!"

He turned to Magpie, who stepped forward with his lockpicking tools. Within seconds, the door opened and the human and Arajak were reunited. Magpie glanced down the corridor to where the goblins were agitating and spitting. He looked at R'sulek-Entah and noticed she seemed subdued.

"Pheromones," she answered his unspoken question. "If I concentrate, it seems I can make myself unappetising to them. However, we must hurry, as it is somewhat tiring."

"Help me with Elise," he asked.

Between himself and Gunboy, Moonchild was gently carried up the stairs, with R'sulek-Entah behind them, a buffer between them and the goblins, who were following at a frustrated distance. When they reached the top, Goldfish was putting the final touches to a basic rope bridge. Between all of them, they contrived a sling for transporting the now unconscious Moonchild across the chasm. When the humans were across, R'sulek-Entah traversed the rope, using her wings to help her balance. She was clearly too tired and too badly injured to fly. Then Goldfish cut the rope, stranding the goblins where they were.

"We may need you to do that again," Magpie said to R'sulek-Entah, aware of what he was asking. "Can you manage it, if you have to?"

The Arajak nodded, but she didn't seem certain she would be able to.

So, with Gunboy supporting R'sulek-Entah, and Magpie and Goldfish carrying Moonchild, they made their way from the palace. As it happened, they didn't meet any more goblins, for which R'sulek-Entah was grateful. The final test was crossing the palace grounds. If there was a Kalaszan vessel in the vicinity, they were risking being fired on, but they reached the gates unmolested. Either it was gone, or it hadn't bothered with them. They didn't know, and didn't care. Once through the gates, Magpie put in the call to Control for an emergency teleport to sickbay. Seconds later, their ordeal was over.

Epilogue

Munich, Bavaria, 2507

When they gathered in Moonchild's quarters, it was to say goodbye. Their little party was a sad affair, commemorating fallen comrades, as well as the Empire-wide devastation. Entire worlds had been lost, survivors being rescued in handfuls in some places. The only solution in many cases was to neutralise the entire planet to ensure the total destruction of their new goblin populations. But it also served to break up the team, marking the end of an era.

Goldfish and Sarah had six years of catching up to do, and they couldn't do that if his commitment to the military came between them. So, with some regret, he'd resigned his commission.

"I'm still on the reserve roster," he explained. "But I'll only be called up in the direst emergency."

R'sulek-Entah and Gunboy still had their children on Ara'Sayal. They had to go and try to retrieve them. And R'sulek-Entah felt it was important, now the Balsari had been so viciously removed from the universe, and the Empire had been decimated, to attempt to repair the damage between the Arajak and what remained of the Empire.

Magpie had also come to a decision. "I need to find the other clones," he announced to the rest of them. "They're the nearest I have to a family. I'm going to find them and live with them, maybe get Project Firewood started again."

Moonchild looked quite stricken when he'd said this. "Is this what you really want?" she'd managed to ask.

"I have no choice, Elise," he told her. "I have to do something to carry on the work Seraph was doing. He sacrificed everything for me, to give me a second chance. I owe it to him to take that chance. Please, Elise, it's important to me that you understand this."

"I understand, Will, of course I do," she smiled, but her eyes held tears. "You have my blessing. Go find them. And take care of yourself."

"Thank you," he took her into a tight hug. "I'll stay in touch. I promise."

They held each other for a long time. And finally kissed.

***

With his mustering out benefits, Magpie bought himself a small ship. He filed a flight plan with the civilian authorities and set off on his journey to find his family. Moonchild watched him go. Slowly, she turned away from the observation deck window and made her way back to her office.

Sitting behind her desk, she picked up the anachronistic block that pronounced her identity to any who sat opposite her. She still couldn't get used to it. Brigadier Elise Washington. She'd failed to save the Emperor, and they'd promoted her. There were things about Admiral Saastemoinen and General N'Komo she'd probably never quite figure out. But they'd been appalled by the knowledge that the Emperor had been behind the genocide of the Balsari and this was probably their way of applauding his demise without being accused of treason. The new Empress was settling in and seemed genuinely concerned that the image of her family was so badly tarnished. Her uncle, she realised, had done so much damage, and it was her job to repair as much of that damage as possible. Moonchild knew that she'd sent a personal message for the Queen with R'sulek-Entah and Gunboy when they'd left. There wasn't much left worth calling an empire, but what there was seemed to be in safe hands.

Moonchild pondered her new role. Now the Balsari were no longer a threat, there was no immediate need for an organisation like S.T.A.R.T., so her duties had been widened to incorporate general security from any threat from outside the Empire. She wasn't sure if she could enjoy the job. It wouldn't involve as much field work. She wondered if they thought she was getting too old for that, or if they thought a break from her normal operating procedure would help her get used to the fact that this was a different position. Many of the people under her new command had followed her from S.T.A.R.T. anyway, so she felt she had some leeway.

She went home, trying to decide if she wanted the job after all. Maybe she should just quit. Resign her commission, like the others. She'd done it before, had those two years when she'd married Maek Newark and run the bar. But she knew she wouldn't. They'd tempted her back then, they'd do it again. She was too much a soldier to turn aside from the defence of the Empire. No, she would die in her uniform, or they'd retire her when they deemed it necessary. She'd just keep fighting until she couldn't fight any more.

When she got home, her lights were on. Drawing her pistol, she stepped into her living quarters.

He was waiting for her.

"Will!"

"Hello, Elise," he said, from his usual chair. "I let myself in, I hope you don't mind. It's a lovely security system you've had installed. Took me entire seconds to get past it."

"Will," she repeated. "You've come back. Why?"

"I was wrong," he spread his hands, almost apologetic. "They're not my family. You are. I belong here with you, Elise. Because we're a team, and we should be together."

"Oh, Will," she crossed the floor and wrapped her arms around him. "You know S.T.A.R.T.'s been dismantled, don't you?"

"Yes," he said. "I've been thinking about that. We could go freelance. 'Space-Time Oversight Patrol'. What do you think?"

"Hmm. 'S.T.O.P.'," she mused. "I like it. It has a certain ring to it. I'll give you an answer in the morning."

He smiled but, although their faces were almost touching, they did not kiss. That memory lingered, but that was all it ever could be. They were just two old soldiers serving the Empire.

"Goodnight, Elise," he whispered, and made for the door.

"Goodnight, Will," she answered quietly.

And she watched him from her window as he disappeared into the night and the future.

Afterword

Thank you for reading this far! I'm assuming you didn't just skip the last couple of hundred pages and come straight to the back, but if you have, well, thanks for at least buying the book!

On the off chance you've enjoyed this novel, and are interested in what else I've written, the best thing to do is go to http://www.amazon.co.uk/ and type Raphael Merriman into the search box. This is a growing list, and I will be adding to it regularly, so please keep checking.

I'm also on Facebook: https://www.facebook.com/Raphael-Merriman-809830522461388/?fref=ts so feel free to catch up with me there!

You can find me on Twitter: https://twitter.com/Namir_Rem

And if that's not enough, here's my Goodreads page: https://www.goodreads.com/author/show/11393306.Raphael_Merriman

I'll try and respond to all communication, as long as it's not rude!

Thanks again!

Acknowledgments

I would like to take a moment to mention a number of people who've been instrumental, directly or indirectly, in the process that culminated in the writing of this novel.

In no particular order, they are:

Les Pope, my English teacher at Moor Grange High School in Leeds. I used to raid the stock room for exercise books to write my stories. He caught me red-handed and, when I confessed I wanted to write a novel, he responded with, "A novel? A novel? Here, Merriman, take the book. And I want to read it when it's finished!" Of course, I never finished any of those early efforts, and probably the world is better for it, but here (better late than never) is the novel I owe him.

Dave Thomas, my teacher at St Margaret's School in Horsforth. He also encouraged me, and promised me, "I'll buy a copy of your first book." I'm holding him to that.

Elizabeth Newby and Steven Waling, tutors on the creative writing evening classes I attended. Elizabeth and my fellow students helped me hone my talents, while Steven's innocuous photo, coupled with a fellow student's comment of, "I don't see how you can turn that into a science fiction story," resulted in the novel you now possess.

Andy Roan, who first got me to post my short stories on MySpace (yes, it really was *that* long ago), Alan Claxton, my bandmate from Scarred For Life and Sharlock, who publishes his own work on Kindle, a route I've followed and enjoyed, and Kevin Wood, an old friend and bandmate whose own book ("Runaway's Railway") has given both myself and Georgia much pleasure. I thoroughly recommend you check them all out. I might even get commission on it.

rolffimages for a fabulous cover!

And finally, thank you to the *real* Elise Washington. You know who you are, and why.

Raphael Merriman
December 2015

Printed in Great Britain
by Amazon